CLIMATE WARS

MIKE PENNEY

Cover Image by Keith Draws Cover Art

ISBN: 1547069945
ISBN-13: 978-1547069941

CONTENTS

ACKNOWLEDGMENTS

Many thanks to Sightline Institute, a vital part of The Thin Green Line. Sightline Institute is an independent, non-profit research and communication center - a think tank - located in Cascadia and readily found on the web at sightline.org. Utilizing Sightline's researches and resources proved truly invaluable and enlightening in the composition of this novel, and to Sightline I am extremely grateful.

Greenpeace.org published in September 2014 their insightful, yet chilling research titled "The Kingpins of Carbon and Their War on Democracy." This valuable work is recommended for anyone concerned about global warming and how the fossil fuel oligarchs have conducted a multi-decade war on democracy; it also aided in painting a more colorful backdrop for this novel.

Thanks also to orkin.com and especially their "Pest Library." Fascinating facts about flies and other insects in this novel were gleaned from this unique source; the "Pest Library" is recommended for hours of enjoyable reading - if, of course, one is so inclined.

Special thanks go to several individuals that were of great help during the revision process for this novel. In particular, Jim Hagerty, Jim Hoyt, Tootie Warner, and my daughter, Noelani Penney, graciously took their time to thoroughly review this work page-by-page; their recommendations and suggestions proved most valuable.

Any failings and errors that remain are my own; nevertheless, heartfelt appreciation goes out to these folks.

MIKE PENNEY

.

PROLOGUE

Breaking the remote canyon's silence and serenity, the first bullet from the high-powered rifle ripped into Ali's very pregnant belly with pinpoint precision.

The second bullet, coming after only a momentary delay, penetrated the center of her forehead and exploded into her brain.

Chris Soles, reading in his director's chair while his lover dozed in the late afternoon sun, didn't immediately register what had just transpired. The gunshots had been startling, but when he saw blood from the gaping hole in Ali's head beginning to soak the pillow, he suddenly comprehended what was happening.

With an instinctual immediacy, Chris sprung from his director's chair to behind the rock Ali's body was reclining on, for what little cover it could afford. All at once he realized Ali was either dying or dead just above – as was their baby they had so many hopes and wishes for.

Chris knew they could have easily taken him out – but why didn't they?

From somewhere up higher on the southern Utah canyon wall, an electronic bullhorn began to blare.

"Put down your weapon and come out with your hands up!"

Weapon, thought Chris, what weapon?

"You are wanted for the murder of the woman and this entire canyon is surrounded!" the voice over the bullhorn bellowed. "You have no choice but to surrender. Come out with your hands up!"

The entire situation was surreal. Empire had killed Ali and their baby, and now they were going to frame him.

"Come out with your hands up and surrender! You will not be harmed!"

"Yeah, right," Chris mouthed silently, as he swore to himself. They were going kill him or frame him: either way he was a dead man.

On the boulder above Chris, blood was beginning to trickle down from the bullets that had entered Ali's pregnant womb. There was nothing he could do for her now – or their baby. There was only one choice: he had to cross the open space to get better cover behind the boulders in front of the cave.

Turning over so he was on hands and knees, Chris darted forth; he bolted and zigzagged as fast as he could to reach temporary safety behind the entry boulders. Two or three shots ricocheted off the sandstone walls above him, as he rapidly scrambled past the entry boulders and into the cave.

Again the thought struck him that Empire's marksmen could easily have killed him – so why didn't they?

Inside the cave, Soles flicked on the three strings of carnival lights with a familiarity garnered over time. It was the same cave in which he and Harry Wimple had grown hundreds of thousands of psilocybin mushrooms before old Wimp returned to the Void; it was the same cave he and Ali had thought themselves safe for so long from Empire's thugs and hounds.

But it was all over now: they were coming after him.

Without hesitation, Chris snatched a headlamp and one of the two emergency packs he and Ali always had hanging on a rack by the cave entrance. After turning the headlamp on and fitting it in place, he switched off the carnival lights. With the backpack secured, Chris began cautiously trotting into the depths of the cave.

A map of the subterranean labyrinth was etched into his mind by now after all the trips he'd made to export the mushrooms they'd grown. When he passed the underground stream, Chris knew it wasn't far from the opening on the other side of canyon walls where Wimp had poached electricity from power lines of the Western grid.

Daylight was fading as Chris finally found his way to the small exit in rocks at the far end of the formerly hidden cave. He knew it would take Empire some time to find his escape route, even if they'd already entered the cave in pursuit.

But it didn't really matter at this point. Old Harry Wimple, in his paranoia after all the years in prison, had wired the entire cave with explosives. "Just in case..." he always said.

Removing his headlamp and stashing it in the backpack, Chris stuck his head outside and gazed about. He observed nothing but the familiar sandstone formations and buttes in the distance. Realizing when he went out in the open there would be no hiding from helicopters or drones, he shrugged; there was no choice regarding the matter.

Returning his attentions inside the cave, Soles located the four detonator switch boxes Wimp had mounted into the rock wall on this end, precisely as he had done at the cave entry.

"Just in case..." Chris remarked in homage to Wimp, as he sequentially began to flip each switch.

Wimp had assured him there was a delay built into the system to permit escape, but he didn't recall how long it was – and surely didn't intend sticking around to find out. Quickly exiting the hole in the rock wall, Soles began running downhill toward a cleavage of weathered sandstone. Feeling vulnerable in the open, he stopped momentarily and turned around upon reaching the rock outcropping.

Nothing was happening. He feared the worst.

Chris waited a few more seconds; he then realized he had to get going. No matter what, he had to be miles away as soon as possible.

Before he had taken three steps though, a deep rumble came from the bowels of the earth. And then there was another, and another, and another. He turned back.

A blast of dusty smoke was being expelled from the opening he had just exited and landslides began at various points on the mountain above.

Chris had eluded Empire's clutches for now, but there was no time to gloat.

Spinning on his heels, he took flight into the growing dusk as if his life depended upon it – which indeed it did.

* * *

Several hours and miles later, Chris Soles found the shelter he'd been seeking. It wasn't so much a cave as a hollowed out stone refuge formed by eons of wind and weathering. These southern Utah canyonlands were peppered with hundreds if not thousands of similar hideaways.

Chris knew scores and scores of them because it was where he had secreted tens of thousands of magic mushrooms over the last several months, as Ali grew more and more pregnant. They surely hadn't wanted to be caught with so many Schedule 1 drugs if the cave was ever discovered; furthermore, they didn't really know what to do with them since Gaia/Universe had been destroyed. The best solution available was to stash them hidden away in the naturally dry havens such as where he now huddled.

In this crude shelter, and with a brief respite from running for his life, the full impact of what had happened to him in the last few hours began to hammer down. Though it was growing colder with each passing minute into the night, his heart pounded with passion as he thought of Ali and his love for her. They discovered themselves to be soul mates in the short months they'd been together; they couldn't get enough of each other and looked forward to every new day. Best of all, they both welcomed the challenges of the future by the celebration of a new beloved human being that would be the product of them both.

Drawn up into a fetal position for warmth and with his backpack for a pillow, Chris's brain began to scream with pain at the loss of Ali and their unborn child. Their future together had been destroyed, eradicated. And his life would now be one of misery because of it. Never had he loved a person more than Ali; going forward he felt destined to be the shadow of the man he once was.

Wallowing in despair and gloom, his thoughts lashed out at the emissaries of Empire, the people that pulled the trigger on Ali and their child. Why didn't they aim at him instead of Ali? He was clearly in their sights as well. And what depths of evil was in the hearts of those that commanded Empire's assassins to do such a thing?

How could he not hate the men that did this? How could he not hate Empire and its oligarchs, the Kingpins that were leading the species downward in a spiral of self-destruction? The depths of hate that Chris was immersed in both poisoned and strengthened his soul, until it became too much, too overpowering.

When the dark brooding nearly reached the limits, it was the life-lifting love for Ali that brought him back. He would dwell on their laughter together, the feeling of the new baby in her belly, and their plans for the future – until inevitably – the regrettable loss of all that had been right in his world would haunt him once more. And with it came the depths of hate for those that had caused that loss.

Into the gloomiest hours, Chris vacillated between his love for Ali and his hate for the others. It was somewhere in the base of his soul that night, however, that it all came together. At some point in murkiness of mental turmoil, he drifted to a state of mind that wasn't at all intellectual, but rather a powerful understanding, an instinctual comprehension.

It was then that his love for her and his hate for them became the same thing. The extremes met out on the outer edge and Chris realized they could not be opposites. They were the same thing. It was simply the way all things were...

As his soul stilled, he marveled how transparent everything had become. Stretching out on the hard rocks, he took in their comfort. Breathing in and breathing out became more regular for Chris; finally, at peace, he slid into an effortless slumber.

***

The dawn light gently aroused him in his sandstone shelter. Rubbing his eyes, Chris gazed upon a world the like of which he'd never experienced. Even in those pale early hours, the colors of the arid landscape were more brilliant than he had ever observed. And the thin clouds to the east, just above where the sun would soon be rising, appeared to throb with intensity.

Sucking in the cool and crisp early morning air, however, brought it all back to him. The horror that was yesterday assaulted his mind.

If there were the slightest chance Empire believed him to be alive, they would unquestionably pursue him.

What was it the big DEA agent told him when he surprisingly set him free?

"Fully realize those in power will do everything they can to chase you to the ends of the earth," he had warned. *"They know about you; they've already spied on your conversations and life. Run to the ends of the earth and hide yourself well, for they will certainly be after you for as long as you live."*

Yes, Chris acknowledged, Empire was after him and the pursuit would never end.

But where could he hide himself well? Where must he go?

Instantaneously, Chris realized only one option was feasible: he knew he had no alternative but to head northwest – toward Cascadia!

CHAPTER ONE

Sapphire MacKenzie was as resplendent in addressing the throngs of protestors she helped organized, as she was defiant.

"You see," MacKenzie continued to explain, "we're governed by what one political theorist called an inverted type of totalitarianism. It's a totalitarianism whereby corporate power has seized all the levers of governmental control and thereby rendered the citizen impotent."

She paused for effect. "But I tell you what: it's our planet too! And we're going to take it back!"

A collective roar arose from the sea of dissidents surrounding MacKenzie in every direction. They were in eastern Oregon along the Columbia River, occupying the Port of Morrow near the town of Boardman. It was a hot day in this arid land on the last Friday in June – June 28th to be precise. It was also the last day of the current Supreme Court term.

"Yes," MacKenzie repeated, "it's our planet too and we're going to take it back for future generations!"

Another collective outcry erupted from the masses that had

gathered; simultaneously, thousands of Cascadia's Doug flags were pumped up and down in the air. Sapphire permitted the crowds as long as they desired to fully express themselves.

When it was time, she carried on. "We the protectors recognize there is a sacred trust we must fulfill and pass on to future generations. We are obligated as stewards of our times to give them a planet that nurtures and sustains as earlier generations have passed on to us!"

Sapphire MacKenzie let her words sink in as she gazed all about her from the top of the bridge over the railroad line on Ulman Boulevard. With their thousands from all over Cascadia, from British Columbia and Alberta, from Washington, Oregon, Northern California, Montana, and Idaho, they had seized the high ground here three days ago and set up the microphones and speakers. The activists had also established encampments and locked themselves into human chains across the railroad below, as well as at several strategic points on the railroad lines further east in the industrial area.

From atop the bridge Sapphire could see the massed troops and tanks of Empire in the distance creating a vast semi-circle about them for miles. As far as could be observed in the flat lands beyond were fully laden train cars waiting on sidings. She could also easily see the hundreds and hundreds of empty barges anchored on the Columbia River waiting to be loaded with coal – depending on today's Supreme Court decision.

It was an untenable situation, MacKenzie was quite aware of that, but she would not be deterred.

"Indeed, we will uphold our sacred trust to future generations and defy the Kingpins of Carbon," she asserted. "No more will we tolerate their WPD's, their Weapons of Planetary Destruction! Here we make our stand and forge our destiny today – no matter how the Supreme Court rules!"

Another cheer exploded from the crowd as the Doug flags pumped up and down.

"Of course," she acknowledged, "you all are quite aware why we are gathered here today at the tiny Port of Morrow in such numbers. The proposal to float coal down the mighty Columbia River on barges so as to export it and make a quick buck has been around for years.

"It has repeatedly been rejected by the Elders and Stewards of Cascadia, but Empire and the Kingpins of Carbon – with their endless litigation and bottomless corporate funding – have never backed down," Sapphire asserted. "For years the case bounced around in lower courts until finally this term, it made it to the Supreme Court. And of course, if the Court rules in favor of the fossil fuel industry, this case would effectively open any and all avenues to shipping and pipelines, and selling fossil fuels at will. And then our planet, in short order, will be rendered uninhabitable for our species."

All this was news to no one, but MacKenzie had an objective, a target she was aiming at.

"So reasonably, what will the Supreme Court decide?" she posed, giving the throngs a moment to stew.

"We all know the answer to that as well," Sapphire replied to her own question. "The big money from the corporations and the Kingpins of Carbon long ago bought out the Congress. Then, in the last election, a bigoted and bombastic, billionaire carnival barker conned his own way into the Presidency – and with his inexperienced cabinet of fellow billionaires and millionaires – they were welcomed with open arms by the billionaires of the oligarchy...producing a pack of corrupt cronies, one and all.

"With a Supreme Court vacancy awaiting the new President's decision, he promptly appointed a rigidly idealistic conservative to take the place of the Justice that had passed away. Then later, when one of the four liberal-leaning judges died and another was forced to resign for health reasons, the new President appointed two new Justices that have always sucked the fossil fuel teat for money."

She delayed momentarily and then tossed in: "And may I add that one of the new Justices appointed was Senator Dudley Gassack from Idaho – a true traitor to Cascadia!"

A round of boos, disgusted catcalls, and imitations of flatulence filled the air when Gassack's name was mentioned.

"All we have left are The Two," she continued, "two elderly female jurists who are essentially powerless, but nevertheless instill the best hope we have. The Two represent all that is left institutionally that care about future generations over short-term corporate greed that pillages our planet and debilitates us all. And yet – though esteemed – The Two are indeed powerless, as are we The People."

Not wasting a second more, Sapphire MacKenzie wanted to know what chance they had with The Seven firmly in control of the Supreme Court. "Does it seem like we are facing nearly impossible odds? Is it a reality that all is hopeless? Are all our concerns for the planet and the welfare of future generations a miserable waste of time?"

The gathered masses grew silent even as the Cascadia Doug flags fell limp. Silence reigned, waiting for the words that would follow.

"Our odds are impossible if we strive to work within Empire's corrupt system," she acknowledged quietly.

All were focused upon the striking six-foot tall woman, her shoulder length brown hair, alluring body, and passionate demeanor. Those close enough could see the animation in her brilliant blue eyes, but even those at the distant reaches garnered optimism from the courage of her convictions.

"We can no longer be subjected to the oligarchs and their corrupt corporate governance," Sapphire declared definitively. "The only way things will alter for future generations and our planet is to foment radical change. And that will become our strength. No longer will we waste effort on reform, for we embrace a vision that makes compromise impossible.

"We have severed ourselves from the formal structures of power, and in those grassroots is where our strength arises," MacKenzie asserted. "If, and when, the Supreme Court decides against us today, we will hold our ground until the aggressors of the Earth tear us from our perches; we will dissolve if necessary into the background of our beloved Cascadia – only to arise ever stronger!"

The applause, the cheers, the clamor of approval lifted skyward as if it were one voice. Once more the thousands hoisted their Cascadia Doug flags and Sapphire MacKenzie took note.

"Always keep close to your heart," she encouraged all, "what the Cascadia Doug flag symbolizes in our naturally beautiful bioregion here in the Pacific Northwest."

Stepping away from the microphone momentarily, Sapphire borrowed a supporter's flag and held it high as she returned.

"The blue bar at the top represents the moisture-laden sky above, our lakes and rivers, our inland waters, the Salish Sea, and the Pacific Ocean," she spoke into the mic. "The white in the center represents the snow and the clouds, and the green represents the evergreen forests and fields of the Pacific Northwest. The solitary Douglas Fir tree stands for endurance, defiance, and resilience. All these taken together symbolize what our Cascadia is about!"

Sapphire MacKenzie abruptly hoisted the pole she was holding with its flag into the air and pumped it up and down.

In response, the masses gathered about her began thrusting their flags to the repetitive chants of, "Cascadia, Cascadia, Cascadia..."

Several minutes later, as the chanting finally began to trail off, a low and distant rumbling began to emanate. Seeming to vibrate through the ground itself, the sea of protestors occupying the Port of Morrow became progressively more aware of a foreboding, and incoming threat.

From her vantage point atop the Ulman Boulevard bridge, Sapphire MacKenzie quickly discerned the source for the growling mechanical disruption. The vast semi-circle of Empire's "National Guard" troops had activated their armored personnel carriers, their humvees, tanks, and paddy wagons; they were transiting down arterials toward their occupied Port hub as if upon spokes on a wheel.

Sapphire readied herself to address the crowd about the coming forces when an aide interrupted by whispering into her ear. She requested that the message be repeated and when it was, she nodded, standing once more at her full height to address the protestors.

"I've just been informed," MacKenzie announced, "that the decision has come down from the Supreme Court of the United States. To no one's surprise, The Seven have prevailed over The Two. Coal barge shipments down the Columbia River can begin immediately; the oil and liquefied natural gas will roll unceasingly on our rail lines, and new pipeline plans crisscrossing Cascadia will be allowed to go forward unabated. And the future of our species is now in greater peril than ever before!"

The noise of a thousand approaching motors of military equipment grew palpably louder with each passing second. Soon Empire would be atop them all and begin clearing a way for the dictates of the corporations and the Kingpins of Carbon.

"The time of confrontation will soon be upon us; we will not shirk our responsibilities to the future!" Sapphire displayed no fear, only resolve, and the gathered throngs fed upon it. "Prepare yourselves: engage in peaceful and passive resistance, knowing you are doing the right thing! We of the Cascadian resistance truly are The Thin Green

Line! Long live Cascadia and future generations!"

The words were barely out of MacKenzie's mouth and the cheers had only commenced when the initial troops were upon them and tear gas canisters began launching at random. Those with gas masks put them on; others in the direct line of fire retreated with all haste.

From atop her perch on the bridge, Sapphire knew it would all be over in mere hours. She had experienced scenes such as this too many times before. The tear gas and pepper spray would rise and fill the air, and the nightsticks would fall. The paddy wagons would be filled, and likewise all local jails and detention centers. Sapphire fully realized with the size of this crowd the cellblocks up in the Tri-Cities in Washington would likely be at capacity as well.

Here at the Port of Morrow resisters on the railroad tracks would have their linked chains cut away by troops with bolt cutters; they would be arrested, and the trains would begin to roll. The boxcars laden with coal would pull to the water's edge, barge after barge would be loaded, and the Kingpins of Carbon would finally enslave the mighty Columbia.

Nearby, on the embankment leading up to the bridge, a tear gas canister exploded. Sapphire and friends about her hastily donned their gas masks. Defiantly, they all stood their ground as they watched humvees and paddy wagons part the crowd, approaching from the south.

Sapphire MacKenzie was well aware of what was coming next. She only hoped her benefactor could get her released on bail in a timely manner. For there was an important and very secret meeting next week on July 4th in Port Townsend, Washington – her hometown – that she could not afford to miss.

CHAPTER TWO

Garfield Taylor sat motionless with night vision goggles trained on the Maxwell brothers. They were across Washington State's Highway 2, the Stevens Pass highway, as they labored above the East Portal of the Cascade Tunnel. He was tucked away on a natural surveillance perch Billy Maxwell had discovered while Garf and Billy's brother Timmy were planting explosives atop the relatively less protected West Portal of the Cascade Tunnel the previous evening.

Garf was relieved the Maxwell brothers were working together again. There was no pleasure in being ordered around by someone six or seven years younger, even if Timmy was an explosives expert for a major Northwest excavating contractor. Timmy and Garf didn't particularly like each other either; it was only Timmy's loyalty to his older brother Billy, and Garf's symbiotically beneficial working arrangement with Billy that brought Garf and Timmy together at all.

Yet Garf Taylor knew his difficulties with Timmy were only a blip on the radar when it came to their overall mission and his destiny as a leader. Timmy was merely another tool he must adeptly manipulate if revolution in Cascadia, and beyond, was to become a reality. And it would become a reality...

Squinting through the night vision lenses, Taylor surveyed the scene beyond the Maxwell brothers looking for anything untoward. Billy and Timmy were a moderate distance below Highway 2, and approximately the same distance to the tall chain link fence with reverse angled barbed wire on top, to repel anyone with ambitions of scaling the fence. They were also relatively close to the heavily locked access gate from Highway 2 with similar barbwire above.

Within the fenced area was a tall triangular tower with a surveillance camera up high. For all they knew, there were probably sensors mounted inside the area as well, but they had no intention – anymore – of breaching the boundary. Where Timmy and Billy were currently planting their explosives was still directly above the tunnel and train tracks, so their main plans were intact. The garnishes they wanted to add as emphasis had to be aborted, however, as too dangerous.

Inside the confines of the fencing was not only the East Portal of the tunnel itself, but also the fanhouse and supporting buildings to address ventilation issues in the nearly eight mile long tunnel under the Cascades. To reduce problems with fumes, fanhouse doors close on the East Portal and huge fans blow cool air through the tunnel to purge the fumes. While this "tunnel flushing" is being conducted a tremendous racket ensues; it was this cover Taylor and the Maxwell brothers had originally intended to use to plant explosives in critical areas of the fanhouse.

Unfortunately, such tactics were deemed too risky so the exclamation point at the end of their nearly week long statement-in-the-making was abandoned. In the end, the statement itself would say all that was needed.

They had met up in the Seattle area last Friday, June 28th. It was the same day as the protests and police chaos at the Port of Morrow in eastern Oregon, and the same day as the Supreme Court decision – the results of which was a surprise to no one. In fact, the timing of those events dovetailed perfectly with Garf's planning for their statement. With so much police and military attention devoted to the Columbia

River coal barge protests, a splendid diversionary smokescreen was permitted them.

In Timmy Maxwell's oversized pickup truck loaded with explosives and camping gear, they stayed that night at a campground relatively close to the popular tourist destination of Multnomah Falls, on the Oregon side of the Columbia River. Not too many miles from the campground, railroad tracks that ran along the Oregon side of the Columbia crossed Oneonta Creek. It was on the steel girders that supported the railroad bridge that Timmy secured the first of his dynamite packages. He then wired them with timers of double cell phone backup so as to explode simultaneously with the rest of their planned targets.

The railroad bridge over Oneonta Creek was a fair distance from Interstate 84 that also followed the banks of the Columbia, but the scenic two-lane highway used mostly by tourists was close enough to the railroad bridge to cause collateral damage if someone was driving by when the bridge blew. Taylor and the Maxwells regretted the possibility, yet accepted the fact that such things happen in war.

Because of unexpectedly heavy traffic in the area, it took them two nights, Saturday and Sunday, the 29th and 30th of June, to complete the relatively simple job over Oneonta Creek. On Monday morning, July 1st, they headed east on Interstate 84. At Hood River, Oregon, the saboteurs crossed on the toll bridge over the Columbia River to White Salmon, Washington; they then headed east once more to a rest area just past Lyle, Washington. The rest area was on a scenic hillside overlooking the Columbia, under which the train tracks that paralleled the mighty river were forced to enter and exit tunnels on both east and west sides.

Although the entire drive on Monday had only taken a little more than an hour, the three men dallied here by lounging and hiking about until darkness fell. Having thoroughly surveyed the area by light of day, it took only a few hours to dig holes as Timmy specified. His main intent was for maximum downward concussion on both rail tunnel openings at the extreme reaches of the mountainside containing the centrally located rest area.

When their work was complete and timers synchronized with those set on the rail bridge over Oneonta Creek on the Oregon side, they slept discretely at the far reaches of the rest area for the remainder of the night. And even though there were "No Camping" signs, they were left undisturbed.

Early on Tuesday morning, July 2nd, the revolutionists drove further east along the Washington side of the Columbia. Turning eventually north onto U.S. Highway 97, they traveled north for several hours along the east side of the Cascade Mountains on Highway 97, and Interstates 82 and 90. Going through the town of Leavenworth and then just past Berne – where the East Portal of the Cascade Tunnel was located – Billy Maxwell was dropped off with camping gear, camouflage clothing, binoculars, and night vision goggles.

That night, while Billy Maxwell went into surveillance mode in preparation for the following evening, Timmy further schooled Garf on planting explosives over railroad tracks at the West Portal of the Cascade Tunnel. Again, Timmy synchronized the detonations over the tunnel entrance to the special time they had chosen for their fireworks show. When finished, they slept nearby off a little used, bumpy and rock strewn forest road under a clear sky filled with millions of stars.

This morning, the 3rd of July, Timmy and Garf had traveled back to the east side of Stevens Pass to meet Billy at a pre-designated camping area not far from Berne. Billy conveyed his opinion that the fanhouse was too dangerous to blow, but that they still should be able to set explosives above the railroad tunnel before it crept too deeply under the Cascades.

Garf's planning had been well thought out and unique; in fact, he prided himself on it. It was the same kind of out-of-the-box thinking that the 911 plotters had used on the World Trade Center buildings and he admired such scheming. Yet where the 911 attackers had slaughtered thousands of innocents for little substantial reason, his people would be making a first strike on an out-of-control danger that threatened all – Weapons of Planetary Destruction, or WPD's.

Transportation was the Achilles' heel of fossil fuel WPD's and it was transportation arterials that his revolutionists would strike down first. After this fireworks show, Garf was firm in the knowledge that a new day would be dawning in Cascadia, a day all Cascadia was waiting for, and the day a defiant Cascadia would begin leading the way to the inevitable worldwide revolution.

All at once, Garf's attentions were snatched away from the Maxwell brothers below to a small light bobbing along the fencing as it went downhill past the support buildings and Highway 2. Someone with a flashlight appeared to be coming uphill along the fence – toward Billy and Timmy – but whoever it might be was still far enough away to not clearly discern.

Without wasting a second, Garf spoke into the microphone of the two-way radio that would be received by Billy Maxwell's earphones.

"Time to chill, Billy," Garf said calmly into the radio. "Do you hear me, Billy? Time to chill."

Immediately, Billy was whispering in Garf's ear over the radio, "What's up?"

"You have a flashlight coming up at you along the fence: don't make a sound."

For three minutes, then four, then five, the man with the flashlight continued his uneven pace along the rough ground next to the perimeter fence. When he was only perhaps one hundred yards from the spot above the tunnel where the Maxwell brothers had been digging, a dog began to bark from behind him.

The watchman seemed to face a moment of indecision as the flashlight turned back down the fence, up the fence, and back down again. The dog's barking became more insistent; the flashlight turned and began going back down the hill at a rapid rate.

Garf watched the man ramble away. When he was comfortable a steady retreat was underway he again spoke over the radio.

"Billy, the flashlight went back down the fence line. You should be okay for now," Garf informed him. "How much longer do you have?"

Clearing his throat, Billy replied, "Timmy was just ready to set the timers when you had us freeze. Then all we got to do is cover our tracks and get out of here."

"Good." Garf was relieved. "Make haste."

"Will do."

Ten minutes later, Billy radioed that their work was complete and they would begin making their way up to the highway. Garf surveyed the area for danger once more; when all was clear he made his way down to Highway 2 to meet them.

Even without night vision goggles on, it would have been easy to detect which Maxwell brother was in the lead up to the highway. A solid block of muscle, older brother Billy moved like a semi-trailer coming down the highway. Stealthy and circumspect because of the circumstances, he stormed up the hill nonetheless, exuding even in the dark an aura of defiant power and independent strength.

The form of younger brother Timmy following was a study in contrasts. Where Billy was barely five feet seven inches tall and seemed almost as wide, Timmy was a more gangly five foot eleven inches, lithe and slippery. Both shared similar facial features, nonetheless: the square jaw, the blond hair, the blue eyes, and Marine haircut were surely gifted them both by whoever their unknown father was.

Garf and the Maxwell brothers met at the center of the Stevens Pass road.

"We've done them all now!" Billy whispered triumphantly. Silently, each exchanged a hearty high-five in celebration.

Without another word, the saboteurs fell in line and walked briskly up the dark highway. Timmy's big pickup was parked hidden off a forest access road about fifteen minutes away. Though traffic was relatively light over Stevens Pass this late in the evening, whenever headlights were noticed in front or in back of them, the three quickly scrambled off the road for cover and to avoid detection.

Upon finally reaching the pickup truck, they hurriedly deposited shovels, picks, backpacks, and other gear into the bed of the truck. Garf dropped himself thankfully into the back seat, while Timmy drove and Billy rode shotgun. None of them spoke for several miles as they headed west back up the Pass. Each dwelled in his own thoughts until they passed near the location of the West Portal of the Cascade Tunnel.

With the spell of silence then seemingly broken, Garf congratulated the two brothers for their efforts.

"You both did a damn good job over the last several days," he told the Maxwells, "and you should be proud of what you're doing for Cascadia!"

"If only we could have set that fanhouse to blow too," Billy exclaimed from the front seat. "That would have been the icing on the cake."

"Don't worry," Garf reassured him, "the cake, or cakes, that we've prepared will be all we need."

Timmy, driving downhill towards the city of Everett that was more than an hour away, had his thoughts focused on other matters. He asked his brother if their younger sister Carolyn was still expecting them at such a late hour.

"I told Sis we'd be crashing at her place late tonight over a week ago," Billy said confidently, "so she'll be waiting for us."

"Sometimes, I think you take her too much for granted," Timmy tossed back at his older brother.

"She'll be ready," Billy assured him.

For several miles nothing more was said. Next to Timmy, Billy eventually appeared to grow drowsy while the silence from the back seat likely meant Garf was already asleep. Tired as well, Timmy was afraid he might drop off at the wheel unless he engaged in conversation with his fellow conspirators.

"So," Timmy began in a sharp voice that visibly roused his brother, "are you two still planning on attending that secret meeting in Port Townsend tomorrow?"

"Of course we are," Garf shot back, quite awake. "It has much to do with the future of Cascadia."

Suddenly Billy was laughing out loud. "Timmy, you know Garf wouldn't miss it. Sapphire MacKenzie is supposedly going to be there!"

There was an edge to Garf Taylor's voice when he replied, "A lot of people important to the future of Cascadia are supposedly going to be there. And we intend to see who we can recruit to our side, for our purposes."

Timmy couldn't help but poke a little fun at Garf.

"I'm sure recruiting a looker like Sapphire MacKenzie would no doubt serve many of your purposes," he suggested.

Next to him, brother Billy sniggered.

"We have a mission to accomplish," was Garf's curt reply in utmost seriousness.

Fully roused now and smiling to himself, Timmy Maxwell knew driving the rest of the way to Carolyn's apartment in Everett would be no problem.

CHAPTER THREE

Quimper Jones had always been a bit of an oddball, even by Port Townsend standards.

Sapphire MacKenzie's earliest memories included "Mister Q," as he was affectionately called by the children of the town.   He was everyone's favorite story-time reader at the Port Townsend library over the decades. A librarian for as long as most living memories stretched back, Mister Q always reminded Sapphire of a leprechaun with a magical, mystical pot of gold hidden somewhere just out of reach.

He was short, only five foot three or four, with a pointy jaw, prominent cheekbones, ruddy cheeks, and a twinkle in his eyes. Reinforcing the leprechaun aura, Mister Q dressed mostly in shades of light green to forest green and preferred disappearing into the forest around town rather than sharing conversation with his contemporaries after a day of work at the library.

Even now in his elder years, Mister Q was quite animated, seeming to transfer his exuberance to others with a mere smile, wink, or a nod. And he was doing a masterful job of entertaining and diverting attention of all those gathered in the old house, who were still waiting on someone of import to arrive.

Mr. Q had bought the old Victorian mansion several years ago. It was one of many still remaining from the 1800s on the hill overlooking Port Townsend Bay to the east. After his Uncle Rich had passed on and left him a tidy chunk for the old house and more, he quit working full time as a librarian, although he still cherished conducting regular story-time hours for the kiddies.

With his inheritance he also bought a small piece of property across Port Townsend Bay on Marrowstone Island, just south of the old Fort Flagler, and it was here he lived. The property didn't have much more than a shack with a wood burning stove, yet it was in this solace that he grew his prized rhododendrons – when he wasn't restoring the Victorian mansion, or reading tales to children.

Most of the nearly four thousand square foot building they were now sitting in had been beautifully revived, but Mister Q had skilled artisans doing some sort of remodel or upkeep project nearly every summer. No workers were present though this July Fourth; the old Victorian had been transformed into a popular bed and breakfast and was instead filled with guests, guests specifically chosen and specially invited.

They were all crowded into the Great Room on the first floor and most were gray, silver, and bald headed seniors in their fifties, sixties, seventies, and some eighties. These Elders of Cascadia nearly looped the periphery of the big room in multiple rows, except against one wall where there were three groups of tables and chairs.

Sapphire and fellow Free Cascadia activist leader Polly Hawser, from Vancouver/Victoria, were situated at the center table. A chair next to Sapphire intended for Glenn Aaron, the Free Cascadia leader from Portland, remained empty because his wife had gone into labor late last evening.

At the table to Sapphire's left sat Tomas and Linda Hernandez, representing the group Commons Rising. Sapphire met the former

Linda Sutton years ago when both worked as raft guides on the Snake and Salmon out of Riggins, Idaho. Even though Linda was now busy with two children under five, the former river guides tried to keep in touch when they could. Slightly behind and in the shadow of Tomas and Linda were two empty chairs. It was for whoever would fill these two chairs that everyone was apparently waiting on.

On Sapphire's right were Garfield Taylor and his brute of a friend, Billy Maxwell. Sapphire was wary of both – especially Billy – even if she had aided Garf in the past, and most recently by penning the basics of his soon to be released Manifesto.

She studied Garf as Mister Q was thanking everyone for attending, and then beginning introductions of all Elders in attendance. Somewhere in his mid-thirties, Garf always struck Sapphire as someone gifted, but also someone broodingly intense. With a swarthy, dark-hued complexion, his piercing brown eyes were fixed deep in sockets that spoke of inherent danger. Fortunately his raven black hair and beard were always cropped and trimmed fastidiously; otherwise, he would have looked straight off a wanted poster for an anarchist/terrorist of the early 1900s.

He was also taller than her six feet by three or four inches, yet lanky, striking one as perhaps underfed as a youth and unable to fill out. Still, Garfield Taylor was never lacking in virulent energy. In fact, there was something about him that made you keep your eye on him; there was something about Garf that warned he might explode in your direction if you weren't paying attention.

Even now, as Sapphire watched Garf's eyes follow Mr. Q's introductions of the Elders and Stewards, she could observe the fuse that was always burning, as well as the anger and the bitterness just below the surface. It was as if he realized the cards he'd been dealt were bad, but he had to play them anyway. In return, retention of some kind of dark powers seemed to be a Faustian trade he'd been granted - and he was emboldened to exercise them.

And yet, for all that, Sapphire respected and even liked the man. Although uncertain of his ultimate methods, Garfield Taylor was a dedicated revolutionist. It seemed his type would be necessary if Cascadia could ultimately repel the Kingpins of Carbon and create a new future for coming generations away from the current destructive path.

Garf and his muscular block of a comrade, Billy Maxwell, dropped into a whispered conference that reflected impatience and a demand for action. They seemed to disagree and Garf began to stand as a result. With a mere tug on the forearm, Billy had Garf seated once more. Billy spoke something into Garf's ear and reluctantly Garf stilled.

Sapphire was tired of the delay as well; she was ready to get on with the reason they had all journeyed here on the Fourth of July. As the introductions of the Elders came to an end, she hoped Mister Q could fill in further with something besides a Victorian home tour – with its six fireplaces, its beautiful newel post at the grand stairway, the bands of decorative shingles and the diagonal juxtaposition of the entry, and on and on – before the late and missing participants arrived.

Instead of a home tour, Mister Q began speaking on a topic he was quite well acquainted with: the town of Port Townsend, Washington, a place he'd known for seventy-seven years.

"So, I welcome you all to our beautiful little city of Port Townsend," Quimper Jones pipped with pleasure. "Those of you that have been here a few days, and those that have traveled here previously from afar, are aware of what a charming little place this burg truly is."

The diminutive host earnestly cast a grand welcome to all attending. Even though Garf Taylor simmered with sullen impatience, smiles were on the faces of the vast majority of the seniors gathered.

"As we wait for the remainder of our participants invited by consensus to arrive, let me tell you a little bit about the history of the city you are visiting, and why it is important to this vital meeting we are conducting today," stated Mister Q. "When Port Townsend was founded in the 1850s, speculators believed that with its safe, secure harbor, it would become a major port on the West Coast.

"By the 1880s Port Townsend was indeed a well-known seaport; it was prosperous and full of promise. During this time many of our Victorian era homes were built. The railroads were supposed to connect Port Townsend to boom times and it was this speculation that drove the rush to build so many buildings for shipping of goods and timber.

"Unfortunately, from around 1893 to 1897 a depression struck and nearly a quarter of the national railroads went broke," he explained shaking his head. "The rail lines that were built ended up on the east side of Puget Sound, in Olympia, Tumwater, Seattle and beyond. Port Townsend was nicknamed the 'City of Dreams' – because all those early dreams of wealth and prosperity failed to materialize..."

Mister Q continued to tell those gathered in one of the old Victorian dreams more about the early history of the town. Sapphire MacKenzie, however, had heard these tales since she was young; her thoughts began to drift as she gazed at the little leprechaun and remembered the one book he suggested she read when she was maybe eleven or twelve.

It was following a family camping trip to either the Cascades or the Olympics, she didn't recall which, and back in the library afterwards, Sapphire remarked to Mister Q how she couldn't understand the clear cutting of the forests she had seen, that rendered entire mountains devoid of trees. Already to her young mind, she declared that to be a criminal act.

Mister Q said little in reply, though he did offer her a book from the library. It turned out to be "The Monkey Wrench Gang," by Edward Abbey. For almost two years it was her favorite book and she read it repeatedly. The spell eventually wore off, however, as for her the book became stale, juvenile, and lacking true seriousness. From then on for years, she studied on her own everything she could get her hands on regarding revolution – genuine and authentic revolution. Revolution, she truly came to believe, was the only avenue open to preserve the species and planet in the face of greed, corruption, and the destruction of the supporting environment.

As she gazed upon the magical little man entertaining all with his tales, Sapphire knew she was in the presence of a true subversive – a genuine librarian.

Her musings were disrupted only seconds later, by a door opening off the great room to a sitting room beyond, which eventually led to a rear entrance to the house. It was the same access she had used so as to be less noticeable to any of Empire's operatives that might be watching the house.

Through the door walked an indistinct, common looking man perhaps in his early forties. A pretty girl followed him in; she was easily half his age and could've been his daughter, except for the lack of facial resemblance.

These two were apparently who Tomas and Linda Hernandez were waiting on, as was Mister Q, and everyone else. Upon spotting Tomas and Linda at their table, they greeted each other, offered apologies for their tardiness, and took their chairs behind Tomas and Linda.

Mister Q, seeming relieved that the final participants had arrived, began to wind up his fill-in remarks to get to the meat of the day's gathering.

"And so, although Port Townsend was once called the 'City of Dreams' in relation to dreams unfulfilled," he sighed, "from this day hence, this July Fourth, America's Independence Day, we want to re-envision Port Townsend as a 'City of Dreams' where forging a new destiny for coming generations gets formally launched. We want to dream in this city, today in Cascadia, a new mental paradigm to lead us forth in order to overcome the downward spiraling death grip the oligarchs and corporations have on our lives – and our planet!"

So much passion, so much earnest enthusiasm was suddenly emitted from the elfin statured man that his audience was completely enthralled. Before Mister Q began speaking again, Sapphire took note that even Garf Taylor was irrepressibly drawn in.

"We all know the situation we are wallowing in and that is what has brought us together today," Quimper Jones factually declared. "We are all aware the Kingpins of Carbon own the most powerful corporations; they have duped the people and bought out the representative government of the former democracies; they have installed their own patsies in the court systems to forestall any checks and balances. And this is true in both the United States and Canada, the two governmental entities that presently rule our Cascadia as their fiefdoms."

Mister Q stalled momentarily as he wandered about gathering his thoughts. When he drew close to the table where Tomas and Linda sat, Sapphire caught the eye of the man sitting behind that had arrived late. He was staring directly at her; instinctively – though not wanting to – she averted her eyes. Sapphire had never met him before; she wanted to know who he was...

"We all also know what happened last week in the U.S. Supreme Court," continued the little leprechaun. "The Seven ruled with the fossil fuel Kingpins and barges loaded with coal have already begun floating down our Columbia River. The ruling also effectively opens unlimited pipeline construction throughout our Cascadia, and even more tanker train cars of oil and natural gas across our Cascadia for the eventual befouling of the global atmosphere and the demise of our species."

Quimper Jones ceased speaking and gazed into the eyes of the audience.

"Within Empire's corrupt system, we commoners have little if any power to change these realities we face. We now come to the root reason of why we are all here today, and why a consensus of Elders and Stewards have invited the groups of these particular younger participants seated at the tables before us to this 'City of Dreams.'"

Determined to muster a pot of gold from the invited participants, Mister Q turned and addressed them directly.

"There is only one question we ask you all today; there is only one question all of Cascadia now needs the answer to." Quimper Jones laid it all on the line. "Tell us: how best do we conduct the coming Revolution?"

***

Mister Q let his question hang for several moments before backtracking slightly.

"Indeed, a Revolution beginning in Cascadia seems a foregone conclusion," he admitted, "but the questions we lay before you young leaders is as much about how we conduct the Revolution, as it is where subsequently we will go with it. In fact, these questions interpenetrate until they become indistinguishable."

Quimper Jones scrutinized the participants at each of the three tables. In the open space available between participants and Elders, he then began to roam about, musing.

"We need to recognize where we are going and how to get there," the little leprechaun began, "and we can only do that by understanding who we are and what Cascadia is to us."

Rhetorically, he posed the question: "So, what is Cascadia?"

Without hesitation Mister Q responded to his own query.

"Cascadia is as much an ideal, as a specific geographic region," he stated factually. "It is a bioregion identified with environmental stewardship, self-sufficiency, and sustainability. We strive to attain bottom-up, local autonomy, local food networks, and local economic ties. We share a dedication to open source, dynamic and associative governing models. In short, Cascadia is everything that Empire is not."

With one hand sweeping in the direction of the gathered seniors and back to the invited participants, Quimper Jones stated that it was the desire of all of the Elders to pass along a sustainable Cascadia, one that nourishes and nurtures future generations.

"We, the Elders and Stewards of Cascadia, understand our time is limited," he declared, "and we offer whatever wisdom and resources we have available to those of you with the best laid plans at this critical time. We have seen this moment approaching over the decades – this corporate coup d'état in slow motion – but have been unable to derail it."

Mister Q was poised to continue when Sapphire's attention as well as all the others were shifted to an interrupting voice seated in the back row of seniors.

"Excuse me, sir," a white haired man respectfully stated while rising to his feet, "but before we get too far into things, I have something to add."

"By all means," Quimper Jones responded graciously, "anyone here is welcome to express themselves at any time."

"Thank you," said the old man, "and I'll try to be brief." He cleared his throat. "The introductions went rather quickly, so let me tell you who I am once more. My name is Thaddeus Upton and I'm a farmer from southwest Alberta, not too far from Lethbridge."

The elderly gentleman paused and looked about the room.

"Now, I'm not even certain folks would technically call where I come from 'Cascadia,'" Upton admitted. "And that, my friends, is why Cascadia is even more of an ideal, than simply a bioregion. The Kingpins of Carbon have raped our Alberta, they've raped North Dakota, and they've raped Wyoming. They've raped the planet and threaten the existence of coming generations.

"If you do things right, if your Revolution is just and fair," the old man proposed, "you will find the common peoples of the world will stand with Cascadia in their rebellion against the oligarchs of Empire. The idea of Cascadia will unite us all. And as I told my young friends who arrived late when they visited my farm, we do have substantial resources, individually and thus collectively. People of Alberta and elsewhere will flow to your cause – if you can do it right!"

Applause erupted within the great room of the old Victorian house as Thaddeus Upton sat down once more. Sapphire, however, wasn't so much caught up in the clapping of hands as she was drawn to the mysterious strangers seated behind Tomas and Linda that the old man had referenced.

Once more, as Sapphire glanced toward the ordinary looking man and the younger woman, she caught his eye fixed on hers. This time she peacefully held his gaze before turning back to Mister Q as he began speaking again.

"Thank you for your comments, Mr. Upton," Quimper Jones beamed, "and for traveling so far to join us in our City of Dreams on this most important occasion."

Mister Q then addressed all those gathered.

"Indeed, we are all on a journey toward the discovery of a new future for us all," Jones made it clear. "We are questing toward Cascadia. There can be no peace, no future for coming generations until a new, far-seeing mental paradigm of Cascadia is conjured and achieved."

Turning on his heel, Mister Q was directly in front of the table where Sapphire and Polly Hawser were seated. He smiled at the vibrant young woman he had known since she was a child.

"I think it is finally time to hear from our invited guests about how we should conduct a Revolution," he simply stated.

**

Sapphire MacKenzie smiled kindly back at the little leprechaun.

"Being among the most visible activists in Cascadia, you need little introduction to those of us here," began Quimper Jones. "Our concerns are naturally focused on the physical brutality you and others suffered at the hands of Empire's enforcers during the coal barge protests at the Port of Morrow last week. We hope all are progressing toward better health."

Attention was immediately fixed upon the sling Sapphire's left arm dangled in, but more so on Polly Hawser's forehead bandage and black eye.

After an awkward moment, Polly merely said, "Thank you, but it could have been worse."

Sapphire quickly picked up on Polly's sentiments.

"It wasn't pretty," she admitted, before changing the subject. "But I do have some very good news for you this morning. Just before arriving here, I learned that Glenn Aaron – our fellow Free Cascadia organizer who couldn't be here today – and his wife are celebrating the birth early this morning in Portland of a beautiful and healthy baby girl. This news couldn't be better!"

Some of those assembled cheered while smiles adorned most faces.

"Our congratulations to them!" Mister Q joined in. "Another new life enters the world on this most solemn day, another new future that we must make our responsibility and duty to sustain and cherish."

Quimper Jones again spoke directly to Polly and Sapphire. "So, for the sake of the future, how best do you believe we should go about the Revolution for the benefit of coming generations and the nurturing of a sustainable planet?"

Polly and Sapphire, both a bit stunned by the magnitude of the question, conferred in whispers for a moment. A few seconds later, it was Polly who spoke.

"I've had constant headaches since the beatings last week at the Columbia River protests," she demurred, "so my thoughts aren't coming together too well right now. But it doesn't matter that much; Sapphire and I are of one mind on these issues, so I'll defer to her."

"Again, we are sorry things didn't turn out so well in Oregon," Mister Q said to Polly with compassion, "and hope you feel better soon." Directing his attention to Sapphire, he asked, "How best do you think we should go about things?"

All eyes were focused on the commanding and striking young woman with the brilliant blue eyes. Gathering her thoughts took little time, and even less to begin expressing them.

"Your question, Mister Q, is not an easy one to answer in only a few sentences," Sapphire MacKenzie admitted. "But I can easily talk around it enough to point us in a good direction."

Sapphire began by starting at the end destination. A new country, a totally new sovereign nation that would become a model for the rest of the world is what the ultimate goal of the Revolution must be, she explained.

"The oligarchs of Empire, especially the Kingpins of Carbon, have achieved unchecked political and economic power," Sapphire proclaimed. "They have rendered the people disposable and pushed us into a corner. A true populist revolt in Cascadia is the beginning; the sovereign nation of Cascadia is the end goal."

"Make no mistake about it – from beginning to end – this is a *class war* we are engaged in," she took pains to point out. "In their unbridled greed and avarice the rich declared war on us, and they have very nearly won. They care nothing about self-sacrifice for the common good; they are a cancer on true democracy!"

Coming into her own, Sapphire MacKenzie slid her chair back from the table and rose to stand tall. Intensely, she gazed about the room.

"Aristotle knew these oligarchs long ago," she noted. "With the rise of an oligarchic, plutocratic state, he realized there are only two avenues that may be chosen. One route is to enslave the masses by means of ruthless and savage tyranny. Today we see that totalitarianism enforced by a police state.

"The other option Aristotle clearly perceived," Sapphire recalled, "was that the destitute masses would rise; they would revolt to remedy the imbalances of power, money, and privilege."

Sapphire paused, surveying all those in attendance.

"This battle, this class war, has been waged over and over throughout human history," she pointed out. "The only thing is: this time it's different! This time our oligarchs, our Bastards of Carbon, have the capability of bringing down the entire species with their single-minded greed and lust for power and dominance. Never before has the mantle of such dire responsibility been laid at the feet of current generations.

"We have to make a choice," Sapphire challenged everyone. "We have to take one of Aristotle's options and only one is open to us and coming generations. We will not submit: we must revolt!"

The fiery words, the passion and emotion enthralled nearly all in the room, much like her speeches before a sea of protestors. The only visible exception, perhaps, was Quimper Jones.

Jones had taken a seat when Sapphire was given the floor. Now, he rose and approached her.

"With all due respect," he said calmly, steadily, "I believe all here are in agreement about the necessity of revolt. The question I put before you once more is: how best do we conduct the Revolution? What are to be our methods?"

The smile on Sapphire's face was triumphant.

"That's incredibly simple, Mister Q," she insisted. "We merely do whatever works! That's how all successful revolutions throughout history have been conducted."

Gently chiding her, Quimper Jones stated they were all looking for something more specific.

"More specific?" Sapphire countered. "How about something more logical too? It would make very good sense to get behind the Transition movement and build Transition Towns away from fossil fuel dependence, toward permaculture, and a more sustainable future."

Directing everyone's attention to those seated at the table on her left, she mentioned, "Or maybe with all of us being commoners, we could enthusiastically join efforts with my friends Tomas and Linda Hernandez here, and work to alter the status quo by a Commons Rising approach. Or perhaps, Garf Taylor and his friends have valid and pragmatic approaches as well.

"The bottom line is, Mister Q and all, we must do whatever works," stated Sapphire quite emphatically. "Our central difficulty is that nothing we propose can even be raised as subject matter or valid material for discussion with the oligarchs and Bastards of Carbon. That will not happen until we gain an equal foothold with them in the yes or no proposition regarding the production of fossil fuels."

"And just how do you suggest we get to that point?" queried Jones.

Sapphire exuded a nearly visible aura of confidence.

"That's simple too," she grinned. "The only way is to thwart their ability to produce and pollute with fossil fuels; then they will begin to listen to us. And the only way to thwart them is to cut off their shipment and supply lines; it's their Achilles heel. When the S.O.B.'s have their lifeblood supply lines disrupted and cut, they will be forced to talk with us."

From those seated in rings about the tables, a woman's voice called out, "Are we talking about eco-terrorism again? Here in Cascadia we saw how well that went over twenty to twenty-five years ago."

"Whatever works," Sapphire responded. "Listen, our purpose must be the same as Martin Luther King wrote in his 1963 letter from the Birmingham city jail: 'we must create a situation so crisis packed that it will inevitably open the door to negotiation.'"

She let that hang only a second, then added, "Or we might remember as well what Gandhi said in 1932: 'Those who have to bring about radical changes in human conditions and surroundings cannot do it except by raising a ferment in society.'"

Silence reigned for a few long moments before Sapphire concluded.

"We will raise a ferment in society," she promised, "and we'll do that by any methods that work to foment revolution. After all, that's what a revolution is all about."

***

Stroking his pointed chin in thought, Quimper Jones thanked Sapphire MacKenzie for her contribution. "Your thoughts and efforts toward change in Cascadia are highly regarded and always appreciated." He was about to say something else, but stopped short.

Turning toward Tomas and Linda Hernandez, Mister Q redirected his query.

"I pose a similar question to you," he stated with equanimity, "how do we best conduct the coming revolution? And please don't be hesitant to propose specifics, if you wish."

Tomas and Linda conferred briefly among themselves, then turned to the stranger sitting behind them and his young female companion. Seconds later, Tomas rose to speak. As he stood, Sapphire again locked upon the guest unknown to her behind her old friends and wondered whom he could be.

All eyes in the great room now focused on Tomas Hernandez, his clearly Hispanic features, his dark hair, brown eyes, and slightly bushy eyebrows. Of moderate height and build, he was about five feet ten, around one hundred sixty pounds. Tomas was a little more formally dressed than most others in attendance this July Fourth in his button down shirt and slacks, but he wore them comfortably. His face spoke of friendliness and good cheer; he was obviously someone easy to be around.

"Thank you, Mr. Jones, and everyone that was kind enough to invite us here," he said graciously. "We'd be most glad to respond in detail to your question, yet to preface my statements – and with all due respect to our friend Sapphire MacKenzie and the alliances she has established – I have no doubt with the rising once more of the commons, we have already begun fomenting the revolution."

"What bullshit!" Garf Taylor erupted from the table on the other side of Sapphire. "You obviously have no conception of what a true revolution is all about."

"Please, Mister Taylor," Quimper Jones stepped in, "you will certainly have an opportunity to express your views. Please, may we allow Mister Hernandez to continue without interruption?"

Garf didn't return comment; he simply seemed to snarl as he sunk back in his chair.

Quimper Jones motioned Tomas to continue.

"It is already underway," Tomas Hernandez asserted definitively. "Whether Cascadia becomes a new sovereign nation or even a de facto country, it will be commoners, by commoning, that must lead the way into the new day. As commoners, we surely have the numbers to determine the sway of the future – and we will!"

Hernandez paused and studied those he spoke to. Nodding his head, he stated, "For too long we have allowed the private plunder of our common wealth. The aberration of private property allowed the greedy and power-hungry to commodify what actually belongs to all, so that a disproportionate profit may be stolen by the few.

"For hundreds of years the Market and the State have colluded to enclose and privatize portions of the commons – that which should be held by all," he added, "and then after making their profits, have made the commons their dumping ground. Examples are everywhere. Oil companies steal out of the ground what actually belongs to us all, and if pristine wilderness areas are damaged or underwater ocean spills pollute the sea, well, that's a problem for the commons. Timber corporations rape and pillage our public forests. Industrial trawlers obliterate coastal fisheries without any thought of sustaining the resource for all. Mining companies pay the government a small fee to extract the common wealth of us all, then we commoners are left to clean up the environmental damages for decades thereafter. And of course there's the ultimate example: the decimation of our global atmosphere by human caused climate change and the threat to all species on our planet."

Tomas ceased speaking momentarily.

"I could go on and on with examples and you could too," he admitted. "It's been said economic enclosures are more than just merely appropriations of resources. They are also attacks on communities and their practice of commoning. And I couldn't agree more."

Once again, Tomas Hernandez paused. Moving out from behind the table he began to roam the small open space previously occupied by Quimper Jones.

"So perhaps you wonder," he posed rhetorically, "how the commons might rise once again?" Tomas turned directly on Garf Taylor. "How might the revolution in Cascadia already be underway?"

Without allowing Garf wiggle room, Tomas turned and addressed all again.

"Let me tell you something simple about all commoners," he spoke as if revealing a secret. "Whatever our commons may be, we *care* about it. We have a relationship with our commons; we have a history with our commons. It's *our* forests, it's our groundwater, and it's *our* air that we all breathe. We have traditions and rules among ourselves that preserve *our* common interests into the future, and simultaneously punish thieves and slackers that violate the common interest, the common wealth.

"It's *our* money," Hernandez stated emphatically, "and that is why commoners join cooperative, not-for-profit community banks. Because it is *ours*, and we *care*, other commoners focus on free, open source software. Still others care about what we eat and thus concentrate their commoning efforts on Slow Food activism and permaculture. And then there are commoners sharing urban gardens, seed banks open to all, academic researching, and online wikis.

"The involved commoner cannot help but see the revival of the commons as an organizing principle for social change," he declared, "and the foremost manner in which we challenge the neoliberal state by advancing an anti-capitalist agenda. As the commons continue to rise, as our numbers swell, we push and provoke the State/Market system into assuming a more sympathetic and benevolent aspect. Slowly, they begin to work with us as they see our commons approach is ultimately in their best interest as well."

Garf Taylor could take it no longer.

"You people are completely deluded!" he nearly spat out. "If you really believe that crap, Empire has already played you for fools and will crush you at their leisure. What a bunch of bullshit..."

Quimper Jones sprung out of his chair. "Mister Taylor! I don't believe Mister Hernandez has finished yet; you will restrain yourself."

Garf insolently shrugged his shoulders and smirked.

"Please carry on, Mister Hernandez," Quimper Jones implored.

An out-of-character scowl rose on Tomas's face as he glanced at Taylor. Shifting his attentions back to his audience, Hernandez noted that at long last, the various commons were becoming a force that the collusion of the State and Market had to confront and deal with on a more even playing field.

"It is because of the Commons Rising movement that a seismic shift is occurring in our relationship with Empire." Tomas had no doubts. "As most of you are aware, Commons Rising is a loose coalescing of vast numbers of commons especially in Cascadia. Together we espouse transparency, fairness, and democratic action, as well as social cooperation and environmental stewardship. The numbers of commoners and commons joining Commons Rising swells with each passing day. Our revolution will erode the ground Empire has maintained for millennia; we are already dissolving them from within."

Hernandez turned to confront Garf Taylor directly.

"We are already the new Cascadia; the turning of the tide is underway," he affirmed. "We have already created the Revolution!"

***

Sapphire watched Tomas strut calmly back to his table and sit next to his wife. Again, they conferred with the stranger behind them, even as Sapphire sensed the collision course they were all on drawing ever closer.

She was well aware of the methodology Tomas, Linda, and Commons Rising proposed, but at Garf's request she had also composed the underpinnings for his soon-to-be released Manifesto. If the revolution in Cascadia was to be successful, trouble was surely brewing; the bumps in the road ahead had to be leveled or the cause would suffer.

Smiling to herself as Mister Q yielded the floor to Garf Taylor, she watched him rise. This was all going to be very interesting...

"Without any due respect," Garf snarled directly at Tomas and Linda, "I say it once more. You've been duped, you're being played for fools, and are completely clueless when it comes to creating a genuinely effective revolution!"

The viciousness of Taylor's tone caused Tomas Hernandez to physically recoil. He began to reply but a calming touch to his forearm from wife Linda induced restraint.

"As Sapphire suggested," Garf railed on, "Empire will only listen to us and begin to negotiate when we have standing in their eyes – because they feel threatened. The only way they'll come to the bargaining table is if they are brought forcibly."

Staring down Tomas Hernandez and speaking directly, he declared, "If you seduce others here and throughout Cascadia to follow your passively milquetoast, namby-pamby approach of Common Rising, Empire will have you in their pockets and under their thumbs forever."

Stepping out from behind the table, and ostensibly still lecturing Tomas, Garf Taylor's line of sight bounced among the gathered Elders. "But perhaps you need to be reminded of the true objectives, as well as the ways and means, of the fossil fuel giants – the Kingpins of Carbon – and maybe only then will you comprehend that a Commons Rising approach is far too little and far too late.

"You must not understand the immensity of the fossil fuel reserves," Garf theorized, "and the intent of the Kingpins to exhaust it all. Already scientists say the fossil fuel giants have many times more carbon in their reserves than we can safely burn. So what do they do? They spend $100 million a day to search for more. The Kingpins of Carbon are determined not to stop until they exhaust it all and our planet in the process.

"In their senseless and self-serving greed, the fossil fuel giants have made war on all the rest of us and created a greenhouse-gas planet," he posited. "Their weaponry and weapons systems include deep-sea oil drilling, all the fossil fuel powered cars on the roads of the world, fracking, pipelines, natural gas and oil rail tankers, coal-fueled power plants, and gas stations.

"Unfortunately, their weapons systems are too vast and far-reaching to successfully confront everywhere," admitted Taylor. "There is only one thing we can do to achieve a measure of success before they destroy our planet's atmosphere and eventually kill us off. The only avenue open for the benefit of future generations is to strike where they are the weakest, in their Achilles heel, as Sapphire called it. We must vigorously attack their weapons delivery systems, their supply lines and routes, if we are to bring them to the negotiating table."

Garf spun and faced Tomas Hernandez directly.

"Only then will they be forced to recognize and deal with 'commoners'" he sneered, "and only then will the Revolution in Cascadia begin!"

All was quiet momentarily until the frail elderly woman that had spoken earlier about eco-terrorism again raised her voice. She re-introduced herself as Molly Boxwell from Bend, Oregon.

"Eco-terrorism will get us nowhere," she stated in no uncertain terms. "All it did twenty or so years ago was get people arrested with no results. And even worse, it created a backlash against us in the press and the repression of our causes. Eco-terrorism is still terrorism; it will hurt us in the end."

Garf Taylor's entire focus was suddenly on the old lady from Oregon.

"This is not terrorism," he nearly barked at her. "This is war, a *just* climate war, that we must commit to if future generations are to be given a chance at surviving on this planet. The Kingpins of Carbon are making war on the entire planet; we will draw a line in the sand in Cascadia. We will stop them here. We will win this revolution by the same methods revolutions have always been won through history: we will violently overthrow the oppressors!"

From the opposite end of the great room, a man in his fifties was abruptly on his feet. "I stand firmly with Mr. Taylor here," he shouted. "For those of you that don't recall, I'm Ted Steele from Sandpoint, Idaho. And I say if we're going down – which it pretty much looks like what will happen anyway – my opinion is we go fighting and screaming. I'll stand right next to you Mr. Taylor; I say we take the battle to them!"

"Damn right!" Garf heartily agreed. "It's time to go on the offensive!"

Without warning, something in Linda Hernandez snapped. Standing, pushing her blond locks out of her face, she nearly screamed at the warmongers.

"Are you people out of your mind?" she wanted to know. "Don't you realize what you're suggesting is insane? You can't have a guerilla war in Cascadia and hope to defeat a global Empire!"

Garf laughed in her face. "You surely can not – if you do not try."

A male voice arose close to the elderly lady from Oregon. "If you violently attempt to attack Empire, the Kingpins of Carbon, and their weapons delivery systems in Cascadia, you will be obliterated by the superior force of their police state. It's as simple as that."

This comment gave Garf Taylor another opportunity to sneer in derision.

"That's precisely how Empire has taught you to think," he dictated, "and that's why you buckle under and future generations are in danger."

Now it was Tomas who was back on his feet and addressing Garf. "You will ruin everything we have worked for," he stated calmly, "you will destroy the true revolution if you succumb to violence.

"Because of widespread dystopian narratives in our contemporary culture," Tomas suggested, "people like you believe only from the ashes of revolution or societal collapse can come new, fair and just, forms of social order and governance. In truth, I'd venture to guess that you have no plan whatsoever how to go forward after your 'revolution.' There is indeed a more benign and responsible way to achieve a clean and hospitable environment, where individual initiative and collective obligation define a new commons-based governance. But violence will only destroy all that!"

"Hogwash and bullshit!" Garf spat back. "You rattle on with empty theory that produces no concrete results! You're nothing if not a bag of wind and full of crap!"

At once, Mister Q stood and attempted to bring some civility to the disagreement when he was overruled by several other voices adding to the fray. Some shouted their support for Garf Taylor, while others proposed a more pacifistic approach. Still others in the mostly elderly gathering were urging their fellow participants to calm and relax, while some seemed readying to depart.

The din in the old Victorian mansion grew louder and louder until the stranger sitting behind Tomas and Linda Hernandez began to rise and walk among them. His motions immediately caught Sapphire's eye as he rambled directly into the center of the verbal melee.

At first, she could barely hear him chant over the noise of the gathered. When he repeated his words again once more – "Peace, peace, peace," – she could hear him more clearly.

Things quieted even further as he repeated, "Peace, peace, peace." When all finally grew silent, he lifted his hand about chest high and let it drift from left to right as a benediction of sorts.

"Peace, peace, peace," was all he said.

***

Transfixed, even stunned, all in attendance slowly retook their seats. Even Garf and Billy – who seemed ready to take on all comers – shuffled behind their table to their chairs.

Sapphire couldn't initially comprehend how the stranger could project such calmness in the midst of chaos; he seemed to exude a confidence and control without any effort whatsoever.

And yet to Sapphire, the presence emanating from the man visibly clashed with his appearance. To scrutinize him out in the open and not laying in wait behind Tomas and Linda was to observe someone very common and ordinary. He had few distinguishing marks; he was easily forgettable, easily lost in a crowd.

The stranger's brown hair was cropped conservatively and his eyes were gray, non-threatening, and dull. His attire, his entire appearance, lacked any and all ostentation; his modesty seemed a perfect cloak, a stealthy modus operandi that only lent his aura more command and majesty. And perhaps that was why she was instantly drawn to him...

"My name is Chris," said the stranger, breaking the silence. "I know many of the Elders and Stewards gathered here today, and many others throughout Cascadia that could not attend this gathering."

Turning, he faced the tables and chairs occupied by Sapphire, Garf, and their companions. To them, he spoke, "But I do not know you."

Moving toward Garf's table, he halted momentarily as if he'd forgotten something. A slight detour brought him to where he had been sitting behind Tomas and Linda. Quietly, he asked his young companion for something and from a backpack she extracted two small packages.

As if gliding without a sound, the man calling himself Chris was quickly in front of Garf Taylor and his friend, Billy Maxwell. He placed the gift his young female friend had given him before them on the table. It appeared to be something with a hard case inside of a purple velvet bag, with a drawstring drawn tight.

Again, he introduced himself and stuck out his hand in comradeship.

"We gather here for a similar cause," Chris stated amiably.

At first Garf was reluctant to shake hands, but after eyeing the unknown intruder for several long seconds, he finally offered his hand without rising from his chair. Next to Garf, Billy Maxwell stood, and Chris's non-descript hand was lost in one of Billy's mighty mitts.

Shifting the few steps it took to be in front of Sapphire and Polly's table, Chris gifted a similar velvet bag before them. Once more he introduced himself, then held out his hand first to Polly. Both women stood and Polly stuck out her hand. Deftly, Chris touched her fingers and turned them so as to kiss the back of her hand.

He turned to Sapphire and their eyes electrically sparked on to one another. Chris lifted his hand toward the arm without the sling, but Sapphire couldn't let go of his eyes. When finally she lifted her hand,

and he kissed the back of it just as he had Polly, Sapphire felt a shudder of anticipation rocket through her entire body.

It seemed an eternity to Sapphire as their eyes had relocked upon one another after the greeting, but when he turned away and she caught sight of Chris's pretty companion, there was nothing but daggers coming from the young girl's face.

Centering himself in the open area between the tables and the gathered Elders in their chairs, Chris began easily, naturally.

"We are all gathered here today supported by similar motives," he began. "We all recognize the necessity of transforming Cascadia and rest of the planet into a sustainable and habitable environment – or we face inevitable demise.

"To do this, our quest must bring all of Cascadia to a higher level of awareness by triumphing over the obstacles that are now finally great enough – and by conquering them – all engaged will rise to that higher plane of human awareness," stated Chris.

Perhaps under his spell, Sapphire sensed something of the supernatural seemed to surround Chris, almost as if he carried a metaphysical vision of destiny on his shoulders. Garf Taylor, on the other hand, purposely emitted a very audible yawn.

Undeterred, Chris carried on.

"The essence of our questing towards Cascadia must be a deep, inner journey to become ourselves," he asserted, "and free from the tyranny of patriarchal dominance and exploitation. Only then can we learn to cooperate as an interactive Global Community before we self-destruct."

Pointedly, Chris directed his speech toward Garf. "As we overcome the obstacles in our way, the methods of this quest towards Cascadia must begin and end by *rejecting the patriarchy through non-violence.*

Otherwise, Cascadia's revolution will be like all those of the past: it will merely become a patriarchal reincarnation of what was overthrown."

"I don't understand this at all!" Garf was suddenly jumping to his feet and interrupting. "Didn't we just go through all this? Don't you understand that Empire will never see us as a threat — unless they are threatened?"

"You are quite correct," Chris passively agreed as he faced off with Taylor, and everyone waited for the fireworks to explode. "Please relax and take your seat once more because you are indeed quite correct."

Warily studying the intruder, not exactly sure what to make of him, Garf Taylor hesitantly found his seat again next to his muscle-bound friend.

"Yes, you are quite correct, sir," Chris said kindly, but sharply. "I agree: you don't understand this at all."

Taylor was leaping to his feet, yet before he could interrupt, Chris posited, "I do not shy away from the idea of violent revolutionary overthrow because it is too radical. No, quite the contrary, the problem with violence is that it is not radical enough!"

"What the fuck are you talking about?" Garf exploded.

"It's very simple, sir," Chris replied courteously. "If we utilize violence believing we can secure a better future than we have now, we are actually stigmatizing that future by the means to secure it."

Garf was baffled. "What?"

"To rise to a higher level of awareness, to secure a truly sustainable planet for future generations," Chris carried on unruffled, "we must truly become radical enough. We must reject the patriarchy through non-violence. We must become radical enough to reject the greed, exploitation, and warring mentality we have all inherited from the instilled culture of patriarchy. When that blight is removed from humankind, there will be no choice but true revolution and Cascadia will lead the way!"

"More and more bullshit!" Taylor pronounced. "You puke theory worse than your friend Hernandez over there. You will both be under the thumb of Empire forever if you take no action!"

A female voice abruptly cut into the tense air. Mister Q, attempting to derail another verbal melee, asked Sapphire to repeat what she had just said.

"Could you repeat that please, Ms. MacKenzie?" requested the elfin man.

"Certainly," she replied. Sapphire realized she'd been at least partially released from the mystique surrounding Chris. "I said: 'the people's patience is not endless.'"

"And that might reference what?" inquired Mister Q.

Sapphire sighed and stood. With her arm limp in its sling and appearing weary, she explained.

"In 1961, in South Africa, Nelson Mandela and his group Umkhonto we Sizwe issued a statement in which they said, 'the people's patience is not endless,'" Sapphire noted. "They then went on to say: 'the time comes in the life of any nation when there remain only two choices: submit or fight.'"

"I wonder," Sapphire mused, "has this time finally come to Cascadia?"

Without wasting a beat, she also recalled what Mandela and his people had stated next: "We shall not submit, and we have no choice but to hit back by all means within our power in defense of our people, our future, and our freedom."

Again, she posed rhetorically, "Has this time finally come to

Cascadia?"

"Damn right it has!" shouted Billy Maxwell, jumping to his feet. "The people's patience is not endless!"

Next to him, Garf Taylor declared, "For the sake of future generations, we will take the climate war to Empire! It is a just and honorable war; it is Cascadia's war!"

"Not so fast!" interrupted the stranger. So powerfully did the man calling himself Chris speak that all others grew silent. "Violence has no place in the true revolution; you will not be permitted to promote the patriarchy in Cascadia!"

Astounded, Garf turned on Sapphire MacKenzie.

"Who the fuck is this guy?" he demanded to know. "Hell, I bet he's not even from Cascadia!"

"I have no idea who he is; I've never met him before in my life," Sapphire admitted. "The Elders of Cascadia invited those in attendance. They said everyone could be trusted."

Interrupting, Chris responded directly to Garf. "To answer your question, I'm originally from Southern California, by way of Arizona and Utah."

Garf felt vindicated. "So there you go – I could smell it! You're not even one of us. You don't belong in Cascadia and cannot speak to its future!"

Suddenly, a gray-headed old man in bib overalls was interrupting from the second row. He reintroduced himself as Henry Fisher from Little Fort, British Columbia, and noted he had moved from Manitoba to B.C. as a young man.

"Everybody comes from somewhere," the elderly man chided Garf, "and I stand firmly behind Chris."

From the other side of the room, a woman said only that she was of the First Nations people in Alberta. "My people have been in Cascadia longer than our memories. Yet we have come to know Chris in recent years and we too stand behind him."

Directly in front of Sapphire's table, a skinny man with thick spectacles stood and reminded everyone he was a retired professor from Ashland, Oregon. "I too stand firmly behind Chris Cadia; I wouldn't be here if it wasn't for him being in attendance."

At the mention of Chris's surname, Sapphire did a double take.

Behind the retired professor, a member of the Lummi tribe near Bellingham, Washington, stood and vouched his support for Chris as well. At once, many others began to rise, and as they did Chris lifted a hand, thanked them all, and bid them to be seated once more. He then turned to Garf Taylor.

"I give you fair warning," Chris said openly. "Do not promote violence in the name of Cascadia's revolution. For if you do, you will find formidable opposition. I will thwart you at every turn."

Garf simply could not believe what he was hearing. Laughing in derision and scorn, he snatched up the gift in the purple velvet bag that Chris had left on the table earlier.

Without hesitation, Taylor heaved the present back at its donor. Chris deftly snagged it out of the air and waited for whatever was coming next.

"You sanctimonious bastard," Garf snarled. "Mark my words: you too will resort to violence when it serves your ends. We are all humans; that is part of our nature."

Chris disagreed. "We go down the wrong road – again – if we choose that path."

"Don't fool yourself," Taylor shot back. "You will adapt yourself to a more flexible path when the time comes."

"Never," Chris avowed. "We're talking about a paradigm shift for the species. Violence must be rejected."

Garf shook his head and laughed again derisively. "A fucking deluded idealist: that's all you are!" Taylor turned to his companion. "C'mon Billy, we're out of here."

A deathly silence reigned as everyone watched the two men storm toward the door at the end of the great room, which led to the hallway toward the front exit of the old house. Before departing for good, however, Garf spun and addressed all in attendance.

"As Representatives of Future Generations," he spoke forcefully, "we declare formal Independence for Cascadia – as of today. I guarantee that tomorrow you will wake up to a very different world. The climate wars have begun!

With that, Garf Taylor turned and slammed the door shut behind him.

***

While the noise from the crashing door receded, heads were shaking as all eyes in the great room of the old Victorian mansion slowly fixed on Chris.

"A short fuse, perhaps?" Chris mused aloud in reference to Garf Taylor.

"Possibly." Sapphire MacKenzie immediately replied. "And yet, he could be quite valuable to the new Cascadia we all seek. What's more, if you know nothing of his history, you cannot possibly gauge the depth of his dedication."

"Fair enough," Chris responded passively, "please clue us in."

Ostensibly speaking to all, Sapphire nevertheless locked eye-to-eye with Chris in a peaceable exchange among equals, as she began to tell her tale.

"If you don't know anything about the Everett Massacre, or Bloody Sunday, on November 5, 1916, go look it up," Sapphire suggested. "I'll only tell you there was a serious depression in Everett, Washington, and the Northwest – and labor unions like the IWW, or Industrial Workers of the World, the 'Wobblies,' had become organized.

"Several hundred of them met in a Seattle hall, then steamed north toward Everett to protest," she continued. "To be brief, local business bought out the authorities and hired 'citizen deputies,' or vigilantes, to repel the 'anarchists.' A firefight ensued when the Wobblies tried to take the docks of Everett.

"Garf Taylor's great-grandfather was one of those who was wounded that day, and though he made it back to Seattle aboard a steamer, he was later tried and spent time in jail, before finally being released." Sapphire paused and nodded her head. "The great-grandfather, in Garf's grandfather's eyes, was a true hero and leading crusader for justice of his time. And he drilled precisely that into a young Garf when he came to live with him after Garf's father's suicide.

"Garf has told me the suicide of his father affected him severely," Sapphire revealed. "Garf's father suffered from depression, grew deeply disillusioned, and became convinced that the world his father and grandfather hoped for would never come about. Death became – in the suicide note – 'a better alternative than false hopes.'"

Sapphire ceased speaking momentarily, took her eyes away from Chris's steady gaze, and looked about the room. All attention was focused on her; she returned her attentions to Chris.

"Garf Taylor believes with all his heart that he has something to prove to his dead father, and simultaneously vindicate the hopes and dreams of his grandfather and great-grandfather," explained Sapphire.

"By waging war on WPD's, Weapons of Planetary Destruction, Garf is convinced he can justify their vision and carry the good fight to the oligarchs and fossil fuel Kingpins."

When it became obvious that Sapphire was finished, Chris shrugged his shoulders.

"Mr. Taylor's motives may be deep and genuine," Chris allowed, "yet his questionable methods will not be permitted. If he and his comrades attempt to promote the patriarchy by utilizing violence in Cascadia, they will be thwarted at every possible juncture."

For the moment, Sapphire MacKenzie was not willing to engage in that argument one-way or the other. And fortunately, there was no need to since Chris's pretty young traveling companion had caught his eye with a hand signal.

Chris strolled to where she was sitting behind Tomas and Linda and bent over to discuss something. He then conferred briefly with Tomas and Linda before shaking their hands. His young female companion then stood up.

To all of those assembled, Chris announced, "I've just been informed that we must be departing to meet a prior engagement." He shook his head and shrugged his shoulders. "I'm sorry we couldn't agree on a unified strategy today as we all had hoped. But we will eventually – we must – for the sake of Cascadia. Thank you nevertheless for inviting us here to Port Townsend!"

Saying no more, Chris and his young friend made their way to the sitting room door that led them to the rear exit of the old house. When the door closed softly behind them, Mister Q rose to address them all.

***

Standing before those remaining, Quimper Jones appeared as bewildered by the chain of events, as were most of the Elders. He shook his head and began fumbling toward an explanation.

"I'm sorry, but what we just experienced was not what any of us expected today," he apologized. "Like most of you, I anticipated a unified plan with which to confront our fossil fuel adversaries. Instead, it looks like we must proceed valiantly into this Revolution with divisions among us. I fear Port Townsend might well remain the 'City of Dreams' – unfulfilled."

"Don't take it too hard or too deep, Mister Q," consoled Sapphire from behind her table. "Almost every revolution has internal divisions."

"Is that so?"

"Indeed," she assured him. "During the French Revolution, the Montagnards and the Girondins were both united against the monarchy of Louis XVI and the Feuillants, a conservative party of revolutionaries. They differed over the Montagnards execution of Louis XVI and the direction of social and economic ideologies after the Revolution. The Montagnards came out on top by gaining control of the National Convention, even as Girondins were being arrested and executed. It wasn't too many months after that Maximilien Robespierre, a Montagnard, helped to lead the Reign of Terror.

"Other examples in other revolutions abound," noted Sapphire. "In the Russian Revolution, the Mensheviks and the Bolsheviks were united against the tyranny of Czar Nicholas and the exploitation of workers. But the Mensheviks believed the revolution was necessarily bourgeois while the Bolsheviks insisted on centralization and dictatorship of the proletariat. We all know that the Bolsheviks were the victors in that disagreement.

"In the Haitian Revolution, though they were against French colonial rule, the Mulatto landowners and former slaves were divided as to how to conduct the uprising," she continued. "And don't forget Castro. During the Cuban Revolution, the Student Revolutionary Directorate, or DRE, initially opposed him."

She paused and gazed about the Elders and Stewards of Cascadia packing the room. Confidently, Sapphire nodded her head.

"Yes," she stated, "almost every revolution has its internal divisions, so why should Cascadia be any different? I even sense divisions among the Elders gathered here. That is why it is vitally important whom you decide to throw your support and resources behind. It is vitally important because you – and I – know one thing for a fact. If there is to be a viable and sustainable future for our species on this planet – there will indeed be a revolution – and it will start in Cascadia! We are The Thin Green Line!"

At once, several Elders about the room were on their feet clapping and cheering. Mister Q felt the electricity in the air; he joined in, as did many others. When the din finally died down, Jones spoke up.

"There will be a revolution in Cascadia," he agreed, but continued in a cautionary mood. "Our hopes can only remain high for the future of our planet and species though, if a house divided can indeed stand."

CHAPTER FOUR

Stuck in the stop-and-go traffic on Scottsdale Road heading south, Stone McClelland slapped a huge hand on the steering wheel in frustration.

"Dammit all!" he swore, as he glanced at his watch. If it weren't for the multi-vehicle pile-up that closed Phoenix's eastside 101 freeway and forced all traffic onto Scottsdale Road, he'd easily be at work at the Tempe Town Lake Festival on time. Now, he wondered if he'd even make it there by the time the Fourth of July fireworks were scheduled to begin.

Inching forward, bumper-to-bumper, McClelland felt the claustrophobia of being trapped on the roadway, as well as that caused by the three-sizes-too-small, security rent-a-cop uniform he had to wear for the job with this new company. It was the largest uniform they had, he was told, and if he made it through the probationary time period for new hires, they promised to order him custom fit clothing.

Stone looked down on the uniform he was wearing and was disgusted. Likely, he'd never get the new uniforms because he'd never make through the probationary period. This was probably just another job he'd get released from, or quit in frustration. Sighing, he still couldn't believe how far he'd fallen since he quit the Drug Enforcement Administration.

Even if the uniform was small and tight, at least in the years since the DEA McClelland took pride in keeping in tip-top physical shape – for whatever that was worth at this point.   Yet even if his imposing physique appeared unchanged, he knew in his heart he was like a bear declawed.   Where in the years with the DEA he was a commanding presence, now he was more hesitant, always allowing others excess space.   He knew his eyes carried a flicker of doubt as well, and uncertainty often worked its way onto his countenance.   Now too, he tended to seek the shadows where before, he cast them.

Worst of all, Stone McClelland knew precisely the root of his problems – but he had no idea how to resolve them anymore than when he'd quit the DEA years ago.

A green light allowed several cars ahead of Stone to cross the intersection in all lanes.   McClelland, in his aging Toyota, was fortunate enough to cross at the tail end of the line.   When he saw emergency vehicles with lights flashing entering the next crossroad – East McDonnell Drive – and stopping at the center of the intersection, he knew he was doomed.

Everything suddenly felt even more hopeless than he already knew it was.

If it wasn't for Lorien, he had no idea how he'd be able to keep going.   He'd talk about his problems with her and she'd tell him to quit torturing himself.   But there wasn't a switch he could just turn off and on.   And that was especially so when he was firmly stuck in the middle.

Ever since the government massacre at the Gaia/Universe compound, his psyche had been split in two.   On the one side was his family's tradition of serving their country and all the years he spent in the DEA.   But at the same time there was no way he could justify his own government's slaughter of so many innocents by its police state.

Because of that juxtaposition, he was a man without a compass, disillusioned and unable to map a course into the future; his life was stagnant and lacking purpose.

Compounding his dilemma were his own actions after the massacre. Although what he did was buried away from the official records, in every waking moment Stone vividly recalled the day he let the prisoner walk free after the government slaughter. It was the wrong thing to do – but it was the right thing to do.

The prisoner had been some minor assistant of the psychedelic mushroom Spore Master hired by Gaia/Universe, that all the government had been searching for back then. The Spore Master was captured on a northern Arizona road and died the same night in a Navajo Nation holding cell. The next morning, the government's fiery attack on the Gaia/Universe compound killed all those inside still holding out. Learning of the slaughter a few hours later and racked with disgust, Stone released the prisoner following assurances from those holding him that the Spore Master's capture and death would be the only records officially logged.

Several months thereafter, government forces finally discovered the hole-in-the-wall secret cave in southern Utah where the Spore Master had been growing millions of illegal mushrooms, as Stone knew they eventually would. The mainstream press made it into the biggest story to come out of the Southwest since the massacre at Gaia/Universe.

In a horrific firefight, a former functionary at Gaia/Universe and assistant to the Spore Master, one Chris Soles, had killed several government agents along with the woman he had either kidnapped or drugged into living with him in the secret Utah cave. Fleeing in desperation into the cave, Soles had detonated tons of explosives prewired in the cavern. An entire mountain came crashing down on the subterranean chamber.

Even though no magic mushrooms were ever recovered and no body could be excavated under the crush of a mighty canyon wall, wanted posters went up for Chris Soles across the continent. The sensationalism surrounding the story wasn't hurt either by the revelation that the woman the mushroom assistant had either kidnapped or doped was a family member of the prominent, multi-billionaire, fossil fuel magnates – the Dellenbach Brothers.

Stone had followed the story closely; all the while knowing his actions in releasing the prisoner had repercussions far into the future – although he could not know what they might be, nor if they be positive or negative.

And it certainly didn't become any easier when stories of a nearly mythic "Chris Cadia" began to surface in the Pacific Northwest – the "Chris Cadia" that was rumored to gift small packets of psilocybin mushrooms upon first meeting. There were those that said he had to be the same Chris Soles that somehow escaped from the crush of a mountain descending upon him. Others, however, repudiated such nonsense by explaining these tales were only concoctions created by those fomenting revolution in what they were calling the sovereign state of "Cascadia."

Whatever the truth regarding the claims, Stone McClelland admitted it probably didn't matter much for him – one way or the other. He was already confronted by bigger questions that he couldn't begin to answer. His life was tormented by his government's actions as well as his own, with no resolution in sight when he quit the DEA and certainly none now. He was stagnating as he had been for years, and likely would be into the foreseeable future.

With little hope, McClelland shifted his attentions to the emergency vehicles still in the intersection ahead. He wondered if it was already too late, or if things would ever get moving on time...

***

"Sorry, Whitey," she spoke softly into the phone when he finally picked up, "I know it's late on the east coast."

It took him a moment to respond, as if he were waking up. "It's not a problem, Sapphire, you know you can call me anytime if you need to."

A tinge of remorse took her momentarily. "I guess I didn't need to talk to you tonight; I just wanted to chat about the day's events." She shifted into a more neutral tone. "How was your Fourth of July?"

"Uneventful," he replied curtly. "Just taking care of my wife and her debilities. How was your Fourth? Did you attend the local fireworks display?"

"No," Sapphire replied. "It started raining hard just before sunset, so there was no point in going out. I did attend the meeting though here in Port Townsend that I told you about."

"Oh yes, the meeting..." Whitey acted as if merely recalling in passing the secret meeting, though he knew from the moment his cell phone rang that this was what she was calling about. "So how did it go there today?"

"The gathering with the Elders and others was interesting," Sapphire stated nonchalantly. "I'll tell you about that in a minute, but first I just wanted to thank you again for sending someone to bail me out so promptly last week at the Port of Morrow and tending to my medical needs."

"It's never a problem; you know that," Whitey assured her. "How is your arm doing now?"

"Better," was all she said before turning the tables. "And how have you been?"

"Me?" He snorted. "It's the same old thing as usual. The nose is to the grindstone with the family business, and though my wife's cancer is supposedly in 'remission,' she's always in pain and in need of continual care, it seems. As always, I'm trying to live my dreams vicariously through people like you."

Whitey's unfortunate circumstances were burdensome for her as usual. Still, she thanked her lucky stars that he had seen fit to back her financially for years in order to effect positive change in the world. She was always left speechless by his good heart.

"So the meeting today," Whitey eventually injected when nothing was forthcoming from Sapphire, "how did things work out?"

An audible sigh from Sapphire carried over the phone. "Unfortunately, it all fell apart in squabbles."

"Squabbles?"

"Yes, squabbles," she reaffirmed. "And it's deplorable since the Elders of Cascadia gathered with such good intentions. What they wanted to know was how best to conduct the coming Revolution and where to place their resources. But it all fell apart without resolution when some of the invited participants simply walked out of the meeting."

"So what happened?"

Sapphire ignored his question.

"I'll tell you, Whitey," she exclaimed, "sometimes I just get so exasperated I'd like to pack it all in and go float the Salmon for a few days."

"So would I," he agreed with a chuckle. "You meet the nicest guides on the river."

She laughed and both were momentarily swept up in their own reminiscences of the time years ago when they met on the Salmon River in central Idaho. She was a young river raft guide and he was a client on a weeklong river trip with several east coast friends.

"So why did everyone get so upset in Port Townsend today?" Whitey queried, bringing them both back to the present moment. "What made everything so volatile?"

Once again she sighed. "Well, the Elders brought in some people with diverse viewpoints regarding how to conduct the coming revolution; maybe because of that, it was doomed from the beginning."

"Who was there?" Whitey inquired with a seeming lack of emotion, although he very much wanted to know.

"Some people I already knew, and some I'd never met."

"Anyone I've heard of?"

"I think you're aware of Tomas Hernandez," she stated. "He is one of the spokespeople for the new coalition of groups calling themselves 'Commons Rising.'"

Whitey mentioned that he was aware of the mounting coverage in the alternative press about Commons Rising. What he didn't mention was the thorough investigation his people had already begun conducting on Tomas Hernandez.

"Well, what Tomas said," Sapphire continued, "really ruffled the feathers of some of the other participants. He had the temerity to declare that because of the Commons Rising movement, the true revolution was already underway. One faction didn't exactly see it that way; they advocated violent and immediate attacks on the fossil fuel industry."

"Who were they?" Whitey asked without thinking.

It was an awkward moment. Sapphire never told him quite everything; she only knew him so well, after all. It was only a natural precaution she supposed, but she only told him just enough to justify his continued support without too many specifics.

"I didn't really know who the people advocating violence were," she sidestepped with a lie. "They were participants the Elders had invited to give their viewpoints."

Whitey knew well enough to let it go. He always attempted to be cautious and remain objective, never expressing his own opinions. This time though, he was aware he'd nearly stepped over a line.

Sapphire carried on undeterred, ignoring Whitey's faux pas.

"And then the most unnerving thing of the day occurred," Sapphire declared. "The meeting had descended into chaos with those advocating violence getting into it with others promoting non-violent revolution, when in the midst of it a stranger I'd never met arose from his seat. He had been behind Tomas Hernandez. When he walked among all, things began to calm by what seemed to be the singular power of his presence.

"I've never experienced anything like it, Whitey," she asserted. "An almost hypnotic aura emanated from the man and he gave me and others small presents. He was most courteous and kind — but then informed those advocating immediate attack on the fossil fuel, Weapons of Planetary Destruction, that violence would not be permitted in Cascadia's revolution. He said he would thwart those clambering for violent attacks at every turn."

"What happened after that?"

"Those promoting what they called a 'just war' on the Kingpins of Carbon threw their gift from the stranger back at him and stormed out of the meeting, proclaiming a new day would dawn tomorrow on the revolution in Cascadia," she explained. "They also added quite threateningly, 'The climate wars have begun!'"

"And what did the gift-giving stranger do then?" wondered Whitey.

"He left shortly thereafter as well." Sapphire felt at a loss. "It wasn't too long following his departure that the meeting broke up completely."

Although Whitey contributed nothing verbally, he was satisfied with the outcome.

"On my way out, however," Sapphire was compelled to toss in an addendum, "I asked one of the Elders conducting the meeting who the gift-giving man calling himself Chris actually was."

The Elder simply told her to open her present.

"So that's what I did," she explained to Whitey.

Inside the velvet bag the stranger had given her was a hard case for eyeglasses. Inside the case she discovered ten to fifteen small mushrooms, dried from stalk to cap.

"So the stories are true then?" Sapphire said she asked the Elder. "He really exists – the one they call 'Chris Cadia?'"

"That's for you to decide," was all the Elder replied.

"But he looks nothing like the wanted posters from the Gaia/Universe days," she had objected.

Sapphire said the Elder had laughed knowingly. He then told her, "A good plastic surgeon can do wonders. Or then again – maybe it's not the same person at all."

Whatever else was said by Sapphire for the remainder of the phone call went in one of Whitey's ears and out the other. Very politely, he terminated the call as soon as possible.

Immediately after Sapphire was off the line, Whitey went to the contact list on his phone and tapped another number in haste.

***

The phone call went directly to voice mail. He left a message, then studied the time on his cell phone. Ten minutes passed, then eleven, twelve. All he could imagine was that Father must be extremely busy on this Fourth of July.

After eighteen minutes, when Theodore Dellenbach called from Oklahoma City, he began by apologizing to his son.

"I'm sorry, Whitley," Dellenbach began in his gruff, tobacco-raspy voice, "but we've been very busy with our annual Fourth of July fete for new members of The Club. As usual, there is a lot of potential dark money to be contributed and we must treat the newcomers well. Your Uncle Paul is in charge for the moment, but I must return soon."

"I understand, Father," Whitley replied. "Perhaps I shouldn't have troubled you this evening."

"No, no, no," the elder Dellenbach chided his son. "I don't have much time though; were you able to make contact with your source?"

"I know you're busy, so I'll try to be brief," he assured his father. "Yes, as I hoped, I was able to speak with her."

As concisely as possible, Whitley passed along the gist of what Sapphire had told him about the secretive meeting in Washington State, called by a collection of so-called "Elders" to foment revolution. He reiterated how different participants had diverse views regarding how to proceed, and how the entire gathering disintegrated in arguments without any final resolution.

"So it always is with the democratic rabble," the old man grunted. Displaying impatience, he asked, "Anything else?"

"Yes, Father," Whitley replied. "Some of the leaders of the new commons based coalition calling themselves 'Commons Rising' were in attendance. I believe these people may pose a genuine threat to us over the long term and we should begin to address it."

"Baloney!" Theodore Dellenbach tossed back. "We've talked about this before. They are no different from the labor unions and such riff-raff. It's taken years of steady effort – just like our efforts to suppress the votes of the minority whiners – but unions and their like have been emasculated. The same will happen with these commoners and their new 'Commons Rising' movement."

"Respectfully, Sir," the son said with some gravity, "I'd beg to differ; from what my people have uncovered, this peril is something that bears our attention."

"Perhaps later, Whitley, but not at this time." The elder Dellenbach was brusque, while simultaneously allowing his son the dignity of breathing room. "Now, is there anything else?

"Yes, Father."

"Well, get on with it!"

Noting his elder's unwillingness to be further deterred, Whitley quickly launched himself into the source's report about the mysterious stranger that handed out gifts to participants of the meeting that he'd never met. He further explained that when his source opened her gift, there were several psilocybin mushrooms inside the small container.

Suddenly, Theodore Dellenbach was fully engaged with his son's revelations.

"So is this the person we've heard about?" wondered the father. "Might this 'Chris Cadia' be more than the mysterious legend we've been told about in your reports?"

"I believe he might actually be the Chris Soles that deceived and despoiled our Alice," revealed Whitley. "And somehow, Soles escaped the mushroom cave explosion, only to reappear years later in the Northwest as the nearly mythic 'Chris Cadia.'"

"If there was only some way to get to him," the old man mused.

"There is."

Theodore Dellenbach's attentions immediately shifted from its primary focus on dark money and new donors of The Club, to the capture of one Chris Soles. As a Dellenbach, it was only natural to seek vengeance on the man that had deluded, deceived, and turned traitor their dear Alice, his youngest sister's daughter.

"So how do you propose to find and take down this Chris Soles, this 'Chris Cadia?'" queried the old man.

"I think one of my operatives may have a lead that could prove interesting," Whitley explained.

"Go on."

"Okay," the son replied. "I know you were overseas and very busy at the time Uncle Walter passed away. It was around the same time Alice was released with other captives from the Gaia/Universe compound, before troops were forced to storm the hold-outs."

"Yes, of course, I distinctly remember those days," recalled Theodore Dellenbach. "I couldn't get to Walter's hospital bedside because I was tied up in Asia with a coal deal that was at deadline."

"Well, right about that same time," Whitley continued, "the Spore Master that was growing all the hallucinogenic mushrooms for the whack-job leader of Gaia/Universe, Bruno Panoka, was captured on a northern Arizona road. Unfortunately, long before he could be brought to trial, he died of an apparent heart attack the first night he was in a Navajo Nation holding cell."

"Okay, I remember that."

Whitley went on to explain that interrogators interviewing Gaia/Universe captives let go at the same time of his cousin Alice's release, definitively identified Chris Soles, a former functionary at Gaia/Universe, as having been assigned as an assistant to the Spore

Master.

"At the time, it was widely assumed Soles had been back at the cave, tending the grow op and missing all the action," noted Whitley. "But I don't think that's precisely how events unfolded – and therein may be our key to capturing and exacting retribution on Chris Soles, or 'Chris Cadia' as they now seem to be calling him."

Theodore Dellenbach inquired after his son's suspicions.

"In all the official records," Whitley commenced, "only the so-called 'Spore Master,' Harry Wimple, had been captured by the Navajo Nation police and placed in their holding cell. He then apparently died of natural causes that evening. There was a DEA agent that had been working on the task force to locate the hidden mushroom cave; he visited the Spore Master in his cell the evening of his capture, and then went back to the detention center the next morning. Later, he filed his report and that was that. An open-and-shut case one might think, eh? But I have facts that seem to lead in a very different direction."

Intrigued, the father said nothing and the son continued.

"It's taken some time," the son began, "but one of my undercover investigators following-up on long forgotten details hooked up with someone that had been involved that day during the arrest of the Spore Master. My operative casually approached him one night in a bar in Gallup, New Mexico. Over a few drinks, this guy told my man what he already knew – that he lived in Gallup, but worked about a half hour away in Window Rock, Arizona, which is the seat of the Navajo Nation government.

"Right now, this guy is some kind of mid-level paper pusher in their bureaucracy," noted Whitley, "but several years ago he worked for the Navajo Nation police. Over a few more drinks they got onto the topic of the Spore Master and his arrest. The former policeman told my operative there was an assistant with the Spore Master and, after the Spore Master died, the DEA agent in charge took him into custody the next morning."

"Interesting," the elder Dellenbach responded, "but did the former cop say why the official records were altered so as to make no mention of the assistant?"

"At the time, he thought the DEA agent and his handlers were simply going to dispose of him, so it was an easy way to tie up a loose end," Whitley explained. "Later though, after the government discovered the secret cave, he figured they simply perpetuated the cover-up since the prisoner must have escaped before he could be killed."

"So this DEA agent is obviously our key," the father intuited, "to finding Chris Soles or 'Chris Cadia' in the Northwest."

"Quite correct, Father," agreed Whitley. "Besides being the only person who truly knows the events of that day, he knows Chris Soles and must have something on him."

"But were they complicit that day?" asked the elder Dellenbach. "If so, the DEA agent should face charges."

"Or maybe Soles did escape that day," posed the son, "and maybe the DEA agent would like to make right his shortcomings. We can't know what scenario we're facing until we can confront the man. The bottom line, however, is that he and Chris Soles share some dark secret – and we can use that to get to the man that ruined our Alice."

"Sounds reasonable," judged Theodore Dellenbach. "So where does the government have this agent working now?"

"Oh, he's no longer with the DEA," Whitley replied. "He quit immediately following these incidents. Apparently he was tired of living away from his longtime girlfriend while on various assignments. He finally married her and they live full time in Scottsdale, Arizona, now."

"So what is he doing?"

"Humph," snorted Whitley. "He mostly works dead-end security jobs that pay barely above minimum wage."

"Do you think you can recruit him?"

"I think he needs a raise in pay," the son quickly rejoined.

Theodore Dellenbach laughed richly.

"You're as wily as your Uncle Walter was," the father lauded. "I knew you'd do him proud by taking over his duties."

"I take that as quite the compliment," declared Whitley.

"And well you should," said the old man.

With their conversation concluded and both satisfied, Theodore Dellenbach bid his son farewell and returned to the new donors and their dark money.

CHAPTER FIVE

If Carolyn Maxwell hadn't volunteered for the optional workday on Friday, July 5th, maybe she wouldn't feel so trapped. Maybe she could have enjoyed a four-day weekend for once, like most everyone else, and could have escaped her cage for at least a brief respite.

As she finished dressing and putting on her make-up, however, it was impossible to ignore the fact she was simply fooling herself. To tell the truth, she was as trapped by circumstances as any twenty-three year old woman possibly could be. She was desperately cornered and there was no way out; it made her bitter and she shouldn't be so bitter at twenty-three.

Carolyn's dark thoughts were momentarily interrupted by the realization that she had failed to turn the coffee maker on before her shower. From the bathroom of her small single bedroom apartment, she marched hastily to the kitchen and flipped the switch.

Dully, she stared at the empty pot waiting for the start-up sounds.

Carolyn would have loved to take four days off in a row, but she had no choice. She had to work whenever she could to pay her bills – especially all the student loan bills. And she swore she'd eventually get the education loans paid off – in at least thirty or forty years…

But getting an education, at the time, seemed the only way up and out. Growing up through a childhood of poverty in Springfield, Oregon, just outside of Eugene, Carolyn and her two older brothers were raised by a single mom, until she died when Carolyn was only fourteen years old. By then, they were living in Everett, Washington, and her brothers helped all they could to get her through high school.

Even in those early years she recognized she was waylaid by circumstances beyond her control; still, Carolyn was determined to make something better of her life. She was accepted for college at Western Washington University in Bellingham, worked her ass off, and finally graduated with an accounting degree.

Still staring at the coffee pot, it vaguely registered in her mind that the coffee was almost ready. She mused how so many of her friends said she was incredibly lucky to find an entry-level accounting position with Boeing right after graduation. And maybe that was true. Many of the people she knew in college could either find no work with their degree, or were relegated to taking intern positions, which were not much more than glorified slave labor.

Sure, she thought sardonically, she was fortunate enough to secure a job coming out of college. That along with her overbearing student debt burden enabled her to climb the success ladder all the way to indentured servitude.

The whole system was insane…

If she would have had a little more courage – and a few more brains in her head – Carolyn admitted to herself time and again, she should have taken the route her freshman roommate, Ingri Rud, wisely chose. Ingri barely had enough money for freshman year through grants and scholarships, and realized she couldn't make it any further. The two girls became best of friends that year and Carolyn was sad to see her go.

But in retrospect, Ingri was a lot smarter and luckier than Carolyn had been with the whole college thing. After contacting distant relatives in Norway to get a foothold, she was eventually able to obtain an education at no cost. Not only that, but like in other Scandinavian countries, she was also able to get a small grant to help with living expenses. And now Ingri was working on an advanced degree, and thinking about taking up permanent residence in Norway when she was finished with school.

Of course, Ingri realized that the free education and other social benefits meant higher taxes, but to her it seemed like a fair trade off and better for the individual and society as a whole.

From Carolyn's enslaved perspective, she would be hard pressed to disagree with Ingri. Sometimes she simply couldn't believe what the American capitalist system was doing to its own people. Where in the world is the prevailing mentality coming from when it puts a strangling choke hold on its own young people, just when they are trying to get started? Preying on each other seemed the American way, but all that added up to for Carolyn was to be part of a nation rushing headlong toward its own demise.

She knew she was up to her neck in that trap and wanted out.

Shelving such thoughts, she noticed the coffee pot she'd been gawking at had finished the brew cycle. Carolyn poured herself a cup, added some milk from the fridge, and then sat at her kitchen table in front of her laptop that was in sleep mode.

Awakening the computer, she waited for the wifi to connect. Carolyn opened a new window to a national news site she always glanced at first, before clicking toward other sites more relevant to her own life.

Leaping off the screen, in enormous bold font and all caps, was the headline: **"TERRORISM IN THE NORTHWEST!"**

Today, she suddenly realized there was nothing more relevant in her life than the national news.

There were several related stories under the headlines and it was confusing at first. Skimming through the articles, it appeared there had been several explosions on different rail lines during the evening hours of July Fourth. As a result, shipping by rail in the Northwest was grinding to a halt.

Apparently, rail lines on both the Washington and Oregon sides of the Columbia River were severely affected. A main railroad bridge had been demolished on the Oregon side of the river, and a tunnel several miles away on the Washington side had suffered serious damage.

The biggest story of all, however, was further north in central Washington. An oil tanker train had been trapped approximately halfway through the nearly eight mile long Cascade Tunnel, when explosions closed both ends of the tunnel. Because of ventilation issues within the tunnel, authorities feared for the lives of the train's crew – even though they carried required emergency oxygen supplies. Unfortunately, the explosions had disabled all communications so the state of the crew was unknown. Workers were nevertheless scrambling to clear the major cave-ins at the east and west portals of the tunnel.

In a related article, the authorities said these incidents of terrorism were a 'temporary disruption' and all resources in the Northwest would be put in motion to apprehend the terrorists. The President himself would be addressing the nation at noon eastern time from the Oval Office regarding these developments.

If Carolyn felt trapped by circumstances before she read the national news, now it seemed she was almost smothering below ground in a buried coffin.

Her very first thoughts upon reading the stories were about the involvement of her older brothers. Still, she simply wouldn't admit to that possibility. But as it grew on her, it became more than a possibility.

It was more like a probability.

All she need do was consider Billy's prison time and the reasons for his criminal record. Add to that Timmy's excavation expertise in explosives, and their madman friend Garf Taylor – and she knew they were suspects – at least in her mind.

They hadn't said anything about what they'd been doing when they came in late a couple nights ago and crashed on her couch and floor. The next morning in passing she'd only heard mentioned that July fifth would be a new day for everyone. The comment made no sense then; unfortunately, it did now.

Carolyn was genuinely worried for her brothers. She didn't want to see Billy go back to jail and she surely didn't want to see Timmy join him.

Suddenly, she was very worried for herself as well. She had to stand by her brothers: after all, they were the only family she had. And yet she had no desire to get snared into their crimes and end up with them behind bars.

All at once, Carolyn realized she had to get going or she'd be late for work. She took a final sip of her coffee and poured the rest down the sink.

As she grabbed her purse and headed toward the door, Carolyn couldn't get it out of her head that she was involuntarily walking into another ambush some cruel fate had preordained for her, and one she could never escape.

CHAPTER SIX

The documents began arriving throughout the day on July 5th, although all of them were postmarked on July 3rd. All were identical in content, even as they were mailed from over forty different post offices in Cascadia.

Most were sent to local television and newspaper outlets; by early afternoon the national media, as well as social media, had picked up on it and were in an uproar over what was proclaimed. Fair it might be to say that after the news of the bombings along vital train routes in the Northwest, the document provided the one-two punch that the perpetrators must have been seeking.

It read:

REPRESENTATIVES OF FUTURE GENERATIONS

MANIFESTO

As of this July 4th we, the Representatives of Future Generations, declare our independence from the corrupt system of governance perpetrated by the fossil fuel corporate oligarchs.

These Kingpins of Carbon – the corporate oligarchs and their cronies – have waged a multi-decade war on our democracy in their lust for greed and power. All our institutional systems have been taken over and tainted by this corporate elite. They buy political elections, they run a police state, and they own our universities, nearly all media and communication, and our judiciary.

"It's just business," they tell us of Future Generations. But we of Future Generations no longer buy into their business model. We no longer passively accept Empire's endless wars of imperialism, nor their unabated drilling and fracking. We reject the squalor and suffering they inflict on this planet in the name of corporate profits. The Kingpins of Carbon have fought valiantly to eliminate regulations that protect the environment. They sow the seeds of doubt about climate change and use their bought-and-paid-for politicians to stall climate change legislation.

The Kingpins of Carbon terrorize us all with their version of the End Times. They have created Weapons of Planetary Destruction (WPD's) that are rivaled by only one other WPD system: a nuclear holocaust. After such an exchange of nuclear weapons, the planet would likely experience a "nuclear winter," whereby Earth, darkened by copious smoke and soot, would rapidly grow colder. A loss of crops would ensue, and the species would perish.

The Weapons of Planetary Destruction that the Kingpins of Carbon actively promote are of a slower time scale, yet every bit as noxious as nuclear destruction. Because of the obsessive burning of fossil fuels, we are faced on a planetary scale with a series of irreversible calamities that will burn our species and most other life off the face of the Earth.

All humanity, and all species, are thus at risk; fossil fuels must remain in the ground and we must transition to a fossil fuel free future. At a bare minimum, Representative of Future Generations demand: 1) the immediate elimination of fossil fuel subsidies, 2) no new drilling or fracking; what is in the ground must remain in the ground, 3) no new pipelines whatsoever and, simultaneously, 4) the building of a real plan of The People that reduces greenhouse gas pollution and is founded on renewable energy.

Representatives of Future Generations are not, however, naïve enough to believe the Kingpins of Carbon would willingly even talk to The People about such proposals. We would never even get their attention.

Therefore, from this July 4th henceforth, we as secular earth dwellers declare a holy climate war on the Kingpins of Carbon and their Weapons of Planetary Destruction, for the sake of Future Generations. The July 4th strikes on the railroad lines are merely our opening salvo; in the coming days we will attack and destroy any and all weaponry of the Kingpin's WPD production systems. The targets are endless: drill rigs, gas stations, fracking operations, pipelines, railroads, fossil fuel terminals, transport trains and trucks, as well as executives, lawyers, and accountants of the most profitable corporations in history – the fossil fuel corporations.

We speak the language of Revolution! Our climate war is intended to maim and disable the machinery of fossil fuel corporate power. With the delivery systems adequately crippled, we begin to pull back from the precipice of ultimate disaster. Then too will we begin to force the corporate elite from power – and so commences the epic confrontation between our corporate masters and ourselves!

Representatives of Future Generations will strike first in what will become the newly liberated and sovereign nation of Cascadia. Others across the continent and throughout the world will willingly join the quest to save our world from impending doom. We are legion; we will become invincible. We are the many, and the corporate Kingpins of Carbon and their cronies are the few.

We are Representatives of Future Generations and Future Generations are us!

CHAPTER SEVEN

"I saw the way you looked at her," Kiri said factually.

"At who?" replied Chris.

She smirked at him. "Like you don't know."

"What are you talking about?"

"Like you don't know," repeated Kiri. "Give me a fucking break; you're pathetic." She sighed, then chuckled and shook her head. "Of course, I mean the most beautiful and famous Sapphire MacKenzie."

"I still don't know what you're talking about," Chris objected.

"Ha – sure you do!" Kiri laughed openly in his face. "You were almost drooling, you know."

Chris shrugged his shoulders in resignation. "Well, I can't do anything with you," he noted weakly.

Kiri grinned, knowing full well she had him where she wanted.

"No, you probably shouldn't," she agreed, "but someday you'll be compelled to. I sense it."

Uneasy with the direction of yet another conversation, Chris strove to be judicious.

"You're a sweet girl," he spoke neutrally, uncomfortably, "and we'll just have to see what the future brings."

At once, Kiri began laughing lustfully. "You are so easy to paint into a corner!" she enlightened him, to her own delight. "Yes, we'll see what *comes* in the future..."

With a flourish of her natural bubbly enthusiasm, Kiri then informed Chris she was going to stroll about the deck of the ferry before they landed on Whidbey Island.

That was yesterday after the failed meeting convened by the Cascadia Elders, and they'd found their way to the Port Townsend-Whidbey Island ferry for the quick thirty minutes passage. Today they were on another ferry – a British Columbia ferry – on an hour and a half trip from Tsawwassen on the mainland to Swartz Bay and Victoria on Vancouver Island.

He thought about her now though, as she had strolled off on the ferry deck yesterday, seemingly so confident and insouciant, which no doubt was a side effect of her youth and vivaciousness. As usual, he'd watched the sway of her hips, her striking figure, and the straight brown hair tied in a ponytail as she sauntered down the deck.

Kiri was indeed much younger than he; at twenty-two she was about half his age and strikingly pretty. Her bangs fell just above her eyebrows, she had a dimple in one cheek when she laughed, and green eyes that sparkled. And she never failed to confound and perplex the hell out of him.

It was like that today and yesterday, as well as a few years ago on the very first day he ever met her.

And how could he forget that?

For several days he had been sick on a fishing boat coming down from Prince Rupert, far north on the B.C. mainland, after meetings with First Nation Elders about the fossil fuel terminals up there and their expansion plans. Most of the time on the water had been on inside passages with very little open ocean transits, but it didn't matter since he wasn't much of a seaman.

It was with great relief when Captain Ole parked his boat in the Comox marina about midway down Vancouver Island, and handed him over to Knute Thorson, a local Elder in the Comox valley. Knute was a jovial, welcoming soul, somewhere in his mid-fifties, that one couldn't help but like. Knute informed Chris he was going to spend the night at his home in Cumberland, up in the hills a bit, yet not too many kilometers away. He and his wife Lila were old hippies, Knute sniggered, but a warm meal was awaiting him, as well as a stable bed not subject to the roll of the waves below.

Cumberland turned out to be a funky little town, the perfect place perhaps for a couple of old hippies to call home. In the early 1900s a vibrant Chinese population inhabited the area, Thorson told him as they drove, and worked the coal mines in the area. Today it was a beautifully green and lush throwback to another era, a place where strip malls and most fast food joints were noticeably absent.

Towards the end of Dunsmuir Avenue, as it transformed from a main street into a road with aging rattletrap houses, Knute Thorson finally stopped and invited Chris into his home. Entering the small house he was greeted by Lila Thorson, a petite yet gregarious woman, with gray streaks beginning to show in her waist length brown hair. The evening meal had already been prepared, but first Mrs. Thorson offered Chris a cup of tea with which to relax. She then called her eldest daughter down from upstairs.

Knute and Chris took seats in the small sitting room off the kitchen. While waiting for the girl to come downstairs, Lila served Chris and her husband tea, and told him about her daughters.

"Kiri – who is upstairs – is our eldest," Lila told him, "and her sister Freya is down in Victoria going to university. Kiri went to UBC, University of British Columbia, over in Vancouver for a few years, but now she's, um, taking a breather."

By the way Mrs. Thorson spoke and how she looked at her husband after mentioning, "taking a breather," Chris could tell the mother wasn't entirely pleased with the daughter's vacation from schooling.

Interrupting herself, Lila directed her voice upwards once more. "Kiri, dear," she called, "tea is ready, and we'll be eating soon."

"I'm on my way down, mum," the girl called from above.

As the young woman descended the stairway, Chris was struck dumb by how attractive she was. Petite like her mother, yet with the clearer bodily definitions of youth, the girl was dressed casually, much as the college student she had been until recently.

They exchanged greetings and pleasantries, and Kiri took a cup of tea. Knute wanted to know of Chris's recent travels, so he did his best to oblige. As delicately as could be managed, the conversation thus turned on travel by boat, days of off-and-on seasickness, and how glad he was to again be on solid ground.

When it came time for their evening meal, they all feasted on Lila's shepherd's pie, one of her specialties, Chris learned. Knute quizzed Chris about the fossil fuel terminals up in Prince Rupert, and then informed him of the multiple businesses he was involved in around the Comox Valley, as well as being an active participant in the local transition town movement. Mrs. Thorson joined the conversation from time to time, and also spoke of her avid interest in permaculture. For the most part their daughter Kiri was silent. She merely observed Chris quite intensely, almost to the point of it being uncomfortable for him.

After the meal, Mrs. Thorson showed Chris to his room for the night, which was actually Freya's room. She also told him to collect whatever laundry he needed done and to bring it down after he took a shower, so it would be ready for his departure in the morning.

Following a pleasing hot water cleansing, Chris dutifully brought his laundry to Mrs. Thorson. She had been chatting with her husband and daughter in the small drawing room and stood to take his bag of dirty clothes. Lila Thorson said she'd get another pot of tea brewing after depositing the laundry in the wash machine, and that he should sit with her husband and daughter.

Chris nodded but as he approached, Kiri abruptly stood. She looked him in the eye, as if examining him. She said nothing at first, but then smiled and nodded her head, like she'd made the right choice. Without a word, she turned and marched up the stairs.

Stunned by the girl's sudden departure, Chris wondered if he'd said something to offend her during dinner.

"Not at all," Knute laughed robustly. "She's just gone upstairs to pack."

"To pack?"

Knute Thorson's face was all smiles. "Sit down, Chris. Her mum and I will explain."

A little bit later, Lila Thorson brought a steaming pot of fresh tea into the sitting room and served them all. Chris was puzzled as he patiently waited for Kiri's parents to explain something about their daughter to him.

Finally, after a sip of hot tea, Knute asked Chris, "What do you understand about prescience?"

The question caught him off guard.

"Prescience?" pondered Chris. "Isn't that where you know about things before they happen — something like foreknowledge or foresight?"

"That's close enough," Lila replied.

"The thing is," Knute explained, "Kiri's always had the ability to a certain extent."

"And it often has more to do with emotions, than events," added the mother. "You have to understand that the event that eventually occurs is of secondary importance; the reality Kiri experiences is in the emotion she feels beforehand."

Upstairs, the very audible sounds of water rushing through pipes told Chris that Kiri was stepping into the same shower he'd stepped out of a short time ago.

"Tell him about the puppy the girls had when they were young," Knute urged his wife.

"Yes, dear, that's a good example," replied Lila.

Briefly, Mrs. Thorson explained her daughters once had a retriever for only about two months. One afternoon Kiri came home from school, took the pup into her lap, and cried and cried before finally going upstairs to do her homework. She wouldn't say what was bothering her at the time, but a few days later while the girls were at school, the pup got out of the backyard and was killed by a car in the street. When Kiri learned what happened, little emotion was displayed. She was already fully aware of what would transpire; by then it just became the accepted nature of things.

"We could give you innumerable examples," Knute stated, "but suffice it to say she often feels things before they happen – we've seen it too many times. That's partially why we give her pretty wide leeway in what she chooses to do."

"And maybe, Knute," Lila interjected, "maybe this is precisely why she said she couldn't go to university this term."

"Maybe so," Knute mused, as if a precise explanation was beyond his ken.

Chris was admittedly lost as to where the Thorsons' conversation had taken them, and Knute read it on his face.

"Chris, let me explain," offered Knute. "Ever since Kiri was maybe eleven or twelve, she's been telling her mum and me that someday she would leave with a Master, a Teacher, whenever he or she finally appeared."

"Over the years we kind of grew used to it," Lila tossed in, "and kind of let it ride, because you can never be quite sure what Kiri senses."

"So anyway, tonight," Knute took up the tale, "while you were taking your shower, Kiri sat us both down before we could start doing the dishes. She informed us that the Teacher, the Master, she had been waiting for all these years had finally arrived."

"Chris, she also told us that tomorrow morning she'd be going on the road with you," declared Lila.

Chris was so taken aback and flabbergasted that he was rendered speechless. From upstairs he heard the water for the shower shut off and all was silent.

After a moment or two, Knute Thorson added, "Naturally, we suggested she might consider talking it over with you."

"And wouldn't you know it," his wife sighed, "typical of Kiri, she just shrugged her shoulders as if it were a done deal. She then said she'd be going up to her bedroom to pack and that's when you came down the stairs."

In total disbelief, Chris sat stunned, shaking his head. All he could eventually muster was, "I don't know what to say."

The Thorsons gave him time to collect his thoughts.

"Is she seeking some kind of apprenticeship?" he queried without expecting a reply. "Such a venture would be a grave responsibility. She is a beautiful young woman half my age; for me it would be a very solemn undertaking. Does she know what she is asking? Does she understand what life on the road is like and the constant danger I face from Empire? I don't ask this lightly."

Chris seemed to pass some kind of judgment in Knute's eyes. He nodded in agreement. "Yes, it would be a most solemn undertaking for you and one laden with grave responsibilities indeed."

"But we've also grown to trust Kiri's prescience," Lila Thorson said reassuringly. "And if it's right for Kiri, and it's right for you, well then, it's right for us. Why don't you think about it for a while and talk with Kiri when she comes down. In the meantime, Knute, you can put yourself to work helping me with the dishes."

As the Thorsons made their way to the kitchen, Chris sank, more than a little stunned, into the armchair he was occupying. He was totally lost in thought until he heard footsteps descending the staircase.

When he looked up, all he could see was a very beautiful young woman before him. For a moment, he doubted his resolve. She was wearing shorts and a loose yellow top – and obviously braless. Her shoulder length brown hair was still damp from the shower, but smartly combed. The green eyes sparkled and the smile was enticing. Once more, Chris questioned his resolve.

"So," he began, as she took the chair across from him, "your parents tell me you're interested in coming along with me on the road."

The grin didn't leave her face for an instant. Factually, she told him, "I'm going to find my Way. And I'll take you along as a Teacher – if you can measure up to the task."

Chris couldn't help but chuckle. "What makes you think I'll take you along?"

"I've already sensed that's part of my Way," Kiri stated without doubt. "I knew it long before I ever set eyes upon you."

"That's what your parents told me," he remarked. "So...I guess I'm saddled with you?"

She snickered, then snorted, "You'll call it one of the luckiest days of your life if you ever saddle with me."

Her saucy reply was unanticipated, yet her spunk amused him.

Chris plainly stated, "That's not what I meant."

"It's okay," Kiri assured him with a twinkle in her eye. "Sometimes I can feel what you think, even before you feel it."

Chris took her statement at face value before he turned more serious.

"What you don't know is how much danger you'll be in if you go on the road with me," he cautiously informed her. "You don't know my history; Empire is always seeking me."

Kiri shrugged her shoulders. "I've felt the forces; I've weighed the odds."

Clearly, Chris could see she didn't understand the gravity of the situation. He explained how he was always on the run from Empire, always becoming someone new. In fact, he explained to her, tomorrow he was meeting with Elders in Victoria that were supplying him a new Canadian passport, in a new name, and with a new phone to go with the new identity, along with other new documents. If she were to go with him, she'd have to leave her passport and personal documents here; she'd have to leave her former life here and assume a new one.

Then he intended to catch a ferry from Swartz Bay to Tsawwassen on the mainland, where a van was waiting with B.C. plates and registered in his new name.

"After that, with the new identity," Chris continued to detail, "if you choose to go, we cross the border at the Peace Arch and hope we aren't detained, because border crossings are always risky when Empire is searching for you. Are you sure you still want to travel with me?"

Not intimidated in the least, Kiri laughed heartily.

"Sounds like an interesting day," she smiled, "and I hope you're up to it. I assume we'll be leaving early. I'm going to tell my parents goodnight, then finish packing. I'll see you in the morning and I hope you don't oversleep."

Kiri had left him shaking his head in amazement that first evening; he was shaking it even now as he awaited her return from the washroom on another ferry back to Swartz Bay and Victoria, B.C.

***

Walking briskly down the private concourse to one of the Dellenbach Brother's Gulfstream jets, the cell phone in Whitley Dellenbach's suit jacket began to ring.

In stride, Whitley retrieved the phone from its pocket and glanced at the caller ID. He halted to take the call. The reception was good here and they had to talk.

"Hello Father," Whitley spoke clearly, "I'm glad you called."

"I received your message earlier," the elder Dellenbach explained, "but I've been in a series of meetings."

"I figured as much."

Theodore Dellenbach emitted a tense sigh. "I'll be honest with you, Son, this 'Future Generations' terrorism in the Northwest has us all concerned."

"That's one reason I'm traveling with all haste to Arizona," Whitley attempted to reassure his father. "My people down there have arranged a meeting for me with the former DEA agent I was telling you about. He's probably our only direct link to Chris Cadia – our Chris Soles – and Soles was likely the mastermind behind the terrorism."

"If in fact he is," the old man replied directly, "it's imperative indeed that you move quickly to get this DEA man on board and short circuit the terrorists. Your Uncle Paul, myself, and our top advisors fear an exponential outbreak of further violence if not quashed immediately. And in the meantime, with the major railways closed through the Northwest, we're losing millions daily if our oil, coal, and natural gas can't get to market."

Whitley sought to be encouraging.

"Father, as you've taught me since I was a child, The Plan can encompass and override periodic disruptions such as this," he stated clearly and positively. "In our family, your father, your generation, and now mine have labored for decades to establish the free flow of capital around the world, as well as the free flow of capital into elections. It's been a multi-year project, but we've been able to successfully downsize the government and eliminate the majority of regulations that are harmful to healthy business practices. We've sown doubt and discredited our enemies that seek to destroy our industry, and we've packed the courts with our allies from the highest in the land to the lowliest municipal judge – so as to protect our backsides. Labor unions heard their death knell years ago and our ongoing restrictions on the voting rights of the minority rabble are in their best interests. It's just like Uncle Walter always told me: 'We must shepherd the rabble in the right direction, for it is in their own best interest.'"

The elder Dellenbach did nothing to disguise a chuckle of pleasure. "My brother taught you well; I sincerely wish he was still with us now. With this new terrorism threat, perhaps what he taught involving this work you've voluntarily undertaken will become more important than ever."

"Father, there is no need to worry," the son spoke confidently. "All the amassed power is on our side. Furthermore, our police forces are omnipotent. Terrorists like this Chris Cadia will not be allowed to succeed."

"Good. Do what you can in your own way to end this as soon as possible," commanded Theodore Dellenbach. "These incidents of terrorism must not be allowed to become a contagion. "

"We will do what we have to," Whitley assured his father. "Whenever I have the slightest doubt, I think about The Plan, and then the quote from the obituary in the New York Times that you had me commit to memory when I was only nine or ten."

Laughing expansively, the elder Dellenbach took great pleasure in his son. "Do you mean the quote about Ayn Rand and her philosophy?"

"Yes Father: 'Selfishness is good, altruism is evil, and the welfare of society must always be subordinate to individual self-interest.'"

The old man emitted a smirk rich with satisfaction. "Get out to Arizona, Son, and look to our self-interests..."

***

Chris was where Kiri had left him when she excused herself to the ferry washroom, sitting amongst scores of others before the large flat screen TV in the cafeteria dining area.

The news was depressing; stories continued unabated about the railroad terror strikes in Washington and Oregon, as well as the desperate plight of the train crew trapped within the eight mile long Cascade Tunnel.

Things looked bad, very bad for Cascadia's future and, initially, Chris assumed the dour expression on Kiri's face as she returned was concordant with the disheartening news reports.

Sitting next to Chris, Kiri uncharacteristically took his hand in hers. He looked at her; she glanced at the TV and away.

Uncertain as to what was on her mind, Chris attempted to make conversation.

"Looks like we'll have much that was unexpected to discuss now with the Elders in Victoria that couldn't attend the Port Townsend meeting," he offered.

Kiri granted him a fleeting look; she then shrugged her shoulders as if all that were of little import. She also clasped his hand a tad tighter.

Following a prolonged silence, Chris asked, "You okay?"

She shook her head in the negative.

"It's about my cousin's friend," she revealed. "It just struck me when I was returning from the washroom."

Waiting patiently, Chris said nothing.

When she was ready, Kiri stated in no uncertain terms, "She's troubled and danger is closing in on her. But that might not be the worst of it."

"No?"

"Not at all," replied Kiri. "I fear I may have to help her, and that could well make matters worse for her."

To be certain, Chris was lost. He gave her hand a kindly squeeze. "Tell me what's happening with your cousin's friend. Maybe by talking out her circumstances, we can find some solutions. What seems to be causing her problems?"

Kiri turned and gawked at him obliquely. "Life," is all she said.

Once again, Chris found himself waiting for Kiri to speak. When finally she did, it was only to seemingly change the subject. She pointed at the TV screen, as the newscasters rambled interminably about the bombings further south in Cascadia.

"I know you're thinking what I am," she mentioned, not taking her eyes off the television.

"Yep," he agreed. "It's very likely we met the terrorists yesterday in Port Townsend."

"Yes, that," she said, "and how we might get to them and become a deterrent."

Kiri then asked Chris if he remembered the companion sitting next to Garf Taylor yesterday.

"You mean that muscle-bound hulk?"

"Yeah, that's who I'm talking about," said Kiri. "I'll have to research it further, but if I'm right, I'm pretty sure I know of him."

"So who is he?"

"Well, I've never personally met him," she began, "but if I'm correct, I know his sister, Carolyn. I think I once saw a picture of him taken long ago in a football uniform."

Kiri went on to explain that her cousin, Ingri Rud, and Carolyn Maxwell were roommates during their freshman year at Western Washington University in Bellingham. Kiri was attending UBC in Vancouver at the time and she often visited the two girls in Bellingham, while occasionally the two of them would travel the short distance over the border to visit her.

The three girls were very close that school year, until Kiri's cousin Ingri decided to go to school in Norway the following year. Kiri and Carolyn got together from time to time, but it seemed less and less as the months went by.

"When I first met Carolyn," Kiri recalled, "her oldest brother Billy was already in prison. She didn't like to talk about it because she loved and cherished both her brothers; after all, they had helped her scrape by and finish high school after their mother died when Carolyn was fourteen or fifteen, I think."

"What did her brother go to prison for?" wondered Chris.

"Well, if I'm right," Kiri qualified her suppositions, "he got mixed up with some extremist environmental group at the University of Washington. It was the last thing anyone imagined happening after he won a football scholarship with the Huskies, but apparently he was involved in a series of arson based, eco-terrorism attacks against logging companies and lumber yards, as well as the firebombing of everything from excessive luxury homes to gas guzzling Hummers and SUV's. Eventually, he was caught and convicted of those crimes, plus plotting to blow up dams and power stations. I remember he was supposed to be in prison for many years, but now it looks like they finally let him out – if that is Carolyn's brother."

"If Garf Taylor's companion is your friend's brother," Chris mused, "we must do what we can – possibly with her help – to thwart them from further attacks. If not, our quest for Cascadia is in grave danger of failing. We need to mentally depart the patriarchal mindset and its inherent violence. Do you think you can get in touch with your friend, Carolyn?"

At first, Kiri didn't answer the question directly. Her thoughts seemed to drift. "Well, apart from her brothers, or maybe because of her brothers, Carolyn seems to be in trouble now."

"Then you must contact her," urged Chris.

"Yes, but I don't know how far I can or should go beyond that," Kiri replied, tempering her agreement. "She might be able to help us – or I might be putting her life in extreme danger."

"You can only do the best thing you can do," noted Chris amicably. "You will know when the moment comes."

Kiri nodded and squeezed his hand tight.

"I know..."

CHAPTER EIGHT

By early evening on July 4th, Garf Taylor and Billy Maxwell were securely ensconced in one of the safe house apartments they maintained on the west side of the Cascades. After departing the failed meeting in Port Townsend, they drove to Kingston and crossed Puget Sound on the ferry to Edmonds. Without any stops, they then motored south on Interstate 5 through Seattle and exited the freeway at Federal Way.

They picked up pizza and drove the short distance to the apartment. By then the predicted rain had started in earnest and they were able to dash from the vehicle to the safe house without being noticed by any of their neighbors. Not that any of their apartment neighbors would necessarily care, however, for this apartment – like others they maintained – was in a high transit area where no one got involved in other's business.

After devouring their pizza, Garf and Billy drank whiskey and played cribbage while waiting for the TV news about their fireworks to come in. It started slow with alerts being flashed at the bottom of the screen, but by 9:40 PM regular programming was off the air. All coverage for the next several hours was focused on a series of explosions that had closed major rail routes in Washington and Oregon. Garf and Billy retired that evening jubilant in the knowledge their mission had been a success.

Upon waking the next morning and tuning in for the latest developments, however, they realized they had exceeded all expectations. Learning they had reaped the unanticipated windfall of a tanker train being snared somewhere in the darkness of the nearly eight mile long Cascade Tunnel, Taylor and Maxwell were nearly giddy. Particularly with the bonus of this being an *oil* train trophy, that fact in particular would only be highlighted and emphasized when the Future Generations Manifesto hit the news later in the day.

Naturally, those in control of the media weren't yet focusing on the fact that the train was carrying fossil fuel Weapons of Planetary Destruction; instead, they were all over themselves in a wringing of hands for the poor train crew trapped in the tunnel and their ultimate fate. Neither Garf nor Billy shared such sentiments. To them, those of the train crew were merely foot soldiers of the enemy and deserved whatever fate might befall them.

Around midday, as the initial elation of their successes from the previous evening was winding down into accepted reality, and before the Future Generations Manifesto would declare their intent to the world, Taylor and Maxwell began brainstorming about strategy and future strikes directed toward WPD's and the fossil fuel Kingpins.

"So tell me again what is happening with Timmy and the rest of the explosives," requested Garf.

"The original plan for my brother is good," Billy assured Garf. "He took his remaining leave at work to help us plant the charges and is on schedule to quit the excavation company next Friday. Between now and then, he'll steal another sizeable load of explosives that we'll take out toward Grays Harbor."

"Does the construction company suspect anything?" Garf wondered.

"Not as of now."

"But they will."

"Yeah, that's for sure," Billy agreed. "With my record and Timmy's expertise in explosives, the Feds will eventually put two-and-two together. But Timmy's got his tracks covered for a while. His bosses know he's registered for community college in the fall, and he's talked up a trip to the Yukon and Alaska till then. So he'll be able to drop off the radar."

"Assuming, he can make it safely through next week," Garf said ominously.

"He'll make it," Billy assured him.

"What about Carolyn?" asked Garf. "We need someone to do the phone shuffle and help with the logistics. Is she willing to do that and still keep her full time job?"

"Don't worry about my sister," Billy replied. "She'll do what she's told. It was the money I had stashed away before prison and what Timmy could earn in construction after Ma died that kept her alive and got her through high school. She owes us big time; she'll do what she's told."

Garf nodded. "Speaking of prison, what about your contacts that have been released from Monroe Correctional?"

"All I know is after a few more strikes by Future Generations, independent cells in Cascadia will be ready to erupt," Billy promised. "I'll get the word out. We agreed to carry the climate war to the police state when the time came. That time is nearly here. You'll see."

"I'm looking forward to it."

For a time, the two conspirators spoke of possible immediate implications resulting from the rail line bombings and the imminent release of the Manifesto. After some discussion, they reaffirmed their original plan to lay low for a few days to observe developments, and then meet Timmy next Friday to take explosives out towards Grays

Harbor.

"One more thing, Billy," inquired Garf, "where are we at with the testing of the hydraulic spreaders? Are we getting close enough to be able to implement them?"

Maxwell responded in the affirmative. "My buddy, McNeil – who I know from the joint – told me a couple weeks ago that he was fine tuning them and they should be ready soon. He's a good mechanic and designed the spreaders based on a type of hybrid car jack. They're supposed to be quiet, easy to move, and can be pumped by one man. He also said he's got a special spike puller so derailing a train should be easy when the rails are spread enough."

"Good," acknowledged Garf. "Where's he testing the spreader out?"

"Right under their noses," Billy chuckled. "McNeil's using an abandoned siding up by the Cherry Point refineries, north of Bellingham. He's not easy to get in touch with, but I'll try to contact him in the next few days and see if the spreaders are ready."

Billy was going to mention something else about derailing trains, when he was confronted by second thoughts. He wondered aloud if they ought to shift their attacks away from railroads, at least for a time, considering how all of the authorities' attention would be focused on them after last night's success.

"No, I don't think so, Billy," replied Garf. "At least not yet. I think we stick it in their eye. We should probably do one or two more jobs on rail lines to make them think that's all we care about. Then we're wide open; maybe we shift to fossil fuel terminals for a while. Or maybe a pipeline. Or maybe an oil company exec. And then – then wherever we choose."

Billy issued a grim sneer. "Just like it said in the Manifesto – the targets are endless."

***

He wasn't sure; he might be mistaken. But no, that couldn't be the same car that appeared to be tailing him down I-5 to the meeting in South Seattle this morning. Or could it be?

No, Tomas Hernandez tried to assure himself, the odds were against it. After all, how many brown four-door, imported sedans were on the roadways of greater Seattle at any given time? More than enough, he answered himself; it was entirely possible that similar looking cars could be behind him at any given time.

Once more Hernandez glanced at his side view mirror to see the suspect vehicle in the next lane a few cars back. This time he was nearly certain he was being followed; it had to be part of Empire's intimidation tactics.

But even if they weren't on his tail, he knew it was essential to keep his guard up. That much was clear ever since the incident a few months ago.

Keeping a wary eye on his mirrors, Tomas accelerated on the Alaska Way Viaduct that ran alongside the Seattle waterfront. He was nearing the ferry terminals and heading north past downtown Seattle. The brown sedan was keeping pace with him; Hernandez nevertheless actively attempted to chase any and all unfounded paranoia from his mind.

It was a problem, he realized, that every progressively focused person must be facing today after last night's bombing of the railroads. Everyone knew knee-jerk, brute force retaliation would soon be coming from Empire, but one couldn't be certain when and where. The trick was to recognize the threat, yet not succumb mentally to before the hammer of reprisals came down. That was the only way to still pursue the illusion of freedom.

Tomas had tried to voice that conviction in the Commons Rising gathering just concluded in South Seattle, but he didn't know if he'd made much of an impact. Even though everyone had come together in solidarity of purpose, the terrorism of July 4th had transformed July 5th into a day of second-guessing and scowls of worry.

They were all representatives chosen by their own respective commons throughout Cascadia and all were committed to transforming individual consumers and employees into commoners with collective interests. All sincerely believed that a great rejoining of production and governance was in its incipient phases with commoners participating in both. Together they looked toward the day when the market no longer controlled production and the state no longer made the rules. And with the rising of the commons, the commoners would make it happen.

Still, those in attendance also recognized the advances they made would be incremental within their own commons. It didn't matter if the commons were of lawyers working toward green governance, or seed bank commoners preserving a collective heritage, or even Tomas's N-Triple-C construction commons, they all understood the commons to be an organizing principle for a campaign of social change.

The many different commons would slowly and steadily work for that change among their own interests, but it was also evident to all that if they came together and labored toward widespread common interest, much could be accomplished because of their shared philosophy and sheer numbers.

A very simple strategy had thus naturally found its way to the forefront.

At an early convening of Commons Rising representatives, and as a symbolic centerpiece of the Commons movement, it was suggested they join forces to protect the one predominant commons they all shared – that being the global atmosphere.

"You can't get a bigger commons than that!" someone had remarked to the amusement of all, and so the scope of Commons Rising's initial mission had been launched.

There were many suggestions how Commons Rising might take back a safe atmosphere for future generations, and all understood it would only be done by persistent and arduous labor. Today's meeting was to have focused on rallying against yet another giant rig being readied in Puget Sound for arctic oil exploration – especially in the face of the recent disastrous oil spill in pristine Arctic seas.

However, because of the unfolding terrorism on local rail lines, many Commons Rising representatives were in a dither. Some spoke of an upcoming sea change in future events, laden with retaliation and backlash. Others openly worried about infiltrators and spies, and being attacked from the inside. And some were probably much like Tomas himself, dancing with one's own paranoia and attempting to overcome it.

By meeting's end today, more focus had been concentrated on the disturbing events of yesterday than proactive planning for the future. The Commons Rising gathering had adjourned with a sour stomach, wait-and-see type resolution that was satisfying to no one.

The fact that Hernandez had fairly well founded suspicions as to the saboteurs' identity as a result of yesterday's meeting in Port Townsend gave him no comfort either. As much as he couldn't condone their actions, neither could he go to the authorities and attempt to turn them in. That would be too close to collaborating with the enemy for his liking. The only thing he could do right now – like many others perhaps – was watch his own backside and observe how events transpired.

At the thought, he glanced in the mirror while approaching a stoplight. Hernandez realized he'd been driving automatically; he was now heading north on 15th Avenue West and not far from the Ballard Bridge. Fortunately, neither rear view nor side mirror held a brown four-door sedan, so Tomas slowly dismissed his prior apprehensions.

In any case, he lauded himself for the decision to avoid the Interstate freeway home to Edmonds, about fifteen miles north of

Seattle, even though these roads were slower going and filled with stoplights. The pace seemed to fit his mood better; it gave him time to take in the sights like the ship canal he would soon pass over on the Ballard Bridge, and possibly allow his mind to wander away from the day's constant news reports of terrorism and bombings.

Still, he knew his thoughts wouldn't stray too far, since those events were most likely a game changer – one way or the other – when it came to how Empire and its police state would now interact with everyday citizens. It truly was a shame the Northwest rail bombings occurred, especially since individual commons were successfully eroding traditional market/state collusion and control, while proving to be a viable alternative to the status quo.

Of course, Commons Rising was only in its early stages, yet carried a potential to someday entirely undermine the current dominance of Empire's power structure. And that was most clearly demonstrated by the viability, strength, and reach of individual commons such as the New Cascadia Construction Commons, or the N-Triple-C.

Hernandez had trained as an architect and joined the N-Triple-C shortly after it formed. In the beginning, the commons was put together by an architectural firm, a moderately successful developer, and a failing labor union. N-Triple-C became an employee-owned and controlled cooperative that promoted a livable wage for all, as they constructed affordable and green homes and buildings for the north Seattle to Everett community.

In less than a decade, the N-Triple-C exploded into a construction dynamo and community asset. The commons enlarged to include suppliers such as logging companies promoting strict forest management, as well as consumers whose purchases from and investments in N-Triple-C were validated by the commons as part of the community trust.

Detractors claimed the New Cascadia Construction Commons was corrupting the free market system, and colluding to fix prices, limit supply, and control the marketplace. N-Triple-C and their green governance lawyers always responded, however, with language that essentially said the commons stood outside of the market by virtue of how they produce their product and how they govern themselves. It was often like walking a legal tightrope, but the commoners understood that as an inherent risk. The reality was that there could be no question the commons were a threat to the state/market system.

So vocal and active had Hernandez been over the years in promoting the interest of the N-Triple-C commons, that perhaps it was only natural he was chosen by his peers to be their representative when the new Commons Rising group had been formed in Cascadia. As a result, his architectural duties were cut approximately in half and the remainder of his work hours were expected to be dedicated to Commons Rising issues.

That seemed all well and good until after a Commons Rising meeting in Bellingham. Tomas had stopped at the Community Co-Op close to home and, coming out of the market, was accosted by a couple of thugs in the parking lot. They wore ski masks and it was nearly dark, so he never could have identified them. They told him in no uncertain terms to lose his interest in unions – he told them he dealt with the commons – and they subsequently delivered several blows to the body that left him laid out on the parking lot asphalt.

Perhaps Tomas should have reported the harassment and assault, but after what happened to his sister and her two children some years ago in Arizona, he was extraordinarily wary of police and authorities in control.

Snapping out of his reminiscences, Hernandez realized he was already in Northgate and about to turn onto Aurora Avenue, or Highway 99, for the rest of his ride north to Edmonds. Instinctively he checked the mirrors without catching sight of a trailing sedan – and knowing he had good reason to be cautious.

The danger was out there: the forces of capitalist market enclosure

– the mechanisms driving Empire's depersonalizing system – do not like competition. Time and again, history has displayed that they are brutal and uncompromising when it comes to dismantling and demolishing the commons. Because the commons threatens the state/market power base, Empire's governments and bureaucracies have no qualms about sending their agents and operatives on covert missions to disrupt and even obliterate those who might stand in their way.

And the threat could only be exponentially greater, Tomas aptly reasoned, after saboteurs successfully attacked the very lifelines of Empire – their fossil fuel arterials.

CHAPTER NINE

Business was brisk on Saturday morning, July 6th, at a run-of-the-mill, franchise coffee shop restaurant in Scottsdale, Arizona.

Whitley Dellenbach lingered at the hostess station as harried employees hustled by delivering coffee and breakfast to patrons, while the hungry formed a line out the entry door waiting for their turn to be seated.

Dellenbach easily recognized the big man he'd come to meet. He was sitting in a booth a short distance away, next to the windows with a view of the parking lot and palm trees. The former DEA agent had no inkling who was coming to meet him; the encounter had been entirely orchestrated by one of Dellenbach's operatives.

When Whitley was satisfied, he strolled past those waiting at the front of the hostess line and sauntered directly to the booth where the big man was sipping coffee. The ex-DEA agent watched him approach – as he appeared to observe everything else transpiring around him – and instinctively seemed to know Whitley was whom he was waiting for.

"My name is Whitley Dellenbach," he said by way of introduction. He offered his hand but Stone McClelland was initially reluctant to reciprocate with a handshake. Instead, he took time to scrutinize the man that had requested this powwow.

To McClelland's trained eye, it was obvious from the start that everything about this character was calculated. All gestures were deliberate and nothing in his body language seemed undetermined. He was in his mid-forties, a little over six feet and probably around one hundred seventy pounds; Stone couldn't envision an ounce of fat on the man's frame.

Dellenbach's most predominant feature, however, was his striking Aryan appearance. With sharp angles accenting a thin face, with brilliant blue eyes and very blond – no, almost white – eyebrows and precisely cropped hair, McClelland imagined if it had been a different time and place, Dellenbach as a child could have been a poster boy for the Hitler Youth. In spite of that, he did seem friendly enough – like a rattlesnake at rest.

Finally shaking the proffered hand, McClelland introduced himself. Dellenbach slid into the booth across from guest, but before he could speak, Stone McClelland had a few things he wanted to know.

"So what's with all the cloak-and-dagger surrounding this meeting?" asked the former DEA man.

"Cloak-and-dagger?" Dellenbach replied innocently.

"Yeah," Stone declared. "Some guy I've never met contacts me out of the blue, and tells me that some other guy I've never met might want to hire me for a job, but won't tell me what his name is or what the job is – so I guess that seems a little cloak-and-dagger."

"So why did you show up? What else did he tell you?"

"He said," McClelland began slowly, "that the possible job was related to the arrest of a Spore Master in northern Arizona several years ago."

"So there we go," said Dellenbach, satisfied. "Obviously it was enough to spur your interest. Suffice it to say, I came to tell you a few stories, see if you might be interested in a new job, and pay for your breakfast, of course."

Having little to reply, Stone McClelland merely grunted.

A waitress abruptly appeared and introduced herself as Karen. She asked Dellenbach if he too wanted coffee while handing menus to both men. Whitley nodded affirmatively and Karen hurried off.

"Yes, let me tell you a few stories, Mr. McClelland," he glibly commenced. "To reintroduce myself, my name is Whitley Dellenbach, though my close friends call me Whitey, but of course I wouldn't know why."

Working past the smugness, it was obvious to Stone and he wasn't impressed.

"If you've never heard of the Dellenbach Brothers, spend a few minutes on the Internet to learn a bit about my father and uncles, and our family," Whitley requested. "Our family has many interests. Some years ago, a favorite cousin of mine named Alice was working undercover at the Gaia/Universe compound in the Arizona desert. You've heard of it perhaps?"

Stone McClelland was impassive; he waited for Dellenbach to continue.

"Anyway, my dear cousin was turned and deceived by one Chris Soles," he stated factually. "Somehow they both survived the turmoil that spelled the end for Gaia/Universe and then Soles spirited Alice away to a remote Utah cave. That's where he happened to have been growing illegal psychedelic mushrooms with the Spore Master – who happened to be arrested one day in northern Arizona. Perhaps you know the rest of the story?"

Still McClelland sat emotionless, unperturbed.

Dellenbach was nevertheless gracious. "Well, if you don't know, I'll tell you. It took several months, but federal agents eventually found the secret Utah cave where this Chris Soles, we learned later, had kidnapped and imprisoned our Alice against her will. With the federal agents closing in, Chris Soles murdered cousin Alice and escaped into the cave that was pre-wired with explosives. It was generally assumed he had died in the explosion and cave-in, but my sources suggest he might be very much alive in subversive Cascadia and plotting revolution."

Dellenbach was interrupted as the waitress returned and poured him coffee. She asked them both what they wanted to order for breakfast, while standing fast at their booth. The men made their selections and she was off.

"Obviously, if this Chris Soles is still alive, he must be brought to justice," Dellenbach stated definitively. "I'd be remiss if I didn't admit it was something personal for me as well, but there's more to it than that."

Stone McClelland sighed; he was ready to cut to the chase. "So how do I fit in?"

A complacent smile arose upon Dellenbach's Aryan features.

"To get there, we should start at the destination, instead of the departure point," he stated enigmatically. "I'm sure you've heard about the bombings on the Northwest rail lines a couple days ago and the manifesto that was issued by a terrorist group calling itself 'Future Generations?'"

"Who hasn't?"

"Well, let me tell you another little story that will get us to our destination," Whitley kindly offered.

For several minutes before their breakfasts arrived, Dellenbach related a tale about one of his people that had been having a drink at a bar in Gallup, New Mexico. He told Stone how his man had tracked down an individual that had formerly been a police officer for the Navajo Nation. His man began plying the other with alcohol. The former policeman had been on duty the day a certain Spore Master and his assistant were arrested and detained in a holding cell. Unfortunately, the Spore Master died from a heart attack that evening in the cell.

"And the next morning, according to the ex-Navajo cop, a certain DEA agent appeared and took the assistant into custody," Dellenbach told McClelland, his eyes narrowing to slits. "The official records made no note of anyone but the Spore Master being arrested and detained, but the former Navajo Nation policeman is willing to testify about what really happened."

Whitley Dellenbach knew he was fudging the facts a bit with the "willing to testify" line, but it didn't bother him.

"Now, I imagine an investigation into the matter could easily be opened," Dellenbach surmised, "but I for one think it'd be a waste of time to bring charges about how the Spore Master assistant ended up back in the hidden cave – and with my dear cousin Alice. More profitable for all, I believe, would be a scenario whereby a certain former DEA agent might somehow choose to recapture the assistant that got away."

Stone McClelland was quite aware he was being coerced and worked into a corner, and it pissed him off. Nobody pulled that kind of intimidation shit on him and got away with it. He was nearly ready to jerk this dickhead out of the booth and toss him through the plate glass window toward the parking lot outside.

"Nobody threatens me like that," he snarled ominously.

"It's not a threat at all," Dellenbach smiled slickly. "Let me tell you the rest of the story."

Stone was within an inch of clobbering this preppy bastard.

"I'm not sure how much you know about separatists in the Northwest that want to establish their own sovereign nation called 'Cascadia,'" Dellenbach continued, "but part of the currently prevailing mythos up there has it that an almost supernatural being shows up from time to time, hands out psilocybin mushrooms, and is a strongly unifying force in the push to open rebellion. They call this character 'Chris Cadia.' Sources tell us that this person is likely Chris Soles and also quite possibly behind the railroad bombings and these Future Generations terrorists."

The bigger picture came into view for Stone McClelland; accordingly his animosity toward Dellenbach began to evaporate. At the same time, he was outraged and shamed by his own actions in letting the Spore Master's assistant go free.

"So you want me to travel to the Northwest and find him, eh?"

"You will be generously compensated," Dellenbach assured him. "You will also be given access to intelligence resources through people in our government."

Stone McClelland stewed the matter over for several minutes in silence. During that time, the waitress brought them their breakfast orders. Whitley Dellenbach launched himself into an omelet, while McClelland picked hesitantly at his two eggs over-easy and hash browns. By the time Dellenbach was nearly finished with his meal, Stone directed his attention back to the man sitting across the booth.

"Supposing I accept your job offer," he began, "how do I go about it? Am I to simply head to the Northwest and look for a mythic figure handing out mushrooms?"

A wry grin attached itself to Dellenbach's lips. "I suggest you start out by contacting a very public figure, a protest leader named Sapphire MacKenzie. Tell her whatever you must to gain her confidence and doors will likely open for you. I cannot tell you why, but under no circumstances whatsoever can you reference my family or me in your discussions with her. If that occurs, all will be lost and your investigation will be effectively terminated. Do you understand?"

"I think so," Stone said tentatively. He cleared his throat. "Assuming I someday track down this Chris Cadia – Chris Soles, what then do you want from me?"

"Very simple," Dellenbach replied. "When you find him, pretend to befriend him. However you do it is up to you. Then we want to acquire several things we believe are likely in his possession."

"Like hundreds of thousands of illegal magic mushrooms?"

"To keep those from potentially poisoning the minds of America's youth would certainly be something we are after," said Dellenbach. "But there's more. There is supposed to be a detailed list of subversives and revolutionaries that Bruno Panoka, the former head of the diabolical Gaia/Universe cult had collected. In her undercover work at G/U my cousin Alice had secured a copy of this list and, very likely, Soles has it now.

"If we can find Soles and disrupt his network," Whitley carried on, "we may be able catch the terrorists calling themselves Future Generations and short circuit any further nonsensical rumblings about a sovereign Cascadia. And finally, we want Chris Soles to stand trial for all his crimes – which includes the murder of my cousin."

Stone McClelland slowly nodded his head. "So how long do I have to decide if I'll take the job?"

"You have until noon."

"Noon?"

"Noon, today," Dellenbach emphasized. "Call my man, Roger, before noon. He's the one that contacted you to set up this meeting; I believe you have his number?"

"Yes."

"Good," affirmed Whitley. He glanced at his wristwatch. "Now it is time for me to depart. Very likely, this is the last time you will ever meet me personally. Anything you need from me goes through my man Roger. If you accept this employment offer, Roger will make certain a substantial sum is wired directly into your bank account on Monday morning – before you fly to the Northwest that same day to begin your investigation."

Dellenbach took a final sip of coffee before rising from the booth, shaking McClelland's hand, and leaving.

Stone watched him walk toward the cashier's station. He paid with a large bill, didn't wait for change, and was out the door.

Still picking at his half-finished breakfast, Stone McClelland was fatefully aware what his decision would be regarding Dellenbach's offer. Of course he would agree to hunt down Chris Soles – he had little alternative. He was ambivalent about his own motives, but what else could he do?

And why, really, did he let Chris Soles go in the first place? It was an especially troubling question in light of Soles wreaking so much murder and destruction thereafter. And what in the world made him think he could no longer serve the country he had been so loyal to for so long? If the truth were to be told, McClelland wouldn't be accepting Dellenbach's offer for the money, so much as to answer questions deep within his soul.

Yet there was one overriding concern: how would Lorien take his decision? After he quit the DEA, he swore to her life would change; he would be at home and become a true partner. With that promise she had finally consented to marriage, but now what would happen? If he went back to work for what its detractors called "Empire," would he still have his wife – who was really, and truly, his life?

CHAPTER TEN

For the sixth time in as many days, Kiri Thorson was listening to the phone number she had dialed ring and ring and ring. She was poised once more to hear Carolyn Maxwell's reserved voice come on the line announcing she wasn't available, and to please leave a message.

This time, however, the ringing simply stopped and the line went silent.

Surprised, Kiri waited and wondered. Eventually she mustered, "Carolyn?"

The silence lingered until it was broken with a quiet, "Hi, Kiri."

Kiri was jubilant. "Carolyn, I finally got a hold of you!"

Again there was an uneasy silence.

"I'm sorry I didn't take your calls or return your messages," Carolyn apologized, "but there are problems. And it's better you don't get involved."

"So why did you answer now?"

"I guess I needed somebody to talk to."

"I'm here," Kiri replied. "What's wrong?"

"Oh, part of it's my job," she said dismissively. "And my bills – especially my student loan bills. I feel like I'm trapped and can never get ahead."

Intentionally, Carolyn changed the subject. She noted how they hadn't spoken in such a long time and was curious what Kiri had been up to.

Kiri evasively stated she had a position as a traveling "intern" for the transition movement. She made the journeying about sound attractive and mentioned she'd seen many places she never dreamed existed in Cascadia.

"How did you get such an awesome job?" wondered Carolyn. "Was it through your father and his work with the transition movement in Canada?"

"Sort of," Kiri replied vaguely.

Carolyn plied Kiri for tales of her travels and the two chatted amiably for a short time. Running low on small talk, Kiri casually dropped that she'd seen Carolyn's brother, Billy, at a recent meeting in Port Townsend.

Carolyn was stunned and surprised. At first, she could say nothing.

"It was a day or two after that," Kiri admitted, "that I sensed some kind of internal conflict. That's why I've been trying to call you."

Carolyn knew well of Kiri's sixth sense and it relieved her. She told of her recruitment by her brothers and the subsequent forced entry to their troubled world. She didn't want to do it, but she owed everything to Billy and Timmy.

"It has to do with the railroad explosions, doesn't it?" Kiri surmised. "And the new group calling itself 'Future Generations?'"

Carolyn was astounded. "How do you know that?"

"I was at the meeting in Port Townsend," she reminded her friend. "I heard Billy's friend, Garf Taylor, speak. Then I put two-and-two together. I'm here to help you, Carolyn."

On the other end of the line, Carolyn Maxwell broke down in tears. For several minutes the sobs continued, interrupted only from time to time by plaintive statements such as, "I don't want them to get hurt and go to jail," or, "Billy completely controls Timmy," or, "They've done so much for me and I'm so worried for them," and "I'm so scared of Garf!"

When Carolyn finally gathered herself once more, Kiri assured her that she was on her friend's side. She also attempted to summon some positivity.

"Listen, Carolyn," she said, "if your brothers were involved with the railroad bombings, at least no one has been killed yet. I heard late last night they finally rescued the train crew from the Cascade Tunnel and all are alive. That's a good thing."

Kiri continued by mentioning that she was associated with people who asserted change in Cascadia, first and foremost, by incorporating non-violence.

"I know you don't want your brothers hurt or going to jail," said Kiri, "so if we could deter them from their present course without them getting arrested or doing more harm, that would be best for all. Maybe then they'd see the error of their ways and begin to back off. Let me try and help you; I think I know people who can be of assistance."

"Oh, Kiri, I'm so thankful you called!" Carolyn gushed. "I thought I was in this all alone."

"Well, you're not," Kiri assured her. "So let's begin with your role. What do they want you to do?"

"I'm supposed to continue working my present job at Boeing as my cover," she replied, "but at the same time be their logistics hub and run the phone shuffle."

Doing a quick mental calculation, Kiri realized Carolyn would have a direct line to whatever plots and schemes Future Generations had coming down the pipe if she was helping coordinate logistics. Assuming, of course, if her brothers kept her fully informed.

Serving as the phone shuffler would take up a good deal of Carolyn's free time, though Kiri couldn't currently perceive how this might work to the advantage of Chris and herself. Because of the overbearing electronic surveillance by Empire, phones had to be circulated constantly and new ones were regularly required. Their phones were aided by a series of apps capable of generating or deleting private phone numbers for one time use to, in theory, stay one step ahead of Empire. Still, it was a cat-and-mouse game as Empire's technicians relentlessly attempted to back door the apps, so new phones were constantly shuffled.

The Elders in various Cascadia locations took care of all this for Chris and Kiri, but she was curious how Carolyn could handle this task.

"Where are your new phones coming from?" asked Kiri.

"From Billy's friends," Carolyn replied. "He's got an extensive network of ex-cons like himself – mostly from Monroe Correctional – that have vowed to support the cause when the time comes. My brother brags that many of them have formed sleeper cells with ordinary people the cops would never suspect, and when the time comes..."

Carolyn let her statement hang in ominous disapproval and Kiri picked up on the vibes.

"So what are they up to now?" Kiri wanted to know. "What do we do to keep somebody from getting killed and, at the same time, calm the entire situation down?"

As Carolyn had only learned she would be working with her brothers a few days ago, she wasn't fully aware of their current plans. All she knew for sure was that Timmy would be quitting his job at the end of the week, and they would be moving stolen explosives after that.

"Stolen explosives?" Kiri was aghast. "You mean they have more of them?"

"A lot more, from the way they were talking this week," said Carolyn. "Timmy has been stealing them little by little from the excavating company he's been working for the last several years.

"They have a cache somewhere near Clatskanie on the Oregon side of the Columbia," Carolyn continued, "and they're moving the last of what Timmy has stolen along with a sizeable stash already out by Grays Harbor into a hidden away, abandoned cabin. I don't know exactly where it is, except I gather it's somewhere north of Aberdeen, off the 101 Highway on the road to Humptulips."

"What in the world could they be planning to do with all that?" wondered Kiri.

"I don't know," Carolyn admitted, "and it scares me to death. But that's not all."

"What do you mean?"

"When they stopped here in Everett a few nights ago, Billy and Garf were on their way to visit someone who lived north of Bellingham," Carolyn revealed. "Apparently he has some hydraulic spreaders ready for them."

"Hydraulic spreaders?"

"I'm not certain exactly what they are," she said, "other than they're capable of spreading railroad tracks enough so a train will derail. They were talking about the trains serving the big Cherry Point refinery, so I'm afraid they might be planning something up there."

"We can't let them do that," Kiri was insistent. "It would be an environmental disaster. On top of that, the governmental backlash would destroy hopes of a new Cascadia before it could get really started."

"But I don't want my brothers arrested and thrown in prison," Carolyn pleaded. "They're my only family and that's all I've got."

"All the more reason that we find out what they're up to and stop them as soon as we can," Kiri asserted. "I'll do all I can to help you."

"Do you mean it, Kiri?" Carolyn needed to know. "I don't know how to thank you!"

"I promise," Kiri told her friend.

***

By prior arrangement, Chris slipped inconspicuously into the back seat of the graying, fifty-four year old woman's car as she slowed in the mall's parking lot. Kiri was already in the front seat; the driver, Mrs. Sutton, greeted him as he closed the door.

Nearly an hour ago Chris had dropped Kiri off in Everett. She waited a short while and then caught a bus to the Transit Center in Lynnwood, about a twenty-minute ride.

After leaving Kiri in Everett, Chris had driven straight to the Lynnwood Transit Center. He deposited the van they were now driving with British Columbia plates in the middle of the thirteen hundred plus slots for park-and-ride users. He then hopped on one of the regular scheduled buses to the Alderwood Mall and lolled about in a predesignated pickup location.

Like clockwork, Mrs. Sutton had stopped for Kiri, then Chris, precisely on schedule. She had then driven straight to her home in Lynnwood, with Chris and Kiri ducking low as a precautionary measure the last few blocks before pulling into the driveway and pushing the remote to close the garage door behind them. Just in case, similar tactics would be employed during the morning rush hour tomorrow when it was time for Chris and Kiri to secure their van and travel on.

About a half hour after Mrs. Audra Sutton arrived home with her surreptitious guests, Tomas Hernandez and his wife, Linda – the former Linda Sutton – arrived at her mother's house with kids in tow. The grandkids, four-year-old Cassie and three-year-old Kyle, were pure energy in their rush to embrace their Grandma, and Audra Sutton returned a similar level of emotion as best she could.

Gradually relocating to the kitchen, Tomas temporarily put the fresh salmon he had bought for dinner in the fridge; Linda did the same with the salad and dessert she had been carrying.

Addressing everyone in the kitchen, Audra Sutton suggested, "Why don't you all have your discussion before we eat, and I'll take two of my favorite grandchildren in the backyard to play for a while?"

Young Cassie and Kyle, realizing they would have grandma all to themselves for a time, were overwhelmed with excitement. Tugging, pushing, urging Audra to move faster toward the patio door, the youngsters shouted about all the activities they wanted grandma to engage in – everything from swinging on the swing set, to going down the slide, and playing games.

After the patio door closed and the energy in the kitchen assumed a more normal level, Linda offered everyone beverages from her mom's refrigerator. They all then sat comfortably around the kitchen table.

"So what is happening," Tomas initiated things, speaking to Chris, "that can't be discussed over the phone?"

Chris turned to look at Kiri. For a couple of seconds they exchanged eye contact. Chris then returned his gaze to Tomas and Linda across the table. "I think I better let Kiri explain."

Nodding at Chris, Kiri turned to Tomas and Linda.

"I could go into detail about unexpected connections," Kiri began, "but it is probably better that less is mentioned. Suffice it to say we have a reliable source within Garf Taylor and Billy Maxwell's organization who is willing to put their own safety in jeopardy to help us deter them."

Somewhat surprised, Linda and Tomas exchanged glances.

"This seems to be some kind of windfall we'd never have expected after the Port Townsend meeting," mused Tomas. "Whatever we can do to avoid violence works ultimately to the advantage of the commons and a new Cascadia."

From the periphery of his vision Tomas could see Linda and Chris nodding in agreement, while Kiri absorbed the focus of his thoughts.

"To help your friend at all – to insure a sustainable vision of a Cascadia that we all share," Tomas logically deduced, "we first need to know what Taylor and Maxwell have planned."

"Right now, our friend doesn't know specifics regarding what they've been scheming," Kiri continued. She did, however, mention how their friend had spoken of two caches of explosives that Maxwell and Taylor had stowed away. "One of them is located somewhere near Clatskanie on the Oregon side of the Columbia."

Before Kiri could mention the other stash, Tomas interrupted. "That's in easy range of many potential targets. Close by is the Port Westward fuel transfer terminal, and across the Columbia is the massive terminal in Longview, Washington, and the two big oil storage and transshipment sites next door in Vancouver, Washington. Further west of Clatskanie, toward the coast is Warrenton, Oregon, where the new oil pipeline from Canada terminates. Warrenton is also where the coal now allowed to barge down the Columbia will be loaded onto foreign bound ships. There's no shortage of attack sites."

"And that's only for one cache of the explosives," Chris reminded Tomas. "Kiri, tell them about the other one."

Briefly, Kiri explained how Garf and Billy were supposedly relocating the explosives they already had stored out by Grays Harbor in central western Washington, to an abandoned cabin somewhere north of Aberdeen off the 101 Highway. Consolidated with this stockpile would be the remainder of the explosives Timmy had stolen from his soon-to-be former excavation company.

"There are no lack of targets out that way either," Chris interjected. "At Grays Harbor, in Hoquiam, there are already two monstrous oil transfer terminals. The new bulk liquid facility at Terminal 4 also came on line last year and with its faulty security record, it would be a tempting prize. Remember too, all these terminals are served by railroad lines which could also be an obvious objective."

"Related to that," Kiri inserted, "is what our friend told us about hydraulic spreaders."

"What are those?" asked Tomas.

To their understanding, Chris explained it was apparently a tool used to derail a train. Assumedly, after the spikes along rail lines were pulled, the hydraulic spreaders would widen the rail lines just enough so the trains would derail.

"With rail lines throughout Cascadia overburdened by fuel tanker cars already, a derailment anywhere could be an environmental nightmare," Tomas exclaimed.

"Well, apparently they are currently focusing on Ferndale and Cherry Point north of Bellingham," Kiri informed them. "At least that's what our friend said."

"And train derailments up there would wreak havoc," added Chris. "Not only are there a couple major refineries in the area, but there's also one of the world's largest coal transshipment terminals – and everything comes in by rail."

For a couple minutes silence reigned at the kitchen table as they took in the scope of potential devastations that could be the handiwork of Garf Taylor and the Maxwell brothers – if indeed they were the likely "Representatives of Future Generations."

Linda Hernandez, having said little so far, brushed blond hair away from her face and brown eyes. She'd taken in what the others had said and now openly wondered if they shouldn't just turn them in.

"I mean, if you think about it," Linda reasoned, "that might just nip all this in the bud. And if that's not the solution, what are our other options?"

Tomas, sitting next to Linda, took his wife's hand in his. "I've thought of that too," he admitted, "but as much as I despise Garf Taylor and his methods, I simply cannot side with Empire. Even if I knew where they were and how to get them, bringing their heads on a platter to the fossil fuel Kingpins is not something I can bring myself to do."

"Kiri, what do you think?" asked Chris.

From the look on her face, it was apparent she enjoyed being treated as an equal and that her traveling companion valued her opinion more with each passing day.

"I promised our friend that I'd try to help," was all Kiri said initially. "It's better that I don't say anything about our friend's circumstances, but we've got to do something to render some assistance and possible deterrence, or it might adversely effect events down the road."

"I agree completely that we have to do something, given the knowledge we have from your friend, Kiri," Tomas concurred. "Since the railroad bombings everyone with an opinion knows something has to be done; now, with this information it is incumbent on us to make the correct decision. We must somehow act."

"How about this," Chris mused. "Linda, what if you had a word with Sapphire MacKenzie? She seemed to know Garf Taylor and maybe she has the means to contact him. And if she does, maybe she could pass along the information that 'people' have told her the Feds are in surveillance in the Grays Harbor area concerning an illegal weapons transfer. Maybe that would slow them down or warn them off. What do you think?"

"I don't know about that," she replied. Linda went on to explain that Sapphire had her own ideas about action, politics, and revolution. Sure, they were good friends as raft guides in Idaho, but when it came to suggestions related to political action, Sapphire had her own will and called her own shots.

"Well, maybe just put a bug in her ear," compromised Chris, "and let her run with it in any direction she chooses."

"Okay, I'll get in touch with her if I can," Linda said, somewhat reluctantly.

"That can't be all we do," Kiri objected.

"I agree," Chris responded. "Maybe it's also time for an anonymous tip from the public."

"A tip?" asked Tomas.

"Indeed, a tip," replied Chris. "You know how since the train bombings Empire's been pleading for information from the public? The hotline number has been smeared all over the media."

"Yeah," replied Tomas.

"Well, I figure I might give that number a call tomorrow," said Chris. "Maybe tell them a little, but not too much. Then between Sapphire's possible warning to Garf and stirring up the heat in his area of operations, maybe Taylor and the Maxwell brothers might be scared off. Who knows, maybe even some of the explosives might be seized and eliminated from the equation."

For another ten minutes they attempted to come up with further options. Unfortunately, however, with their limited knowledge of the apparent saboteurs' plans, there wasn't much more they could do.

They settled on Linda attempting to contact Sapphire tomorrow, while Chris would deposit an anonymous tip on Empire's hotline.

And, finally, it was time to go out back and play with the kids, before eating a delicious dinner and enjoying one another's company.

***

The next day, with the help of Linda's mother, Audra, Chris and Kiri safely retrieved their van and headed south toward Oregon. Traffic was slow as they worked their way down the Interstate into Seattle. Chris and Kiri had expected the same so it mattered little; in fact, it worked to their advantage if anything.

As it turned out, they still arrived a little too early at the Pike Place Market which overlooked the Elliott Bay waterfront and downtown Seattle. The place hadn't yet filled with its normal touristy throng, which would have been ideal for Chris's purposes. Regardless, the place was beginning to bustle and come alive for another day of business.

He found a nearby parking spot easily enough and Kiri waited in the van while Chris went about his self-assigned task. Restaurants inside the public market were already doing a brisk breakfast/lunch business as he entered, while craftspeople were setting up their wares as antique, collectible, and comic book shops opened their doors.

The produce stands were beginning to attract buyers as well, though Chris knew he would be well on his way to Oregon before the fishmongers began attracting crowds by tossing huge salmon to one another. What he had to do here could be done quickly and because it was such a busy scene, it didn't really matter that his location could be detected by Empire's ever-vigilant electronic surveillance.

Stopping in front of one of Seattle's oldest head shops seemed ironically fitting for the call he intended to make. From a pocket, Chris extracted a burner phone. It was one of several that various Elders had supplied them with and was probably bought with cash, at locations distant from where the Elder lived or worked. This phone happened to be an old flip phone model that would be perfect for his simple purposes.

Chris had memorized the railroad bombing hotline number, although he needn't have gone to the trouble since the number was nearly omnipresent in the last week on radio and TV, billboards – and even the electric banner ad directly across the market flashing at him – as he simultaneously punched in the numbers on the burner phone.

A recording greeted his ear, telling Chris he had reached the hotline for information about the Northwest railroad bombings, and to please leave his message after the beep.

Chris did just that: "You might want to know the group calling itself 'Future Generations' could be moving and consolidating explosives somewhere north of Aberdeen, Washington, into a cabin a little ways off the 101 Highway, on the road to Humptulips."

That seemed to say it all, so Chris ended the call.

He turned the phone off, then popped the back off and removed the battery. With a cloth he had purposely brought along, Chris then wiped down the battery and then the phone.

Taking great care thereafter to touch either with only the cloth, he made his way through the market arcade toward the exit where the van was parked. At the first trash can Chris came to, he tossed in the small battery that quickly lost itself in the early rubbish of the day.

By the busy entry/exit door of the market, Chris casually deposited the burner phone into a larger trashcan. He then made his way toward the waiting van and Kiri, and their eventual Oregon destination.

CHAPTER ELEVEN

A week after Stone McClelland met with Whitley Dellenbach in Scottsdale, McClelland was busy burning another day in his hotel room near Seattle-Tacoma International Airport.

The local morning TV news, only because it was so bad, had diverted his focus from wondering if and when the protest leader would contact him, to a realization that he had to get in touch with her soon – if he was to have any chance of forestalling the insurrection that was threatening the Pacific Northwest.

Violence had erupted the previous evening from the suburbs of Vancouver, B.C., to the city streets of Portland, Oregon, but the majority of the destruction occurred in the state of Washington. Random gas stations had been shot up and damaged, parked oil tanker trucks were vandalized, and even unoccupied luxury vacation homes were set ablaze. The sheer number of incidents was as astounding as it was appalling.

According to a communiqué issued by the group calling itself "Representatives of Future Generations," there would be more such "statements" in the weeks to come. "Sleeper cells across Cascadia are now awakening," they proclaimed, "and the fossil fuel Kingpins should take note."

As McClelland watched countless video feeds of arson fires in the night, and heard first-hand reports of fuel truck drivers and gas station owners being shot at and scared witless, Stone knew it was more imperative than ever that he get in contact with this Sapphire MacKenzie. If she could indeed get him in touch with Chris Soles, maybe he could stop this madness.

Stone had arrived Monday evening and took a room at this SeaTac hotel. On Tuesday he'd driven his rental car to downtown Seattle, then hopped a ferry to Bainbridge Island where MacKenzie and her protest people had their small office. McClelland was told she was out of town and unavailable for a few days, yet an assistant promised to pass on a note to Sapphire if he cared to leave one.

With little other option available, Stone fudged a tad and wrote that he worked for the Drug Enforcement Administration. He requested a casual conversation rather than formal interview. He also made a point to mention that she was not under investigation, but that the meeting could perhaps be mutually beneficial. For contact purposes, McClelland left both his phone number and personal email address.

And then he began to wait, and burn day after day away. For diversion, he toured the greater Seattle and Tacoma areas. He ate salmon at a waterfront restaurant and frequented a couple nearby brewpubs.

He had lunch with Bertie Stanton, an old friend from the Las Vegas DEA office that had wrangled an interagency transfer to the FBI in Seattle. Bertie, a wiry black man with a hearty laugh, was glad to see Stone. He was also quite appreciative to be back home in the rainy Northwest, and out of the Southwest deserts.

After the lunch with Bertie a couple days ago, Stone had returned to his hotel room to wait. And he had waited, waited, and waited some more.

Of course, he had long conversations every night with Lorien and wished he could be back home in Scottsdale with his wife. Every evening Lorien was as encouraging as she had been when he returned home a week ago and told her about the meeting with Whitley Dellenbach.

She knew the story regarding the release of Chris Soles and how it tore him up. She told him the only way he would find any peace with himself was to go to the Northwest and finish it however it must be finished. She framed it as a necessity, as a duty to himself – and he loved her for it.

Lorien was correct of course: he had to do whatever he must to tie his own loose ends.

McClelland's reveries were interrupted by the signal from his phone. When he realized the television was still blaring reports about last night's string of terrorism, he turned it off as he passed by on the way to the nightstand that held his phone.

Snatching it up, McClelland tapped the messaging app. The text message that just arrived read: "I can meet with you in our Free Cascadia staff offices on Bainbridge Island on Monday. I hope 10:30 AM is a good time."

It was signed: "Sapphire MacKenzie."

***

"I tell ya," Timmy Maxwell stated enthusiastically, "whenever I'm out Grays Harbor way, I gotta stop by the Ding-Donger restaurant in Hoquiam; they've got the best clam strips in all of Washington state."

"Who eats clam strips in a burger joint?" his brother Billy replied disdainfully, as he sunk his teeth into a double cheeseburger.

"I do," Timmy shot back. "And it's a shame you haven't acquired a more discriminating sense of taste."

"Fuck you, kid," Billy chuckled, giving his younger brother the finger.

Downing one of the restaurant's trademark Green River milkshakes, Garf Taylor laughed at the Maxwell brothers. "You two should eat whatever you damn well please. You've had a very successful day so far, after a very successful night."

"No question about that," Timmy agreed. "Even if he doesn't know the refined difference between a burger and a clam strip, I'll have to go so far as to admit my brother has one hell of a sleeper cell network out there just waiting to arise."

"Yep," Billy beamed. "Last night was a good test of how ready we are. And now they all go back to sleep until it is time to awaken once more. It's guaranteed to drive Empire insane when they can't find anyone to persecute."

"Best of all," Garf pointed out, "just like we planned, last night's attacks took any possible heat off us out here. Empire's Gestapo is gathering in force in urban areas from Portland to Vancouver and Victoria, and we're here in the boonies moving hundreds of pounds of explosives virtually carefree in broad daylight."

Garf directed his attention to Timmy. "And speaking of explosives, I have to say once again what a great job you did accumulating all that stuff, Timmy. As soon as we get the rest of them moved to the cabin this afternoon, we'll be ready to take the revolution directly to the Kingpins of Carbon."

"And then we begin to raise some hell for the sake of Cascadia and Future Generations," Billy stated ominously, while purposely flexing one of his mighty biceps for show.

Timmy Maxwell reacted more cautiously than his brother.

"I don't know if you guys heard it on the radio in your truck,"

Timmy mentioned in warning, "but when we were coming back south down the 101 toward Hoquiam after stashing the first load, on the news they said it was very possible martial law would be established throughout the Northwest as a result of last night's attacks."

"So much the better," replied Garf.

"What do you mean?"

"If Empire establishes martial law, it works to our advantage," Taylor unequivocally stated. "Cascadia is a tinder box, just waiting to explode. If martial law is declared, people won't tolerate the oppression. Cascadia will openly revolt."

"The sooner the better," Billy tossed in, "by whatever route it takes."

Garf Taylor nodded in agreement. "So let's get done with our lunches and head to the storage unit in Aberdeen. We should be able to load the two pickups, hide the crates at the cabin, and be done in a couple of hours."

"And then the planning for open revolution gets very serious," Billy promised.

CHAPTER TWELVE

"So what's been bothering you since you got home from the emergency meeting?" Linda wanted to know.

It was the first opportunity they really had to speak. When Tomas arrived just before the evening meal, the kids had been all over him before they'd eaten; then after dinner it was the daily bathing adventure and story time. Cassie had fallen asleep easily, but when a major three-year-old fit overtook Kyle, his older sister was awakened and upset. Forty-five minutes later both children were finally asleep and Linda could finally talk one-on-one with her husband.

Gathering his thoughts, Tomas hesitated, as his face grew darker.

"Sometimes it's difficult to get through to others at the Commons Rising meetings," mused Tomas. "After last night's terror attacks, many commons representatives were scared shitless and didn't know where to turn."

"What do you mean?"

Tomas took his wife's hand. They had wandered into their own bedroom after the kids were finally asleep and now sat together on the edge of the bed.

"They don't adequately understand the threat all commoners and commons are facing," Tomas began, "and because of that lack of comprehension, they generally misapprehend where the danger is coming from."

Linda said nothing in reply; instead, she waited for her husband to continue.

"The thing is, most of my fellow representatives from different commons that make up Commons Rising see the perils now facing them as arising from the outside," explained Tomas.

"Many got up this morning and heard the news about all the violence last night by Future Generations and suddenly they're overwhelmed with fear. Part of it is rational because the capitalistic state/market system is by nature diametrically opposed to a commons based system that's founded on principles of sharing and cooperation. They also know the terror attacks last night are a perfect premise Empire might well use to come down hard on the commons, in a wide-ranging backlash on any opposition they perceive. But as I tried to explain, the dangers we face when it comes from Empire is not merely from the outside; more, it's from the inside."

"I don't know if I understand what you're saying any better than your fellow representatives," admitted Linda.

"It's about infiltrators," replied Tomas, "but that's just the beginning."

As briefly as possible, Tomas attempted to recount what he had related at the emergency meeting of Commons Rising earlier that afternoon. Such things had happened throughout history of course, but he initiated the discussion by bringing up J. Edgar Hoover and the FBI's "Counter Intelligence Program," or "COINTELPRO," as it was called. Fully involved in government authorized political repression, agents were called upon to "expose, disrupt, misdirect, discredit, neutralize or otherwise eliminate," the activities of social movements and their leaders.

The FBI began this in the early decades of the 1900s by subverting and repressing communism, socialism, and labor movements. As time went on the civil rights movement was harassed by the government, as were dissident protest groups such as the Black Panthers, Students for a Democratic Society, and the American Indian Movement, among others. Even though COINTELPRO was exposed in 1971, extensive internal spying persisted during anti-war protests and up through the Occupy movement and beyond. For any group deemed "subversive," FBI field operatives were directed to: "create a negative public image for target groups, break down internal organization, create dissension between groups, restrict access to public resources, restrict the ability to organize protests, and restrict the ability of individuals to participate in group activities."

"Most of my fellow representatives seemed to take this somewhat nonchalantly," Tomas explained, " as if they've heard it all before."

"Well, they probably have," replied Linda.

"But it's worse than that," countered Tomas, "and I tried to make the point."

Tomas told Linda of recent reports of global corporate espionage programs that are out of control, with as many as one in four activists possibly being private spies. Corporations had been facilitated by government agencies to do their infiltration and spying, while simultaneously having investigations relating to non-violent civil disobedience classified under its "Acts of Terrorism" designation. Not only that, but the FBI's involvement in corporate espionage was institutionalized through "InfraGard," a little known partnership between private industry, the FBI, and the Department of Homeland Security. Further, active-duty CIA agents were reportedly allowed to moonlight for the highest bidder. And all this, Tomas had told them, only further incapacitates the civic sector in the face of the corporate and wealthy elites.

"So what do you do about all that in relation to the commons?" Linda asked. "How do you protect yourself?"

"I tried to make the point at the meeting that the best we can do is be extremely aware," he explained. "We are vulnerable from the inside, so the violence of Future Generations serves to inevitably undermine the emerging power of the commons. Also, because of the violence, I'm worried about much more than talk of mere martial law and curfews."

"How so?"

Tomas shook his head. "The corporate state, Empire, is an ossified beast; it can only react in the way such calcified states respond. In fact, it has all the levers readied to do so. It will use all the apparatus available for surveillance and security – to shut down dissent with force. Under the National Defense Authorization Act, Empire can also use military forces to carry out domestic policing. And they will. I fear, I worry, that we will soon see armed soldiers patrolling our streets."

"If so," Linda pondered, "what can we do about it?"

"I don't know," murmured Tomas. "And that's what worries me; that's what been bothering me since the end of today's meeting."

"I know what we do," Linda shot back. "In fact, there's only one thing possible: we take the best care of our kids that we can."

***

Observing all posted road regulations and speed limits, Garf Taylor and Billy Maxwell drove north out of Hoquiam, Washington, on the 101 Highway, their pickup bed loaded with crates of explosives. Timmy Maxwell followed ten minutes behind with his pickup load, as had been the case in the early morning hours during their first run to the remote cabin.

The drive was lush with greenery; the Hoquiam River came into view from the east at times and there was an occasional residence along the roadway that had been carved out of the surrounding forest.

About ten minutes out of Hoquiam, they passed a nursery then exited Highway 101, turning left onto Ocean Beach Road. Several more minutes took them to a little used, rough dirt road on the right that paralleled a creek. Within this new tunnel of vegetation, the going was slower until finally they came to a rickety bridge that crossed the stream.

Though appearing precarious, the bridge was sound enough to travel over, so they cautiously proceeded once more. A short distance beyond the bridge was one overgrown road to the right that seemed to disappear into the dark green enwrapping it, then another that turned to the left that was very similar about a half mile further on. Billy, who was driving, chose to turn down the second overgrown road as he did earlier in the morning.

Suddenly, however, he stopped short.

"I see it too," Garf observed quietly.

A bush they had cut and loosely implanted on the side of the road, yet still within easy range of a vehicle, had been run over and pushed to the side.

"Someone's driven in here since this morning," Billy said, suspecting the worst.

"No question about it," replied Garf.

Quickly, a range of possible alternatives sifted through Taylor's mind.

"Listen, here's what we do, Billy," he proposed. "You back out and meet your brother on the road, since there's no cell phone coverage around here. Tell Timmy not to come in with his load. Tell him to wait somewhere by that nursery. After that, come back and wait on the other side of the bridge."

"What are you going to do?"

"I'm going to see what's happening at the cabin."

"Maybe you might need a little muscle to accompany you," suggested Billy.

"Not this time," Garf objected. "Your first priority is protecting those crates of explosives. I'll take a quick look around and we'll go from there."

"Okay," Billy agreed.

Slipping out of the truck and closing his passenger side door as quietly as possible, Garf Taylor began sneaking forward as Billy started backing the pickup out.

Garf was extremely wary as he crept toward the cabin that was still several hundred yards away. Sunlight filtered through the cool rain forest canopy, but it wasn't enough to dispel the feeling of claustrophobia that began to surround him in this underpass of green.

Coming closer, he heard them long before he saw them. One man's voice carried through the vegetation; his companion's speech was muffled. Likely, Garf suspected, that meant one man was outside keeping watch, while the other was tearing the floorboards up – under which they'd hidden the first load of explosives.

When Garf was close enough to catch sight of their car outside the cabin, he ducked more fully into the undergrowth. The car was a shiny, American made, four-door SUV; it reeked of Empire and its agents, something totally foreign to this remote location.

Taylor debated what to do and in the end there wasn't much choice. If Billy had been here, it's quite possible he might have simply killed the men. Yet to Garf's mind, that wasn't necessarily the wisest alternative in these circumstances, or for their long-range plans.

Slowly, he rose and began backing off and away. When he judged he was safely out of sight and earshot, Garf broke into a run in the direction of the old bridge over the creek.

By the time he made it to the bridge, Billy was just driving up on the other side. Winded, Garf slowed to catch his breath and gather his thoughts.

Obviously, it was very disappointing to lose the weaponry already hidden. Apparently, they'd somehow been tracked as well, but at least the big pickup trucks they were using had been rented with false I.D.'s, and those would be near impossible to trace.

But to lose the explosives in the cabin was a blow to the plans of Future Generations, to be certain. Still, that cloud at least had a silver lining.

As Garf walked across the bridge to Billy's waiting truck, he chuckled – it wasn't a total loss.

No doubt Empire's agents would find and confiscate that first load under the cabin's floorboard. But if nothing else, they would surely also find the dummy note he'd intentionally planted – just in case – between a couple crates.

It read: "T.L. Make sure you get the rest of the blasting caps."

And Garf had signed it: "Chris Cadia."

***

Driving north up Interstate 5 in Oregon, Kiri fell asleep about half way between Eugene and Salem. The Sunday public radio news show was on, but she appeared blissfully unaware, her head resting on a pillow propped against the passenger door.

It was understandable that she dozed, however, since she had stayed up later than Chris, talking around the campfire, laughing, and singing – with people they had never met before, people they were now close with, and people they would stay in contact with. And like other such gatherings, after breakfast this morning and before departing, Chris had gifted small presents of magic mushrooms to those in attendance.

It had all been generated by a single name off his former boss Bruno Panoka's secret list of invaluable contacts. This name belonged to a young man that inherited a farm next to a river east of Eugene, east of Springfield, and along the Jasper Lowell Road. Like similar gatherings as a result of that list, contacts had been established and underground networks had been set up of like-minded individuals for that day in the future when the quest for Cascadia was to be realized.

After a communal feast and swimming in the river, everyone gathered round the fire into the later hours of the evening. As was often the case, Chris grew tired before Kiri felt sleepy. Accordingly, he retired to his sleeping bag in the tent they had erected, next to others on the grassy fields between the farmhouse and the river.

Sometime later Kiri joined him in the tent. Slipping into her own sleeping bag, she spooned and snuggled tightly in next to him, of which Chris was only sleepily aware.

It was curious, this arrangement, yet it was often how they slept on the road. Or, for that matter, it was similar to how they slept in a bed – both being adequately clothed during a stay in an Elder's house, or in the safe house cottage they'd been loaned in the woods close to Poulsbo, Washington.

Lost in thought as he drove north through the northern outskirts of Salem, Chris admitted to himself their sleeping arrangements were curious to be certain, but it seemed apropos – considering the relationship he shared with Kiri was perhaps the most atypical relationship with a woman he would ever have imagined.

They were close; in fact, they were very close. They were much more than brother and sister – yet certainly less than lovers. Chris knew, and though they never spoke directly about it, Kiri must surely have sensed as well that if they were to become lovers, it would sever the duty and responsibility he'd pledged Kiri's parents when he agreed to take her on his travels – ostensibly as some kind of apprentice.

If the truth were told, however, Chris never really understood what that was to entail. If indeed he were to be some kind of teacher, he imagined he was probably failing miserably.

During their first several months of travel together, Chris thought to fulfill this seeming obligation by bringing up a discussion of the opposites, how they could come together, and how they were ultimately the same. That was how his old mentor Harry Wimple had guided him. And it was the only way he knew to provide a path for Enlightenment – as that was what he assumed Kiri expected of him – when she chose to leave her parents and friends and follow him.

For all his efforts though, he might well have been bellowing into the wind. Kiri had no interest whatsoever in any of that and, with a wave of her hand, she simply dismissed the subject whenever he brought it up. One time, she told him point blank that she wasn't interested in anything that smelled like Eastern philosophy.

Kiri explained how she and her sister Freya had found a book of koans on their parent's bookshelves in their early teen years. They had gone through an entertaining stage of reading the seemingly nonsensical stories and questions – such as the widely known, "What is the sound of one hand clapping?" – that supposedly could shock one into an Enlightened state. Yet the sisters would laughingly make up their own fantastical answers and that had turned out to be sufficient. To Kiri, the sum of all that must merely be a game, whereas in reality she was encumbered by a prescience she fought to comprehend.

After explaining her rejection of the need for Eastern thought that day, she'd tilted her head and scrutinized him with curiosity.

"You don't really understand what it's all about do you?" she queried.

"What do you mean?"

"The Teacher-Student thing," Kiri had simply replied. "Education itself."

Chris had shrugged his shoulders. "I'll be the first to admit that. I didn't go looking for a student."

"Well, as a Teacher you've got a lot to learn."

"Like what?" he tossed back. "I told you I never intended to be a teacher."

"First, you don't just throw things out there," she simply pointed out. "You let the Student learn by example. What else is there that is of true value?"

"I'm not a teacher," he reemphasized.

"Well, just be yourself then," she pleaded. "That's all I really need."

Realizing the futility of his efforts, Chris had let it go at that point and resolved to let happen what would. Abiding upon that course, they became better and closer friends in spite of their age difference, trusting each other a little more each day, while enjoying shared experiences.

It wasn't until one day several months ago, however, that they stumbled upon a peculiar, yet amicable chord that seemed to bond them in a way that only two like souls, perhaps, can understand and relate to.

They had been driving down a road following the Fraser River in central British Columbia when they came upon a large buck deer that had lost its life in a collision with a vehicle. It was sprawled out on the side of the road with guts ripped open, and covered with thousands and thousands of flies.

As they slowly passed the dead animal, Kiri remarked, "I don't think I've ever seen so many flies."

"Yeah, it's a shame," Chris replied. "He was a beautiful creature."

A kilometer or two on, Chris mused in passing, "You know, there are a lot of flies on this planet."

Kiri thought his comment humorously quaint. "Yeah, so?"

"So sometimes when I think about it," he drawled, "I often wonder if there are more flies on the planet, or more gallons of water."

She chuckled at him. "What are you talking about?"

"I'm serious," Chris averred. "It's a good question. Are there more flies on the planet, or more gallons of water?"

"Well, judging by that poor animal we just passed, I'd have to say flies," Kiri posited. "With that many flies in such a relatively small area, it boggles the mind to guess how many flies must be on the entire planet. They are everywhere and a pest to everyone."

"I'm not so certain," Chris mildly objected. "Think about it the next time we go from the mainland to Vancouver Island to visit your parents or meet with Elders. Think about the hour and a half ferry ride and all that water we have to cross. Think how deep it is. Think about how many gallons you'd have to scoop out if you wanted to empty the entire Salish Sea. Then remember that it's only one relatively tiny body of water. When you think of all the lakes and oceans on the planet, now that's a lot of water. Likely, there's more gallons of water than the total number of flies on the planet."

"Not so fast, buster," Kiri shot back. "Remember that the nature of water is to be a fickle thing. You think you've got some and then it evaporates. Suddenly you're left with nothing at all! At least flies are constant and dependable."

And so, on and on it would go. One of them would postulate a fact either in favor of there being more gallons of water or more flies on the planet, and the other would counter. During their travels they would often change sides in the defense of either water or flies, and often their discussions became quite involved. So much so, that when they were in their safe house cabin near Poulsbo, or other locales with secure Internet connections, they often took to researching flies or water to prove a specific point.

All such enjoyable nonsense became a game of wits between themselves, and most certainly something they shared only among themselves and no others.

Even now, as Chris realized he was passing Wilsonville, Oregon, and maybe a half hour from downtown Portland, he began thinking about reminding Kiri how there were at least 120,000 species of other kinds of flies besides the common house fly. But she had awoken and was murmuring something with her head still nestled into pillow.

"What did you say?"

"So is it true?" she wondered. "I mean, is it like the radio just said?"

"What did the radio say?"

Kiri didn't answer his question; instead, she asked one of her own.

"You're just like Santa Claus, eh?"

"What the hell are you talking about?"

"Or maybe you are more like God."

"Huh?"

Kiri straightened up in her seat and let the pillow rest on her lap. She turned toward Chris as she brushed back her hair.

"Honestly, I think Santa is a better fit in your case."

"I don't have a clue what you're talking about."

"Apparently not," she agreed. "I guess you weren't listening to the news on the radio."

Chris replied he was lost in his own thoughts as he drove.

"Well, I didn't know you could be in so many places at once," Kiri admitted. "You are kind of like God or Santa Claus."

Saying nothing, Chris let her enjoy her little joke, even as he awaited explanation.

"I could have sworn I spent yesterday with you," she smiled, "outside Jasper, Oregon, along a pleasant stretch of river."

"Yes," he stated patiently.

"How is it then that the news reports say after nearly catching the culprits, the authorities discovered a cache of explosives in western Washington," Kiri asked, "and can directly link the terrorist group Future Generations and one 'Chris Cadia' – also known as the wanted Chris Soles, from the Gaia/Universe days – to the hidden explosives?"

"So they found them, eh? One must give Empire credit for such a boon when working off a single tip," he observed. "And somehow, I've been tied into being connected with the whole thing?"

"Yeah, but not like God or Santa Claus though," Kiri admitted. "In their theology, I'm guessing it's a lot more like the Devil."

CHAPTER THIRTEEN

On Monday morning, Chris and Kiri were unexpectedly waiting to board the ferry in Seattle. It would take them across Puget Sound to Bainbridge Island and, after a short drive, to their safe house cabin in the woods near Poulsbo.

As prearranged, they spent the previous evening southeast of Seattle in Maple Valley, at the home of Cascadia Elders Todd and Sasha Tharp. The Tharps were close friends of the Carlsons, the Elders that had gifted them their cabin.

The plan had been to travel east from Maple Valley, across the state to Spokane, Coeur d'Alene, and northern Idaho for more meetings and future planning. With the Tharps, however, they more fully digested what had happened since Friday evening when they arrived at the farmhouse not far from Jasper, Oregon.

As the Tharps explained in great detail how extensive the terror attacks had been Friday night, then told them about news of the recovered explosives on Saturday and how Future Generations' terrorists had barely escaped – plus how Chris was supposedly involved, according to authorities – Chris and Kiri's immediate plans came into question.

Watching the Sunday evening news they heard talk of curfews and possible martial law being imposed. The specials aired last night on TV, however, were what really sealed their decision to return to Poulsbo and lay low for some time. On several major networks were slickly produced "documentaries" detailing the time Chris Soles spent with the discredited cult, Gaia/Universe, his months as an assistant to the cult's psychedelic mushroom Spore Master, and his murder of a member of the powerful Dellenbach family, before he somehow made his improbable escape from a Utah cave explosion.

As if each of the specials they watched with the Tharps were made in collusion but spliced together differently, Chris Soles – who reportedly had become the mysterious "Chris Cadia" in subversive Cascadia – was suspected to be behind the Fourth of July railroad explosions, the eruption of the reign of terror last Friday night, the explosives discovered on Saturday, as well as the mastermind behind the terrorists calling themselves "Future Generations." Photographs from Chris's Gaia/Universe days were prominently featured, as were the wanted posters distributed after reports of the murder of the Dellenbach heiress.

Chris noted that Kiri's normally chipper mood had deteriorated as Sunday afternoon progressed. By the time they reached the Tharp's residence she was down in the dumps; after they finished watching the news specials following dinner, Kiri appeared to be wholly depressed.

Having traveled together for so long and spending so much time together, Chris probably should have known better. Unwittingly, he initially attributed her heavyheartedness to what they'd been viewing on television. The first indication that it was something deeper that only she could sense, was when it didn't phase her one way or the other that he suggested they change plans and hightail it to Poulsbo and lay low.

As they later sat together on the edge of the guest room bed before turning off the lights, Chris asked what was on her mind.

It took Kiri a while to answer. "I'm not certain," she replied. "It's ambiguous."

He waited for her to say something else, but when she didn't after several minutes he decided to recline into the open covers. Like a statue, Kiri continued to sit unmoved.

Eventually, she quietly remarked, "There's a very large darkness in our immediate path. It'll pass, but it will still be there."

With his head on the pillow, Chris waited for more, but that was all she said.

Kiri stood, walked toward the bedroom door, and turned off the light. She returned to the bed, snuggled in next to Chris and, adequately clothed as usual, they soon drifted off together without further words.

Now, as vehicles began loading on the ferry for the short thirty-five minute trip to Bainbridge Island, Kiri mentioned that she wanted to use the restroom once they were parked. The hour plus drive from Maple Valley to the Seattle ferry terminal in Monday morning traffic, combined with the coffee they shared with the Tharps, was taxing Chris's bladder as well. After they were parked in line on the ferry's lower deck, both exited the van and climbed the stairs to higher levels. On the way up to the ferry deck that held restrooms, cafeteria, and observation stations, Kiri asked Chris if he could do her a favor.

"I know you'll be done before me," she mentioned, "so could you maybe get me another cup of coffee? I didn't really sleep so well, and one cup this morning wasn't enough. I'll meet you in front of the women's restroom closest to the cafeteria."

When Kiri next saw Chris, she was just exiting the restroom. Quite out of character, he was hustling toward her with two steaming cups in hand, pale and quite upset. She had never seen him like that.

"Let's go – now!" was all he said.

Almost stumbling down the stairs to the vehicle deck, Kiri called out, asking what was wrong.

"Later!"

Finally in the van, when he furtively sunk into the driver's seat, Kiri noticed as he passed her coffee that his hands were shaking. His face was ashen and he stared straight ahead.

"So what's the matter?" she asked.

Still attempting to gather himself, Chris couldn't utter a word at first. A short time later, when finally he could speak, his voice was raspy.

"Remember when I explained to you the reason they were after me when we first met," he began, "and I said I was framed for the murder of my girlfriend?"

"Yeah," Kiri replied, "and you were at the cave in Utah where you'd been assistant to the Spore Master – but escaped through a secret exit before you blew the cave up."

"You got it," Chris assured her. "But there's more to it than that."

Chris quickly recounted the events he was involved in the day before the slaughter by Empire at the Gaia/Universe compound in south central Arizona. Explaining he was traveling from the Utah cave with a reluctant Harry Wimple – the Spore Master – Chris told Kiri he was determined to do anything he could to prevent an impending disaster at the compound.

"Unfortunately though, we were stopped by Navajo Nation police before we could even get out of northern Arizona," he recalled. They put us in adjoining holding cells. A while later, an agent from the DEA came in; he wanted to talk to Wimp. I was taken outside, so I don't know what passed between the two. After the DEA guy left they returned me to my cell, and old Harry Wimple said he was not going to go back to prison. Instead, he told me it was time for him to return to the Void."

"To the Void?"

"Yep, that's what he said," Chris replied. "So Wimp starts meditating and about fifteen or twenty minutes later, he falls over dead in his cell."

At the memory, Chris shook his head.

"I started raising all kinds of hell after that," he continued. "The guards examined Harry then handcuffed me, and locked me in the back of a patrol car for over an hour. Eventually, paramedics arrived in an ambulance; I suppose they confirmed he was dead and took away the body. After that, they threw me back in the bare cell and I spent a sleepless night on a cold cement floor."

Chris ceased speaking momentarily, lost in thought.

"The next morning," he recalled, "the DEA cop came back. He had the Navajo Nation cops cuff me, and then I was escorted to the back of the big guy's car. To this day I can't believe it, but he drove me to where Wimp's truck was still parked — at the scenic turnoff where we were apprehended — and he let me go! The big frigging DEA cop just let me go!

"Why did he set you free?"

"I have absolutely no idea why," exclaimed Chris. "All I know for certain is that if he wouldn't have let me go, I have no doubt Empire would have killed me like everyone else associated with Gaia/Universe."

Kiri didn't understand where Chris was going with all this until he turned in his seat to face her. In spite of him being so distraught, there was a wry grin on Chris's face.

"Kiri," he said in disbelief, "that big DEA agent is on this ferry! He looked directly at me as I passed by him, but there was no acknowledgement whatsoever that he recognized me."

"Are you sure it was him?"

"I'm absolutely certain," returned Chris. "For obvious reasons, that's one person I could never forget."

"Well," Kiri rationalized, "your plastic surgeon should be commended."

"Oh, I've thought that many a time," he admitted. "But why the hell would the big DEA guy be up here now? It can't be a coincidence; it must have something to do with Empire's media blaming me for the Future Generation violence."

Kiri agreed that the combination of events could suggest that conclusion, but also it was important not to overreact as a result of undue paranoia.

"You're probably right, Kiri," acknowledged Chris, "but the appearance of the DEA agent at this point in time likely means only one thing."

"And that is?"

Chris sighed. "Empire has set their dogs loose in the form of the one person on this planet that I literally owe my life to."

***

After Stone McClelland boarded the ferry to Winslow and Bainbridge Island as a foot passenger, he purchased a cup of coffee on the upper deck level. He then found an open booth table with a window on Puget Sound, and spread out some of his research paperwork.

The relationship between Whitley Dellenbach and Sapphire MacKenzie, the strikingly attractive activist he would soon meet on Bainbridge, was a continuing puzzle to him. Ever since Dellenbach had suggested he contact Sapphire – and yet under no circumstances could he reference Dellenbach when they met – Stone's curiosity had been piqued.

At Whitley's suggestion, McClelland had researched the Dellenbach Brothers Empire, which had been extraordinarily easy to do. He had also scoured the Internet for information about Sapphire MacKenzie. For all his prying inquisitiveness, however, Stone had been unable to establish any definitive link between the two. In fact, the worlds inhabited by the Dellenbach clan and Sapphire MacKenzie seemed to be mutually exclusive, as well as diametrically opposed.

Of course, McClelland had been vaguely aware of Dellenbach Industries, the Dellenbach Brothers, and their enormous oil and chemicals conglomerate, but the more he read, the more he was thunderstruck by their megalomaniacal pursuit of limitless power and control. Like many Americans, Stone didn't pay a whole lot of attention to politics, because he saw most politicos as blowhards that didn't accomplish much more than lining their own pocket books. Scrutinizing facts about the Dellenbachs, McClelland was convinced that these robber barons were some of the most prominent puppeteers controlling your everyday politician and greasing the entire system with their vast wealth.

More than merely buying Congress and disenfranchising liberal voters, the Dellenbach Brothers appeared committed to weakening the rights of workers, cutting taxes for the wealthy, reducing social welfare programs, gutting regulations for businesses like their own and, of course, sowing doubt about climate change while actively opposing any action to reign in fossil fuel pollution.

Beyond the Dellenbach's public role, Stone dug up what little he could relating to the family's famously hushed personal interrelationships. In particular, he focused on Alice Cope, the cousin Whitley Dellenbach told him had been murdered by Chris Soles. Because of the notoriety produced by the murder, there was at least some information pertaining to this member of the secretive Dellenbach clan.

Cope's mother was the youngest sister of Walter, Theodore, and Paul Dellenbach, and from what Stone had been able to detect from old news reports, Alice was working undercover at the Gaia/Universe compound for her Uncle Walter. Alice and a number of other captives had been released the day before the compound was stormed and she had flown immediately to Boston to be with her dying Uncle Walter.

Almost as a footnote in the more obscure researches McClelland conducted, he found a singular reference to Alice's disappearance – apparently the same day as her uncle's death, and on a flight back to Arizona. There was no further mention of Cope anywhere until her alleged murder by Chris Soles at the hidden mushroom cave in Utah.

Whitley Dellenbach told Stone his cousin had been kidnapped and drugged by Soles before he murdered her, but something about that didn't feel right to McClelland. Something told Stone she didn't fly back to Arizona in such haste just to be kidnapped.

If there was a sharper contrast to the Dellenbach Brothers' overreaching dark dominion, to Stone McClelland's mind it could clearly be observed in the person of Sapphire MacKenzie. A lower middle class child of the working class, the salt of the earth, Sapphire and everything about her upbringing had been modest. Her father was a shipwright building wooden boats in Port Townsend, Washington, and her mother had been a grocery clerk. Sailing about Puget Sound had been the family passion as Sapphire and her younger brother grew up. She had, in fact, been named Sapphire for her brilliant blue eyes – the eyes her father equated with the color of water at the middle of the ocean he'd encountered on a sailing voyage to Hawaii before she was born.

Shifting his papers as the ferry steamed its way across Puget Sound, Stone found what he was looking for when he came to the magazine article he'd copied entitled, "The Genesis of a Natural Rebel." It was a fairly recent piece that sought to detail the early rebelliousness of the now most widely known activist throughout Cascadia, Sapphire MacKenzie.

In one anecdote that Stone found particularly telling, Sapphire related to the magazine's author what had occurred during a school bus ride in the eighth or ninth grade. She was already seated on the bus, and when it stopped to pick up her friend Hailey and others, there was the normal clamber to get aboard. Sapphire was saving a seat for her friend, but as Hailey slowly worked down the aisle, some boy reached up into her skirt and felt between her legs. Hailey was naturally upset; she told Sapphire what had happened.

"I was so pissed," MacKenzie told the magazine interviewer, "that I went up and slapped the boy silly."

When Sapphire returned to the seat next to her friend, Hailey was grateful. She was also embarrassed; she admitted what startled her as much as the assault was that she hadn't shaved her legs. Sapphire was aghast. She told Hailey how ridiculous it was "they even make us think like that." And from that day on, Sapphire told the article's author, she quit shaving her own legs in protest.

As they drew near the ferry landing in Winslow, an announcement came over loudspeakers urging drivers to return to their cars and for foot passengers to prepare to disembark. In response, Stone gathered up the papers he had strewn about the tabletop before him. He stuffed the research into a daypack he'd brought along, finished the remainder of his coffee, and then stood to enjoy the rest of the voyage on the observation deck.

Once outside, the views were fantastic. It was a beautiful summer day and behind the green of Bainbridge Island, the Olympic mountain range stood out in perfect clarity. Because of the angle of the boat's approach to the terminal, if McClelland looked back he could also catch sight of downtown Seattle's prominent skyline. When all this was over, Stone promised himself, he would bring Lorien up here for a nice long vacation.

After disembarking and making his way through the ferry terminal, Stone glanced at his watch and realized he still had a little time before his appointment. Sapphire's office was only a short distance away so he killed the extra minutes by gazing at sailing yachts in Eagle Harbor, and taking a short stroll along the waterfront trail.

Two minutes before the appointed time of ten-thirty, Stone McClelland stood in front of the building over which hung an enormous Cascadia Doug flag. Above the entry was a sign denoting the Free Cascadia offices within, and a banner below that read, "Part of The Thin Green Line!" From his researches, McClelland knew the Cascadian resistance called themselves "The Thin Green Line."

Inside, the same receptionist greeted him as before. He announced himself and she requested that he be seated. The receptionist then disappeared behind a door off to the side of her desk.

A short time later, the door reopened and McClelland was asked to follow the receptionist. They entered a well-lit, moderately sized room with nine or ten cubicles clustered about. A more or less straight walkway led to Sapphire MacKenzie's station at the far end of the room.

The receptionist introduced him to Sapphire, then departed. Languidly, and lacking an overt display of respect, MacKenzie rose from her chair to greet him. For a few brief moments they studied one another.

McClelland's first reaction to the tall and comely young women was to agree with what he had read: her eyes were the bluest of blue eyes he'd ever seen. She was dressed casually and comfortably for the pleasant summer day in shorts and a loose fitting turquoise top. The cold and indignant air she projected, however, buffered her pleasing appearance.

They shook hands haltingly and MacKenzie motioned for him to be seated.

"So what do you want to see me for, Mister DEA agent?" she demanded to know. "I don't do drugs; I foment revolution."

Stone was taken aback, feeling this was getting off on the wrong foot. But he'd been here before.

"Well, I don't have anything to do with drugs either," he attempted to assure her. "Actually, I retired from the DEA several years ago. I'm up here looking for someone and if I can find him, it might be beneficial to both of us."

Sapphire laughed not only in disbelief, but also in ridicule.

"How could you possibly help me?"

Forthrightly, McClelland replied, "With information."

Again, her reaction was one of incredulity. "Information about what?"

"Intelligence about people in your organization," he said cryptically. "Plots against you."

Sapphire MacKenzie couldn't believe what she was hearing.

"Now, how are you going to deliver that?"

"I still have contacts in government that owe me favors."

This guy was simply too much, she mused to herself.

"Assuming that's true," she shot back at him, "what's in it for you? Who are you looking for?"

Stone McClelland laid it bare. "I'm looking for a man named Chris Soles; he's also being tagged as 'Chris Cadia' these days."

Sapphire couldn't help but burst out laughing.

"That's pretty rich," she observed. "You and just about everybody else in the government are looking for him, I reckon."

Sapphire's amused demeanor quickly chilled. With a snarl, she said, "If I was half your size, I'd physically throw you out of my office right now."

She shook her head. "Look, we're very busy organizing for a well publicized blockade in Portland next week, in order to stop another vital support ship bound for the Arctic oil fields. So if you don't mind, the exit is that away."

MacKenzie pointed toward the door but Stone was undeterred.

"Let me repeat: I don't work for the government," he stated emphatically. "This is a personal matter and I've been told you might be able to contact Chris Soles."

"Who told you that?"

"Sources."

Sapphire's chuckle was derisive. Pointing again, she said, "The exit is in that direction, Mister DEA agent."

"Former agent," corrected Stone.

MacKenzie's patience was running thin.

"Look, if I knew who you were talking about and that he really existed, I'd say you're looking for the wrong person," she informed him. "Anybody that's in the know and spreads rumors about a mythical Chris Cadia says he is thoroughly committed to non-violence as a way of unshackling and freeing ourselves from our patriarchal heritage. Who you're looking for does not exist. You are after the wrong guy, Mister DEA agent."

"How do you know that?"

Sapphire smiled smugly. "Sources."

Stone started to say something but Sapphire cut him short.

"You know what this whole Chris Soles, Chris Cadia, thing that's erupted over the weekend smells like to me, Mister DEA agent?"

"No, what?"

"It smells precisely like one of Empire's dark, subversive counterplots," she admitted, "where the police state is turned loose to go after authentic non-violent activists working to change a corrupt system — then the authorities paint them as violent extremists and terrorists, only to viciously hunt them down, attack them, and destroy the movement. It's the classic, standard operating procedure for a dying intransigent Empire; it's what we deal with every day around here."

She had had enough. "I'm not going to keep repeating myself, Mister DEA agent. The exit is right down that way."

McClelland finally rose to leave. "That's fine; I can find my own way out. But the next time you see or talk to Chris Soles, Chris Cadia, physically describe me and mention an old pickup truck. Mention also a scenic turnout on a highway in northern Arizona. And, if you don't mind, tell him he owes it to talk to me. Here's my card."

Sapphire allowed McClelland to deposit his card on her desk. "You're barking up the wrong tree, Mister DEA agent."

Politely, Stone McClelland thanked Sapphire MacKenzie for her time.

As he marched off toward the exit, Stone was left with the impression that she probably wouldn't, or couldn't, contact Chris Soles, or Chris Cadia – even if he truly existed.

CHAPTER FOURTEEN

"When there is nothing to do," Chris had told her, "then we should do nothing.

But after several days of doing nothing, this was getting ridiculous, thought Kiri.

"Don't worry," he said repeatedly, "something will break. In the meantime, let's go for a hike."

Or make a loaf of bread. Or clean out the gutters on the cabin. Or take another hike. Or sew up that old pair of jeans. Or cut firewood. Or stack firewood. Or clean out the van. Or take another hike. Or do Internet searches on quantities of flies and gallons of water.

It was getting ridiculous.

In their cabin on the other side of Liberty Bay from the town of Poulsbo and backed off into the woods on a hill, they felt safe enough. They were ensconced away from the media's incessant rattling of dragnets and possible terrorist sightings, yet the waiting for whatever was going to "break" was driving Kiri nuts. She didn't understand how Chris could be so indifferent to something that realistically might not come at all; even as he was so serenely confident something poignant was on the way.

Hells-bells, Kiri thought, as she prepared her pack for another hike through the woods with views of the Bangor Trident Submarine Base to the west, wasn't she the one that had been gifted prescience? She had indeed, yet she sensed nothing but an increasing quotient of boredom with each passing day.

And then, with Chris waiting outside on the porch just before they were to set out on their hike, Kiri's cell phone began ringing.

She didn't recognize the caller I.D., but she recognized the voice. Calmly, she sunk onto the sofa in the front room.

"Kiri, I'm on my break at work," Carolyn spoke softly, "so I can't talk for very long."

"I'm glad you called," Kiri replied. "I've been wondering how you're doing."

"Just my normal bundle of nerves, anymore," Carolyn attempted to joke. Purposely she attempted to change the subject. "I don't know if you had anything to do with the discovery of the explosives last weekend, but I was really glad nobody got hurt or arrested. After all that, I thought my brothers and Garf would realize how crazy this is, but it didn't work out that way at all."

"What do you mean?"

"Well, if anything, it emboldened them," Carolyn stated. "Even though the government is touting how they recovered some of the explosives, my crazy brothers and Garf think they're almost bulletproof since the authorities are blaming that Chris Cadia guy for everything. Now they imagine they're free to strike anywhere."

"Anywhere?" Kiri realized Carolyn was getting to the reason she'd called. "So what's next?"

"It's not good, Kiri," said Carolyn cautiously. "It could be a real environmental mess."

"Where is it going to be?"

Carolyn didn't answer the question directly. "As their cover, they're planning on using the upcoming Portland ship blockade protests that Sapphire MacKenzie and her Free Cascadia people have announced."

"What do you mean, 'as their cover?'"

"It's like what they did when they planted the railroad bombs," Carolyn explained. "While the government had vast resources swarming to control the Port of Morrow coal transfer protests and the media made it a national circus, Garf knew they would be virtually unwatched while they planted their explosives on vital rail lines. It'll be the same thing next week when the Arctic oil supply ship tries to leave Portland: while all eyes are focused there, my brothers and Garf intend to blow up at least one giant storage tank containing nearly four million gallons of oil."

"Where is it?"

"That's the huge problem."

"How so?"

"It's right on the Columbia River," exclaimed Carolyn. "If they succeed, it'll be an environmental nightmare. Can you imagine how devastating four million gallons of oil in the Columbia would be? Or if they destroy two tanks and eight million gallons of oil?"

"Are they mad?" Kiri nearly erupted. "Don't they understand they'll damage their own cause?"

"I don't know," Carolyn equivocated, "I'm beginning to think their cause is to stop the Kingpins of Carbon at any cost."

"So where is this place?" asked Kiri.

"Have you ever heard of Clatskanie, Oregon?"

"Not really."

"Well, it's not in Clatskanie, but the port is pretty close on the Columbia," explained Carolyn. "The area is northwest of Portland and a little closer to Longview, Washington than out by the coast towards Astoria. It's a real pretty area, but it won't be anymore if there's a major oil spill."

"Is it a refinery then, or what?" Kiri wondered.

"Oh no, it's not a refinery at all," replied Carolyn. "As I understand it, the place was built as an ethanol plant, but years ago it was bought out by oil people, then used more or less as a transfer station. My brothers say they had permits to only load so much oil onto ships, yet supposedly for years the company running the operation blatantly violated the restrictions of the permit and moved millions of gallons more than allowed. And now, with the new Supreme Court ruling and the lifting of the ban on foreign exports of US crude, there will be no limit as to how much oil can be shipped abroad. Unless, of course – as my brothers and Garf believe – unless, there are no storage tanks for the incoming oil rail cars, and the outgoing oil freighters."

"Holy crap," swore Kiri. "So when is all this going down?"

"That's tricky," said Carolyn. "It all depends when the blockade in Portland hits its crescendo. Everybody realizes the oil supply ship will leave the dock and make it through the protestors eventually, so precisely when the situation is most tense in Portland, will be the same time the oil storage tanks are blown up."

Taken aback, Kiri was at a loss how to respond. Carolyn picked up the slack, however, mentioning how she didn't want to see a massive oil spill – anymore than she wanted her brothers arrested.

"Is there anything we can do?" Carolyn wondered.

Kiri did all she could to reassure and comfort her friend, until Carolyn realized it was time to return to work. Upon hanging up though, Kiri felt she could use a little reassurance herself.

She found Chris waiting patiently on the wood bench outside on the front deck. As she walked through the front door he snatched up his daypack, ready for a hike.

Kiri shook her head. "I don't think it's time for a stroll in the woods."

"No?" he queried.

"No," she stated firmly. "Something finally broke – and we've got a problem."

***

"At last I've been able to read the report your people put together, Son," said Theodore Dellenbach, "and I find it very disturbing."

"Thanks for going through it, Father," replied Whitley, "I realize it was quite lengthy."

"Justifiably long, because it was very complete," the elder Dellenbach acknowledged. "This mobbing of the rabble under the theoretical umbrella of the commons – and then their supra-group of Commons Rising – is a potential future nightmare for our system's enduring success, should it come to pass."

"I agree, Father," Whitley admitted, "and we've begun to take steps to turn this rising tide, as I suggested we should at the end of the report."

Theodore Dellenbach laughed huskily; the laugh was followed by the hack of a decades-long smoker into the phone. "I'm sure you'll get this threat under control, Son, and I approve of the resolutions you bring up in the report's concluding chapter. On another front, it looks like our police forces have had some luck in uncovering a cache of terrorist explosives."

"While barely missing some of the Future Generations terrorists at the same time," added Whitley. "It is just a matter of time, however: the terrorists will likely be captured sooner than later."

"Which of course brings us to your project with the former DEA agent," the elder Dellenbach recalled. "Where is that at?"

"It's underway," Whitley replied in a neutral voice.

"Meaning?"

"Meaning the ex-DEA agent, Stone McClelland, had an initial meeting with Sapphire MacKenzie."

"And?"

"And according to my man, Roger," Whitley related, "after McClelland explained why he'd come, and who he was after, MacKenzie threw him out of her office.

"That doesn't sound too promising," observed the Father.

"There's more to it than that," the son countered. "He told Roger this mission to find Chris Soles through the activist Sapphire MacKenzie was a total waste of time. McClelland was discouraged; he wants to quit. He also told my man if the entire government is mobilized searching for Chris Soles, aka Chris Cadia, how could he do any better than all of them? In his own words, McClelland said, 'Tell Mr. Dellenbach I'm going to quit and return to my wife in Arizona. I'm not going to take his money; it just wouldn't be right.'"

Once more, Theodore Dellenbach was chuckling into the phone. "It sounds like you've got a live one on your hands. If you can hold on to him, I think you've got him hook, line, and sinker."

"I agree, Father, he's a keeper; his integrity is his undoing," said Whitley. "And that's more or less what I told Roger when he reported to me. I told him to let McClelland go back to his wife for a few days or a week – and to keep the money we're paying him, with our compliments. I had Roger tell him not to be discouraged. The seed had been planted and the message will get through."

"Are you certain of that?"

"I know Sapphire," Whitley stated with confidence, "and she doesn't let things go. The meeting will bear fruit, we must just be patient."

"I hope you're right, Son," said Theodore Dellenbach. "Eliminating Chris Cadia and the Future Generations terrorists would surely erase many of the short term problems and instability we currently face in the Northwest. When it comes to longer term issues, however, suddenly things aren't so bright."

"What are you getting at, Father?"

"In my mind, I keep going back to your report about the rising of the commons, Son," the elder Dellenbach replied. "I worry less about your unwitting source of information Sapphire MacKenzie and all her thousands of activists, than I do if the conception of the commons actually catches fire among the unwashed and unnumbered."

"I can concur, Father," replied Whitley, "especially in light of the fact that protestors have always been around and will always be around."

"Yes, and it's much more than that," agreed Theodore Dellenbach. "If the masses willingly join something like the commons – based on sharing, instead of privatization and self-assertion by the strongest and smartest – our current structure of society will rapidly begin to erode from within."

"Of course, Father, you realize that as a primary point the report attempted to address," noted Whitley. "It took our people decades to emasculate labor unions and those were energized and goaded by money, a very strong inducement. But if the rabble falls fully under the sway of an *idea*, an ideological movement, money has more than met its match with them."

"And that is why you must move forward with all haste implementing the action plan at the end of your report," the elder Dellenbach asserted. "Even as we deal in the short term with protesters, terrorists, and the likes of this Chris Cadia, a concerted and aggressive effort must be launched to eliminate the Commons movement."

"That is well underway," the son assured the father. "We already have people planted that will feed us information, as well as infiltrators that will disrupt and promote dissension in the ranks. And as has been the case through history, when the elite must deal with the hoi polloi, we will use the rabble's own thick-skulled thugs and vigilantes to do our enforcing when the police are not there, or must look the other way. The rise of the commons is a credible threat; it must be eradicated."

"I agree, Son," said the father. "Eradicated."

***

"Are you sure we're in the right place?" Kiri asked again.

"I hope so," Chris replied, growing weary himself.

The knocking on the door continued, but this time he wasn't going to open it. At least not until it was the exact series of knocks they were told to wait for.

"Even if it is the right place," Kiri noted, "this restaurant is plenty busy during the midday rush and I'm sure some families have to go."

"Or change their babies," acknowledged Chris, "but this is where

Linda told us to meet her. She was reluctant enough to come in the first place, so I'm just following instructions." He sighed. "I was told to come to the seafood restaurant on the hill in Poulsbo overlooking the marina and the bay, then go to the family restroom at the end of the hall past the male and female restrooms. So we did that. Then I was told to take the 'Out of Order' sign off the back of the door, hang it on the hook on the front of the door, then sit and wait for the designated series of knocks and she would be there. So we did that – and here we are."

"I don't know," Kiri said warily, "but something doesn't seem right if she isn't here by now."

Chris was compelled to agree, though he didn't say anything. Instead, he gazed about the restaurant's family bathroom for perhaps the twentieth time. On the wall opposite the door was the washbasin with a mirror on the wall. To the right was a diaper changing station and to the left was an open toilet without a stall. Two folding chairs were together on each side of the room and a mop within a mop bucket was next to the door.

Kiri and Chris were seated against opposite walls facing each other, both feeling quite conscious about being out and about again, and away from the safety of their cabin and woods. With nothing much else to do, Kiri eventually snatched up her purse from the chair next to her, retrieved her phone, and checked the time. She shook her head and replaced the phone.

"I think I've got to pee," she said, standing.

Chris shrugged his shoulders as Kiri stood and walked the few short steps to the toilet. Without a second thought, she dropped her terry cloth shorts and panties and sat down. As she relieved herself, Kiri glanced at Chris and he calmly returned her gaze.

At first, many months ago, such an incident would have proven awkward to both, but by now they'd seen each other naked enough times, that it didn't really matter any more.

From the toilet, Kiri asked Chris, "How much longer are we going to wait for her?"

"A little while longer, I guess," he replied. "She's an old friend of Linda's from their raft guide days in Idaho, and if Linda says she'll be here, I'm hoping she will."

Kiri finished, pulled up her panties and shorts, and flushed the toilet. Just then, so also came two quick knocks on the restroom door, followed by a pause, then two more rapid knocks.

As Kiri made her way to the sink to wash up, Chris nodded to her and moved to open the door. The lock clicked open as he turned the knob, and Sapphire MacKenzie entered the family restroom, locking the door again behind her.

"Thanks for agreeing to meet with us," said Chris.

The combination of the noise from the flushing toilet and water running from the sink as Kiri washed her hands, gave Sapphire pause.

"Am I interrupting something?" wondered Sapphire.

"Not at all," Kiri replied, without turning from the sink, "I just had to pee."

After she dried her hands with a paper towel, and then deposited it in the nearby wastebasket, Kiri turned to discover Chris and Sapphire transfixed upon one another, just as they had been at times during the meeting in Port Townsend.

When Linda Hernandez helped arrange a meeting to talk about Future Generations' plans for the oil storage tanks near Clatskanie, Kiri had wondered if Chris and Sapphire would be star struck by each other again – and apparently that was the case.

Their shared gape dropped, however, as both became aware Kiri had turned to them. Chris, courteous as always, noted that he believed the two women never had a chance to meet at the Port Townsend gathering, so he introduced them.

Kiri and Sapphire kindly shook hands and exchanged pleasantries.

Most curiously, at least to Kiri's mind, Sapphire said, "I've wondered who you were ever since I saw you sitting behind Linda and Tomas at the Port Townsend meeting."

Taking the remark as a compliment, at least for now, Kiri said nothing as Chris once again thanked Sapphire for taking the time to get together. Without really thinking about it, Sapphire took a seat opposite the wall where Chris and Kiri were settling into their folding chairs that had been leaning against the wall before they entered.

"So, the way Linda explained it to me," Sapphire began without prelude, "you have credible information that someone is planning a terrorist strike that would cause catastrophic environmental damage."

"And we need your help to avert it," added Chris.

"And you need my help..." Sapphire mused.

Without mincing words, Chris stated unequivocally, "We know that Garf Taylor and Future Generations are behind it."

"Garf Taylor?" she queried. "So?"

Sapphire stared incredulously at Chris. "Garf Taylor is a friend. He's a true revolutionary; we need people like him or Cascadia will never become a reality. Besides, how do you know he's the mastermind behind it? I've been hearing all week how 'Chris Cadia' is in charge of the Future Generations 'terrorists.'"

Before Chris could reply, Kiri jumped in. "We know Garf Taylor is behind all this; it's credible because we have a friend in their organization that can't be named for their own safety."

Sapphire scrutinized the younger woman for a long moment before nodding.

"Fair enough," she acknowledged. "So tell me a little more about what's happening."

Briefly, Chris explained to Sapphire the sabotage scheme as best he understood it. He talked about the location on the Columbia River, as well as mentioning the target being massive oil storage tanks. Speaking about the environmental damage from such a spill into the river, Chris made the point that no matter how good a friend Garf Taylor might be, such heinous acts would be an unacceptable outrage on the planet that could not be condoned. Finally, he made note of the timing of the attack, which was supposed to coincide with the time the Arctic oil supply ship would attempt to break through the protestors in Portland, head down the Columbia, and out to sea.

"So, what do you want from me?" Sapphire asked Chris. Obviously, she was dubious.

"We need your help," he replied. "Talk to Taylor if you think that would work, or maybe..."

"Or maybe what?" Sapphire demanded. "Are you asking me to abandon the blockade – by means of holding a potential environmental disaster over my head and on my conscience? That won't fly. The blockade goes on no matter what."

"So," Kiri interrupted. "Why can't you just be in two places at once?"

Sapphire turned to the other woman in the bathroom.

"What are you talking about?" she snapped, before shifting her attention back to Chris.

"Let her explain," he suggested. "After all, it's her idea."

"Okay. Explain." Sapphire seemed quite uncertain about Kiri.

"I think you can prove yourself and your movement twice as strong if you can be two places at once," Kiri began. "I've read reports that you'll have anywhere from twenty-five thousand to forty thousand protesters at the blockade next week. At the height of things – precisely when Future Generations intends to blow up the oil storage tanks – you could send maybe five or ten thousand to Clatskanie to interrupt what otherwise might be an environmental disaster. Call it a 'flash protest' if you will; it will be a statement about the overseas shipment of oil that pollutes our common atmosphere, as much as it will be about a blockade of continuing oil exploration in the Arctic. You'll raise awareness in two places at once and Cascadia will be twice as strong for it."

"It simply won't work," Sapphire disagreed. "Even if we get fifty thousand in boats to blockade the Arctic oil ship, we'll need each and every one of them."

"More than that," Chris interjected. "You'd need Empire's Navy to have a truly successful blockade. And, sorry, but I'm afraid they are precisely the armada that will ultimately open the blockade and escort the ship safely to the ocean."

"Are you trying to say in the end we don't have a chance?" Sapphire shot back.

"I'm saying precisely that," Chris stated emphatically. "You can not ultimately succeed against the forces of Empire with your blockade; that's why we are suggesting that you make a show of your power and influence in two places at once."

"You gain great face that way, as well as double the media coverage," Kiri added. "And you help avert a possible environmental disaster."

For several minutes, Sapphire's brilliant blue eyes darted between Chris and Kiri as she churned over what they had proposed. Eventually, she shrugged her shoulders.

"I have to talk to my fellow organizers about this," Sapphire conceded. "Then I may talk with Garf, or we may have a go with your 'flash protest,' or we may – I don't know. But whatever we do, we can't have a major oil spill in the Columbia, can we?"

Both Chris and Kiri agreed that would be the last thing they wanted to transpire.

"Now, before I go," Sapphire spoke directly to Kiri, "I have to talk with him about a personal matter. So, if you don't mind..."

Kiri was shocked to realize she was being dismissed. As she slowly stood to step outside, it was clear Kiri took umbrage at what she considered a snub. In response, she fired visual daggers in Sapphire's direction while departing.

After the restroom door closed, Chris informed Sapphire, "That wasn't necessary."

"She's very smart, and very pretty," Sapphire countered with a smile, "but too young for you, you know."

"You don't understand our relationship at all," he countered. "Kiri is a friend, a very good friend."

"Uh-huh." Sapphire nodded knowingly, then changed the subject.

"Several days ago, someone I never met before was in my office," she stated. "He was looking for you."

Chris said nothing.

"I hadn't seen you since Port Townsend and didn't know if or when I'd ever see you again," Sapphire admitted. "So I sort of blew him off and kicked him out of my office."

Still, Chris was silent.

"And then Linda called a couple nights ago and said you wanted to meet with me," she continued. "For what it's worth, I brought the guy's card along in case you want it."

From her purse, Sapphire retrieved the card, stood, and crossed the restroom to hand it to him. Still sitting, Chris read the name and studied the contact numbers. None of it made any sense to him and he told her so.

"He also asked me to describe him if I ever came across you," she said, "so I will. He was massive, as huge as any pro football player, and said he was a former DEA agent."

Chris visibly recoiled.

"He also suggested that I should mention to you an old pickup truck and something about a scenic turnoff in northern Arizona," Sapphire recalled. "Oh yeah – and he said you owed it to him to meet up. Does any of that make sense?"

Chris said nothing in reply, but Sapphire could tell he was visibly shaken.

"I better get going now," she announced. "I've got to talk to some friends about stopping a potential oil spill."

Still stunned, Chris nevertheless rose in a show of politeness. He mouthed something about how he appreciated her taking the time to meet.

Sapphire grinned as she took one of his hands in hers. Once more, their eyes locked up. She squeezed his hand.

"Please take care of yourself, okay?" she admonished him. "I look forward to seeing you again – and not on the nightly news in handcuffs."

Speechless, Chris was aware she had loosened her grip on his hand, and was turning to the restroom door.

On her way out, Sapphire announced, "I'll tell your little friend she can return."

As soon as Sapphire departed, Kiri entered – and she was hot.

"So what was all that about?" she demanded to know. "How personal did you have to get with her?"

With thoughts reeling, Chris shook his head. He'd never seen Kiri like this. Simultaneously, he was still trying to recover after being sandbagged by news about the cop that had set him free in Arizona.

"I have no idea why she didn't want you to hear what she told me," Chris pleaded. "It was merely about that DEA agent I saw on the ferry. After he got off, he apparently visited her office looking for me."

"Oh, I have every idea in the world why she had to speak with you 'personally,'" Kiri fired back. "Even though I'm not the famous and beautiful Sapphire MacKenzie, I'm a woman just like she is – and I know precisely why she wanted to speak 'personally' with you!"

It took Chris five minutes to calm Kiri down. And it took another five minutes for him to assure her that the only thing that had transpired while she was outside was the revelation about Stone McClelland. He even showed her McClelland's card, but that didn't fully appease her.

Still in a huff as they finally departed the restaurant and made their way to the van, Kiri told him in no uncertain terms it was all a trap.

To be honest though, Chris didn't know if she was referring to Stone McClelland, or Sapphire MacKenzie. Or both...

CHAPTER FIFTEEN

A little after four in the morning, the pounding began on Carolyn Maxwell's apartment door.

Groggily, she slipped into her robe hanging on the bedroom door and tied it fast about her middle. Turning on the hallway light, Carolyn lurched toward the living room and the insistent knocking on the front door. Through the peephole was her older brother, Billy; she turned the deadbolt and opened the door.

Billy rumbled inside, followed by three other men she'd never met.

"What's going on?" Carolyn wondered, not even half awake.

"Just put some coffee on, Sis," Billy demanded. "We're meeting up here and then heading east. We'll only be a little while."

Carolyn shook her head as her brother's friends collapsed on the sofa. Billy followed her into the kitchen. She retrieved ground coffee from the refrigerator and began filling the pot with water, even as Billy wanted to know about food for breakfast.

"How about some bacon and eggs?" he asked. "And maybe some pastries? I'll start cooking while we wait for the others to arrive."

Waking up ever more and growing annoyed, all Carolyn said was,

"In the fridge."

Just as Billy started to open the refrigerator door, the knocking began all over again on the front door.

"I'll get it," said Billy, leaving the refrigerator open without a second thought as he hustled down the hallway.

Carolyn set the coffee to brew. She then closed the fridge in time to see down the hall that her other brother Timmy was entering with three others. She didn't know two of them that arrived with Timmy, but the third was a guy named Joseph, who sometimes brought her phones for the phone swaps.

With the coffee brewing, Carolyn pulled a dozen eggs out of the fridge and what remained of a pound of bacon her brothers had left before they departed to Clatskanie. Billy hadn't returned to help, so Carolyn put several strips of bacon in a pan to fry, then began breaking and scrambling eggs. When the full pot of coffee was ready, she put several cups on a tray and took everything to the living room to distribute.

She hadn't heard any more knocking, but Garf Taylor had just arrived too. There was a lot of grumbling going on; apparently things hadn't worked out too well in Clatskanie. Carolyn preferred not to pay attention to it. And then Timmy was complaining there wasn't enough coffee to go around, and Billy was ordering her to brew another pot.

That was fine by her as she had bacon cooking and scrambled eggs ready to put on the stove – and didn't really need to listen to a roomful of male bellyaching. At least they were all still alive and not in jail, was all she could focus upon.

By the time the next pot of coffee was ready, the first batch of bacon and eggs was prepared as well. Carolyn delivered the coffee and a few additional mugs, and then returned to the kitchen. She put the bacon and eggs in separate serving dishes and grabbed paper plates and utensils from the cupboards.

Back in the living room, she dumped everything on the coffee table in front of the sofa and told all to dig in. Without hesitation, the men clambered forth for the food, but the grousing carried on unabated.

One of the guys she didn't know was complaining about all the bright lights. Or, more specifically, about the bright lights from the helicopters.

"If it wasn't for those damn choppers, with their lights on all over the place," he declared, "we still could have blown those storage tanks."

"You fucking dufus," Garf Taylor swore, "the helicopters and all the troops and the media were there because the protesters were there. As soon as they showed up we didn't have a chance to accomplish what we came for. It's sheer luck we got out of there with all our stuff intact."

"Well, I'll tell you one thing," stated a scraggly man Carolyn didn't know, "if all those protestors had stayed in Portland, maybe that blockade might not have failed last night."

Carolyn, pouring out the remainder of the coffee pot so she could presumably brew another, clucked derisively to herself. What a fool he was: she'd seen the TV news last night and how a flotilla of U.S. Navy ships made way for the Arctic oil supply boat. All the little people in kayaks and private boats were simply no match.

"Who is to say all those protesters came out of Portland anyway?" posed Timmy Maxwell.

"I'll be the first to say it," Billy immediately replied to his brother. "From where I was on lookout, I saw Polly Hawser, one of Sapphire MacKenzie's fellow organizers, carrying the Cascadia flag and leading the march on the front gates. She and all those people should have been down in Portland with Sapphire."

"Yeah, they damn well should have been," Timmy agreed. He

turned on Garf Taylor. "So what's the matter, Garf? Doesn't Sapphire love you any more?"

Cautious laughter erupted and even Carolyn was forced to stifle a snigger as best she could.

Garf Taylor glared truculently at everyone in the room. To Timmy, he snarled, "Fuck you, kid."

Any lingering chuckles dissipated at once.

"Okay, let's finish up here and head out," ordered Garf. "We leave separately as we came, and we meet up on the other side of the Cascades at the restaurant I told you about outside of Ellensberg. I'm out of here first, then everybody else get going."

Without any further delay, Garf set the paper plate that had held his breakfast on the coffee table, along with his fork. A sullen and bellicose air followed him out the door.

Carolyn was relieved they would all be going soon; she began gathering used coffee cups, utensils, and used paper plates to return to the kitchen. Billy told the men he'd come with to prepare to depart. He then helped Carolyn carry stuff to the kitchen.

Depositing everything on the countertop over the dishwasher, Carolyn asked Billy where they were going.

Her brother laughed. "East for sure, other than that I'm not entirely certain. For some reason, Garf's holding back on the plans. He's apparently going to clue us all in on the exact location in Ellensberg. All I know is that it has to do with the new hydraulic spreaders."

Taken aback, Carolyn shuddered. "Just be careful," she pleaded.

"I always am, Sis," he smiled, giving her a peck on the cheek.

Billy turned back down the hallway, joined his friends, and departed.

By the time Carolyn put coffee mugs and utensils in the dishwasher, and paper plates in the trash, Timmy was shouting his good-byes from the living room. After they were gone – and she was finally all alone again – Carolyn returned to the living room for a final inspection to see if there was anything else for the dishwasher.

Walking down the hallway in a state of semi-shock after all the unexpected visitors, only now did she fully realize she was still in her robe after being awakened by the pounding on the door.

There were two coffee cups she previously missed on the end table by the sofa, yet as she moved to retrieve them, there came pounding once more on the front door.

Through the peephole Carolyn saw Garf Taylor. She opened the door and he came in, closing it behind him.

"I forgot something," he stated, almost brutally.

She took a step back, and he kept coming. He closed in on her until her back was against the opposite wall. With his left forearm pressed hard upon her and just above her breasts, Garf slammed Carolyn against the wall. At the same time his left hand grasped firm onto her left breast, while his right hand slipped through the folds of her robe below. She had only been wearing panties to sleep in, but there felt no barrier whatsoever as he vise-gripped her labia between his right thumb and the rest of his fingers.

"I forgot something," Garf Taylor repeated, his clasp above and below unrelenting, "I forgot to tell you we may have someone in our midst we can not trust."

Carolyn was nearly paralyzed, afraid to death to say anything.

"But before we get to that, let me give you a word of advice," he warned.

Still frozen, Carolyn was speechless.

"For your own well being, don't go laughing at me because of your brother Timmy's sick jokes. Sapphire still loves me," he stated. "Do you understand?"

All Carolyn could do was nod her head.

"The other thing I wanted to make sure you understood is that my plans rarely go awry," Garf declared, his dark eyes boring into hers. "Things that should have succeeded haven't worked at all of late; I think there's a traitor in our midst."

"So what do you want me to do about it?" she finally managed.

The uncomfortable grips both high and low continued.

"You run our phone shuttle and coordinate logistics," he replied. "You, if anyone, should be able to detect who might be using our very secret plans against us. If you even suspect it, *I* want to know about it. Do you understand? I don't want you to tell your brother, Billy; I don't want you to tell your dickhead brother, Timmy. I want you to tell *me*. Do you understand?"

Carolyn nodded in fear.

"No, speak to me," ordered Garf. "Do you understand?"

In a weak voice, she murmured, "I understand."

"And do you know what happens if you fail me, or lie to me?"

"No..."

Bypassing her panties, Garf rammed two implacable fingers up inside her forcefully enough to lift her off the floor.

"This is what happens; do you understand?"

Carolyn nodded and her eyes began to fill with fluid. "Yes, yes, yes; I understand."

"Good, that's what I wanted to hear."

Slowly, he lowered her to the ground and removed his hands from her body.

As Garf turned to the front door and departed, Carolyn slumped powerless to the floor.

There was nothing she could do but lose herself in a torrent of tears.

***

In the shower Carolyn began coming back to herself after the shock of the morning had knocked her numb.

Regardless of what had already happened today, she realized she still had to go to work so she could pay off a pittance of what she needed to live, to pay off a pittance of her student loan bills, and thus be able to go back to pay off a pittance more of everything tomorrow.

As the water cascaded from above, Carolyn consciously and repeatedly washed and rinsed below, hoping enough scrubbing would erase the degradations of that early hour away, while nevertheless retaining doubts regarding the efficacy of it all.

After drying, getting dressed for work, and putting her make-up on, she realized she still had a little time before she must depart. She settled at the kitchen table for the lack of anything better to do. Carolyn knew she was hungry; contrarily though, after this morning she couldn't stomach the prospect of eating. She toyed with the whim of turning on the morning news, but concluded that she really needed to talk to someone. And that someone had to be Kiri.

Unfortunately, the phone went to voice mail as soon as it rang. At first, she thought not to leave a message, as she much preferred to speak with her friend in person. Ultimately though, Carolyn acknowledged the need to convey information overrode the very personal affronts she might or might not eventually share with Kiri.

She began very tentatively: "Uh, Kiri, this is Carolyn. I'm sorry I missed you this morning. I'm on my way to work pretty soon, so I probably won't be able to speak with you until this evening."

Carolyn paused, trying to gather up what she really needed to say.

"My brothers, Garf Taylor, and several others were through my apartment here in Everett early this morning. It looks like the disruptions the protesters caused made it necessary to abandon the strikes on the oil storage tanks, so that's a good thing. If you were somehow able to trigger those protests, I can't thank you enough."

Once more, she paused before continuing. "But the bad news is they're all headed east with the new hydraulic spreaders. I fear that might mean a train derailment.

"I have no idea where it might be," she said with regret, "because Garf wasn't telling anyone the specific location until later. I found that curious at first – but I discovered why, later on."

She cleared her throat. "After everyone left, Garf came back to my apartment. He said he suspects someone is revealing Future Generations' plans. Since I'm handling the logistics by contacting everyone from the lists he gives me and so on, I'm supposed to inform him of any suspected spies."

Carolyn couldn't bring herself to say how Garf had emphasized his orders.

"Just from his actions though, Kiri," she said to the message recorder, "I'm afraid he might suspect me."

Carolyn sighed heavily. "I really don't need any of this," she stated. "Call me or I'll call you tonight."

Five minutes after hanging up, Carolyn was still lost in thought at the kitchen table. She felt better having made the call to Kiri and leaving the message, even if they hadn't been able to converse. Carolyn knew when they spoke Kiri would share rational and encouraging words, because that's the way Kiri was. And it made Carolyn comfortable to muse upon it.

A short while later, as she was walking toward the front door to leave for work, Carolyn involuntarily glanced at the wall Garf had pinned her against.

She shuddered. All that washing and scrubbing and rinsing hadn't worked any better than she imagined it would.

As she walked out the door, she felt him inside her – rough, cruel, and domineeringly invasive.

CHAPTER SIXTEEN

Panting nearly in unison as the moment came, and then passed, she lay atop him afterward, hot with release. Slowly he withered to the point that their bodies disjoined; she slid off him to the side, and he cuddled her inward.

It had been like this, morning and night, since he had returned from the Northwest. Lorien and Stone couldn't get enough of each other; it was almost like they were meeting again for the first time.

Eventually though, it was time for her to shower and prepare for the wellness center and her first acupuncture patients of the day. Stone dozed until Lorien called to tell him the shower was open. He reluctantly withdrew from bed, knowing he once again had to try to decide what to do with the rest of his life after the shower.

When he finished and was mostly dried off, Lorien was beckoning him from the breakfast bar in the kitchen.

"Stone, I think you better get out here and check what's on the news this morning," she called.

Judging by the immediacy in her voice, he wrapped the towel about him and made his way toward the kitchen.

On the small TV at the end of the breakfast bar countertop was a fiery scene, accented by enormous flames and billowing black clouds of smoke. It looked to be in an arid region with sagebrush and scrub vegetation. The reporter on the scene was interviewing a fire fighter; both were at a great distance from the towering inferno in the background.

"As local responders, there's little we can do with an explosion of this magnitude," the fireman was explaining, "other than isolate the area, and allow the episode to burn down to the point where we can finally extinguish it."

"Do you have any idea how many oil tanker cars were involved in this derailment?" prodded the reporter.

"No sir, I can't say that I do," replied the fire fighter. "I heard one of the derailments on the railroad line up between Odessa and Lamora was close to one hundred tanker cars. But it doesn't make much difference, really."

"What do you mean by that?"

The fireman sighed. "One of those railroad oil tanker cars carries about 30,000 gallons of crude. Most local fire departments can't handle a gas tank fire of nine or ten thousand gallons. And here we've got maybe forty or fifty tanker cars with thirty thousand gallons of crude each that exploded into fire when the train derailed. There's nothing we can do but let it burn."

The reporter thanked the fire fighter and the station cut back to the news anchors in the studio. Stone looked at Lorien, while shaking his head and tightening the towel around his middle.

In grave tones, the woman anchor began recapping the events of the prior evening in east central Washington. Apparently, during the course of a four and half hour time period, three trains derailed on three separate lines, roughly in the shape of a right triangle. Two of the trains were strictly carrying crude oil tanker cars; the third train was loaded with a mix of oil, potato, and onion cars.

Because each derailment was within twenty to forty miles of each other, the TV news announcers said the local responders could see each other's fireball in the distance against the dark night sky. The male anchor stated that was a result of the phenomenal quantity of crude oil that was burning.

The train that derailed furthest north was between the small towns of Odessa and Lamora, eventually destined to carry the crude through the Cascade Tunnel, and was hauling close to one hundred tanker cars. It was estimated 80-90 rail cars had exploded into a fireball after the derailment.

"When one oil tank car ignites," the man on TV explained, "the heat can set off a chain reaction, causing adjacent cars to explode into a fireball as well."

About thirty-five miles south of that first derailment and just outside of the town of Lind, the second train to derail was hauling an estimated fifty-five oil cars and around forty more carrying a mix of potatoes and onions. This was the smallest of the fires from the three derailments, yet still much too big to do anything other than let it burn out.

The final derailment, which occurred more than four hours after the first, was situated about twenty-five miles east of Lind, near a lonely crossing on a country road. This train derailed with eighty-five tanker cars of crude, all carrying 30,000 gallons, and all on fire.

"So do the authorities have any word," the female anchor was asking her male counterpart, "what the suspected cause of these derailments could be?"

"Well," he explained, "investigators probably can not get close enough for several days to search for clues, but already there is abundant suspicion that terrorism is involved. The derailments simply cannot be regarded as coincidental, since they were so close in time and proximity."

"Are there any suspects at this time?"

The male anchor nodded his head. "Well, at this point it's still early. No group has claimed credit for these incidents, and the authorities haven't made any formal statements. Judging by much of the speculation that's being tossed about, however, it doesn't take a genius to believe the eco-terrorist group, 'Representatives of Future Generations,' and their reputed leader Chris Cadia, might well be behind these attacks. After all, they did claim credit for the Fourth of July railroad bombings. And, needless to say, these latest incidents are all the more grim and consequential with at least nine railroad worker deaths."

Stone McClelland couldn't take it any longer. From the countertop, he snatched up the TV remote and turned it off.

He was dead serious when he turned to Lorien.

"I have to go back up there," he declared, his iron jaw set. "I have to do something; I have to do anything I can to stop this madness. These people, those of Future Generations, have no idea of the forces they are ultimately dealing with."

"What will you do?" asked Lorien.

"I don't know," he answered honestly. "Maybe I'll start by contacting my friend Bertie Stanton. I told you about him. He used to be with the DEA down here and ended up getting a transfer into the FBI, so he could move back to Seattle where he's from. The FBI is undoubtedly investigating all this; Bertie's got to know something."

"You do what you have to do, Stone," said Lorien. "And don't worry: the two of us will always be together even when we're apart."

McClelland stared deep into the eyes of his wife. "I love you."

"I love you, too," she smiled.

"It's just that I have an obligation to stop all this," Stone murmured in excuse, "since I was the one that let Chris Soles go."

"Like I said before, you have an unfulfilled duty toward yourself," replied Lorien. "So go northwest – and try to fulfill it."

* * *

"After all the bullshit about detection systems being wired into the rails, I guess it didn't make any difference after all," Billy Maxwell noted as they watched more news coverage of the oil train derailments.

"Maybe it's because we were in the middle of nowhere," replied Garf, "or maybe the sensors didn't work or weren't deployed. It doesn't matter; we were more successful than we could have imagined. We were hoping to snare at least one train hauling oil; instead we got three."

Billy grinned. "I guess that just goes to prove there're too many trains hauling crude."

They were holed up in a cabin owned by Garf's cousin on Hauser Lake, north of Post Falls, Idaho, roughly between the Spokane, Washington, and Coeur d'Alene, Idaho. After their three teams finished sabotaging the three different train lines using hydraulic rail spreaders last night, all had disbursed in random directions with Garf and Billy hightailing it to this remote cabin well out of the limelight.

The news reports were already coming in fast and furious by the time they arrived at the cabin and switched on the television. With each story, with each on-the-scene interview, Garf and Billy grew more excited and giddier with success. High-fives were repeatedly exchanged and the toasts of whiskey and beer had energized and crowned their achievements.

Midday had come and gone, and as the TV droned on, Garf announced more beer and some chips to eat were what they both needed. As he made his way to the cabin's small kitchen, Billy's phone began to ring. Garf stopped and turned, but Billy waved him off after checking the caller I.D.

"It's just my Sis," Billy explained. "Go ahead and get the chips; I'm hungry."

Answering the phone, Billy was brief. "What's up?"

"Hi, Billy," said Carolyn. "You wanted me to call you back in a couple hours for an update."

"Yeah, so what's up?"

"Well," she said, "they've all reported in except for numbers 2, 6, and 8."

"That's not good," Billy judged. "Why haven't they called?"

"How should I know?" Carolyn replied a tad indignantly. "I don't even know who I'm talking to when they call. I'm just doing what you told me and telling you the numbers that call in and say they're okay."

"It's all right, Sis," allowed Billy. "You done good. Call me back if anything changes."

Garf was returning from the kitchen with food and beverages as Billy was hanging up.

"What did your sister have to say?" he wondered.

"Everyone has reported now except for 2, 6, and 8," Billy informed him. "And that's not good."

"No, it isn't," agreed Garf. "Especially since they were the ones that were supposed to send the media outlets the 'Communiqué from the Hypotenuse,' from Ritzville. I guess we'll just have to see what develops."

Suddenly, Billy was chuckling. "I never thought it would happen, but you fucking guessed it, Garf. I didn't think they'd figure out the right triangle thing on their own, but the guys on TV are already calling it the 'Right Triangle Oil Spill Disaster,' or the 'Right Triangle Terrorism,' or the right triangle whatever. I thought for sure it would take the communiqué for all those talking heads to figure they were dealing with disasters shaped in a right triangle."

"Well, it's a good thing that the town of Ritzville is pretty much smack dab on the hypotenuse," smiled Garf, "otherwise it might not have worked so conveniently for the communiqué. But, you know Billy, it's our duty too to add a little flourish, a little art – or is it science? – to the plots concocted by the evil terrorist, 'Chris Cadia.' The media just loves that kind of shit."

Laughing, Billy agreed. "And they'll love even more when the communiqué hits the news tonight or tomorrow morning."

For another twenty or thirty minutes, Garf and Billy watched live coverage of burning oil tanker rail cars shot from helicopters, grave reports of disrupted commerce because of attacks on rail lines, and discussions with "experts" on terrorism in Cascadia. When it all became too much of the same thing, however, Garf turned to Billy and told him something was wrong.

Pointing at the television, Garf stated, "All that success bothers me."

"Why?"

"Let me ask you: why were we able to so brilliantly achieve our objectives last night, Billy," posed Garf, "when before we couldn't even hide explosives in a remote cabin? Or why were our plans to blow up oil storage tanks interrupted by unannounced protests – in a place where nobody ever protests?"

"I don't know."

"I think I do," declared Garf. "I think we have a spy in our midst. I personally didn't reveal plans and assignments for this mission until we split up a few days ago in Ellensburg. And I made certain each group only knew it's own assignment and no one else's. Nobody knew what was happening this time until the very end, and everything worked perfectly."

Billy cocked his head. "So you suspect one of our own people?"

"I don't know," Garf replied neutrally. "Do you trust all our people? You recruited most of them."

"Damn straight, I trust them," Billy fired back without hesitation. "Almost all of them did time with me and I know them inside and out. Plus, they've all sworn an oath to Future Generations; they'll make the ultimate sacrifice if needed."

Garf nodded more for form than anything else. Slowly, cautiously, he inquired, "What about your sister? How much do you trust her?"

Billy Maxwell bristled and the rope of muscles around his neck bulged out.

"She's my Sis," he said, obviously offended. "She trusts me with her life and I trust her with mine. She'd never do us wrong."

"I hope not," Garf replied, his voice calm. "But I sense someone betrayed us earlier. You keep your eyes and ears open for a traitor, and I'll do the same."

"And if we find someone has crossed us?"

"It's no different from when you and I started all this months ago," Garf assured his friend. "If future generations are to have a chance on this planet, the people are either with us or against us."

Nodding his head, Billy agreed, "They live or they die."

"And it doesn't matter who it is," Garf hastened to add.

***

"All I'm certain of," Tomas stated shortly after Grandma Sutton ushered her grandkids outside, leaving them sitting at the kitchen table again, "is that what's happened the last few days is a very dangerous escalation of events."

"No doubt about that," agreed Chris. "The governor's called out the National Guard and on the federal level there's serious talk about the army's involvement in a civil matter. Fossil fuel interests in British Columbia are urging the Premier to follow a similar course, even though he's saying it's all an American problem."

"Although I'm admittedly not a big fan of the gas, oil, and coal industries," Linda interjected, "I fear there're yet those that don't see Cascadia as an indivisible whole when it comes to these issues."

Her husband nodded his head.

"It seems counterintuitive to those in charge," Tomas spoke to Linda, "but B.C. may be targeted all the more by Future Generations, the more they refuse to be involved."

Turning his attention to Kiri sitting across the kitchen table, Tomas wondered, "Speaking of targets, what happened to your voice on the inside regarding these train derailments?"

"My friend didn't have any information about what was going to happen," Kiri replied softly.

For Tomas and Linda's benefit, Kiri briefly explained that her friend had left a message after the men headed east over the Cascades. Unfortunately though, her friend had no knowledge of where exactly they were going or what their plans might be.

"When I was able to get in touch with my friend later on," Kiri recalled, "I was told the withholding of information was likely because Garf Taylor thought there was a spy amongst them. He must have been threatening as well, because my friend seemed quite fearful and on edge that evening."

"Whoever it might be is in a very difficult situation," acknowledged Tomas.

"You know," Linda mused, "sometimes I still wonder if we shouldn't just anonymously turn Garf Taylor in."

Kiri was quick to respond. "If so, we might as well be throwing my friend in jail with all of them for aiding and abetting. And we simply cannot do that."

"Besides that," Chris tossed in, "we'd in effect be colluding with Empire as Tomas said before."

Reluctantly, Tomas concurred. "I think your friend must be very cautious," he said to Kiri, but if we can get more solid information from him or her, possibly we can deter Future Generations from their suicidal course and possibly help your friend out of the circumstances that they're in."

Linda rose from the table and announced she was getting a pitcher of iced tea from her mom's refrigerator. She asked Tomas if he would get some glasses from the cupboard. Back at the table with their beverages, Linda asked Chris about the meeting with Sapphire that she'd arranged.

"Obviously, the results of getting together were successful," Linda noted. "Because of the unexpected massing of protestors at the port near Clatskanie, there was nothing at all in the news about oil storage tanks exploding into the Columbia River."

"There's a lot more to it than that," Kiri blurted, glancing at Chris askew.

Sheepishly, he admitted, "Yeah, there's more to it than that."

Chris purposely turned his attentions to Tomas.

"We first met, Tomas," he began, "because your name was on a secret list of contacts I'd more or less inherited from the former leader of Gaia/Universe."

"Yeah," Tomas responded, "and because of what you told me regarding the background of how my sister and her toddler sons died during the conflagration when the government troops stormed the compound, it made a big difference to me as well as providing closure."

"Well, one thing I never told you completely about before," said Chris, "was perhaps the main reason I survived those times – when likely I should have perished with everyone else."

"We all know the basic story," recalled Linda. "You escaped a cave explosion and made your way to Cascadia."

Chris shook his head. "Like Kiri says, there's more to it than that."

Patiently, he told Linda and Tomas the tale of his capture in northern Arizona, his incarceration for one night in a Navajo Nation holding cell, and his inexplicable release the next morning by a DEA agent.

"After we spoke to Sapphire about recruiting some protestors to disrupt Future Generations near Clatskanie," Chris continued, "she handed me a card from Stone McClelland – the same DEA agent that set me free several years ago. She said he was looking for me."

"Isn't everyone?" quipped Linda.

"Yes, unfortunately they are," Kiri promptly and protectively tossed back.

Chris shrugged off the comments. He then explained to Tomas and Linda how he and Kiri were on the same ferry from Seattle to Bainbridge the morning Stone McClelland apparently had an appointment with Sapphire MacKenzie.

"After I got something hot to drink on the ferry and was on my way to meet Kiri," he recalled, "I walked past the big DEA agent that had set me free. He looked directly at me, but didn't recognize me whatsoever."

"Yet." Kiri's succinctness was on purpose.

Linda and Tomas glanced at each other, both intuiting a rift between Chris and Kiri regarding the issue. Chris chose to directly address that rift.

"Kiri, rightly or wrongly, thinks McClelland's attempting to find me is a trap," he admitted. "At the same time, he set me free. I somehow feel obligated to confront him – and find out what he's really after."

"It's nothing but a trap." Kiri spoke without hesitation. "The DEA agent is the large darkness in our path; I felt it before and I feel it again."

Tomas attempted to move past his friends' conflict. "If you were to meet him Chris, how would you go about it and still be safe?"

Haltingly, he glanced in Kiri's direction before responding.

"Because of the extensive plastic surgery after I escaped from the cave in Utah," he replied, "Stone McClelland couldn't recognize me on the ferry. If I meet him, I'll go as the 'representative' for Chris Soles – and tell him I'll convey whatever the big cop has to say to Chris."

"It's a stupid risk," Kiri bluntly declared, "to go waltzing like that into the presence of a force so ambiguous and dark."

Tomas and Linda looked back and forth at Chris and Kiri as they gawked questioningly at one another. In time, Tomas diplomatically stepped in.

"Well, I'm sure as you churn it over," he said to both of them, "you'll come to an adequate decision you can live with. More to the point right now though, what do we do about Garf Taylor and Future Generations?"

"And not only with regards to their raising the stakes with the train derailments," added Linda, "but what about the affected attitude change with the pretentious and bombastic, 'Communiqué from the Hypotenuse?'"

"By attitude change," wondered Chris, "do you mean cocky statements from the Communiqué like, 'we make a stand here on the Hypotenuse: oil tankers will not from this day henceforth cross over the Hypotenuse of Cascadia?' Sounds like bloviating hyperbole to me."

"I don't know about you," Kiri winked sarcastically, "but I kind of enjoyed the section in the Communiqué where they said something like, 'from time to time we like to take nature into account – since the corporate world of the fossil fuel Kingpins does not – and put natural geometrics to use in the powerful symbol of the right triangle.'"

"Okay," Tomas granted, "they could have used a better ghost writer like I assume they had when securing Sapphire's help with their initial Manifesto, but there are a few really frightening things in there as well."

"I agree," said Linda. "Especially when they say things like, 'we could have taken out an entire town, if we had chosen to do so. In climate wars, such events are likely to be shrugged off as mere collateral damage!'"

"And perhaps they actually could have turned one of those small nearby towns into a gigantic fireball if they derailed the train close enough," Tomas acknowledged. "Empire will ignore the rest of the pompous ranting and use the threat of a town being obliterated as an opportunity to double-down with repression."

"Certainly, that will be used as an excuse by the authorities," agreed Chris, "but what really raises the stakes and instills fear throughout Cascadia will be because of what happened at the city of Ritzville's main post office."

"Obviously though," Linda interjected, "the police didn't have the remotest idea it would work out like that. All they thought they spotted was a stolen car in the post office parking lot. An officer approached the idling car and ordered the lone occupant out; he was searched and no ID was found. The officer cuffed him and was taking him to the back of the police car when he crumpled and fell to the ground. What would you think if you had been that cop?"

"By then," Tomas continued, "police backup had arrived and with guns drawn, began approaching the post office entrance. Inside, witnesses later stated that two men who had just deposited a quantity of mail observed all the police action outside and grew quite agitated. One reportedly said to the other, 'we've sworn allegiance.' And the other replied, 'yes, we have.' A minute or two later, as police were entering, both collapsed only steps from the door."

"The people Garf Taylor recruited have been transformed into mindless zealots," declared Chris. "Biting down on a false tooth filled with potassium cyanide is the ultimate ultimatum."

"And Garf Taylor is the ultimate fanatic if he's convincing his people to commit suicide in order to avoid capture," Kiri added.

"All this is a dangerous escalation indeed," Tomas spoke sternly. "Empire now knows the opposition's level of intensity. Empire will be compelled to match it — and then crush Future Generations by any means possible."

"Of course," agreed Chris, "that is the patriarchal way, the way of war — and in this case the so-called climate wars they are spoiling for.

And we must do all we can to alter both their courses – if our eventual quest to establish an authentic Cascadia is to be realized."

CHAPTER SEVENTEEN

After his credentials were checked at the door of the Executive Lounge in the Honolulu airport, Whitley Dellenbach spotted his father at a table with two gentlemen he didn't know. At the same time, Theodore Dellenbach caught his son's entry. Politely, he dismissed the emissaries that were departing with him shortly to the Far East.

"I'm sorry you had to travel all the way to the middle of the Pacific to meet with me, Son," said the elder Dellenbach, "but I wanted to speak with you in person before I sneak off to secret trade talks in North Korea."

"Oh, so that's where you're bound," replied Whitley, a little surprised.

"Yes, but it's for your ears only," warned Theodore. "I'm traveling with people, friends of ours that work for our government, and it could mean a lot of money to us in the end. But it could be a diplomatic mess if the wrong people find out about it."

Whitley smiled. "If it means a lot of money, I wish you all the success in the world, Father."

Theodore Dellenbach nodded, but then his demeanor shifted.

"I'm having club soda, Son; what would you like to drink?"

"Club soda is fine for me as well."

The elder Dellenbach snapped a waiter to their table and ordered for his son. He said nothing as they waited for Whitley's drink to be delivered, yet this was not uncommon. Theodore Dellenbach often dropped into moments of reflective silence with friend and foe alike.

As the two generations sat across from each other, Whitley scrutinized his father as he had occasion to do over so many years. He was famous for the long face that made his heavy jowls seem thinner, while his prominent cheekbones were offset by droopy eyelids that many mistook at their peril for dullness rather than cunning. What was missing now – and it disturbed Whitley – was the supremely confident, snide smile that ordinarily adorned his features.

After Whitley's drink arrived, his father addressed what was on his mind.

"I'm very concerned about the course of events in the Northwest," the older man stated forcefully. "I fully realize you are too, Son, and that's why you are here today. We have to formulate a workable plan to end these troubles caused by the terrorists."

"I agree completely, Father."

"This terrorism that they call a climate war is costing us millions every day," Theodore Dellenbach declared. "Profits are what it's all about, and every day without profit is another day closer to our demise. Just when things were finally getting back to normal after the Fourth of July bombings, now we have three train derailments on all three major lines carrying crude through the Northwest."

"And to make matters worse, there are people in D.C. calling for legislation to prevent crude by rail," added Whitley. "Frankly, I'm worried."

"That will never happen," the elder Dellenbach assured his son. "Powerful friends that we support tell me we'll have military boots on the ground first – with the full approval of The Seven in the Supreme Court if need be – and it could come soon. All that may happen regardless, but we must be more proactive. We've got our own avenues to exploit and it's incumbent upon us to do so."

"I agree completely, Father."

"So tell me then, what's going on with the ex-DEA agent?

"Well, the good news is that my man Roger tells me Stone McClelland is back in the Northwest filled with resolve," reported Whitley. "Something about the derailments disturbed him deeply apparently, and he's going to start working with some friend of his in the Seattle FBI."

"Well, that's good enough news," the elder Dellenbach half agreed. "But I can already guess the bad news."

"Yes, you can," admitted the son. "So far there's been no contact between Chris Cadia and McClelland."

Theodore Dellenbach sighed heavily enough to cause his jowls to shudder.

"I hate to say it, Son, but maybe it's time to have our coverts bring your activist dupe in," the father asserted. "Interrogation is what she needs to reveal where this Chris Cadia is."

"But I'm not certain she really knows where he is," cautioned Whitley. "I urge patience, Father. The bait is in the water just waiting for the sucker to take the hook."

"I don't think that's enough," Theodore Dellenbach said dubiously. "We've got to move forward more rapidly; we need to develop a comprehensive plan."

Whitley assured his father he had been working precisely in that direction.

"And it has become especially intriguing in light of a new angle we discovered," he revealed. "Maybe we'll be able to kill the proverbial two birds with one stone."

"Meaning?"

"Meaning by doing their homework, my people have discovered something right under our noses all the time that we never knew existed," Whitley stated proudly. "We might well have a link between the problem of the commons and Chris Cadia's Future Generations that we can exploit."

"Yes?"

"Yes indeed, Sir," replied the son. "As you might recall from my reports, a man named Tomas Hernandez is one of the leaders in the supra-group calling itself Commons Rising. Hernandez is a vocal proponent of the dis-enclosure ideology that's fighting privatization and catching fire among the rabble identifying themselves as commoners. Well, several years ago, his wife Linda was a raft guide and fairly close friend with – as you call her – my 'activist dupe,' Sapphire MacKenzie."

"Okay, you've got a connection," agreed the old man, "but where do you intend to go with it?"

"I think it is time for me to get personally involved with Sapphire MacKenzie again," replied Whitley. "Though I've fed her support funds for years and she's unwittingly supplied me with information, I haven't seen her in person since I met her on the Salmon River in Idaho all those years ago. I think it's time for me to see what I can personally draw out of her – and maybe short circuit all the rumbling chaos in the Northwest."

Glancing at his wristwatch and nodding, the elder Dellenbach mentioned, "I've got to get going. If anyone can get to the bottom of this mess that's costing us millions every day, maybe you can do it."

Rising, Theodore Dellenbach shook his son's hand as he also stood.

"Why don't you stay the night, Son?" asked the old man. "Get some rest, get rid of the jet lag, and enjoy Hawaii. Maybe even take in a beach."

Whitley demurred, stating it was imperative that he journey to the Northwest with all haste.

"The beds on our jets are quite sufficient," he stated. "I'll be well rested when I arrive in Seattle."

"May you have a pleasant trip, Son," bid Theodore Dellenbach, "and success in your ventures."

"Same to you, Father," replied Whitley. "Safe travels."

CHAPTER EIGHTEEN

They had waited an extra forty-five minutes for more to show. Unfortunately, at this point, it didn't appear the rest of the representatives were coming. Perhaps half their normal number, only about twenty-five or thirty, had made it to the Saturday afternoon meeting in the rented West Seattle high school cafeteria. By now it must be assumed the remainder would not be coming.

Considering the circumstances, however, the Commons Rising delegates that were in attendance understood the difficulties they were all currently facing. No one realistically expected the five delegates from various eastern Washington and Oregon water commons to make the trip due to travel restrictions in place as a result of the train derailments.

The extra security and resulting delays on ferries could explain why the doctor-patient commons rep and others from coastal Washington were either late or not coming. And the clamp down on the border was likely the reason no one from the B.C./Salish Sea fisheries commons and other B.C. based commons were here. Between all that and random roadblocks throughout Washington State, it was perhaps amazing in itself to Tomas Hernandez that this many Commons Rising representatives had found their way here at all.

Lacking a firm agenda with so many of their comrades absent, those present spoke mostly about the alleged acts of the terrorist group Future Generations and how they might affect commons throughout Cascadia.

Many agreed with Conner Belhaven, a representative from a large seed exchange commons in Oregon, when he stated that the actions of Future Generations could only be detrimental to all commons in Cascadia.

"Empire already sees us as a primary threat to their State/Market system," Belhaven declared. "They will use the terrorism as an excuse to come after us, even though we have absolutely no connection with the Future Generations group and their climate wars."

"And that's precisely why we must stand firmly together," Tomas had proclaimed. "The solidarity of all the commons is what gives us our strength."

There had been murmurs of approval at such sentiments, especially from the ever-dependable Wade Nash representing the forestry commons from Coeur d'Alene and north Idaho. But even Tomas knew his words rang hollow just by the fact that half their number was missing today.

A man that Tomas didn't know very well named Ridley, who was the rep from a Cascadia-wide commons that advocated open source software programming, advocated an all-together different approach.

"I agree that the forces currently governing Cascadia see our anti-privatization campaigns in favor of a sharing economy as a reason to attack us, even if under the false pretenses of connecting us with Future Generations," noted Ridley. "And for that reason it may be fitting to cease activities for a time. We become less visible, we permit these events to blow over, and we surface again when we are no longer a target."

Some agreed with Ridley, and some did not. Tomas Hernandez was one that strongly disagreed.

"We must have solidarity among all commoners," Tomas stated adamantly, "for that is what ties us together. All commons must stand proudly against intimidation by the State, by Empire."

It was just about then that ten or twelve rough looking men filed into the cafeteria and stood next to the wall where the Cascadia Doug flag had been hung. Saying nothing, they glared ominously at the Commons Rising representatives – who fidgeted nervously, feeling threatened.

Millie Hadley, a delegate representing one of the northwest food commons, was fully aware of the intruders but defiantly carried on with what she had intended to say.

"We are miniscule against the might of Empire," Hadley declared, "but we have our constitutional rights and they must respect that."

"Unless you side with the terrorists," the lead thug against the wall interrupted loudly. With an exaggerated display of showmanship he ripped the Cascadia flag behind him off the wall and cast it to the floor.

"We've learned you people associate with those wanting revolution," the hooligan challenged, "and we're going to shut you down."

Hernandez shook his head; he'd seen this shit show too many times. Growing up in Stockton, California, down by the tracks, they'd called these types "hombres." He'd had to fight against them; he'd had to protect his sister and join friends against them. But whatever you called them, first and foremost they were bullies through and through.

"You have no right to threaten us, much less interrupt," Tomas said calmly to the leader.

"Hey, it's free speech, Dude," the lead goon shot back. "We all got it, we're all free to give it."

Hernandez had no intention of backing down.

"This is a private meeting in a rented venue," he stated, deliberately pulling his cell phone from a pocket. "If you don't leave immediately, I'm calling the police."

Insolently, the head hombre looked among his fellow ruffians and laughed. "How do you like that?" he asked them all.

Turning to Tomas, he egged him on. "Go ahead and call the cops: they'll arrest you for trying to destroy the American way of life."

Hernandez stood firm. "If you don't immediately walk out the same door you walked in, I'm calling the police."

At this, the intruders again shared hearty laughter and the leader told Tomas they would leave.

"But we'll be watching you," the head hombre promised as he exited the cafeteria.

Shortly thereafter, some of the representatives abruptly departed while others fell into small groups. Minutes later, those still remaining began to disperse.

As he passed Tomas on his way out, Ridley said, "We must let this all pass over for a time, and come back stronger after the storm."

Hernandez was prepared to rebut, and then Ridley was gone and the Commons Rising meeting simply dissolved.

Hernandez was almost the last to leave and by then the school parking lot was virtually empty. As he approached his car, however, three gangs of hombres came running at him from different directions.

Initially, they pushed him violently about in a closing circle until suddenly his arms were pinned behind him. Four or five solid blows to the gut doubled him over, and dropped him to his hands and knees.

The familiar voice of the head hombre was in his ear. "Tell us about Chris Cadia."

Gasping for air, Tomas mustered, "I don't know any Chris Cadia."

"We certainly don't," said another voice, "but we're pretty sure you do."

"I don't know any Chris Cadia," he protested again.

"That's okay, you will remember all about him," the lead thug promised. "You'll eventually remember because we know all about you."

Still sucking air, Tomas didn't know what they were talking about.

"Yes, we know all about you, Hernandez," said the leader.

"And where you live in Edmonds," claimed another new voice.

"So a few words of advice," the head hombre snarled. "Drop this commons shit, stay away from your terrorist friend, and you'll live a safer life."

"And so will your family," someone else chimed in. "We know where Grandma lives and we know about your pretty wife."

"We also know about your kiddies, little Cassie and Kyle," the leader was talking again. "You certainly wouldn't want anything to happen to little Cassie and Kyle, would you?"

In anger, Hernandez started to rise. "You sons of bitches."

The blow into the chest from the steel-toed boot lifted Tomas into the air and landed him on his back. Almost immediately the lead hombre had a firm grip on Hernandez's hair. Without a second thought he lifted Tomas' head and slammed it down onto the asphalt of the parking lot.

"Consider what we've said, okay?" the leader said as he and his fellow goons left.

Wretchedly sprawled out, it took Tomas some time to come to himself. Finally, dazed and in pain, he rose and stumbled toward his car. He fumbled for the keys in his pocket for what seemed an eternity before at last opening the door.

It was only when he agonizingly moved to sit down in the driver's seat though, that he recalled he'd peed himself when they threatened the lives of his kids.

CHAPTER NINETEEN

"Is this Stone McClelland?"

"Speaking," he said into the phone.

"He never knew your name before, you know," said the voice in McClelland's ear.

"Who didn't know my name?"

"Someone you're looking for."

"Who are you?" McClelland demanded.

"Someone representing him," replied the voice. "The problem is: he's not going to speak directly to you. In all likelihood, and with good reason, he figures he could be walking into a trap."

"So, who are you?"

The question was ignored. "He said he literally owes his life to you. That's why he's willing to have me contact you for him. And I'll convey whatever you need to say to him."

"I'll only talk to him," McClelland shot back gruffly. "That's why I'm here."

"Then you might as well leave," Stone heard in his ear, "because you only talk to him through me."

McClelland immediately perceived the predicament he was in.

"How do I know you represent him?" he countered.

"For starters," the voice seemed to smirk, "he told me about the Navajo Nation holding cells in northern Arizona. He also said it was pretty cold concrete to try to sleep on all night. But that's probably not enough for you."

"Not even close."

"Okay, let's try this," offered the voice. "He told me about when you released him at the scenic turnout where Spore Master Harry Wimple's truck was still parked. He also described the mostly Navajo vendors and booths that were also at the scenic turnout. Are we getting warmer now?"

"It's still not enough," McClelland barked back.

"Okay, we'll try again." The voice was unperturbed. "He said you told him that no one would ever know he was apprehended with the Spore Master. Everything had been arranged, he assumed, with the Navajo authorities in charge. In fact, he made me memorize something else you told him that day. You said, 'The Native American, indigenous people everywhere, understand imperial overreach more viscerally than the rest of us will ever know.'"

The silence from Stone McClelland was utter and complete.

Eventually, the voice on the phone asked, "Is that enough or do you need more?"

"That's enough," McClelland replied sullenly. "When and where do I meet you?"

Stone heard a chuckle in his ear.

"Oh, I'll be in touch," the voice promised. Rhetorically, he then asked, "You like Bainbridge Island, don't you?"

"I suppose."

"Well, when you come to visit," requested the voice, "make certain you are alone and have no ulterior motives in your soul. Because if it's a trap, you'll be left empty handed. Do you know what that means?"

"Not exactly."

"Do you recall what happened at the Ritzville post office a few days ago?"

Stone McClelland's tone was leaden. "I believe I'm aware of what you're referring to."

"Well, just to let you know," the voice explained patiently, "I prefer sodium cyanide to the potassium cyanide that they took. From what I've read, it might, or might not be, faster acting. Regardless, the effects of potassium cyanide and sodium cyanide are identical. Death occurs by hypoxia of neural tissue. Does that make sense?"

McClelland's response was emotionless. "I suppose it does."

"You know what precisely is fitted into my tooth," continued the voice. "Remember, if the meeting you desire is a trap, all I do is bite down and you lose your connection with Chris Soles forever. Do you understand?"

"I understand completely."

"Good. And there's one more thing," the voice hastened to add. "I'm calling on a burner phone that will be destroyed as soon as we hang up, so the caller ID will be useless. Do you understand?"

"I understand completely."

"Okay then, I'll be in touch," promised the voice. "Ta-ta for now, Mister Stone McClelland."

***

He thought they were back when the pounding began on the car window. Still hazy, Tomas tried to turn the key in the ignition to leave. And then the door opened.

Instinctively, he raised his left arm to shield himself from the blow. But there was no assault coming.

"Tomas, Tomas!" cried his Commons Rising friend from Idaho, Wade Nash. "I saw them leaving you on the ground as I came out of the school and ran here as fast as I could."

Hernandez was relieved. "Oh, Wade, it's you. I thought they'd come back."

"Are you okay?"

"I don't know," Tomas replied, a little shaky, "but I think I'm going to have a bad headache."

"Well," Nash declared with certainty, "we've got to call the police."

"Hold on," Hernandez balked. "I don't think so. That just means trouble for us; the police state isn't on our side."

"No way," Wade objected, as he pulled a cell phone from his pocket, "I'm calling the police right now."

Tomas let him proceed. After all, he wasn't thinking too clearly and Wade was the young, energetic idealist that perhaps knew better than he did, for now.

It took the police seven or eight minutes to arrive. During that time, Tomas mentioned it was his inclination that the thugs that roughed him up were probably the hired vigilante type. He also told

Wade what they said to him and how they threatened his family.

"Well, it's a damn good thing the police are coming," Nash proclaimed, "so we can get this all on the record."

Tomas clearly perceived that Wade was deeply affected when he spoke of threats to his family. The pain from Wade Nash's last year was never very far below the surface, and rose to prominence whenever someone else's relationships were threatened.

About eight or nine months ago, in the backwoods of northern Idaho, one of the forestry common's tree planting trucks collided head-on with one of their tree culling trucks and the result was a disaster. Three people died: two were tree planters and one in the log culling truck. Wade Nash's fiancé was one of the tree planters that died and he was devastated.

For several months Nash was overwhelmed, but eventually he began to work through his grief by redoubling his efforts in their forestry commons. For his toil, his fellow commoners had elected him their representative to the new Commons Rising coalition and he undertook his duties with great vigor.

A minute after the first police car arrived, a backup also pulled into the school parking lot with lights blazing. The police interviewed each man separately, then spoke among themselves for several minutes assumedly to check possible divergences between individual accounts of what transpired.

The officers then split Tomas and Wade once again, and asked whether they could identify their assailants, as well as asking for names of those Commons Rising representatives that attended the meeting.

As the cop was inquiring of Hernandez regarding those in Commons Rising, Tomas began to have great misgivings. Saying a bit misleadingly that he'd didn't know everyone in attendance, Tomas only mentioned a few of the more publically known attendees like himself, since the authorities were probably aware of them anyway.

Eventually, after completing their on-scene reports, the officers let Tomas and Wade go without a trip to the station. Wade told Tomas that – depending on roadblocks across the state – he was intending to travel back to Coeur d'Alene, but was going to stop and visit his sister for the evening, halfway across the state in Moses Lake, Washington.

He also insisted on following Tomas home to Edmonds to make sure he made it okay.

"Really, Wade," Tomas protested, "that's not necessary. Except for the headache, I'm doing much better now."

But Wade wouldn't hear of it. He was going to follow Tomas to his house in Edmonds, make sure he was okay, and that was that.

For the most part, they drove the twenty to twenty-five minute trip north on Interstate 5. Nash was on Hernandez's tail for the entire distance and was right behind him when Tomas stopped in front of his house.

Stepping out of his car, Tomas walked back to Wade's pickup truck to thank him for his concern. He also made certain Wade knew the best route from Edmonds to join Interstate 90 for his trip over the Cascades.

Tomas watched as Wade Nash waved and drove off.

As he turned and walked toward his front door, Tomas knew he had to tell Linda about the hombres and their threats. In truth, he was less worried about the hired thugs, than he was about his encounter with the police – and how they would enforce the law.

**

Sapphire knew the voice, but it didn't match the place. Dumfounded, she was at a loss for words.

He repeated his question once more, and this time, added a little more.

"Do you know where the Seagull Café is?" he asked again. He then tossed in, "Just up from the ferry."

"Of course, I know where it is," Sapphire exclaimed. "It's down the street from my office."

"Ah, you know the place!" he rejoined triumphantly. "So if you can take some time off for a cup of coffee, why don't you come join me?"

"What? You're here?" Sapphire was confused and exultant at the same time. "Whitey, why didn't you tell me you were coming? How long are you here for?"

"I'll explain it all at the restaurant," he laughed. "That is, if you'll join me."

"Of course, I will," she said excitedly. "I'll be right there."

It took Sapphire mere minutes to snatch up her purse, exit the office, and then trot down three blocks and across the street to the Seagull Café. Inside, she immediately spotted Whitey sitting at the far end of the restaurant, by the plate glass windows overlooking Eagle Harbor.

Although she hadn't seen him in years, he was as handsome as ever. Slim and trim with perfectly sculpted hair, Whitey projected even at a distance the same dominant and confident aura he had carried when she first met him on the Salmon River. He might have aged some from what she remembered, but in Sapphire's eyes it only made him appear stronger and more appealing.

He stood as she approached and launched herself into his arms.

"What a fantastic surprise!" she proclaimed as they hugged. "It's been so many years!"

"Yes it has," he agreed, smiling. They loosened their grip on one another and sat down.

"When I realized I might have a few hours after a family business trip to Portland and then Seattle," Whitey began, "I thought I'd hop a ferry and see if I could meet up with you."

Very briefly, Whitey explained to Sapphire that his wife's aunt in Portland had recently passed away and his wife had been named executor of the estate. Also in the aunt's will, if his wife couldn't perform, Whitey was designated in her stead.

"So I had to meet with some lawyers in Portland yesterday," he told her, "and then flew to Seattle to meet with an attorney here. We finished up sooner than expected and with a couple extra hours before I fly back east, on the spur of the moment I thought I'd see if I could catch up with you."

"Why, that's very kind," she said tenderly. At the same time, Sapphire recognized the underlying reason he was here was that his wife was unable to perform her duties as primary executor. She felt genuinely sorry for Whitey and his family; accordingly, she asked after the health of his wife.

"Oh, it's not good, it's never good," he admitted mournfully. "I think I might have mentioned she has a cancer that keeps her bedridden most of the time, but that's only the half of it. Before all that started she was struck dumb by a mental instability that rendered her mostly incapable of dealing with the outside world. We've kept it all hush-hush, but that's mostly for her sake."

"I'm so sorry," Sapphire said earnestly, as she reached across the table to take his hand in hers.

Whitey allowed the grasp as he stared into her intensely blue eyes.

"Frankly, Sapphire," he conceded, "I've never felt so alone in my life. And to be honest, maybe that's just part of why I wanted to talk with you in the little time I had."

Abruptly though, Whitey recoiled. He moved his hand away from hers and off the table. "Maybe I've said enough," he stated. "Perhaps the less you know about my background the better it is for you, especially if they ever investigate your money trail."

Once more she felt immensely sorry for this kind and generous man; she vowed to herself to do anything she could to make his life better.

"I think I understand," replied Sapphire, "and I thank you for all you've done for me and the revolutionary cause over the years."

Whitey was about to say something else when a waitress popped up and asked if they were ready to order lunch. Menus were on the table but after a cursory review, Sapphire said she wasn't really hungry and would prefer a latte. Whitey followed suit and the waitress scurried away.

"All that family stuff merely created an unexpected opportunity to visit," Whitey continued. "But besides just being able to see you again, I have some genuine concern about the situation you and others that are particularly outspoken will now find themselves in."

"What others?"

"People from the Commons movement, perhaps," replied Whitey. "And particularly those leaders at the forefront in the new supra-group Commons Rising, like Tomas Hernandez. Do you know him?"

Sapphire nodded. "I think I might have met him at a protest meeting."

Whitey thoughtfully gauged and registered her reply. "But I thought the people from the commons weren't attending your protests, preferring instead to work through their own organizational structure."

With a shrug, she responded, "Well, then maybe I don't know him."

"No matter," Whitey returned briskly. "What I am personally concerned about is your situation."

"My situation?"

"Yes, your situation," he affirmed. "Back east, inside the Beltway, it's being said there are major restrictions coming to the Northwest. Because of the terrorism and lawlessness, a severe clampdown is in the offing. Already central Washington State is trussed up because of the oil train explosions, but more is coming. Likely in the next week there will be a major extension of highway checkpoints, as well as at airports, ferries, and bus terminals. It's going to be a massive dragnet intended to snare the terrorists. Everyone will be affected – especially those prominent in movements against the state."

"That will solve absolutely nothing," Sapphire stated emphatically.

"Why do you say that?"

Sapphire didn't answer his question; instead, she asked him if he remembered what John F. Kennedy said in 1962.

Whitey smiled. "No, but I'm sure you probably do."

She quoted: "Those who make peaceful revolution impossible will make violent revolution inevitable."

Whitey reacted as if he didn't hear, but Sapphire was so enthused by his simply being there that it didn't matter.

"And the revolution, one way or another, is already underway," she emphasized.

Whitey shrugged his shoulders. "Merely a word to the wise," he stated.

Lattes in hand, the waitress delivered the drinks, and asked if Whitey and Sapphire might require anything else. They each replied in the negative and the waitress was on her way.

"What I'm particularly worried about in relation to you is this Chris Cadia and the suicidal fanaticism his people are displaying," Whitey stated unabashedly. "As a result, the government sees a terror group with no moral core; the authorities then, standing on what they believe solid principles, will righteously believe it their duty to crush these anti-humans and any others remotely connected to them. And I'm afraid that could well include you and your people, Sapphire."

"Two things, Whitey," she simply replied. "First, 'the revolutionist is a person doomed.' That's what Sergei Nechaev wrote in the 1800s in his 'Catechism of a Revolutionist.' It was true then, it's true today. He also said that the revolutionist 'has no personal interests, no business affairs, no emotions, no attachments, no property, and no name. Everything in him is wholly absorbed in the single thought and the single passion for revolution.' Those in the group calling themselves 'Representatives of Future Generations' have that single passion. For the cause, they don't care if they are doomed."

Whitey nodded in apparent agreement. "And the second thing?"

"There's something wrong with the big picture we're all getting."

"Meaning?"

"If this Chris Cadia is the same guy I met in Port Townsend on the Fourth of July," Sapphire posited, "then he isn't leading Future Generations. The nature of the guy I met was pointedly non-violent."

"Okay," pressed Whitey, "Then who is actually running Future Generations?"

"I wouldn't know," Sapphire lied. "I'm busy with my own protests and don't have time for colluding with terrorists. And anymore, since the police state seems to know just about everything we plan before we do, I'm sure you could ask the informers that are embedded in our Free Cascadia organization if we deal with terrorists, and you'd get the same answer."

Realizing he'd nearly pushed too far once again, Whitey immediately backtracked. "All that is surely not my concern and I hope you didn't take it that way. I'm just personally worried about you in light of all the escalating civil disorder in the Northwest."

Sapphire gazed deep into Whitey's dignified face and believed she found sincerity there. She smiled at him and he smiled back at her.

Soon thereafter, Whitey was checked his watch.

"I'm afraid I've got to go," he said. "The next ferry is leaving shortly. I'm on a tight schedule to catch my flight and resume my caregiver duties for my wife."

"I'm sorry you have to leave so soon," sighed Sapphire. "And you've hardly had a sip of your latte."

"I'll take it with me," he replied, standing. "But listen, it's likely I'll have to get together with the estate attorney in Seattle again. If so, maybe you could meet me over there."

"Do you mean it?" asked Sapphire, rising from her seat as well, and quite exhilarated. "I'd love to see you if you come back; please do."

"I will," Whitey promised.

They exchanged a quick kiss on the lips. Then, with latte in hand, Whitey hustled to the cashier station and requested a to-go cup for his drink. After receiving his drink and paying their bill, Whitey waved at Sapphire on his way out the door.

Quite charmed, she waved back; she couldn't wait to see him again.

One of the last foot passengers to transit the ferry terminal and find a seat before the boat cast off to Seattle, Whitley immediately removed his phone from a coat pocket. He didn't know if his father would receive the text message in North Korea or after he departed the country, but knew he expected it regardless.

Wasting no time, Whitley keyed in: *"Met with unwitting informant in Washington State today. Little new of substance at this time, but laid groundwork for a spilling of all the beans at next meeting. Hope your travels go well."*

He touched send on the screen and the message was on its way.

CHAPTER TWENTY

Stone McClelland had followed instructions.

Purposely, he had not mentioned the upcoming meeting with his handler, Roger, who represented Whitley Dellenbach. He was coming alone.

He had hopped an afternoon ferry as a foot passenger from Seattle to Bainbridge Island. He had taken a walk on the waterfront trail that began close to the ferry terminal building. He was now in the small park along the trail that was his destination, and he was seated at the picnic table by the time he was supposed to be.

And he had waited. He had been there fifteen minutes now, going on twenty, and nothing had happened.

Above the park were some empty tennis courts and below was a view of Eagle Harbor. On either side was greenery where the waterfront trail entered and exited.

When he found the small park and sat down, a man had already been playing fetch with his Labrador retriever. Occasionally passersby strolled the trail from one side of the greenery to the other, down between Stone and his harbor view. Some of the hikers glanced in his direction; most rambled by without giving him a second thought.

For the lack of anything better to do, McClelland watched the man throw a tennis ball to the dog, again and again and again. The dog was devoted, even obsessed, in his pursuit of the ball, and always laid it at his master's feet upon returning while intently waiting for another toss. The black lab's passion for the game entertained Stone for some time, but eventually he grew bored as his thoughts shifted to Lorien.

He had told only her last night on the phone that he was coming to meet "the voice." He also mentioned how he'd been told previously to bring along "no ulterior motives in his soul."

"At the time," he told his wife, with a chuckle, "I thought that would be something you would say."

"It is something I would say," Lorien had firmly asserted. "It's the only way you'll resolve your conflict."

Stone attempted to object. "But if Chris Soles has caused murder, destruction, and terror, how can I not go with ulterior motives? Especially too, when I'm being paid so generously to pursue him for all his misdeeds?"

"It's very simple," Lorien replied.

"What do you mean?"

"Go there like 'the voice' said," she had directed him, "with no ulterior motives in your soul."

Admittedly, Lorien retained an innate wisdom that he lacked, so he had promised he would do his best. But really, as he sat at the picnic table waiting for someone to show up, was he capable of purging his ulterior motives? It wasn't very likely...

Presently, the guy tossing the ball to his dog took the object of the canine's obsession away and deposited in a nearby backpack. He then extracted a bowl and a canteen of water as he walked in Stone's direction.

Approaching the picnic table, he and the dog drew close to Stone.

"Do you mind if I share a seat and read the paper," he asked, "while my dog gets some water and takes a rest?"

"It's public seating, open to all," McClelland remarked placidly.

From the canteen the man poured water into the dog's bowl and the lab began eagerly lapping it up. After topping off the bowl once more, he snatched a newspaper from his backpack. He opened it up, and pulling his broad brimmed hat fully over his forehead, sat reading silently at the far end of the table. The dog finally finished drinking; he then dropped upon his belly next to the master with tongue hanging out and breathing heavily.

Naturally, McClelland had studied the man as he approached as would anyone by virtue of training long instilled, but in this character he saw only the total lack of anything at all extraordinary. In fact, it was his utter run-of-the-mill commonness that would make him totally forgettable if passing him by on the street.

Compound all that with the blandness he exuded now as he read the paper, and Stone knew why the obsessed Labrador retriever held much more interest for him than his master. Seemingly quite oblivious to Stone's presence at the other end of the park table, it wasn't long before McClelland's attention drifted from his tablemate.

A few minutes later, however, the man at the end of the picnic table apparently began talking to his newspaper.

Staring downward, the fellow appeared quite odd as he asked, "What are you seeking here in Cascadia? What are you questing toward?"

The man didn't appear to be talking to him, so Stone allowed him space to be a flake if that's what he was.

Still focused on his newspaper, the guy patiently inquired once more, "What are you seeking here in Cascadia? What are you questing toward?"

Feeling uneasy, Stone's silence continued. Then the man turned toward him.

"Is it vengeance, power, control, riches," he queried, "or perhaps equality, cooperation, the paradigm for a sustainable future – or what?"

Beginning to guess this might be the person he was coming to meet, McClelland was on guard but nevertheless attempted to answer honestly.

"Maybe it's as simple as justice and clarity," he replied.

"That's a start," the man acknowledged.

"Who are you?" asked McClelland.

The fellow donned a snide smile. "Call me Chris. That's whom you wanted to see, isn't it? Pretend I'm him."

Stone didn't see the same degree of humor in the situation.

"Chris sent me here because he wants to know, first of all," the man began, "why you set him free."

McClelland had no option but to answer as authentically as possible. "I don't know; maybe that's mostly why I'm here."

"Mostly?" wondered the man, raising his eyebrows. "What are the rest of the reasons? More to trap him than help him would be my guess. Regardless, I'm here representing him because you let him go – and he lived. Otherwise, he likely would have been killed with all the rest."

"And what worries me the most," admitted McClelland, "is that I set him free to ultimately commit murder and mayhem."

Immediately the man at the other end of the picnic table was shaking his head.

"That's not him," he averred. "It's all lies, fabrications, power plays, and corruption – everything that's been handed down with our patriarchal inheritance – and that's what he fights against."

Stone McClelland was silent, so his visitor at the public park table continued.

"What he must assume," suggested the man, as his dog rolled on its side to snooze, "is that Empire is behind you, and backing you, in their search for him. If that wasn't the case, why didn't you show up searching for him two years ago, or four years ago?"

McClelland chose to dodge the question. He said instead, "After the alleged kidnapping and murder in Utah, after the rail line bombings and oil tanker train derailments, I have an obligation to myself to get to the bottom of all this and short circuit the ongoing chaos if possible. Because I set him free, I have an obligation to pursue him in order to learn the truth."

"Very honorable," observed the man. "But if there was one thing he could tell you truthfully, it would be that he's done none of that. And yet, you won't listen when I say such things, so let me ask you: what do you want from him?"

Without dwelling at length upon the question, Stone simply replied, "Mostly I want my conscience clear."

"And how do you intend to do that?"

"Well, I suppose," McClelland said tentatively, "if he's the kind of person you say he is, I guess it's a matter of developing trust between us and see where it goes from there."

"I'm wondering how that might be accomplished."

"Start slow, then let it grow bigger," was Stone's reply. "Every organization has its spies and informers that trade information and sow disinformation. I can help him find those that are a threat to him and his organization."

"Sorry," said the man, "but he doesn't have an organization. He merely has a tight and vast network of friends throughout Cascadia that share a similar mindset."

"Well, maybe some of those friends could use some help."

"From who?"

"I still have friends in government that owe me favors."

"Like who?"

"For starters," replied McClelland, "there's a good friend of mine in the Seattle FBI office who's on the task force investigating the Future Generations terror case."

"Interesting," mused the guy at the other end of the table. "And what would you want in trade from him so that the trust you speak of can begin to blossom?"

The answer was simple for Stone McClelland. "Like I said, I feel an obligation to help end all this, one way or the other, by virtue of my having set him free. If he's who you say he is, I'll do what I can to assist him. Keep in mind I already let him go free once."

"And you've been paying for it ever since," observed the guy at his table.

"Precisely," admitted McClelland. "But, by the same token, if he is the person that murdered the girl in Utah and initiated all this terrorism in the Northwest, you tell him direct from me that'll I be the one that will hunt him to the very ends of the earth."

The man nodded. "I understand that, but let me ask again so it's very clear to me. What do you seek from him?"

"My peace of mind," Stone stated without hesitation.

The visitor to McClelland's table studied him for a moment and then nodded.

"I guess that's good enough for now," he allowed. "I'll let him know what you said."

Standing, the man called to his dog. "Okay, Fido, let's go."

Instantly, the black lab was back on his feet fully alert, his tail was wagging, and looked ready to be tossed the ball.

McClelland was chuckling. "Really, your dog's named Fido?"

"Sure, why not?" the fellow returned. "If you can pretend my name is Chris, I can pretend his name is Fido. Besides, he doesn't really care when you bring the ball out to play."

While the man picked up his backpack to depart, Stone remarked, "The cyanide tooth ampoule is a bluff, isn't it?"

"Is it really worth it for you to definitively find out?"

Stone McClelland was silent.

"I thought as much," the man noted.

As dog and master turned uphill toward the tennis courts to exit the park, the master said, "I'll be in touch."

***

After Chris dropped the black lab off at Elders Cecil and Myra Hanson's place on Madison Bay, they thanked him profusely for taking the dog out for some exercise. Their son and his family had left the canine with the old folks while on vacation and, as Cecil admitted, the lab's endless energy was a little too much to handle at their age.

From Madison Bay on the north end of Bainbridge Island, it was easy to hop back on State Highway 305, the main north-south route for the island. In only a matter of minutes he was exiting the lush Bainbridge forest of green and crossing the bridge that spanned the Agate Passage on the way to the Kitsap Peninsula.

His current destination was Poulsbo, maybe seven or eight miles away, but it was coming at him all too rapidly. To say he was more apprehensive and uneasy about the upcoming get-together than he was with his session with Stone McClelland would hardly be an understatement. And with every passing mile, his discomfiture grew.

When Kiri learned he had arranged an encounter with the ex-DEA agent that had set him free, she informed Chris she wouldn't be sitting around their cabin in the woods alone. Kiri told him she would have her own little meeting as well.

"With whom?" Chris wanted to know.

"With Sapphire MacKenzie," she spoke sharply. "We've got a few things to straighten out."

So Kiri had arranged a showdown with Sapphire through her old friend Linda Hernandez. Sapphire was willing to oblige and suggested they might rendezvous at the same seafood restaurant in Poulsbo overlooking Liberty Bay as they did before, since it was a favorite and a friend of hers was the longtime owner. In accordance with her wishes, Chris dropped Kiri off at the Fish House restaurant on his way to Bainbridge, although he had great misgivings about what might be coming as a result. And it was all the more so in light of Kiri's determined and almost grim demeanor before the upcoming confrontation.

The plan was that after his meeting with McClelland, he should proceed to the same family restroom as before. He was then to place the "Out of Order" sign on the door, lock it from the inside, and call telling he'd arrived. Kiri reasoned such measures were a judicious precaution, as it was perhaps better the less the three of them were seen together in public, the safer for all.

Following instructions, after Chris parked and entered the restaurant, he strolled directly to the familiar family restroom. The sign went up and the door was locked; he then called Kiri on his cell phone.

It took her a while to answer, but when she finally did, Kiri told Chris they would join him in a few minutes.

Almost fifteen minutes later, he heard them coming before there was ever a knock on the door. Initially, he didn't believe all the raucous laughter and giggles to be emanating from Kiri and Sapphire, but after the coded knock on the door, the unshackled merriment came right into the family washroom with them.

"Thanks for saving an open restroom for us when we both got to go," Kiri exclaimed.

"It must have been that last glass of wine," Sapphire exulted, all smiles.

"What do you mean 'last glass' of wine?" Kiri asked, while maneuvering directly to the open toilet, dropping her shorts and panties, and preparing to relieve herself. "It was that whole bottle of wine!"

"It must have been," agreed Sapphire.

While she peed, Kiri broke into cascades of giggles once again. "I still can't believe what you told that guy!"

"You should have seen his face!" Sapphire beamed happily. "It was a once in a lifetime expression."

"I imagine so," sniggered Kiri. She finished, pulled up panties and shorts, flushed and moved to the washbasin.

Having no idea what the women were talking about, Chris simply remained silent and thanked his lucky stars they weren't at each other's throat like he'd worried earlier.

Immediately after Kiri moved from the toilet, Sapphire was reprimanding her in jest.

"It took you long enough, girl," noted Sapphire, "I thought I was going to explode waiting for you."

"Well," Kiri shot back, "I was trying to make sure the seat was warmed up for you."

"That's what I love," Sapphire sniggered, "someone that's considerate."

In that small, open room Chris had little choice but to watch Sapphire MacKenzie yank down her shorts and undergarments, then position herself on the toilet. Neither could he close his ears to her strong and resounding stream as it tumbled onto the flat waters below. Feeling a little out of place and a bit awkward, Chris watched Sapphire's relieved expression turn mischievous as she shifted her gaze to him.

"You know," she said matter-of-factly to him, "we've got to quit meeting like this!"

Chris wasn't certain how to reply, but Kiri burst into laughter.

"You are just something else!" Kiri exclaimed to Sapphire.

As Sapphire wiped, flushed, and readjusted her clothing before her turn at the sink, Chris noted, "Looks like the girls have been having some fun."

"*Some* fun?" objected Sapphire, while turning the water on at washbasin, "I told Kiri she's the little sister I never had."

"And I told Sapphire she was the other sister I never knew," averred Kiri.

"Well, you both apparently got on together pretty well in such a short time," observed Chris.

"It's because we talked about nearly everything under the sun," said Sapphire, drying her hands. "And we solved all the world's problems."

"Well, not all of them, but close," Kiri qualified the statement. To Chris, she said, "It was actually a lot of stuff you probably wouldn't understand."

"Yeah," Sapphire agreed, "and we both know more about you than you'll ever know."

They giggled conspiratorially; Chris was definitely the odd one out.

"But don't worry, we're both on your side," Kiri assured him.

"One reason," Sapphire suggested, "is because we figure you're going to need all the help you can get."

"That's just the way it is," Kiri chuckled. "Guys are kind of helpless sometimes."

Chris smiled. "If that's the way it is, then it isn't all bad. I'll take whatever help I can get from you two."

As things calmed a tad, Kiri asked Chris almost as an aside how is meeting on Bainbridge went.

"Productive and positive, for the most part," he replied. "But I'm still not certain what he's ultimately after."

"Just what we thought, huh Sapphire?" said Kiri.

"Yep," she replied.

"Well, at least you've got us two sisters to guide you around the bumps in the road," Kiri asserted.

"True indeed," Sapphire agreed. "We'll do what we can to make sure your backside is covered."

With smiles all around, Kiri announced, "Okay, time to go and time for hugs!"

Without hesitation the two women enwrapped tightly in each other's arms amid expressions such as, "Oh, it was such a delightful time," and, "Yes, we've got to do it again!" before separating.

Turning to Chris, Kiri declared, "It's your turn now; give Sapphire a big hug."

Feeling a little awkward once again, he and Sapphire embraced one another tentatively, and then the hug seemed to grow of itself without restraint. He registered that her ample breasts were hard pressed into his chest, even as each finger on each of her hands was compressing his whole body into her.

And then it was over, way too soon.

Kiri and Sapphire exchanged their final goodbyes. They all then departed their favorite family restroom, in Poulsbo's popular seafood restaurant overlooking Liberty Bay.

CHAPTER TWENTY-ONE

She closed the door to her apartment like she was closing the door on her life.

Again.

But she couldn't let anyone get near; it was too dangerous for them.

Some of the girls in the office had invited Carolyn along for a Friday after work drink, and she wanted to go. It just wasn't a smart thing to do, even if the pressure on her had ostensibly decreased.

Simply put, even now she didn't dare drag others anywhere close to her predicament if she could help it.

The national and local news throughout the day had only heightened her advanced anxiety levels, and justifiably tormented her anew concerning the well being of her brothers. Major announcements from TV, radio, newspapers, the Internet, and social media all screamed of upcoming curbs and controls. Throughout Washington and Oregon they were to gradually go into effect over the weekend and to be fully implemented by the end of the following week.

"Expect To Be Inconvenienced!" the public service announcements blared incessantly from every media source, even finding their way into the cloistered accounting office where Carolyn worked.

An all-out dragnet was promised to limit Future Generations' terrorism opportunities, with the express intent of capturing the insurrectionists – dead or alive – and ending their reign of terror forever.

Specifically targeted would be any and all means of transportation to slow and snare the adversaries of a free and secure America, it was proclaimed. Armed checkpoints were to be established at all traffic hubs, including ferries, bus stations, and airports. Governmental issued picture I.D.'s would be required of all travelers and all information garnered would be submitted to a cloud database to link previously unknown and interwoven connections.

Going even further, all roadways in both states would be subject to the same level of scrutiny. Random, roving roadblocks would be erected on multiple highways and byways, including major interstate highways. No one, and no place, would be exempt from this heightened pursuit of the terrorists plaguing the Northwest.

"Expect To Be Inconvenienced!" were the watchwords being drilled into the public's collective psyche.

With all this going down, and after what her brother Billy told her last night, how could she possibly saunter out for some light-hearted laughs with her co-workers after hours?

No, Carolyn knew she had to go straight home, talk to no one, then close and lock her door. She had to get in touch with Kiri as soon as possible – and not just over the phone, but in person.

At the kitchen table, she opened up her computer. When the wifi connection was established, she clicked the bookmark she needed.

Then, utilizing the next to last burner phone they had left her with before Garf declared a change in tactics, Carolyn tapped in a number that Kiri assured her was safe.

In a text message, she wrote: *"Must meet you in person. Important. Can you make it to Edmonds as a foot passenger on a Sunday morning ferry from Kingston?"* She signed it, *"C."*

Carolyn sent the message and stared at her computer, lost in thought. A few minutes later there was a beep from the burner phone. She tapped on the screen to open the reply from Kiri.

"Absolutely. When/where do we meet?"

Staring at the state ferry schedules on the screen in front of her, Carolyn keyed in the Kingston departure time she wanted for Kiri's trip across Puget Sound to Edmonds.

She continued with, *"You'll see me when you get off. Follow at a distance and act like you don't know me. Got it?"*

"Got it!" was Kiri's immediate reply.

***

"I can't fucking believe it," Billy Maxwell exclaimed. "Are you serious, Garf?"

"I'm deadly serious," Taylor shot back. "As always. After hearing the arrogant comments from B.C.'s Premier once U.S. announced their crackdown, it's time to make him aware of the new reality evolving in this world. It's time he learned first hand that Cascadia is a homogenous bio-region, not separate fiefdoms of domineering Canadian and American business corporations."

"But Dude, we've been doing dry runs at Cherry Point for nearly two weeks preparing for Sunday night," protested Billy. "I thought you wanted our last mission before the tactical transition to strike both awe and terror into Empire's heart by taking out the biggest objective. And there's none bigger than Cherry Point."

"That's certainly true," Garf agreed, "but all players in Cascadia need to step up to the plate if they're in the game, and ex-oilman Premier Hoagland has to be called on to take his turn."

Safely ensconced in a vacation cottage on Birch Bay, in the very northwest tip of Washington, it was only a few quick miles north to Blaine, the Peace Arch crossing, and the Canadian border.   More importantly, they were even closer to massive fossil fuel facilities of Cherry Point, only minutes to the south.

Home to two enormous refineries, railway oil tanker cars were continually arriving and departing on the grid of rail lines surrounding Cherry Point. It was so busy that campers at near by Birch Bay State Park often complained sleep was impossible because of all the noise and vibrations shaking the ground.

Making matters worse, when the new American administration took office a few years ago, burning restrictions for all coal power plants were rescinded and exports of coal jumped exponentially. Responding to the opportunity, the repeatedly stalled Gateway Pacific Terminal at Cherry Point was revived and resurrected, quickly becoming North America's largest coal export facility as had once been projected.

Naturally, security was extremely tight at all Cherry Point facilities. Billy asked Garf if this weighed in his decision to shift targets at this late date.

"Not really," Taylor replied. "I think we could make valid strikes on Cherry Point with the suicide triads we've got prepared. But we are Cascadia. When the Premier of British Columbia makes comments like, 'we stand shoulder-to-shoulder with our U.S. friends and deplore the troublemakers that are intent on disrupting their own country,' or, how he was 'proud and confident that Canadians remained above the fray,' I think things have to change."

"So what do you propose?"

"Aren't some of our triad people from Canada?" asked Garf.

"Some of the best are from Canada," Billy assured him. "But they've all been trained separately and only know the three in their cell, so there aren't any that only represent America or Canada. They represent Cascadia and the hope for future generations."

"As do we all," nodded Garf. "But you can gather some triads with Canadian roots, can you not? I think they'd be particularly interested in a shift of targets at this point."

"Hell yes, I can find the right people; that's always been my job," Billy stated proudly. "But what's the target?"

"The target is perfect," Garf assured his friend. "There's only one hole in the planning that needs to be worked out, but the target is perfect."

"And the target is?" pushed Billy.

"You remember that marine terminal in metro Vancouver?" asked Garf. "It's in Burnaby, below that university up on the hill."

"You mean Simon Fraser University," said Billy. "And the terminal is called the Westridge Marine Terminal. That's where Sapphire's friend Polly Hawser and her people are always staging protests."

"And it's also where the Trans Mountain pipeline terminates," Garf stated.

"You mean the new twin Trans Mountain pipelines?" asked Billy. "The new pipeline was jammed in there a few years ago alongside the leaky piece of shit old pipeline. And that's why they had all the protests."

"Yep, that's the place," Garf acknowledged. "But do you know who the head oil executive was for the company that forced the pipeline deal through and runs the pipeline?"

"Let me guess," smiled Billy snidely, "could it be a certain ex-oilman, now politician, named Premier Hoagland?"

"Indeed, and that makes it the perfect target," repeated Taylor. "Just off the main public road that leads down to the gates of the marine terminal, you can see two enormous storage tanks used for jet fuel, or so they say. What I say – is we use two suicide triads for the mission. They rush the gate together, then one threesome uses incendiaries to blow the jet fuel depots, while the other triad pushes down towards the water to take out the terminal points for the pipelines."

Saying he thought the plan feasible, Billy nonetheless had misgivings because of the heightened level of alert surrounding the terminal as a result of years of protest. He asked Garf, "Is that security perimeter wrapped around the terminal grounds the hole in the plan?"

"Oh, not at all," Garf replied, brushing off the suggestion. "Heavily armed with explosives and weaponry, our people have the benefit of surprise when they storm the gates late at night. After that, they proceed directly to their respective missions. They have nothing to lose: after all, they're suicide squads."

Nodding ominously, Billy still wondered, "So what's the hole in the plans?"

"It's the border," stated Garf. "Of course we'll travel with the triads involved to set them on their mission, but we'll have to get across and back with any of them that live."

"Yeah, and the border is nearly sealed," said Billy, "at least according to the news. But don't worry; I think I can find an open road late at night. Let me get in touch with a friend whose family farm straddles the border between the Lynden crossing and Sumas. The hole in the plan might not be such a hole. Still, what about the rest of Sunday night and the sleeper cells?"

"Just because we're standing down at Cherry Point doesn't mean the sleeper cells shouldn't awaken once more and focus again on maiming everything fossil fuel," Garf replied. "This time, however, we engage only Washington, Oregon, and northern Idaho. Call off all sleeper cell activity in B.C. Let smug Premier Hoagland think the fossil fuel he rams through British Columbia isn't connected with the sleeper cell awakening Sunday night in the U.S. By the time the sun rises on Monday morning, the Premier will realize Cascadia has spoken and he'll be in it up to his ears as well."

Billy laughed luxuriously, sharing his friend's confidence.

"It's a good plan," he lauded Garf, "but I still think we could have made a big statement at Cherry Point."

"Okay," Garf assured him with a smile, "if we so choose, we can always cherry pick Cherry Point later on."

***

Even before Carolyn's mysterious, curious, and somewhat panicked text messages late on Friday afternoon, something was preoccupying Kiri. It distracted her enough to create an unusual distance between them that Chris decided for the time being to leave well enough alone.

She'd been like that off and on for a couple days, but he knew the spell would be broken at least temporarily over dinner. They had been invited over to Bob and Donna Carlson's place, the Elders that had gifted them the safe house cottage on their sprawling, wooded acreage. And sure enough, when they all sat down for one of Donna's superb home cooked meals, Kiri had been quite engaged in discussion of the day's news, including ramifications regarding the government's announced clamp down on its citizens and their rights.

But throughout the day Saturday, she drifted away lost in thought at times when they were taking a morning hike, and later when they were making a grocery list that afternoon. Kiri volunteered to do the shopping this time, since they agreed for safety purposes it was better to be seen out in public together as little as possible.

When she returned, Chris helped her put away the groceries, then observed as her mind floated off once again to some foreign destination. In his estimation, the more this happened of late, the more the tendency was for Kiri to become increasingly glum. And it was thus time, he reckoned, to initiate a suitable diversion.

As the last of the groceries made its way into the cupboards and fridge, Chris offhandedly mentioned, "If you need me, I'll be busy with a project in the bathroom," before he strolled away without another word.

A short time later Kiri, puzzled, approached the half open bathroom door wondering what his project was. She heard the sound of running water from the bathtub spout that was soon thereafter forcefully shut off. Next, Kiri heard water being gurgled into the tub from a container. When the sound stopped, Chris said, "Four."

What the hell was he doing?

Still clandestinely stationed outside the bathroom door, Kiri listened once again as the tub spout shot out water for ten or fifteen seconds and was once more abruptly shut off. Then, the pouring of water in the tub recommenced. When it was over, he announced, "Five."

Kiri opened the door and walked in. Holding a plastic gallon jug, Chris merely smiled and turned back to his project, once more filling the container. When it was full, he poured the contents into the tub with a resounding, "Six."

She watched him take care of numbers "Seven," and, "Eight," and suddenly a mischievous smirk surfaced on her face.

"Oh, so that's the game we're playing," grinned Kiri. "I'll be right back."

By the time Chris was dumping gallons number eleven and twelve into the tub, Kiri had dragged a chair into the bathroom. She positioned it so she could sit comfortably by propping her feet up at the end of the tub. She also had a notebook with dozens of papers she began sorting through.

On went the water, off went the water, and then into the tub.

"Thirteen," he called out, with his back to her.

As the water was turned on once more to fill the gallon jug, Kiri began reading from the papers she'd collected.

"It says here, depending on the species," she noted, "the life expectancy of a fly is eight days to two months, and in some cases up to a year. Also, there're more than 16,000 species of flies in North America alone."

"Ah, there's number Fourteen!" Chris exclaimed. "And we're just getting started."

"And guess what, Chris?" Kiri continued. "Millions of microorganisms may flourish in a single fly's gut, while a half-billion more swarm over its body and legs. Besides that, because they only have two wings, flies land often and thus deposit thousands of bacteria each time they land."

"That's nice," he replied. "Fifteen."

"But what might be really helpful for you to know as you're wasting both water and time," she remarked, "is that it says here when flies feed on waste, they collect pathogens on their legs and mouths. These pathogens are then transferred to food on tables or counters when a fly lands again. Flies regurgitate on solid food then they eat the liquid. They are capable of transmitting disease when they vomit, groom themselves, or just walk on surfaces."

"What a pretty picture you paint!" he exulted. "Remember though, the discussion is about the quantity of flies, not necessarily their more appealing attributes."

"Oh, don't you worry," she shot back. "I'm just getting started too."

"Sixteen!"

"Your efforts are feeble, laughable," she told him. "If you want to focus on quantity, try wrapping your head around this: One pair of flies can produce more than one million offspring through their offsprings' offspring in a matter or weeks."

"Seventeen."

Kiri shook her head, and then scanned her notes. "It appears you're not listening very attentively. Since that seems to be the case, let's concentrate on one single species of those 16,000 species found in North America alone. Okay?"

"Eighteen."

"Okay, that's fine," she answered for him. "Our discussion this afternoon will be on green bottle flies. They're the ones that are about the same size as houseflies and appear metallic green with portions of copper-green. But you're probably more familiar with them because they're classified as filth feeders that develop in and feed on dead animals, feces, garbage, and decomposing plants."

"How pleasant!" Chris smiled. "Nineteen!"

"Even while you're relishing such details," Kiri carried on, "let's train our attention once again, for your benefit, on their copious reproduction capabilities – as in *quantity* of flies. Let's start with a single adult female green bottle fly. She can deposit up to about 200 eggs that hatch and become larvae in 1 to 3 days. Within about 3 to 10 days, fully developed larvae leave and burrow into the soil. The development of the pupal stage takes around 6 to 14 days. After that adults emerge to feed on plant nectar, carcasses, or garbage. Yum, yum, yum! And in only about two weeks, the newly emerged female green bottle fly can begin laying her eggs."

Chris was already filling gallon number twenty-two to pour into the tub.

"It also says here that green bottle flies usually complete three or four generations per year," read Kiri. "All told, one female green bottle fly will lay about two thousand to three thousand eggs in her lifetime. That adds up to a lot of flies, and a lot of offspring through their offsprings' offspring. And that's only one species of flies!"

"And this is only one bathtub," remarked Chris, adding, "Number Twenty-Three."

"So what's that suppose to mean?" Kiri tossed back. "And how high are you going to fill it?"

As water poured into gallon twenty-four, he said, "I figured if I took it up to the overflow drain, that would probably give you a fair enough idea of how many gallons can be in a bathtub. And then I was going to let you imagine how many more were in a swimming pool, or even in a small pond, or a bigger lake. And that's still just for starters."

"Well, it'll obviously take you some time at your rate to even get the tub filled," observed Kiri. "So while you persist in your futile efforts, I'll do my best in attempting to enlighten you regarding the sheer quantity of flies on this planet by investigating yet another single species."

And so the late afternoon delightfully dashed onward as Kiri continued to read from her research and Chris kept filling the tub, gallon after gallon. When the height of the water finally reached the overflow drain and Chris had lost count about an hour later, both were all smiles and quite ready to exit the bathroom.

Together they prepared an evening meal and shared a bowl of ice cream afterwards. A streamed video followed and by bedtime, Kiri appeared more relaxed than she had been for some time. Whatever had been consuming her thoughts for the last several days had departed and she seemed to Chris her normal amicable self.

Appropriately attired as always, they kissed goodnight and she spooned back in next to him in bed, wrapped in his arms. When his erection awakened a short time later as it often did, she seemed to sigh in acknowledgement only to press her clothed backsides snug against it. In such a state, both blissfully surrendered to sleep shortly thereafter.

Yet if entry to sleep was wrapped in serenity for Kiri on Saturday night, the exit from her slumbers on Sunday morning was anything but.

Awakening to a great deal of thrashing about, Chris felt the warmth next to him depart with covers cast back in his direction. He waited for her return but with Kiri's side of the bed growing ever cooler, he finally rose in search of her.

He found her sitting outside upon the bench on the front deck with a blanket wrapped about her. Though the sun had yet to rise, it was a pleasant dawn at the height of summer, even if early. Chris took a seat next to Kiri and wrapped an arm about her shoulders.

For the longest time they sat there like that, unmoving. Eventually, he said, "Tell me what's going on."

Staring straight forward, after a deliberative delay, she merely uttered, "It came to me in a dream this time."

"What is it, Kiri?" Chris gently inquired.

"It's what's been coming into my mind of late," she remarked obliquely, "but this time it came in a dream."

Respecting her silence, Chris simply drew her tighter and she was secure in his consolation. In time, she appeared to change the subject.

"I think the nature of my prescience might be altering," she murmured.

"Really?"

"Yeah, I think so," Kiri replied, still gazing straight forward. "You once said my parents told you about our puppy that got killed by a car, and how I literally saw it happen in my own mind before it occurred. Well, you know what, I think the nature of that experience is changing as I get older."

"How so?"

Turning to Chris, Kiri noted, "For one thing, it's not nearly as direct anymore; it's much more ambiguous. These things come into my mind like a collection of recurrent feelings and events; they almost resemble riddles I have to figure out. It's like the darkly ambivalent aura that we approach and get around – yet it's still there in our way – that I felt before you encountered the ex-DEA agent. And it's like what's been coming at me the last several days, and now in my dreams. But I haven't got this one figured out at all."

"Tell me about it," Chris urged.

Kiri rested her hand on his thigh and said, "Okay."

She then commenced to verbally project for him a repetitive scene of a small, high mountain brook on a beautiful summer day. The tiny stream is trickling happily and peacefully down within its banks, with "Mozart, or one of those guys, playing music in the background.

"The small brook meets and joins others on the journey out of the high mountains, yet it's still a most pleasant day as the water slips and slides over rocks and around curves on its course downhill. Eventually, still teaming with other tributaries, it becomes a raging river – yet all is still well and good in its very naturalness – and it's here the music intensifies, reaching toward a crescendo.

"And then there's the waterfall," she continued, "where this whole massive river is released from the safety of the earth and plunges into the sky. There's a pool far below, but the music simply stops. And that's it."

"That's all?"

"That's it," she assured him. "It's been coming into my mind for days, precisely the same every time, and now it's invading my dreams."

Kiri and Chris sat for some time on the porch bench without speaking further. Both seemed content to be close. Churning over their own thoughts, they caught hints of the sun beginning to rise through the trees to the east.

Later, in preparation for the new security measures that were supposed to be implemented soon – or were already implemented – on the state ferry system, Kiri made a deliberate choice on which set of forged I.D.'s she would travel with. The least likely to raise a red flag, she calculated, would be those supplied by the Elders that showed a Washington State driver's license with a Poulsbo address, along with a student identification card from the local campus of Olympic Community College.

It only took about twenty minutes for Chris and Kiri to drive from their hidden cottage in Poulsbo to the Kingston ferry. From the parking lot near the marina where Kiri would walk to the ferry, it didn't appear that any major checkpoints had been established, but it was only a matter of time.

Before Kiri exited the van in the direction of the ferry to Edmonds, she turned in her seat to face him. They discussed once again the possible ferries she would return on, then prepared to send him on his way in the meantime to the meeting she'd urged him to make.

"And you make sure you tell Sapphire hi for me," Kiri made a point of directing Chris.

"I will," he promised.

Kiri gave him a peck on the cheek.

"Trust her. I guarantee you'll meet someone you don't expect," she said as got out of the van.

Chris watched Kiri walk toward the ferry loading area where the foot passengers collect. When he lost sight of her in the crowd, he turned the van toward Bainbridge Island and his anticipated rendezvous with Sapphire MacKenzie.

***

The unloading of cars from the ferry was well underway by the time Kiri and her fellow foot passengers completed disembarking in Edmonds. She easily spotted Carolyn standing about fifty yards away, near the entry of a waterfront park to the south. When Carolyn was certain Kiri had caught sight of her, she turned and began sauntering into the park casually, but deliberately as well.

A sign she passed upon entering the park informed Kiri this place was called Brackets Landing South. Although charming with a beautiful Puget Sound view, this leisurely playground was small and she was quickly onto what another sign announced as the Edmonds Marine Walkway.

Carolyn occasionally stopped, ostensibly taking in the view, but also making certain Kiri was still trailing her. Whenever Carolyn briefly halted, so did Kiri, with the intent of remaining a discreet fifty or sixty yards behind at all times. She was still close enough to hear the last of the vehicles disembarking from the ferry, as well as the revving of motors a block or two away as waiting cars began firing up their engines to load for the return trip to Kingston.

Where Carolyn could have turned right to walk out to the Public Fishing Pier, she chose instead to continue her meander down the Walkway towards the marina a short distance away, again making certain Kiri was in sight.

As Kiri passed the avenue toward the public fishing pier over the water, and drew close to the marina, she could see lots of people moving to and from the docks intent on boating on a beautiful Sunday morning. To her right as she strolled was dock after dock of boats on either side, and to the left were restaurants overlooking the water and various businesses catering to tourists.

She passed signs for the Port of Edmonds, then the Edmonds Yacht Club, and wondered where they were bound. Carolyn gave no indication as she kept moving on. Regardless, she continued stopping occasionally and gawking like a tourist while surreptitiously checking on Kiri.

Before Carolyn reached the obstructing traffic of boats being loaded and unloaded at the public boat launch, she made certain one last time that Kiri had sight of her. She then proceeded directly to the popular crab house restaurant overlooking the marina and disappeared into the entry door.

By the time Kiri arrived at the Crab Catcher restaurant, she had already seen signs advertising the Sunday brunch that was underway. Through the glass entry doors she could also observe all the patrons in line, waiting their turn for the Sunday morning meal. Kiri attempted to bypass the line, but the hostess in charge snagged her before she could sneak by.

"I'm sorry ma'am," she informed Kiri, "but we've got a wait of about twenty-five minutes before you can get a table."

"Oh, I'm late," Kiri fabricated as best she could. "My friends should already be here saving me a seat; I'll just go find them."

Someone in line began interrupting the hostess with a question and, distracted, she waved Kiri through.

The place was packed and Kiri didn't see Carolyn anywhere. After two trips around the dining area Kiri was almost ready to depart in frustration. And then, there she was, seated at the bar with a stunning view of Puget Sound and the departing ferry to the north.

Carolyn was carrying on a conversation with the bartender. He was good looking with a thin mustache, tall, and slick – and with an all too obvious hankering for Carolyn. The bar had the only open seats in the house and one was next to Carolyn. When Kiri approached, the bartender was so busy making small talk he hardly noticed her.

To Carolyn she inquired, "Excuse me, is this seat taken?"

Her friend acted as if she'd never seen her in her life.

"No, go ahead; it's yours," Carolyn replied nonchalantly.

Kiri seated herself then observed the drink Carolyn had ordered holding a celery stalk.

"Are those any good?" she asked.

Carolyn shared a knowing wink with the bartender.

"These are supposed to be the best Sunday Bloody Mary's in Edmonds," she affirmed.

Without hesitation, Kiri requested the same of the bartender.

As he shuffled away to make the drink, and even when he returned with it, Carolyn and Kiri undertook friendly, innocuous conversation, as might any two young women seated next to each other by happenstance. For the bartenders benefit and for that of anyone else possibly observing, they spoke in banal terms of the splendid summer weather and other light topics.

When the bartender moved on to prepare drink orders for a harried waitress, the two women moved onto other subjects of more topical import. They exchanged firsthand information of what they had observed so far regarding the impending State of Emergency, with more substance coming from Carolyn than Kiri, who had seen little impact as yet across the Sound on the Kitsap Peninsula.

Carolyn had heard on the radio this morning about practice checkpoints for the upcoming week being set up on Interstate 5 and major arterial Highway 99. So, on her drive down from Everett to Edmonds, she had taken back roads and encountered no difficulties or delays.

Nearly halfway through her Bloody Mary, Carolyn seamlessly transitioned into a chat about what could have been a family misunderstanding.

"It involves my oldest brother and his friend who I'll just call 'G.,'" Carolyn rambled on. "He says he doesn't want my brothers or any of their friends involved with me anymore. None of them are supposed to stop by, and none of them are to contact me again."

"Well, that's not very kind," Kiri replied innocently.

"No, it's not," agreed Carolyn. "But actually, it's quite fine by me, because I don't like most of them. And I feel so much better about having my own life all to me. I'll tell you a little secret why."

She leaned close to Kiri as if to convey something special girl-to-girl.

Whispering, Carolyn said, "No one is to have contact with me because sooner or later the police will find out about Billy and Timmy. But my brother's friend G. also said he'd use me later when necessary, but nothing more for now. I personally also think G. simply doesn't trust me."

Carolyn sat back straight up in her chair.

"So in some ways it's good that the pressure is off me," admitted Carolyn. "I feel relieved, better than I have in weeks. Life is back to just my job and all my debt."

She sighed and leaned forward to Kiri again, whispering, "Most importantly, I don't have to worry about being arrested in the immediate future."

Sitting back up, she stated, "It makes my life so much easier, happier. It's almost like I'm floating along, glad to simply be myself again."

Just then, the hostess that delayed Kiri's entrance into the busy restaurant happened by after delivering customers to their seats. She noticed Kiri seated at the bar and inquired if she'd found her friends.

"No, not yet," Kiri fumbled, "they haven't shown up yet. I don't know what's happening."

"They're probably late because of the new roadblocks popping up everywhere," Carolyn tossed in for Kiri's benefit.

The hostess shook her head and shuddered. Before shuffling off, she noted, "It's going to be a hell of a week."

The bartender was still busy at the other end of the bar, and they were alone. Without pretense now, Carolyn picked up where she left off.

"But there's the other side of the coin," she admitted to Kiri. "I'm worried about my brothers; they are the only family I have."

"That's understandable," replied Kiri.

"I told Billy that," Carolyn continued, "and he told me not to fret.

He said he was going to 'watch out for his little Sis, no matter what Garf says.' Besides that, he told me there was going to be only one more sensational attack – and then the tactics would change."

"What are they going after this time?" Kiri needed to know.

"I have no idea," replied Carolyn. "I'm thankfully, yet regretfully in some ways, out of the loop for now."

"Well then, how are they changing their tactics?" asked Kiri.

"Like I said, I'm out of the loop," said Carolyn. "The only thing I know is according to my brother, Garf alluded to the fact that they'd accomplished enough in pinpointing the handiwork of the Kingpins. Now it was time to call out those responsible for the handiwork – whatever that means."

Carolyn then attempted to change the subject matter of their conversation entirely.

"But I've been chattering entirely about myself," she announced. "Are you okay?"

Kiri nodded affirmatively. "My friends are taking good care of me and still want to help you if possible. Let me know if you find out anything that can deter this ongoing madness."

"I will."

"No, really," Kiri insisted. "I'm with you one hundred percent, you know that. Whenever, wherever, you need me: I'm there."

Carolyn's eyes were beginning to tear. "I know that. You're just like your cousin, Ingri; I so miss her being in Norway. It was the luckiest day when I met her and the next luckiest was when I met you."

Finished with his duties at the end of the bar, the bartender approached the two women. Seeing the Carolyn had finished her drink, he asked if she would like another.

"No, I don't think so," she laughed. "One Bloody Mary in the morning is quite enough for me. Besides, I better go; I have a lot to do on my day off."

For the bartender's benefit, she turned to Kiri and mentioned, "I hope your friends make it through the roadblocks and finally arrive in time for brunch."

"I hope so too," Kiri replied, as Carolyn stood to leave. "It was nice to chat with you in the meantime."

"This State of Emergency is going to be a real mess," the bartender muttered before directing his attention to a new couple taking up seats at the bar.

After Kiri finished her Bloody Mary, she paid her bill and began the ten-minute walk back along the waterfront to catch the next ferry to Kingston. About half way there, the recurrent mental projection of the past several days again intruded upon her thoughts.

The little stream began pleasantly following its course out of the high mountains and joining others to the sound of growing symphony music.

Just as suddenly, Kiri was then struck wondering what was going to happen to Carolyn as she went over the waterfall. And how she too would be impacted along with her friend.

After all, they would surely be together one hundred percent – all the way down the falls.

CHAPTER TWENTY-TWO

Sapphire MacKenzie was already seated on the floating dock with feet dangling over the water of Madison Bay when Chris arrived. He had briefly chatted with Elders Cecil and Myra Hanson, from whom he'd borrowed the black lab when meeting Stone McClelland; they told him he'd find Sapphire down by their boat.

The water was still even though the tide was extremely low, so low he couldn't catch sight of her until he stood at the top of the steep-angled walkway to the dock. Cautiously, he made his way down the ramp toward her, while simultaneously taking in how focused she was on the reflective waters of the bay.

Passing by the Hanson's classic motorboat with its polished and glistening teak, Sapphire turned to him as she registered his approach. When she smiled, the petite dimples in her cheeks captivated Chris as much as the affable sparkle she conveyed. Brushing brown hair behind her left ear, Sapphire patted the dock.

"Have a seat," she urged him.

Taking a place next to her and hanging his own feet over the water as well, Chris inquired on how she was doing on such a fine summer morning.

"I'm fine," she replied pleasantly, "but did Kiri get off okay on the ferry to Edmonds?"

"As far as I know," said Chris. "Why?"

"I was just wondering," she stated. "Did you see any troops or police?"

"No."

"That's good; maybe Kiri won't run into any difficulties," noted Sapphire.

She then mentioned she'd stopped by her office earlier. Rather shocked, Sapphire said she'd observed military troops working the newly established checkpoints for both vehicles and foot passengers.

Chris was stunned as well. "I heard they were calling up the National Guard, but I never imagined it would be to harass ordinary citizens."

Sapphire looked him in the eye. "Chris, major demonstrations are inevitable. Difficult times are coming."

She sighed. "We're already beginning to organize, but the police state seems to know our every move. I'm sure we have informers that have infiltrated our ranks and when all hell breaks loose, there will be a sweep that snares even the most good-hearted and innocent among us."

In thought, Chris failed to initially respond. He then asked Sapphire, "What if I can get you information on people Empire has wormed into your organization?"

"How would you do that?"

"Remember the ex-DEA agent that visited you in your office?"

"Yeah."

"I think it may be time I tested the waters to see what he really has to offer," Chris explained.

Sapphire was dubious. "He mentioned something about that when he met with me, but aren't you concerned he could destroy you?"

"Yes," Chris acknowledged. "But I don't view him as an adversary. I believe that's the wrong way to think."

"The wrong way to think?" she objected. "Then what is he, if he's not an adversary?"

"I'm not sure," he admitted. "Perhaps he's just a participant. But I don't know for certain. His actions in the future will define him; he must be given a chance. After all, he gave me one."

Sapphire raised an eyebrow. "Well, it's up to you, but if you can give me help I won't turn it down."

For a short time thereafter, their conversation stalled. Kiri had urged him to speak with her; still, he didn't really know what to talk about. Especially as he was transfixed by how strikingly attractive and fresh she appeared in the morning sun by the bay.

In time he muttered something to the effect that things didn't have to reach a boiling point.

"If only we could turn Garf Taylor and his people from their violent course, we could salvage everyone from Empire's recriminations to come," Chris postulated.

"That'll never happen," Sapphire declared swiftly.

"Why?" wondered Chris. "In Port Townsend with the Elders, I seemed to sense you had some influence with him."

Sapphire didn't respond. Instead, she dropped into thoughts of long ago, a time when she and Garf were both young activists swept up in a cause. Their dalliance was consensual until he didn't want to use a condom. He got rougher and she held her ground.

"Whomever I'm with uses a condom – no exceptions," she'd warned.

His desire eventually overcame his drive for control; he put on a condom and they had sex. It was okay, yet her pleasure in just being with him was diminished. And after that one time, sexual allure for Garfield Taylor was totally lost.

Resurfacing into the present, Sapphire simply stated, "Maybe at one time I had some influence with Garf, but that was long ago. Besides, he's gone so far underground at this point, I wouldn't even know how to contact him."

Deliberately, Sapphire changed the subject.

"Because of this new State of Emergency, I know what I'm going to do," she stated with certainty. "I'm going to protest. So what are you going to do?"

"What do you mean?"

"Kiri tells me she mostly wanders Cascadia with you," replied Sapphire. "She also told me you did the same for years before she joined you. Now, however, your roaming about Cascadia will be severely restricted by the police state. So what are you going to do?"

"If that's the physical case for a time, it doesn't matter," he attempted to explain. "It won't stop what I must do."

She asked him the obvious. "What is it you must do?"

"I'm just looking for something."

"What?"

"I'm not certain," he admitted, "but I hope I know it, if and when I find it."

Sapphire asked him to explain.

"I'll try," Chris promised.

For the next several minutes he spoke of a reputed time long ago in human history, a golden age of humanity, when people organized themselves for the good of the whole through co-operation, shared resources, and a respect for the earth. It was supposedly a time of creative partnership, egalitarianism, and a reverence for the generative power of life that stressed an enduring equality of the sexes.

Unfortunately, he told her, this so-called golden age of humanity was believed to have altered more than five thousand years ago beginning in Mesopotamia, and has marched ever onward to the present day. Characterized by dominance, violence, and exploitation, a male power based hierarchal system was established featuring ruthless and arbitrary rulers, as well as insatiable avarice and control over others at all levels of society.

"I seek to discover that home we once supposedly shared so very long ago," Chris maintained. "What I'm searching for is a journey home, a discovery of the past — yet it is also something that can only be revealed in the future, by creating a new future."

"You know, I'm certain," Sapphire mildly objected, "that there are those that say violence, domination, and exploitation of others is simply human nature."

Chris acknowledged that fact with a nod. "And there are, of course, others that say we've been taught that by those in control; without thinking, we accept the same because it's our patriarchal inheritance."

He went on to tie these thoughts with those expressed earlier.

"In fact, that is precisely why I greatly fear Garf Taylor's violent approach will provoke a similar, if even more powerful response from Empire," Chris elucidated. "It is the way of the patriarchy, not the way of the sustainable Cascadia we must seek."

Sapphire smiled and tenderly placed her hand atop his.

"You have your destiny," she stated simply, "and Garf has his."

"And you have yours."

Chris enjoyed smiling back into the bluest of blue eyes he had ever seen.

"Yes, I have my destiny," she agreed, "and Kiri has hers. But sometimes they align, and I think they have."

Although inclined, Chris restrained from inquiring whose and what destinies she imagined aligning, feeling it better to simply remain unsaid.

Instead, he stood and mentioned it was probably time to get going to pick up Kiri at the first of the possible ferries she may be returning upon. Chris then offered Sapphire his hands to help her up off the dock. Once she stood, however, she didn't let go.

"You know," she said looking into his eyes, "you're very lucky to have found someone like Kiri."

As Sapphire maintained her grip, Chris grew increasingly uncomfortable. "You don't really understand our relationship."

"Oh, I understand it perfectly," she beamed in affirmation. "Remember, Kiri and I are long-lost sisters that finally found each other. I understand your relationship completely. I understand your vow to her parents and how difficult it must be. What you share with her is a beautiful relationship, something Cascadia could cherish."

Still staring back into the deep blue eyes while she held his hands,

Chris was at a total loss for words.

"And you know what?" Sapphire continued. "I think you and I will develop something, in our own way, that's just as beautiful."

Taken a little aback, yet hearing precisely what he would have wanted to hear, Chris murmured awkwardly, "I hope so; I'd really like that."

"Count on it," she promised.

The next thing Chris realized, they were suddenly in one another's arms. Their lips were meeting, and then their tongues were vigorously in each other's mouth. With bodies tightly compressed and squirming enthusiastically, the passion of their kiss kept them engaged for several minutes.

When finally they parted, both recognized that more was likely to be theirs – but it could only be at a later time.

***

After weeks of trying, the restaurant they planned to finally meet up at was not far below Seattle's famous Pike Place Market. It had a waterfront view of Elliot Bay and was surrounded by clear Plexiglas, a barrier in place for outdoor dining on chilly days yet superfluous on sunny summer Sundays like this.

Stone McClelland had arrived on time and taken a table, while Bertie Stanton had called en route. Saying the morning services at his church had run longer than expected, he promised his arrival was imminent.

When Bertie made his entry a short time later, he was a mixture of the affable and apologetic at the same time. Eagerly approaching Stone's table, he shook his friend's hand robustly.

"I am so sorry I haven't been able to get together sooner," Bertie said, making amends, "but with what's going on out there, I'm up to my ears in it at work."

"I completely understand," Stone replied cordially. He took a moment to study his friend, noting his lean and lithe build still quite intact, even if more white was peppering his hair and standing out against his rich black skin.

As Bertie took a seat, Stone voiced his observations, saying, "At least you don't look any worse for wear."

"Ha!" Stanton laughed buoyantly. "We both know all too well how looks can be deceiving."

Conversationally, McClelland asked his friend how church was today with his family.

Stanton cast a sideways look at Stone. "A great bunch of Baptists – that's what we are!"

From the tone, McClelland couldn't tell if Bertie was being genuine or satirical. That was classic Bertie Stanton though; he could slide through any opening while comfortably donning his airs of ambiguity.

A waitress arrived with waters and menus for both of them. Bertie quickly surveyed the food choices and instantly made up his mind. Stone was still churning over the menu when Bertie got right to the point.

"I'm assuming you want to talk about old friend stuff," he stated.

"Of course I do," Stone assured him. "That's why I'm here."

"We're old friends to be sure," Bertie eyed Stone, "but what do you want that won't compromise me? I can only go so far, you know."

"All I want is old friend's stuff," McClelland made it clear. "I wouldn't ask for anything if I couldn't help you. And you know that."

Bertie nodded his head. "I do indeed; that's what old friend stuff is all about in our business."

Seeing the men had put their menus down on the table, the waitress returned and inquired after their orders. Stanton ordered a BLT sandwich without any hesitation while McClelland, still delighting in the cuisine of the Northwest, requested grilled salmon with a house salad. The waitress then asked about their choice of beverages and Bertie stepped in to order ice teas for the both of them.

After the waitress departed and before Stanton could launch himself, McClelland asked his old friend from the DEA days if he remembered the Spore Master of the Gaia/Universe cult.

"Of course I do," Bertie replied. "And I recall you had something to do with arresting him."

"Actually, it was the Navajo Nation police that detained him," McClelland clarified. "I was merely the closest one to where the Spore Master was taken into custody and represented the DEA."

"And he died that night in detention," added Bertie.

"Yes he did," Stone concurred. "And now everyone is desperately searching for the Spore Master's former assistant, Chris Soles, or Chris Cadia, as some call him."

"That's certainly no secret," spoke Stanton, his voice taut.

"Well, I can't tell you precisely why, but I have a connection with Soles," McClelland revealed. "And finding him is something personal for me."

"So you want help from me?" Bertie Stanton was flabbergasted. "Good luck! The entire FBI is looking for him and we can't find him."

"No, I'm not seeking that kind of help whatsoever," Stone assured him. "In fact, I believe I've already found him – or at least his representative."

"You're fucking kidding me!"

Suddenly Bertie was very interested.

Accurately yet concisely, Stone told his old buddy about the basics of the meeting on Bainbridge Island and how Soles's representative attempted to make the point that Chris Soles, or Chris Cadia, was not connected at all with the Future Generations terror group.

"And you believe that crap?" Stanton said, shaking his head. "What made you think this guy was credible at all?"

"He told me things that only Chris Soles and I could know," muttered Stone McClelland.

Bertie Stanton studied his friend long and hard.

"I don't know what you got yourself into in Arizona," Stanton remarked, "but I hope you can get yourself out of it."

"I hope so too," Stone sullenly replied.

Absorbed by their own thoughts, both men were silent for a time. It was only the return of the waitress, laden with their lunches, which brought conversation back to the surface.

"So, I know what I want from you – and that's Chris Soles," said Bertie, as he hungrily tore into his bacon, lettuce, and tomato sandwich. "But what do you want from me?"

McClelland began working on his grilled salmon.

"If Sole's representative gets back to me and says Soles wants information that I suggested I could obtain," he said between bites, "I need info from you to buy his trust with."

Stanton considered while finishing off the first half of his sandwich.

"What type of information?"

"I'm not certain," Stone replied. "I have to wait and see what he wants."

"So that's on hold for now," observed Bertie. "We'll see what he needs when the time comes, but if you can also serve him up when the time comes – of course we'd be interested."

Once again, McClelland took pains to point out the possibility that Chris Soles was not even involved with the Future Generations group.

"That remains to be seen too," Stanton snapped. In a more amiable tone, he continued, stating, "But like I said, I'd do whatever I can to help you – without compromising myself."

For a few minutes both men focused on their lunches. The waitress strolled by and Bertie asked for another lemon for his iced tea, even as he finished the other half of his BLT before she returned.

Without preliminaries, Stanton then pushed onward. "Let me tell you a few of the things we do know about the Future Generations terrorists that haven't been made public as yet. First, the three that committed suicide by biting into cyanide capsules at the Ritzville post office were all in Monroe together."

"Monroe?"

"Monroe Correctional Complex," Stanton formally stated. "It's a state prison a little less than an hour northeast of here. That fact alone affirms a link we'd been pursuing involving two brothers, one of which was a convicted eco-terrorist and who we believe gathered and schooled others in extreme eco-politics while at Monroe."

"And the other brother?" inquired Stone.

"The younger brother was an explosives expert for a big regional excavation outfit," Bertie explained. "He quit some weeks ago supposedly to hike and hunt in the backwoods of Alaska for the summer and had been accepted by a local community college for the fall term. But after an extensive audit by the excavation company revealed an extraordinary amount of missing explosives, we think he might have had other summer vacation plans with his brother."

"What are their names?"

"Billy and Timmy Maxwell," said Stanton. "Billy's the older one and the eco-terrorist that served time at Monroe."

"Any other family?"

"They were raised by a single mother that died years ago," Bertie informed Stone. "There's also a sister and we just started tailing her of late. She has a steady accounting job at Boeing in Everett and appears not to be involved. We'll keep a watch on her; likely though, there's nothing there."

McClelland had finished his salmon and was halfway through his salad. "What else do you know about Future Generations?"

Stanton shook his head. "That they're extremely elusive?" he suggested.

"The best guess we have right now," Bertie mustered, "is that all their communications are dark, fully encrypted to the point that we don't know where to look."

"What about phones?" wondered Stone. "They have to be using them."

"Of course they have phones," Bertie agreed. "But most likely they've been using one-time burner phones, or phones with apps capable of changing numbers every time they're used. Still, our technical people are working on back doors to those apps while simultaneously attempting to assign a signature to the individual phones using the apps. We'll corner them eventually."

Finishing his salad, Stone pushed his empty plates off to the side, as did Bertie.

"Anything else?" asked McClelland.

"Sure," replied Bertie. "Unless we see another general eruption of violence as we did several weeks ago which was attributed by the terrorists as a 'waking of sleeper cells,' we know their focus, their very scope, is limited. In other words, they're not going to spray a random restaurant or concert hall with bullets and bombs. They are not going after anything but fossil fuel related targets, so we concentrate our efforts there. In fact, we're actively working something north of here, up near the Canadian border."

Stanton began to further explain but suddenly the waitress returned to their table. Noticing the empty plates, she inquired about the quality of the meal and if she could bring them dessert. Both men replied affirmatively regarding the meal; both also declined any more to eat. Sweeping up their plates and silverware with a smile, she promised to return with the bill.

"As I was saying," Bertie hopped back in, "there's been unusually heightened activity up by Cherry Point, close to Canada. It's a huge complex with a couple refineries, as well as off-loading and shipping for coal, oil, and natural gas. So it's a natural target for our eco-terrorists who claim they're fighting climate wars."

"What kind of heightened activity are you talking about?"

"It's troubling."

"How so?"

Stanton shook his head. "They appear to be developing new weapons along with everything else."

"What kind of new weapons?"

"Night before last, almost simultaneously at different points around Cherry Point," Bertie divulged, "three of the high-tech heat seeking surveillance drones up there were taken out by some kind of surface-to-air launcher. All of Cherry Point went on high alert, but no one's certain if it signified an imminent attack, mere target practice, or even a diversion."

The waitress returned, thanked them for choosing this restaurant, and then placed the bill on the table between them. Stone snatched it up and Bertie didn't object.

"I'm telling you," Bertie stated explicitly, "these Future Generations terrorists are fanatics. They're as crazy as any radical Islamist and as dangerous as they come. To die for their cause is apparently an honor for them."

Stone totally agreed with his friend. "That's all the more reason I've got to get to the bottom of this with Chris Soles, find out what he's up to, and stop the insanity in its tracks."

Stanton acknowledged similar sentiments and then asked Stone, "How's your security clearance?"

"It's inactive," he replied with a shrug of his shoulders, "but with no red flags as far as I know, if that's what you mean."

"You may need it going forward," Bertie noted. "I'll do what I can to expedite it to active status. Regardless, let's keep all this unofficial between us for the time being."

"That works for me," Stone declared.

"Also," added Stanton, "from now on, I intend to make time to meet as often as need be. Does that work for you as well?"

"By all means," McClelland assured his old buddy.

***

They woke up to what sounded like fireworks around midnight. Further rousing them from their slumbers were multiple and extended siren squeals overlapping themselves in a tangled Doppler effect of comings and goings.

When the noise refused to cease, Linda arose from their bed to check on the kids. Fortunately, both Cassie and Kyle slept undisturbed, although she wondered for how long.

Meanwhile, Tomas opened the front door looking for the origin of the nearby fireworks – and just as quickly closed it, realizing what they heard were not fireworks, but gunshots.

For nearly an hour the occasional firing of weapons could be heard, and then all grew quiet except for the occasional siren of an emergency vehicle passing by somewhere on the streets of Edmonds.

In the morning, news reports from radio and TV were to alter the normal plans for many that day in the Northwest, including Tomas and Linda Hernandez.

Scattered across various locales throughout Washington, Oregon, and Idaho, seemingly random violence had erupted at the stroke of midnight. Resembling the chaos and destruction of several weeks ago, drive-by shootings targeted multiple gas stations, Molotov cocktails were hurled through windows of SUV's and other gas guzzling vehicles, while propane supply outlets suffered explosions and subsequent fireballs as their tanks holding fuel came under attack.

Worst of all, it was being reported a first responder policeman had been captured north of Everett, in Marysville, and killed execution style with a single bullet to the back of the head.

North of the US border, British Columbia was hardly immune to the terrorist violence. In Burnaby, a Vancouver suburb, giant fireballs within proximity to residential neighborhoods set the night sky ablaze when two massive fuel spheres purportedly storing jet fuel were explosively detonated. Down by the water at the same site, also heavily damaged was a major terminal for the transshipment of oil from a main overland pipeline to ocean going vessels. Conflicting reports stated four or five terrorists had died in a shoot-out or by suicide as authorities closed in. It was also believed two or three terrorists had possibly escaped.

British Columbia Premier Hoagland was outraged. Declaring this terrorism needed to be forcefully stopped in its tracks, the Premier was quoted again and again on TV stressing, "Make no mistake: We are at war with Future Generations!"

With the horrific news, for their own safety, people throughout the entire region were advised not to go to work or venture out for the day unless absolutely necessary.

"Stay home and remain calm until order is fully restored," blared the announcements on the television. Otherwise, citizens were warned they would face certain delays, long checkpoint lines, and heightened scrutiny – all designed to capture the terrorists.

Tomas believed staying home from work to be an excellent suggestion, yet before he could telephone the office, a reverse 911 call of sorts came in from his Triple-C construction commons. The priority message mandated that all employees remain with their families for the day, as offices would be closed.

So besides watching news updates from time to time, Linda and Tomas played with their kids most of the morning, reading stories, doodling in coloring books, and enjoying the swing set in the back yard. A little after lunch, however, Cassie and Kyle wanted to take a ride around the neighborhood in their red wagon. Although normally a weekend treat, the parents found no reason to object on this unexpected family day.

The wagon was retrieved from the garage, and after Kyle clambered in followed by Cassie, the family made their way down sidewalks and across streets in the general direction of Edmond's small downtown area. The closer they drew to the quaint and friendly shops and restaurant area, the more troops in military uniform they saw on patrol.

Not far from a favorite bistro was a low slung office building surrounded by yellow police tape. Nothing remained of the street facing windows but broken glass scattered about the ground. A sign in front announced the building as offices for a local petroleum transportation company.

As the Hernandez family approached ever closer to the scene on the sidewalk, with the red wagon and kids in tow, a soldier stepped from behind the yellow tape and intercepted them.

Tomas asked the military man, "What's going on?"

The soldier grunted. "You best take your family home, sir. And lock the doors."

Standing firm and grim, he said nothing else. Linda touched her husband's elbow and nodded her head in the direction they had come from. Tomas wordlessly agreed as he turned the kids and their wagon around.

Back home, later that afternoon, Linda received a phone call from Sapphire MacKenzie. They spoke for several minutes in the kitchen, although Tomas could catch parts of Linda's one-sided conversation from the living room where he was reading Cassie and Kyle a story.

Hearing phrases such as, "I guess it's inevitable," and, "Sapphire, I know you don't have any other choice," he had a fair idea of what they were discussing. When Tomas eventually overheard, "I don't know, I guess you'll have to ask him," he realized his own part of story time would soon be ending.

Shortly thereafter, Linda came into the living room and handed him the phone.

"Sapphire wants to speak with you," she informed him. "I'll take over here."

The exchange of phone and children's book took place, as did the exchange of kitchen and living room.

When Tomas seated himself at the kitchen table, he said, "Hello Sapphire, how are you?"

"Not so good," she honestly replied. "Especially in light of the response to what happened last night. There are military troops everywhere here on Bainbridge Island."

"I'm sure Linda told you they're here too," he replied wearily. "In fact, they are probably stationed everywhere in Cascadia by now. I've long feared this day would come."

"What do you mean?"

"It has to do with the National Defense Authorization Act that passed into law years ago," Tomas explained. "In particular, Section 1021 allows the military to carry out domestic policing, and I think that's why we're seeing troops out on civilian streets. Effectively too, it can be used to shut down all dissent with force. With the flip of the Section 1021 switch, the nation – or more specifically, Cascadia – falls under strict martial law. Canada has recently enacted similar provisions and you can be certain their new right wing reactionary, and former oil man, Premier Hoagland, is already flexing his muscles to our north."

"Well, we have to do something about it," exclaimed Sapphire.

Tomas stated he was at a loss when it came to confronting the greatest military empire on the planet. "What can you do when they have the legal power to crush dissent?"

"We protest anyway," she said defiantly. "We have no choice but to make them play their hand, if that's what they intend. If we don't protest and fight back against their domination and corporate power plays, we might as well simply surrender and never again dream of a free and sustainable Cascadia for the future. And that's one reason for this call; I need your help."

"You need my help?" Tomas replied, somewhat mystified.

"I need your help," she averred, "and more pointedly, the help of a united Commons movement. We have a much better chance of success if the Commons movement can unite with our Free Cascadia protest movement, and then jointly confront the specter of Empire."

Tomas sighed. They had been through this before. While he personally thought it a good idea to join forces with the Free Cascadia movement, a majority of Commons Rising delegates and perhaps even a majority of commoners were wary of such a proposal, fearing it might well be detrimental to the cause of the commons in general. Avoiding confrontation and the inevitable backlash that would follow was seen as preferable to most, if the commons were to effect change in their own way.

Sapphire and Tomas talked about it for several minutes. In the end, he reluctantly agreed, as a result of her insistence, to survey those in Commons Rising regarding their opinion about joining together and working in sync, considering recent events.

For the next hour and a half or so, Tomas worked the phones calling fellow delegates nominated by their commons to be represented in the collective Commons Rising. As he expected, for one reason or another, the vast majority of those he called were outspoken about not joining forces with the legions of Free Cascadia protestors – especially at the present time. In fact, only one individual, his friend Wade Nash from Idaho, had been prepared to fully join and support the Free Cascadia protestors.

One person, however, obviously did not make a majority.

When he called Sapphire back that afternoon to report his results, all he got was her voice mail.

Regretting he had to leave things on a sour note, Tomas informed Sapphire that unfortunately most commons and commoners in general would not be attending any of Free Cascadia's forthcoming rallies.

CHAPTER TWENTY-THREE

"I think we should get started," the voice said over the phone without preamble.

"It's about time," Stone McClelland snorted. "I've been waiting for your call."

Chiding, "Tsk, tsk, tsk," the voice further admonished, "one shouldn't be hasty. All things come to fruition in their own time."

"Why shouldn't I be hasty?" McClelland fired back provocatively and on purpose. "Especially after what Chris Soles and the Future Generations terrorists pulled off last night!"

"Oh, there you go again with your hastiness, as well as jumping to conclusions," the chiding continued. "I keep telling you that Chris Soles is not involved, and you keep refusing to listen."

"Then give me some credible evidence that I'm mistaken," Stone demanded.

"You're playing with a weak hand, Mister McClelland," the voice reminded him, "and anyway, it's your turn first. Remember, I could hang up at any time and you would have no link whatsoever to Chris Soles, or the mythical Chris Cadia."

Stone was forced to acknowledge that simple fact as obvious reality. Accordingly, he attempted to concede as graciously as possible.

"Okay, what do you want from me?"

"Let's start with information."

"What kind of information?"

"Something minor, I suppose, in the grand scheme of things," replied the voice. "Maybe something about infiltrators and informants."

"Regarding any particular party?"

"How about we start with our mutual acquaintance, Sapphire MacKenzie?"

"What's your connection with her?"

"You're being hasty again, Mister McClelland," the voice scolded, "and meddling in affairs of little import at this time. Please think back to the meeting in the park on Bainbridge Island, and look at this request as a test. We are trying to build up trust; do you remember?"

"I remember."

"Good," said the voice. "With that settled, I look forward to calling you back and receiving some information of value within, say, twenty-four to thirty-six hours."

"That's not much time," cautioned McClelland.

"I *trust* it shall be all the time you require," replied the voice. "Are we on the same page?"

"We are," he affirmed.

After hanging up, Stone McClelland sighed and rubbed his forehead with one of his massive hands. He hated being trapped in a situation where he was so powerless to affect the outcome. But there was nothing he could do about it for now, except for the two phone calls he could make.

The first one was to his old friend, Bertie Stanton. Stone told him that he had been contacted by the representative for Chris Soles and needed information as a test of burgeoning trust. Further, he mentioned it had to be something about informants or infiltrators within Sapphire MacKenzie's Free Cascadia movement.

"And get me the good stuff as soon as possible – within twenty-four hours at least," McClelland requested. "Otherwise I might lose him altogether."

The second phone call was to Roger, his contact on the pipeline to his ultimate employer, Whitley Dellenbach. Previously, he had revealed to his handler that he had made credible contact with someone representing Chris Soles, yet explicitly without mentioning any doubts regarding his involvement with Future Generations.

Now he informed Roger that the rep for Soles had finally called back and was requesting information regarding informants inside Sapphire MacKenzie's organization. He also repeated the demand for quality intelligence in a short window of time, or risk the contact disappearing entirely.

After concluding both calls, McClelland reckoned that going forward – if Chris Soles was using his quest for intelligence not merely for the information, but just as much for a determination of trust involved in the interchange – there was no reason he shouldn't do the same. Whatever he got back from Stanton and the FBI, as well as his handler and employer Dellenbach, would necessarily be a litmus test for trust all the way around.

Whenever McClelland had found himself in such circumstances, it always reminded him of the first sting he'd ever been involved in with the DEA taking down a drug kingpin working Las Vegas.

The man was understandably bitter about being hoodwinked and arrested by those he thought he had confidence in, yet he was every bit as enraged at himself for ending up in such a situation.

McClelland had asked him why.

"You never trust anyone," the drug dealer told him. "And I violated my main rule."

He then went on to tell Stone how as a very young boy, just when he was starting to figure out the ways of the world, his father had placed him high atop a ladder he'd hauled into their tenement. With open arms, he demanded that his son leap. The boy did just that, but his father turned away while the child was in mid-air. After crashing hard on the floor, hurt and in tears, the father lovingly scooped him up.

"What you have to learn," the drug kingpin's father had schooled, "is never trust anyone!"

***

"Yeah, everything worked just fine," Garf fired back snidely, "except for that asshole brother of yours!"

"Look, he was upset," Billy Maxwell countered. "We didn't give him anything to do and he felt left out. Plus, he hasn't seen his girlfriend in weeks; he probably doesn't have a girlfriend anymore."

"That's no excuse," snapped Taylor.

"I know, but that's what we're dealing with," was the best Billy could offer. "Besides, Timmy wanted to go to B.C. with us. When you wouldn't let him go, he got pissed off and started drinking."

"Your brother's becoming a fucking liability," Garf took pains to point out. "He never should have been involved with the cell from north Everett. I wanted him away from the action for specific reasons; he should have stayed at home like he was supposed to."

"The thing is, Timmy believes in the cause and wanted to do his part," Billy protested. "And he's known Tom Wilcox of that cell for years."

"So he duped Wilcox into going along," said Garf, "even though he knew he wasn't authorized to do so."

Billy knew he was running out of excuses in defense of his brother.

"And then," Taylor continued, "they capture a cop who had pursued them into an electrical substation, take him up to Marysville, and Timmy — your fucking brother — puts a bullet in the back of the cop's head."

There was not much Billy could say.

In the quiet and relative security of the Birch Bay safe house, Garf Taylor shouted, "Tell me one good reason I shouldn't put a bullet through your brother's useless brain!"

The answer came quick. "Because we absolutely need him for the next phase. He just jumped the gun."

The stall in Garf's retort indicated Billy was correct.

"Well, it's not going to happen again — got it?" demanded Taylor. "And he didn't just jump the gun; he's come very close to imperiling the next phase altogether. We need him, but if future eliminations are to succeed, it's your responsibility to rein in your brother."

Billy knew that would be a tough assignment. Timmy had purposely defied Garf, they didn't care for each other in the least, and now he had to be the diplomatic buffer between the two even more than before. The mission to liberate Cascadia depended on it.

"I'll do what I can," Billy promised, "but he doesn't listen to me and drinking the liquor turns him loose."

"I'm warning you, Billy, get him under control," Garf hissed. "Otherwise the consequences are harsh. Do you remember what we pledged when we started this?"

Billy Maxwell nodded and his reply was stone cold sober. "We pledged that everyone was expendable for the cause."

"Damn right," concurred Garf. "And that means everyone – you, me, and especially – your fucking brother Timmy!"

***

"So the trip to the Far East was a success, Father?"

"Very much so," replied the elder Dellenbach to his son. "Our people in Washington must prop up the regime to an extent, but it opens a vast new hub reliant on our coal, oil, and natural gas. In the end, it's a win-win for all: we're the first to access a new market that's been sequestered for decades, and the lives of their ordinary citizens will be vastly improved."

"And in essence, a painless and admirable coup d'état engineered by you and those we support," Whitley congratulated his father. "It's the American way."

"Indeed," Theodore Dellenbach agreed over the phone. "But upon my return home, I see things have slid from bad to worse in the Pacific Northwest."

"Unfortunately they have, Father," acknowledged Whitley, "yet it's likely events are only following a necessary pattern of progression toward a successful resolution against the forces of revolution."

"Explain yourself," requested the elder Dellenbach.

"Certainly," said the son. "The latest terrorist attacks by Future Generations have invoked Section 1021 of the National Defense Authorization Act and similar laws in Canada. Both countries now have military boots on the ground and in the streets attempting to restore order."

"Yes, we all knew that was coming," the father spoke impatiently.

"Well, the next step in the progression is sure to be resistance in the form of mass protests and demonstrations," Whitley noted. "The great unwashed and unnumbered will protest that their 'rights' are being violated, and then dissent will inevitably be quashed as the military has been authorized so to do in such extraordinary times."

"You've spoken then with your 'unwitting informant?'" asked the elder Dellenbach.

"Just this morning in fact," replied the son. "Ms. MacKenzie is promising major demonstrations sometime next week, or in her words, 'a vast uprising.' I told her I was worried for her safety, for I feared vast reprisals to her uprising."

"How did she respond to that?"

"Precisely as I figured she would," said Whitley. "She was defiant, saying the revolution toward a free Cascadia was all the more determined to persevere."

"So it's all part of the natural progression you visualize, eh?"

"Yes, but this time when the crackdown comes," Whitley promised, "I believe it's time to teach Sapphire MacKenzie and all her people a lesson. The reprisals will be harsh, and I think I'll personally let my 'unwitting informant' linger in jail a while so as to stew upon her actions. I believe that will make her all the more pliant with me when finally she is rescued and bailed out."

"Surely you're not content focusing solely upon the demonstrators during the upcoming crackdown?" asked Theodore Dellenbach.

"Not at all," the son's voice seemed to smile into the phone. "The military troops will do their part to take care of all that, while law enforcement goons in our pay will strike a paralyzing blow to the leaders of the Commons movement. We must cripple them, for they are a far greater threat in the long term than the vocal rabble that will take to the streets next week."

"What else do you have, Son?"

"Nothing but good news, Father."

"Let's hear it."

"By all means," Whitley said almost triumphantly. "You recall the ex-DEA agent on our payroll?"

"I do."

"Well, he has finally made credible contact with a representative of Chris Soles, according to the handler I have in charge of him," Whitley informed his father.

"Merely a representative?" queried the elder Dellenbach.

"It's a valid starting point," the son assured his father. "The last I heard we were waiting on his request for information, so as to build up trust. And once we have his trust, we'll have Chris Soles."

"That's all well and good," the father conceded. "Still, as I recall, you used Sapphire MacKenzie to get to Soles. To me, that points to some kind of definitive relationship between them. How do you intend to utilize that?"

"You're a jump ahead of me, Father," Whitley lauded the old man. "I was getting to that. We're not yet certain what's between them, but we will use that relationship – as well as what the ex-DEA man is working on – to put the head of Chris Soles on a platter."

"It's what must be done," Theodore Dellenbach concurred, "especially after what he did to our Alice."

"Oh, don't you worry, Father," the son pledged, "I will do everything I personally can to see retribution expeditiously dispatched to Soles for the despicable deed he did to the family."

Whitley cleared his throat before continuing. "I guarantee I will do my best to get to him through Sapphire MacKenzie. I have opened the door to her heart; I'll go inside and eat it raw if necessary – to nail Chris Soles."

***

In less than six hours, Stone McClelland had his information back from both Bertie Stanton and his handler, Roger. The next call he was waiting on didn't come in until the following morning, almost exactly twenty-four hours after the initial request for intelligence.

"What do you have for me?" asked the voice that was becoming ever more familiar.

"A few things," McClelland replied. "Are you ready?"

"Quite ready; go ahead."

From the desk of his SeaTac hotel, Stone snatched up the paper containing notes he jotted during Bertie's call.

"I've got one name for you to begin with," said McClelland, "and that's Amanda Pierce."

"Who's that?"

"She's a staffer in Sapphire MacKenzie's Bainbridge offices for Free Cascadia," Stone informed his caller. "In fact, she's one of MacKenzie's primary assistants."

"How long has she been a source for Empire?"

"Probably for about three to four years," calculated McClelland, "but it's quite likely she's not even aware of it."

"How can that be?"

"It's her live-in boyfriend for the last three plus years," Stone replied. "He's a guy named Sean Smith, which I'm guessing is a phony alias. He works part time as a local park ranger, but in reality is some kind of cop under very deep cover. My source also tells me he's been infiltrating subversive movements for years, both on the East Coast and here. Further, he's so good at what he does that it's unlikely the Pierce woman knows anything about her boyfriend's double life."

"Is that it?" wondered the voice.

"No, not at all," Stone shot back. "I have more."

"Let's hear it."

Setting down the paper with notes from his conversation with Bertie, Stone then picked up the next one on the desk with scribbles from his talk with Roger.

"Okay, we've got a number of things here," he began. "First, there's a neighbor in MacKenzie's small Bainbridge apartment complex that's paid full time to keep tabs on her comings and goings, who visits, and tailing her when possible."

"And the name?"

"It's Susan Baxter," said McClelland. "They know each other as friendly neighbors, but that's the extent of it for MacKenzie."

"Is that it?"

"No, there's more."

From the notes during Roger's conversation with him yesterday, Stone told the voice on the phone that Sapphire MacKenzie and Free Cascadia should take a look at a staffer in the Portland office named Wilbur Luckmann if they were interested in infiltrators and informants there.

McClelland then passed along a final bit of information that left the voice on the phone stunned and silent.

After a prolonged period of hearing nothing but breathing in his ear, McClelland asked, "So what have you got for me? This trust business only works if it's reciprocal."

For the longest time, the silence was absolute, unbroken.

When the voice finally came back into McClelland's ear it said, "I'll get back to you after I make some calls; stick close by your phone."

For the next two hours, Stone let some tennis match from Europe run on the hotel room TV, and paid little attention to it. When his phone finally began ringing again, he took the initiative to speak first, and forcefully.

"So what have you got for me?" demanded McClelland.

The voice did not answer the question directly or immediately.

"Some of your information is probably rotten," was spoken into McClelland's ear. "Appropriate people are checking the names you gave me, but what you told me at the end about the commons leader Tomas Hernandez smells bad."

"What part smells bad?"

The voice ignored the question, saying instead, "Let's get this straight. You told me Sapphire MacKenzie and the wife of this Hernandez fellow were old friends. You also told me Hernandez reports to secret domestic terrorist surveillance personnel and is purposely withholding the support of the commons, so that the Free Cascadia movement might wither and die on the vine during the inevitable, upcoming demonstrations."

"Yes, and I also you told the cause of all this was an engineered internal rift between the commons people and the Free Cascadia people," added McClelland. "Hernandez and the people he reports to want MacKenzie set adrift and offered up as a sacrifice – before destroying the Commons movement itself from the inside."

"And I'm telling you there's something very much rotten there," the voice fired back. "In fact, someone you trusted fed you disinformation."

"What in particular do you believe is disinformation?"

The voice would not deign to respond to the question.

"It would behoove you to more thoroughly vet your sources," warned the voice. "And that, Mister McClelland, is what I reciprocate with. I believe you'll ultimately find my information of great value in advancing our little game of burgeoning trust."

CHAPTER TWENTY-FOUR

"I don't know what's going on with my computer, Kiri," remarked Carolyn, shortly after her friend picked up the call and they exchanged greetings. "It's the strangest thing."

"How so?"

Obviously puzzled, Carolyn sighed. "Lately, I've been getting random emails on the encrypted app my brother's tech guy originally installed on my computer. And that's after weeks of being cut off completely from them. Even weirder, all of them show me being blind copied as the recipient."

"So who are they from?" wondered Kiri.

"That's kind of bizarre too," said Carolyn. "Some are from Billy, and some denote no sender at all. Mostly though, since none of them involve me, I don't have a clue why I'm receiving them at all."

"What are they about?"

"The majority of them are more or less routine, I guess," replied Carolyn. "They mention meeting at particular places and at certain times in general."

"That could be very valuable," Kiri noted.

"But only to them," Carolyn shot back.

"What do you mean?"

"It's all coded," Carolyn explained. "Someone giving orders says something like, 'we'll stay in the dirigible at Gullible, Washington, and meet separately at night a half hour from when the sun is over the yard arm.' Or, 'bring three squads of tomatoes to the Toenail House, precisely at mid-morning happy hour.' It's something they apparently understand among themselves, but useless to anyone else."

"Is there anything that makes sense?" asked Kiri.

"Oh yeah – more or less," Carolyn replied, qualifying her answer. "Some of the emails were directives about laying low and going back to sleep for a time."

"That certainly makes sense after all the devastation and destruction they've caused," Kiri observed. "Every soldier and law enforcement official in Cascadia is searching for them, hoping to prevent further attacks."

"Yep, and while the authorities are preoccupied with all that," said Carolyn, "I've also read a couple emails regarding a change in tactics, a moving into a new phase."

"What kind of tactics?"

"It's frightening," Carolyn admitted, "and that's mainly why I needed to call you. They talk about beheadings to come. I think it's more figurative than literal – though for all I know it could be literal too."

"They're planning on killing people?"

"From what I've read," Carolyn said cautiously, "I get the sense that assassination is the next phase, the next tactic."

Kiri exhaled audibly into the phone. "If that's the case, I suppose it isn't too difficult to guess who the targets will be."

"Not difficult at all," agreed Carolyn. "Likely it'll be any big-wig in the oil or gas business. I tell you, Kiri, all this gives me the creeps. And creepiest of all, I don't know why I started receiving the occasional email on the encrypted app again after being cut off weeks ago."

"I don't suppose you can ask your brother," said Kiri.

"I haven't had any contact with either Billy or Timmy for some time now," Carolyn noted. "I don't even know how to get in touch with them anymore. So it makes me wonder with these emails popping up, maybe it's Billy's way of saying he's doing okay. That would be fine, but I fear it could be something much more sinister as well."

"Like what, for instance?"

"A part of me wonders if Garf Taylor isn't trying to trap me," she admitted. "Then again, I don't know; it could just as easily be some kind of glitch in the software that's allowing the occasional random email to get through."

"Well, Carolyn, keep reading them when they show up," Kiri urged. "If anything concrete comes along, maybe my friends can help deter and end this madness."

Carolyn was silent on the other end for the longest time. When finally she spoke, it was quietly to inquire, "Kiri, do your friends include Chris Cadia?"

Taken aback by the unexpected query, Kiri's mind rushed through several scenarios. Even though Carolyn was a close confidant and a dear friend of her cousin Ingri, Kiri was suddenly on guard. She wouldn't give anything away and she couldn't stop from conjuring the worst. Was Carolyn being forced to make this call? Was it being listened to and taped by the surveillance state? Or was Carolyn just asking the question as a friend? In the end, there was only one way to answer and that was with the truth.

"Carolyn," Kiri spoke softly, "Chris Cadia is a mythical figure. He's something many in Cascadia envision as an idealized leader or savior of some sort that has materialized to get us out of this mess – this mess the corporate oligarchs have saddled the planet and people with. But he's not real; we're all in this together."

"Well, myths are often based on fact," Carolyn pointed out. "So if he is your friend, maybe he's the only one that can detour us around an upcoming disaster. Kiri, do whatever you can to help him pay it forward."

Kiri was astounded; it was if her friend hadn't heard a word she said. But it didn't really matter.

"I'll do whatever I can," promised Kiri, "because I know you will too. We're all in this together."

***

After hours of churning it over and over in his mind, as far as Stone McClelland could discern there were two credible alternatives. And since he'd heard nothing further from the representative for Chris Soles, he could only base his deductions on what he had so far.

So at least until further notice, the intel from Bertie Stanton and the FBI could apparently be deemed authentic. Assumedly, Sapphire MacKenzie would quickly get to the bottom of that intrigue. If her chief assistant's boyfriend was not an undercover cop Stone would probably hear about it from Soles' representative; if he was, MacKenzie would likely deal with it and he'd hear nothing back directly.

As far as his handler Roger and ultimate employer Whitley Dellenbach were concerned, the matter was a good deal more complicated. One the one hand, nothing had come back to dispute the information regarding Sapphire MacKenzie's snooping neighbor or the staffer spy in Free Cascadia's Portland office, so perhaps that information was good.

On the other hand, what he received from Roger regarding the fellow named Tomas Hernandez and the Commons movement was branded as disinformation by the rep for Chris Soles. So if this was true, McClelland had repeatedly stewed, what was the motive and reasoning behind it?

The initial answer was easy enough to guess, but that only led to more questions. To begin with, it didn't take a rocket scientist to see that the interests of the mighty Dellenbach Brothers empire with its dominating and exploitative tentacles of corporate control would be in direct conflict with a cooperative grassroots Commons movement that eschewed privatization and promoted the common good.

That was the simple answer, but why was it that Roger and the Dellenbachs didn't think he'd see through the disinformation sooner – via his quarry Chris Soles – or later, eventually on his own? On many levels it was personally insulting as well. Did his employer believe he was a fool or patsy, a minion of theirs without a brain of his own that could figure things out? If such a scenario were true, how far indeed could he trust Whitley Dellenbach regarding anything he'd been told – especially during the recruiting process?

The other alternative Stone McClelland deemed credible as a result of the recent exchange of possible "trusts" dealt with Chris Soles and his representative. For starters, to be as objective as possible in the underworld of the gray and vague, Soles was protecting Tomas Hernandez for some reason. In short, the disinformation claim he came back with could in actuality be disinformation from Soles to McClelland for – for what? The only answer Stone could come up with was to protect Hernandez. But then again, for what, and why?

Following that line of thought, it was possible that Hernandez was on the secret list of contacts that Whitley Dellenbach told him at their initial meeting that Soles had inherited — and that list was part of his mission to obtain when he caught up with Soles. That too hinged upon whether he could believe what Dellenbach told him was true or not. And without more information, Stone didn't know what to make — if anything — of the connection between Tomas Hernandez's wife, Linda, and Sapphire MacKenzie.

Further, because he couldn't yet comprehend the connection between Sapphire MacKenzie and Chris Soles, he had to lean toward the assumption that Soles had some entwinement with the Hernandez people through MacKenzie. And maybe that's why Soles was protecting Hernandez and apparently had his back.

Or perhaps, what he received about Hernandez from Roger was exactly what the rep for Soles said it was: disinformation.

Most perplexing of all, however, were the questions regarding the connection between Whitley Dellenbach and Sapphire MacKenzie. As McClelland's starting point for this entire crazy escapade, he still didn't understand how they were related but somehow sensed this was integral to the mission he was on in the Northwest.

The Dellenbach Brothers and their fossil fuel corporate conglomerates were everything Sapphire and her Free Cascadia movements were against. Yet, for Stone McClelland, whatever was between them was becoming the same glue that held the door shut for him when it came to why he set the prisoner Chris Soles free — and how to liberate his own soul.

The whole mess was complicated and convoluted, yet as far as the recent exchange of information was concerned, Stone leaned toward having more faith in Soles and his rep, than his own employer. Still, there was yet much jabbing and feinting to be swapped and bartered as they moved forward, for it was the only way to play the great game of trust.

***

They had been through the accusations, the disbelief, anger, and recriminations, through the threats and finally the tears.

After Sapphire had told Amanda Pierce about her boyfriend Sean's possible double life as an undercover cop, Amanda was visibly stunned.

"There's no way in hell that could be true," the young woman protested, shaking her head with its stylish cut of short blond hair. "Why are you doing this to me?"

"Because, very likely, it is true," Sapphire replied patiently.

For several minutes Amanda had railed at Sapphire, growing more perturbed and upset by the second. She claimed Sapphire must have some sort of personal agenda against her and Sean; she shouted retaliatory threats at Sapphire and claimed she would do everything she could to bring the Free Cascadia movement down for promoting such vicious lies.

Sapphire sat with cool aplomb through all her assistant's tirades, quite poised and self-assured. She had asked Amanda to stay late, so just the two of them were in the office alone.

"Is that what you really want," Sapphire posed calmly, "the demise of the Free Cascadia movement?"

The question was an awakening slap in the face for Amanda Pierce. From being overwhelmed by rage, she transformed into self-questioning bewilderment, only to finally be overtaken by a torrent of tears that were cried out on Sapphire's shoulder.

When the tears finally ceased, Sapphire helped Amanda back into her seat and handed her a box of tissues.

"Let's take it slow here okay – step-by-step," Sapphire proposed with equanimity. "I understand you love Sean, but really, how well do you know him?"

"How well do I know him?" Amanda shot back indignantly, a little bit of the earlier anger surfacing once more. "I've slept with him for over three years; that's how well I know him!"

While allowing the young woman her dignity but probing onward nonetheless, Sapphire inquired if she slept with him every night during those three plus years.

"Of course not," the assistant snapped. "Sometimes he takes off on hunting trips and recently he went to Alaska to interview for a ranger position."

"Are you certain he went to Alaska?"

"That's what he told me and I believe him."

"Have you ever been on a long trip with him?" wondered Sapphire.

"Only up to B.C. for few days in Victoria," Amanda replied. "Neither one of us has a lot of money for extended vacations."

"When did you meet him?"

"Just after I started working here."

"Uh-huh," nodded Sapphire. "And have you been to meet his family?"

"He doesn't have a family," the young woman blurted. "He grew up in orphanages and foster homes back east somewhere."

"With all due respect, Amanda," said Sapphire, laying it on the line, "he could be anybody. Likely he's a good lover and confidant, but it's just as likely he could be an undercover cop spying on 'subversives.'"

Amanda Pierce at last admitted the possibility, then added, "But you have no real proof. It's just something that someone told you."

"You are quite correct," agreed Sapphire. "So let's set up a little test for him."

"What kind of test?"

"I'll get to that in a minute," MacKenzie promised. "But first let's set some ground rules about the consequences from such a test."

"For instance?"

"For instance," began Sapphire, "if he passes the simple test, he's still your boyfriend. And I will very humbly ask your forgiveness for doubting him."

"And if he fails the test?" Amanda asked.

"If he fails," Sapphire replied, "he's out of your life forever if you want to stay with Free Cascadia – or you're out of Free Cascadia if you subsequently still choose him."

"That's fair enough," the young woman stated. "So what's the test?"

Sapphire smiled. "Like I said, it's very simple. Your boyfriend is the only one that will get this information and we'll see where it goes – or doesn't go. Let him know we plan a mass protest on the downtown Seattle waterfront exactly a week from this coming Saturday. That's about ten days away. We will not be obtaining a permit to demonstrate because they wouldn't issue one anyway, but we will be 'adequately prepared' – tell him that – in expectation of an inevitable confrontation with military troops and police."

"That's it?" wondered Pierce.

"That should be more than enough to get the ball rolling," chuckled MacKenzie, "and then we do a little change-up."

"What kind of change-up?"

Conspiratorially, Sapphire laughed once again.

"I promise you'll be the first to know – when it's time."

CHAPTER TWENTY-FIVE

A mere three days later, on a sunny August Saturday morning in Seattle, Sapphire gazed upon an ever-swelling sea of protestors. Rapidly, they were filling the U.S. Federal Courthouse Plaza and streets beyond, about a mile from the Space Needle. Proudly at her side was Amanda Pierce, adorned in shorts and top colorfully dyed to resemble the Cascadia Doug flag.

Sapphire had already welcomed the demonstrators hoisting thousands of Cascadia flags with preliminary remarks and was now listening to lawyer Ambrose Pike addressing the throng. He was a short man with a bulbous nose and booming voice that sought to illuminate the gathered, so as to redress the constitutional wrongs those in Cascadia suffered at the hands of their government.

"I personally have talked with over one hundred people who have been subjected to searches of their homes and vehicles without warrants or court orders," claimed Pike into the microphone. "Under the guise of pursuing the Future Generations revolutionists, many others have been excluded from their homes, or ordered to stay in their homes by the authorities."

Ambrose Pike pointed an accusatory finger at the tens of thousands still gathering before the Federal Courthouse. "You – yes, you – may be one of these innocent third parties! You very likely have no relationship with the Future Generations revolutionists, but the state and local police, the FBI, and now military troops, are doing whatever they want, while ordering people to permit them to go through their homes and vehicles – all in violation of the U.S. Constitution.

"I've been asked here today to tell every such aggrieved individual in Cascadia what they should be doing in these circumstances," the lawyer proclaimed with gusto.

As Sapphire listened to Pike, she was glad he was able to get up here from Portland at such short notice. The people of Cascadia that had almost spontaneously assembled this Saturday morning needed the information he could provide. More souls than she could have ever imagined now strained to hear what they could from the woefully inadequate public address system that had been put together on the fly, yet the fact that the thousands and thousands were here was really the only thing they all needed.

Sapphire glanced at Amanda in her Cascadia Doug flag garb and marveled how unexpected this entire assemblage was only a few days ago. A day and a half after Amanda confided in her boyfriend plans about a supposed major rally on the Seattle waterfront in nine or ten days, the authorities publicly decried rumors of the same. By legal rights granted under Section 1021 of the National Defense Authorization Act, it was announced time and again in the media, under the current State of Emergency no mass assemblies would be allowed at the downtown Seattle waterfront or elsewhere.

By Friday morning, yesterday, Amanda Pierce knew she had been betrayed along with everything else she believed in. With tears in her eyes she had come to Sapphire and said, "I'm with you and Free Cascadia one hundred percent. So what are we going to do, Sapphire?"

"I told you that you'd be the first to know," she had replied, "and you will. But for starters, we'll be staying in a hotel over in Seattle tonight near the Space Needle. So go home, grab your overnight things and anything special you want to wear when we turn over the apple cart tomorrow."

At the hotel in Seattle and after dining early, Sapphire told Amanda, "It's time for the change-up I told you about."

"What do you mean?"

"I want you to call three friends you feel you can absolutely trust with Cascadia's future," Sapphire explained. "Tell them about a spontaneous mass rally tomorrow at U.S. Courthouse Plaza, at 700 Stewart Street, in Seattle at nine AM sharp. Ask them to attend, then tell them to each call three of their most trusted friends, and each of those to call three more, and so on down the line."

"What else should we do?"

"I'll do the same as you with three trusted friends," Sapphire had promised. "After that we'll get in touch with some people here that can quickly arrange microphones and loudspeakers in the public space shortly before The People begin to arrive."

And did The People ever continue to arrive and arrive, Sapphire thought to herself as she gazed down the steps of the Courthouse to the throng filling the plaza and streets as far as she could see. Presently, the thousands were mostly silent as they listened to attorney Pike as he reminded all of their legal rights when confronted by the authorities.

"If a LEO, a law enforcement officer, stops you in your vehicle," said the lawyer, "you need only produce your driver's license, registration, and insurance cards. You do not have to speak with the LEO or answer any questions. The only other thing you must do is ask the LEO if you are free to depart!"

An automatic cheer burst forth from the gathered masses before the attorney could continue.

"If the LEO tells you no, you are not free to depart," trumpeted Ambrose Pike into the microphone, "you should immediately demand your attorney – and don't budge an inch – as you next ask for LEO's name and badge number. Never, ever, consent to any search, no matter what they promise or threaten. It's likely they will attempt to intimidate and browbeat you with threats of obtaining search warrants for your vehicle or home. But again, don't budge an inch: if they think they can get a warrant, well then, make them!"

Once again, rooting and praise erupted from the crowd amidst the pumping of Cascadia flags.

As the attorney began speaking about keeping track of financial and/or other damages incurred as a result of the deprivation of one's rights, Sapphire began to notice the first indication of the presence of police state authorities. It was happening to her right, along one of the buildings far down the street. From her perch atop the entry steps to the Courthouse, she could detect a line of troops in riot gear worming their way between the building and the crowd. No doubt there would be more, Sapphire fully understood, as all assembled lurched forward to the inevitable outcome.

Ambrose Pike was finishing up by reminding all once more of the importance of documenting the name and badge number of every LEO and what that officer said or did.

"Just because the revolutionists have killed one of their brethren and wreaked havoc on the fossil fuel empire, it does not give them the right to violate your rights!" the attorney stormed in conclusion.

After Pike stepped away from the makeshift podium, Sapphire took up the microphone to thank him for his pertinent information. She then introduced Glen Aaron, leader of Free Cascadia in Portland.

Aaron began to speak softly, yet forcefully. And as he did, Sapphire could see more and more troops and uniformed police slithering into position in response to the spontaneous gathering of so many protesters, with their backs to more and more buildings, their helmets and riot shields before them.

Glen Aaron gained momentum and enthusiasm as he railed against repression and the violation of constitutional rights by Empire's forces in Cascadia. He slammed the cessation of dissent proclaimed by authorities and the attempt to restrict the free exercise of first amendment rights.

"It is time for the true revolution against the corporate oligarchs and fossil fuel kingpins to begin in Cascadia!" Aaron proclaimed to great applause and the pumping up and down of Cascadia Doug flags.

"And I must stress the absolute necessity for non-violence in this revolution," he continued. "We cannot defeat Empire with force, but nevertheless – we can defeat them! We are The Thin Green Line!"

Aaron hoisted the Doug flag he had brought to the microphone high into the air.

"Onward to the revolution and a sovereign, Free Cascadia!" he boomed into the microphone, again to great vocal acclaim.

On cue, a few steps directly below Glen Aaron, fellow demonstrators broke out one United States flag and one Canadian flag. Both were then set afire and as they slowly burned, thousands of Cascadia Doug flags were waving in the air frenetically, and joyfully.

From the gathered masses erupted the repetitive chant of, "Free Cascadia! Free Cascadia! Free Cascadia!"

The repetitive shouts and flag waving continued unabated for several minutes. And as it did, Sapphire could observe that troops and heavily armed tactical police teams had taken the perimeters about the base of nearly all buildings in the area, almost like impenetrable rocks surrounding the shores of islands in an inland sea. With backs to banks, brokerage buildings, and storefronts of multinational corporate retail chains – the edifices of capitalism – the forces of Empire were now nearly all in place and prepared for the inevitable.

Many of the troops and riot squads were close enough that Sapphire could clearly see the batons in their belts, their ballistic vests and body armor, their helmets with swat hoods and spit shields. She realized they all carried a devastating number of offensive weapons, including stinger rubber ball grenades, pyrotechnic pocket grenades, and twelve gauge bean bag rounds, as well as any combination of mace, pepper spray, or tear gas.

Sapphire MacKenzie knew as well as anyone what was coming.

Nevertheless, by the time she stepped up to the microphone once more, she stood forth undeterred. Having quieted, the crowd awaited her words.

Smiling broadly, Sapphire said with great pride, "The call went out to all quarters – and The People have responded today!"

Cheers erupted once again to the chants of, "Free Cascadia," and the hoisting of Doug flags.

When the assembled masses quieted once more, Sapphire wanted to change the subject matter. She told the crowds that they had gathered here at the Federal Courthouse today to demand justice and their constitutional rights during a trumped up State of Emergency, but just as importantly she wanted to reclaim The People's narrative when it came to one of Cascadia's own – that being Chris Cadia.

"Yes, Chris Cadia," she repeated. "You all know the stories about him! Some say he hands out psychedelic mushrooms as a gift upon first meeting. Others say he promotes a new paradigm for the future of our Cascadia, a casting off of our inherited patriarchal heritage, a rejection of hierarchal-based competition, domination and exploitation of others and our planet. In our quest for this new paradigm, still others say he strives to adopt a more cooperative, global community, where gender equality is taken as the norm and the individual matters every bit as much as those whose greed and avarice have taken them to what we now call the top. Some people even talk of Chris Cadia as a spiritual leader, boldly venturing forth into a new sustainable future for us and our descendants."

Sapphire paused and could sense the impact of her words on the thousands before her.

"Some say this Chris Cadia is a living individual," she continued, "some say he's a myth. I say: if he's a real person or not, does it really matter? He was always *our* idea; that's all that really matters! In Cascadia we should be content with the reality that Chris Cadia is an idea; he's an idea for Cascadia to circle round, to quest positively toward for a brighter future for our planet and our descendants!

"Unfortunately, however, the fossil fuel kingpins and oligarchs of Empire have done all they can to usurp and betray our idea," Sapphire carried on. "They've put him in combat camouflage, they have him planting bombs and derailing trains. Of course, this is a typical ploy, standard operating procedure for a calcified, intractable, and corrupt regime intoxicated by it's own obsession for power. They take the good guy, the good idea, and then make it bad through propaganda that undermines the genuine – and thus justify destroying it.

"But we're not going to let this happen with *our* idea of Chris Cadia!" proclaimed MacKenzie into the microphone. "Here, today, we take back our idea of Chris Cadia, be he real – or yes, simply an idea and ideal. Will you stand with me and stand for *our* idea of Chris Cadia – in Cascadia?"

Once again, the gathered masses broke into cheers; they pumped and waved thousands of Cascadia Doug flags to the reverberant chant of, "Free Cascadia! Free Cascadia! Free Cascadia!"

Things began quieting down a few minutes later and Sapphire was prepared to speak more – but suddenly hundreds and hundreds of police whistles pierced the air on a coordinated signal. Spit shields had been temporarily lifted, the whistles sounded again and then a third time, before utter silence took sway over what had been an expressive and raucous crowd.

Even as the troops and riot squads were either donning gas masks or refitting spit shields, loudspeakers from atop the Federal Courthouse began to boom. Like Empire's God from on high, the people were being warned and reminded such assemblies were illegal by law under the present State of Emergency. All in attendance were further advised to disperse immediately.

Already though, tear gas canisters were being lobbed at random into the milling crowd and smoke began to arise.

A single voice cried out in reply, "Free Cascadia!"

Sapphire MacKenzie, still at the makeshift podium, heard the desperate call. Into the microphone before her, she shouted back, "We are the Cascadian resistance; we are The Thin Green Line! And I say: Free Cascadia!" and commenced with the vigorous pumping and waving of the flag in her hands.

Hundreds of others responded. As one, the chant of, "Free Cascadia!" filled the city streets, accompanied by the fluttering of flags.

And then, the military troops and police assault teams moved in with full force.

***

Late that Saturday night – actually, it was early Sunday morning – a deep vibration from heavy pounding on the front door carried through the walls, floor, and ceiling of the Edmonds house, startling awake both Tomas and Linda Hernandez.

They were in total darkness; only the hint of light from a waning moon crept through the bedroom curtains. There was no green glow of time from the bedside clock and there was no reassuring nightlight for the kids in the hallway past their open door.

Suddenly, the pounding stopped and all they could hear were the footfalls of many feet thundering toward them. Tomas was out of bed but before he could reach the bedroom door, they were already through it – maybe nine or ten of them.

Bright flashlights blinded both Tomas and Linda, paralyzing them for a precious heartbeat. And then Tomas was tackled and pinned to the floor. Two strong sets of male hands anchored Linda to her place in bed while at the same time she heard the shredding of duct tape. She fought back, struggled, and started to scream, but the tape applied to her mouth rendered her silent.

Nevertheless, in her writhing about, as flashlights darted about the bedroom, she caught sight of Tomas on the floor just in time to see a hypodermic needle being injected into his shoulder. Whatever drug they gave him worked quickly; mere seconds later his entire body went limp.

When Linda realized how desperate circumstances had become a panic overtook her. Violently, she thrashed about, trying to free her arms while kicking the air with her feet. A brutal slap to her face stunned and rendered Linda inert.

"Don't be stupid," warned a gruff and passionless voice.

With flashlights in her eyes the whole time and overpowered, with her husband unconscious on the floor and fearing for the lives of her children, Linda gave up the struggle entirely.

She heard the sounds of male grunting as several men beyond the flashlights scooped up Tomas and dragged him out of the room.

Someone with a hoarse voice, maybe their leader, informed her about the status of events. "You're husband is being taken into custody for suspicion of aiding and abetting the Future Generations terrorist organization."

Unable to speak because of the duct tape, Linda emotionally rejected the entire notion by vigorously shaking her head. But the flashlight people paid her no heed.

"Now we're going to secure you to the bed," the man with the gravelly voice continued, "and then we'll let your children come in and join you before we leave. You'll be able to escape your bonds soon enough – but your husband will be in custody, perhaps for a long time."

Speaking to his men, the leader barked, "Okay, tape her to the bed."

As he reached the bedroom entry, however, he turned back to Linda and said, "Oh yeah, you'll probably want a copy of the warrant for your husband's arrest. I'll leave it right here on the top of this dresser."

Maybe three or four hours later, Chris and Kiri awoke to a phone call from a very frantic Linda Hernandez. Chris immediately turned on the speakerphone so they both could hear.

With her heart still pounding, Linda spoke rapid-fire and staccato, blending facts and racing emotion into a mostly understandable narrative. She told them how intruders had invaded their house in the dead of night, how the power had been turned off, and how Tomas had been abducted. She rattled off what had happened after being securely duct taped to the posts of the bed, how the children had helped set her free, and with a flashlight she made it to the breaker box in the garage to restore the power. Aided by lights once more, Linda found the side garage door lock had been damaged, the front entry door was nearly off its hinges, and then the warrant for her husband's arrest on the top of the dresser where the leader with the hoarse voice had left it.

When Cassie and Kyle were sufficiently calmed and settled down, Linda said she had called the Edmonds police. The cop that took the report was patient, even empathetic. He said after the unlawful demonstrations and riot control in downtown Seattle earlier in the day, the Federal authorities were now actively rounding up many suspects throughout the Northwest. Apparently, he felt genuinely sorry for them, so after they gathered their stuff together and secured the front door as best they could, the cop drove them in his squad car to stay with Linda's mom.

"I'm just an emotional mess, you guys," Linda nearly screamed into the phone. "My children and I have been traumatized and terrorized, and my husband has been abducted. I just don't know what to do."

Without a solution, she jumped to the next best alternative. "Chris, you've got to do something. You're our only hope; the people of Cascadia are behind you. You've got to do something."

Chris looked up from the phone into Kiri's eyes and didn't know what to say.

But Linda was insistent. "Lead the people of Cascadia out of this mess, Chris. They believe in you."

"It's all a myth," he protested, "and certainly not one of my own making."

"Then use the myth!" demanded Linda. "Bring us all together and get Tomas back."

Chris recognized that such was likely beyond his powers, but he promised Linda he'd do whatever he could.

"I love you, Chris," she said emphatically. "It was a good day when you came into our lives."

He reciprocated honestly, saying he felt the same way about them.

Still somewhat understandably distraught, Linda's thoughts leaped onward. "And what about Sapphire – and all the others that were taken to jail? We saw it all on TV last night."

Kiri graciously stepped in. "We don't know, Linda. But we're worried for her and so many others. The whole world's gone crazy; I don't know if it can get any worse."

Attempting to calm the waters primarily because there was little else possible at this juncture, Chris mentioned, "I think all we can do right now is give everything a little time. Things will sort themselves out. The authorities will find Tomas is in no way connected to the terrorists and they'll likely set him free."

"I seriously have my doubts about that," Linda shot back quite skeptically.

"Why?" wondered Chris.

"You know that warrant I told you about that they left on the dresser?"

"Yes?"

"It was nothing but a blank piece of paper."

***

As the days dragged on, Chris and Kiri knew full well they were trapped and held captive in place, as was the rest of Cascadia.

With the further daily deployment of more and more military troops, a stranglehold on the entire region was effectively seized while individual lives were held in abeyance.

Checkpoints and roadblocks were erected on the outskirts of every town and village, on all major and most minor passages of egress. Entry lanes to freeways were backed up for miles as identification papers were validated before getting on the road, and random spot checks for I.D. popped up at grocery stores, in taverns and strip malls, and even convenience stores and clinics. Strict curfews after the fall of darkness were harshly enforced while commerce everywhere crept closer and closer to a standstill.

Soldiers armed with assault rifles patrolled the city streets, as well as the rural back roads. The citizenry was held hostage, yet they learned quickly not to complain aloud – for if the whispered rumors were true, those that did often disappeared in the night.

And if Empire didn't have full prior control over the mass media before, it most certainly did now. Night after night in virtually all evening newscasts, the current State of Emergency was lauded for bringing a stop to the out of control terrorism, and for providing the necessary riot control after recent mass demonstrations turned into chaos. And, of course, there wasn't a dissenting voice to be heard.

For Chris and Kiri, the absence of Sapphire and Tomas and their own inability to help their friends weighed heavily upon them. There was no news regarding either of them and no way they could obtain any information. Furthermore, they were indeed trapped and held captive where they were. Obviously, it would be futile to venture beyond the Elder's property where they'd been given sanctuary, especially with Chris Soles still being touted as "most wanted" and "the ringleader of the Future Generations terrorists."

As the days edged closer to the end of August, the only release for Kiri and Chris was their hikes through the Elder's property and into the surrounding woods. Still, they were careful even here, always on the lookout for soldiers on random patrol. From the clearing on the ridge they could observe to the southwest, towards the Bangor submarine base, the military troops with their checkpoints on the main Highway 3 thoroughfare. And even if that was frightfully close, as of yet they had seen no foot soldiers on the forest trails.

Returning from a hike around mid-afternoon seven or eight days after Sapphire's arrest and Tomas' abduction, both Kiri and Chris suffered from the torment of the day. The weather was uncommonly hot and humid and, while in the forest, they had been cruelly assaulted by swarms of mosquitoes and flies, as well as a host of other insects they couldn't name and didn't want to know.

They would have preferred to totally escape the bugs inside the cabin, but without air conditioning it was a virtual oven. On the other hand, the outside deck at least offered the hint of a breeze. Kiri brought them glasses of the lemonade she'd prepared before the hike and both plopped with great pleasure onto the outside bench under a shady overhanging roof.

As he was removing his hiking boots and airing out his toes, Chris started it all by comparing the flies, mosquitoes, and various insects that had been torturing them to the current swarm of Empire's police state.

"They're both everywhere and in prodigious number," he complained. "The heat is on and the people are oppressed."

Raising a mischievous eyebrow, Kiri sweetly replied, "That's why there's so much more water. It's meant to be our escape route, an avenue of imagination that we float away on to a new future."

Though Chris agreed in principle, he could already see where she was going. His only alternative was to play the Devil's Advocate.

"You can't escape the flies, mosquitoes, and other insects any easier than the repressive, domineering and exploitative, patriarchal mindset we've all inherited," he warned her.

"Ah, but so much water also means so many possibilities," she cooed. Kiri then confronted him head-on. "Do you know how much water is actually on this planet?"

Before Chris could say anything, Kiri had set down her lemonade, was off the bench, and through the cabin screen door for her notes in the bedroom. Having a darn good idea what was coming, Chris too was off their wooden seat for his folder of papers on the coffee table in the living room.

When both were once again outside, Kiri asked her question again – and even more specifically.

"What is the total number of gallons of water in all of Earth's oceans, seas, lakes, and bays?" she probed.

Chris couldn't come up with a quick answer, so Kiri laid out the facts.

"It's so simple, I'm surprised you don't know," she jabbed with gusto. "The answer is about 3.52 times 10 to the 20th power gallons. And that's a lot of water."

"How do you know that?"

"I asked my phone; it's smarter than God."

Chris threw his hands into the air and moaned in feigned frustration.

"I was afraid we were going to get to that at some point," he whined. "So I reckon it's time we raised the ante."

"What do you mean, 'raise the ante?'" she asked suspiciously.

"I think instead of just flies," he proposed, "we should focus upon the total quantity of insects on the planet compared to the total gallons of water."

"Changing the rules in the middle of the game isn't exactly fair," Kiri protested. "Still, I'd venture to guess there's more water than insects on the planet."

Chris flipped through his folder of papers until he found what he wanted. "Okay, how about this? It says here that there are 200 million insects for each human on the planet and that there're 300 pounds of insects for every pound of humans."

"That's irrelevant and misleading," Kiri snapped in judgment. "Please confine yourself to the stated discussion of either more gallons of water on the planet, or more total insects – which I've so kindly granted you to bring into question."

"Okay, if that's the way it's going to be," Chris began as he shuffled his papers and found what he wanted, "here's something for you to chew upon. It says that at any given time, it's estimated that there are some 10 quintillion – that's ten with eighteen zeros behind it – individual insects alive on the planet."

"So that means there's more water than insects," stated Kiri jubilantly.

"Both water and insects quantities are mere estimates," cautioned Chris.

Kiri shrugged her shoulders. "Well, I can give you unit conversions too."

"Unit conversions?"

"For sure," she smiled. "If you want the amount of total water on the planet in cubic feet instead of gallons, there's 4.704 times 10 to the 19th power of cubic feet. I can also give it to you in liters or cubic meters if you prefer."

"Spare me."

"Well, what if I give you the volume of earth as compared to the volume of earth's oceans?"

Chris dourly remarked, "Your phone is too smart for it's own good."

Still looking at her notes, Kiri further offered, "I can even give you the total volume of the moon."

"Ha!" laughed Chris. "How much water is there?"

"I dunno," Kiri smiled back. "Probably about the same as the number of insects buzzing around up there."

"Precisely my point!" exclaimed Chris.

Moving past the juncture of making much sense, Kiri began tiring of their playful jousting. Standing, she took Chris by the hand and urged him off the bench.

Joining their hot and still sweaty bodies together, Kiri wrapped her arms around him, and he around her.

"Chris, we've got to do something about Sapphire," she said from the heart.

"I'm worried about her too," he concurred with equal emotion. "And Tomas as well."

"And Tomas too," Kiri agreed. "So what do we do?"

Gently, Chris moved his hands under her chin and gazed into her eyes. "We look for guidance where guidance is available."

"Meaning?"

"Meaning we try to tap the wisdom of the aged," he explained. "Maybe it's time to convene a meeting with whatever Elders that can be gathered and seek their guidance."

"So be it then," Kiri acknowledged. "We have to do something."

CHAPTER TWENTY-SIX

At precisely 8:47 P.M. a van, with its sliding side door open, pulled up behind the Fish House restaurant overlooking Liberty Bay in Poulsbo, Washington. Seconds later, two restaurant workers emerged from the back door to the kitchen, hauling a container laden with cans and bottles destined for the recycle bin.

Behind them, the solitary figure of a woman also slipped out the kitchen door, but then ducked into the van and closed the sliding side door behind her.

Because their travel would be within the checkpoints surrounding Poulsbo, there would likely be no roadblocks or demands for identification on the short journey around to the other side of Liberty Bay. Soon, turning on the road that would take them to the cabin in the woods, the woman driving stopped before the padlocked gate at the entrance to the Elder's property. Briskly, she unlocked and opened the gate. She then returned to the van and drove through, only to stop once again to close and lock the gate behind her.

Chris was waiting on the porch of the little cabin and when he saw both Kiri and Sapphire step out of the vehicle together; the three of them were jubilant. He dashed to greet the women and immediately they were all hugging and kissing one another. When the spontaneous joy of the moment tapered down, they slowly made their way arm-in-arm inside the cabin, only to end up at the kitchen table.

The women each decided to have a glass of wine while Chris opted for an ale, and then the questions began.

"We're so glad you're finally free, Sapphire," gushed Kiri. "How did you finally get released and what happened at the checkpoint at the Agate Pass Bridge when leaving Bainbridge Island?"

Sapphire laughed. "The checkpoint hassles were minor compared to getting out of jail. With the travel restrictions and paperwork they now make me carry since my release, all I had to do was show it and they waved us through. But really, it all worked – so far – according to the plans we made this afternoon."

"So you came with your assistant Amanda and the authorities believe you are at her brother's place here in Poulsbo?" asked Kiri.

"Apparently so," replied Sapphire. "But I have to be back on Bainbridge by tomorrow."

"Well, we're overjoyed that you were finally released and can at least be here now," Chris said with a smile. "But what took so long for you to get out of jail? We saw news reports on TV about other protesters getting out mere days after the mass arrests at the demonstration a week and a half ago."

A troubled and puzzled shadow fell over Sapphire's face.

"I'm certain the persecutors within the police state were playing mind games with me," she admitted.

Sapphire then told her friends about being locked down in solitary detention the entire time. There was no interaction with other prisoners, no television or radio, and not a single guard spoke with here.

She told them about a secret benefactor – someone she'd met

years ago when working as a raft guide in Idaho – who had always secured her release quickly in such situations and who had funded her in the past.

"But even he was powerless this time to help me," Sapphire complained. "Empire was doing their best to break me down, but all it did was strengthen my resolve."

Chris and Kiri both smiled.

"We wouldn't expect anything less," remarked Kiri.

Quite happily, Sapphire reached out with her hands to Chris and Kiri on the kitchen table. "I can't express how glad I am to be back with both of you. But tell me, since I've been a little out of touch for a while, what else is happening that I should know about."

Kiri and Chris exchanged glances that spoke of heavy hearts and despondency.

"You probably don't know anything about Tomas and Linda Hernandez, do you?" Chris began.

"No, nothing," replied Sapphire, alarmed. "What's happened to them?"

As calmly as possible, Chris reiterated the events of the night after the demonstration where she and hundreds of others were arrested at the Federal Courthouse in Seattle. He recounted in detail how Tomas had been abducted from home in the middle of the night, how Linda had called them quite panicked in the early morning hours, and how she and the kids were staying at her mom's house in Lynnwood, fearing a return to their own home without Tomas.

"We've spoken with Linda daily using secure phone apps," Kiri added. "She's constantly been calling every governmental law enforcement agency she can get the number of, but no one seems to have any information on Tomas."

"She was back at the Edmonds police station again yesterday," Chris tossed in, "and came up empty handed there as well. They even had the gall to suggest some paramilitary group had abducted Tomas, or maybe the Future Generations people."

"That's utter nonsense," Sapphire declared without hesitation. "Such tactics would do nothing to benefit Garf Taylor and his people."

"We know that and you know that," Kiri agreed, "but we also know the tactics of Future Generations are likely undergoing a dramatic shift."

"Who told you that?" Sapphire wondered. Just as quickly, however, she requested, "No, don't tell me. The less people that know, the better."

"Sapphire," Kiri said in a tone almost scolding, "whatever we know, you can know. We're all together in this and we have to trust each other one hundred percent. Right, Chris?"

"Absolutely," Chris agreed. "We stand united for the duration."

"Well, that's how I feel too," Sapphire said, relishing the authentic support. "So tell me who it is if you want later, but tell me now what the change in tactics for Future Generations involves."

"According to our source," revealed Kiri, "Future Generations appears to be shifting away from destruction of fossil fuel infrastructure and product, and moving deliberately forward into planning assassinations."

Sapphire shook her head. "I hate to say it, but that probably makes perfect sense to Garf Taylor and his followers. If you could take out the Kingpins of Carbon, you not only eliminate your adversary, but you also establish a reign of chaos and terror – which is often the precursor to revolution."

"You're absolutely correct, Sapphire," conceded Chris. "And if their tactics are changing, so must ours."

"What are you proposing?" asked Sapphire.

Kiri answered for Chris. "We're not exactly certain at this point. But with no more public dissension or gatherings being permitted, and the crack down by the police state, something has to be done. So we think it would be a wise choice to gather as many Elders as possible, and as soon as possible, to seek their guidance."

"I think that would be an excellent idea," Sapphire responded enthusiastically. "And it should be in Port Townsend again, in Mister Q's old Victorian mansion."

"But how would we get there with all the roadblocks and checkpoints between here and Port Townsend?" posed Kiri.

"Talk to Bob and Donna Carlson, the Elders that own this cabin," Sapphire suggested. "They'll probably have some ideas."

"And how would you get to Port Townsend?" Kiri asked Sapphire.

"Oh, that'll be a piece of cake," chuckled Sapphire. "I'll secure paperwork that says I'm going to my parents' home in Port Townsend, and I'll meet you there."

Kiri was encouraged by Sapphire's enthusiasm. "Yes, indeed. We'll travel up there one way or another, we'll make a plan of action with the Elders, and we'll move forward together."

"Collectively," Sapphire declared, looking back and forth at Kiri and Chris, "we are one."

Kiri and Sapphire were downright serious, but a smile cracked Chris's lips.

Attempting to inject a little levity, he quipped, "What a great threesome we'd make!"

Sapphire and Kiri looked questioningly at one another for a

moment then, shrugging their shoulders, apparently agreed.

Chris was suddenly taken aback; he had expected laughter, not concurrence.

"On that note," Kiri announced to Sapphire, "you're staying here with us tonight. I have an extra nightgown as well as an extra toothbrush. And, you can use whatever else of mine you might need."

"That's wonderful," Sapphire said with a smile. "And I'm sure Amanda will understand when I don't show up at her brother's house."

"Everything will work out fine," acknowledged Kiri. "Before we go to bed though, and after another hot, sticky day, we're all taking showers."

Politely, kindly, Chris offered to let the girls take their showers first.

Sapphire and Kiri looked askew at each other; both then began shaking their heads.

"No way," Kiri beamed with pleasure. "Remember, we're a threesome."

"Huh?" murmured Chris.

"Yeah," chuckled Sapphire, "and a threesome should surely take a shower together."

The bewilderment openly displayed on Chris's face provoked conspiratorial giggles from the women.

"C'mon Chris," Kiri pleaded, urging him up from the kitchen table. With Sapphire's help, the women marched him toward the bathroom shower as Kiri exclaimed, "This'll be fun!"

Even as they entered the bathroom and Sapphire pulled back the shower curtain, Chris was protesting, "This is only a small tub with a shower head. I don't know if there's even enough room for all of us.

"There's plenty of room," Sapphire assured him. "It'll just take a little teamwork."

Sapphire's comment propelled the female co-conspirators into a paroxysm of giggles once again, as they briskly launched into the business of removing their clothing. Effortlessly, the shorts and panties of both girls dropped to the floor. Because Sapphire was wearing a bra, it took her a few seconds longer to get completely nude than Kiri who was braless.

After Kiri shook out her ponytail, she moved behind Chris to snatch towels from the nearby linen closet. As Sapphire bent over to begin adjusting the water faucets, Chris couldn't help but gawk transfixed by her beautiful and shapely backside. Such fascination and enticement didn't last long, however.

From behind, Kiri declared, "Time to shower, Chris," and with both hands tugging the sides of his gym shorts and then his underwear, Kiri made certain his lower half was unclothed in short order. Eagerly, she then assisted him in pulling his tee shirt over his head.

"I think I've got the water temperature just right," announced Sapphire, "so everybody in!"

Sapphire stepped over the side of the tub first, followed immediately by Chris and Kiri. As the last in, Kiri slid the shower curtain closed, telling Sapphire at the same time to, "Let her rip!"

Laughing heartily, Sapphire called out, "To the first of many threesome showers to come!" as she pulled up on the stopper and released the water from above.

Initially, Sapphire and Chris received the bulk of the water cascading down. Then Chris and Kiri changed places, as Sapphire shifted back, so that Kiri was thoroughly drenched. For the next several minutes a cautious and somewhat awkward dance under the water in such a small space ensued, accompanied by a great deal of hugging, kissing, and the occasional playful pinch, all with the assumed goal that everyone become wet and slippery.

Kiri soon determined thereafter that the women would take turns shampooing and conditioning each other's hair. While that was taking place, Chris was assigned to thoroughly soap up and rinse their bodies.

"And after that," Kiri assured him with a wink to Sapphire, "the two of us will take care of you."

Amidst even more conspiratorial female chuckles, Kiri turned Sapphire away from the flow of water, grabbed the shampoo bottle, and positioned herself behind her. Kiri began working the shampoo into Sapphire's soft shoulder length brown hair while urging Chris onward with his tasks.

Chris had no choice but do his best to oblige. Lathering up both hands, he began at Sapphire's right shoulder and armpit and worked his way down over her biceps and elbow, and on to her forearm and hand. Conscientiously, he followed suit with her left arm. After soaping up his hands anew, he quickly yet studious considered his next task.

With Sapphire's head and shoulders leaning backward as Kiri continued to shampoo her hair, this beautiful woman's breasts and firm nipples stood forth prominently and proudly. In an instant Chris realized he had to keep going. Enthusiastically he began soaping up her breasts and belly, to which Sapphire moaned pleasurably with eyes closed.

Abruptly, with arms suddenly encircling him, she drew Chris tight into her chest.

"Now, soap up my back while Kiri's still doing my hair," instructed Sapphire.

Once again, Chris followed the commands he'd been given. When he finished it was time for more soap and then Sapphire's long, elegant legs. Chris began the feet and between each toe as he assiduously worked his way up to the groin area on each leg.

Lathering up again, he was apparently too hesitant with her crotch area.

"Don't be so timid," Sapphire commanded, placing her hand over his with exacting pressure to assumedly insure proper cleaning.

From behind Sapphire, Kiri announced she had completed the shampooing process and was ready for a rinse before the conditioning formula was applied to the hair. Sapphire squeezed by Chris and stood fully under the shower, while Kiri wrapped her arm around his waist.

When Sapphire had fully rinsed, she squeezed out her hair and all three resumed their prior positions in the confined space of the tub. Kiri poured conditioner out of the plastic bottle into Sapphire's hair, even as Chris gawked at the two girls under the assumption that his duties for the moment were at a standstill.

Sapphire, however, had other ideas.

"What are you standing there for?" she asked.

"Huh?"

"Soap me up again, while Kiri's doing my hair," Sapphire sweetly ordered. "I want to make sure I'm clean after this shower."

More female snickers bounced about the small enclosure and Chris merrily complied. By the time Sapphire had rinsed once again, more and more steam was filling their tight chamber. Sapphire and Kiri exchanged positions for Kiri's shampoo and soaping, and Chris was tasked with the soaping of another lovely female form.

Her body, however, he had seen many times but never touched in the way he now would. Kiri's green eyes were smiling at him, inviting him onward, and he responded with obvious anticipation.

With soapy hands, Chris tenderly, lovingly, and with measured passion, explored inch and crack of her body not once, but twice as he'd been instructed to do with Sapphire. When Kiri completed her final rinse and stepped out of the pouring water, both sets of female eyes focused on Chris.

"Now, it's your turn," Sapphire said to him

A quick shampoo was followed by a quick rinse – and suddenly everything stalled.

Kiri and Sapphire were smiling at each other mischievously, then darting their eyes back in his direction. He knew precisely what was up, for there was no hiding it – especially among threesomes.

With a mind of it's own, his erection had started its steady rise when he was soaping Sapphire. By the time he had finished with Kiri, the darn thing was rock solid and pointing the direction to the heavens.

With a shared wink or two, the women eyeballed it a bit longer before deciding to each take a side of his body and soap longitudinally from shoulders to feet to begin, then decide what to do with the middle thereafter. Accordingly, Chris was generously lathered from neck to toes, while what stood out most prominently was temporarily bypassed.

Completing those chores and full of mischief, the women again winked at each other.

"So what do you think we should do with this?" Sapphire asked Kiri, as her hand firmly wrapped around his penis then stroked it up and down a couple times before letting go.

Kiri's grasp from underneath was equally solid as she too partook of some vigorous play, before setting it free.

"Oh, these boys," she exclaimed, feigning displeasure. "They have absolutely no patience whatsoever."

Once again, Sapphire grabbed him full on and pretended to address the erection, saying, "Don't you know there's a time and place for everything, and that it isn't now?"

Sapphire let loose and Kiri's hand latched on in place. She too directed her words to the stiff and unyielding rod.

"The time is not now," Kiri repeated. "I have foreseen that the time will come, but it is not now."

As before, the center of current attraction in the tight, steamy shower remained unbent and unrepentant.

"So what do we do with this thing?" Sapphire asked Kiri as she wrapped her hand about it once more.

With water still tumbling down upon them, Kiri shrugged her shoulders. "I guess we soap it up, rinse it off, and see if it becomes more civil after that."

Both women again shared a snigger as they busied themselves with lathering him up. Several times during the process as they gently massaged his testicles with slippery hands and soaped his granite hard member up and down, Chris was certain he was going to explode. Before that transpired though, Sapphire and Kiri guided him under the showerhead for a full-fledged rinse.

Upon retrieving him after the dowsing, the girls made a show of acting disappointed by shaking their heads and clucking as if frustrated.

"Look at this thing!" Sapphire exclaimed, securely gripping the inflexible pole once more. "It refuses to be socially acceptable and won't listen to reason."

"Maybe we should just hide it," suggested Kiri.

"Hide it?"

"Sure, that might be our only option," Kiri affirmed.

"You don't mean..." Sapphire's words trailed off.

"No, I don't mean that – not yet anyway," she pledged. "I mean if we just tucked it down between his legs and then closed them tight, maybe it would go away. You know, out-of-sight and out-of-mind."

"I don't know if that's the answer," Sapphire said dubiously, while still holding him fast and stroking him slow. "But let's give it a try anyway. You get behind him; I'll bend it down and push it through to you. Then we close his legs."

Chuckling to himself, Chris played the part of the willing victim. As Sapphire pushed his very stiff cock downward though, his upper body follow suit until he was quite bent over. Sapphire handed the wiener off to Kiri, as they both then attempted to seal his thighs together. When the women were satisfied with their work and believing they had accomplished their mission, Kiri announced she was letting go. And when she did, the imposing missile burst forth without hesitation as if a rocket rising from its silo.

"Well, that didn't work too well," observed Kiri.

"I guess there's only one thing left to do," Sapphire stated definitively.

"What's that?" asked Kiri.

"We kiss it good-bye," was all Sapphire replied.

Sapphire then whispered into Kiri's ear, which caused Kiri to laugh and whisper something back as well.

Moving in front of him and rotating Chris slightly so that Sapphire was directly under the pounding water, she went down on one knee, looked up at him, and said, "Okay, time to kiss it good-bye."

Taking hold of the throbbing unit once again, Sapphire placed her lips on the tip of his penis for a moment. She then opened her mouth and took in maybe an inch or two, all the while tickling and massaging with her tongue. With the warm shower water cascading down on her back, Sapphire eventually withdrew until it was no longer in her mouth. With her tongue, she made slow circles around the tip; finally, there was a very soft kiss at the top of Chris's obdurate member, as well as a final stroke or two of her hand – as if saying good-bye for now.

"Okay, Kiri," summoned Sapphire with a giggle, "it's your turn for fond farewells."

The women winked impishly as they changed places in the tight steamy quarters. When Kiri was positioned squarely under the warm streaming flow from the showerhead, she smiled first into Chris's eyes then dropped to her knees before him. Grasping his shaft at its base with her hand, Kiri perfunctorily kissed the tip, then slowly but surely ingested him entirely to where her hand held a grip at the base.

Just as slowly and surely, Kiri began backing off until he was completely out of her mouth. Then, like Sapphire, she doodled circles about the tip with her tongue before delivering the most tender of kisses to the tip.

"Okay, Chris, you've been kissed good-bye," Kiri declared, as she moved behind him to take a place next to Sapphire.

"Time now for a special treat," announced Sapphire

Smiling all the while, Chris fully realized Kiri and Sapphire were having great sport with him at his expense, but it would have been impossible to enjoy this shower any more than he did. Only in the very back of his mind did he harbor any forebodings of what might be next.

"Since you're taller than me, Sapphire," said Kiri, "maybe you can cover his eyes. I'll hold his hands behind him and we'll march him and his wooden dick straight into the water."

Still the willing victim, Chris allowed the girls to move him directly into the pounding water of the showerhead. They let him enjoy the warmth for several seconds. Then, with a smooth move Kiri shifted her grip so that one hand only held him by the wrists, and one hand was free.

With the free hand, she rapidly reached around him and turned off the hot water faucet. Immediately, the shock reverberated throughout his entire body. Kiri and Sapphire stayed shielded from the cold waterfall as best they could behind him, while Chris endured the brunt of it.

Under such a chilling stream, it didn't take Chris long to become limp as a noodle. Surrounded by female laughter, the water was completely shut off. Both Kiri and Sapphire took time to physically inspect the now shrunken and inert sausage. When satisfied, they kindly took turns with full body hugs in attempts to warm him after their shenanigans.

About an hour later, after towel drying one another amidst much kissing, hugging, and laughter; after the women assisted each other blowing their hair dry; after Chris slipped into baggy sleeping shorts and the girls donned matching nightgowns, they all slid under the sheets of the little cabin's queen size bed.

Positioning Chris in the middle with Kiri and Sapphire on either side, they kissed and hugged each other repeatedly before turning out the lights for good. Getting cozy, the girls laid their heads upon his shoulders. His arms on each side were around them, even as a solitary female leg from each girl was draped over his. Kiri and Sapphire interlocked arms atop his chest by gripping each other's forearm and contentment reigned.

As the minutes passed and all began to calm with sleep's approach, Chris felt a true happiness warm his heart again – for the first time since all those years ago when Empire murdered Ali, and their unborn child.

CHAPTER TWENTY-SEVEN

"Sorry I'm late," Stone McClelland apologized. "The traffic was as snarled as ever; if it wasn't for the security clearance you expedited for me, I wouldn't even be here."

"Humph," Bertie Stanton snorted grumpily. "I assume you've got something for me and that's why you wanted to meet."

"You assume correctly," Stone assured his friend, "but the rep for Chris Soles didn't give me much."

Stanton was visibly perturbed; he needed results. "Look, Stone, did you tell him that we gave up a high value asset embedded in the Free Cascadia movement and emphasize that we've gotten nothing in return?"

"I did."

"So what does he have for us?"

McClelland squirmed in his chair as he gazed absently about the commodious Pirate's Palace restaurant on one of the commercial piers on the downtown Seattle waterfront. The building was wide open with high ceilings and nautical paraphernalia graced all the walls.

Turning back to Bertie, Stone replied, "Like I said, he didn't give me much. But that's mostly because he didn't have a lot because, according to him, the Future Generations people have gone further underground than it's possible to dig."

"Stone," began Bertie patiently, "you know that, we know that; I suppose everybody knows that. But your source gave you something, so what is it?"

"The best that he could offer is that there's a change of tactics coming up," replied McClelland. "Supposedly there's a shift from attacking fossil fuel infrastructure to a focus on assassination."

Stanton was unfazed. "So who is Chris Soles planning on assassinating?"

For the moment, Stone held in check his objections that Chris Soles was even involved with potential assassinations. It didn't seem logical that his rep would be supplying them intelligence for whatever terror plots they may be planning.

"That's all he knew, Bertie," McClelland spoke calmly. "He didn't know who, when, or where. When he did, he said he'd get back to me."

"Well, that isn't shit," blurted Stanton.

Stone acknowledged it wasn't much. "But at least I've still got the connection alive to Chris Soles."

"So you better start jerking his chain," Stanton urged. "The current State of Emergency has the Future Generations terrorists frozen in their tracks, but we still fully intend to bring them to justice."

A waitress that had visited Bertie Stanton before McClelland's late arrival dropped by the table and asked the men if they had made selections for their meals. Bertie replied they hadn't even checked what was on the menu, but he'd take a cheeseburger. Stone assumed the Pirate's Palace would also offer grilled salmon, so he ordered the same.

After the waitress departed, Bertie informed Stone that promising, as well as curious, new developments had surfaced according to his people.

"First of all, our analysts are fairly certain an avowed revolutionist named Garfield Taylor has teamed up with the Maxwell brothers that I told you about before," revealed Stanton. "Taylor and his family have a long and troubled past, with deep roots of hatred for authority over the decades. There is good evidence that Taylor and the Maxwell brothers joined forces a few years ago through a mutual friend – a mutual friend that died in the suicide attack on the B.C. fuel storage depot in Burnaby. Further, it's suspected that they all work under the direction of Chris Soles – or Chris Cadia, as he's also known – although our people don't know yet how that original connection was established."

Abstaining from voicing his doubts once more regarding Chris Soles and the allegations surrounding him, McClelland simply took it all in without comment.

"Fortunately, there is one positive sign that we may be catching up with the terrorists," Stanton informed McClelland. "Our tech people think they may be on the verge of a breakthrough concerning their communications. Regardless of the fact that these people very likely are using phone apps that constantly alter numbers, and that the sim cards are repeatedly being discarded and replaced, our engineers are now using some new kind of algorithm so they'll eventually be able to track specific phones that link to other specific phones. All the technology they talk about is kind of over my head, but the geeks involved believe it's a hopeful development."

"That would be hopeful and helpful indeed," McClelland agreed.

Bertie shook his head.

"And once you think this whole Future Generations terrorist mess can't get any weirder," he stated in amazement, "we now have reason to believe there's an old geezer network out there that's likely involved."

"You got to be kidding me," Stone remarked in disbelief.

"Not at all."

"How old are we talking about?" wondered McClelland.

"There're probably some in their fifties," replied Stanton. "But more likely they are in their sixties and seventies, and probably even some eighties, and maybe nineties."

"But surely they're not planting bombs, derailing trains, and blowing up fossil fuel terminals," Stone McClelland objected.

"No," admitted Stanton, "though it is very possible that they are supplying the terrorists with material support."

"Are you serious?"

"I'm dead serious," Bertie affirmed. "You haven't been here long, so you don't understand the people of this place they call Cascadia. The passions run deep, they are intensely loyal to the bioregion. Many will defend Cascadia to their last breath – maybe even to the point of joining a terrorist revolution."

McClelland remained unconvinced. "How do you know the old geezer network, as you put it, is out there?"

"Oh, that's the easy part," Bertie explained. "It's from compilations of thousands of phone and email interactions. I tell you, these old farts have absolutely no comprehension of tracking technology. And it appears they might have organized throughout the Pacific Northwest – in B.C. and Alberta, Washington, Oregon, and Idaho, and even down into Northern California."

"But how do you know all these old geezers aren't discussing the next vacation, or where they should hold the next gathering to play shuffleboard?" asked Stone.

It was apparent that Stanton's patience was wearing thin.

"With all due respect, Stone, like I said, you simply don't understand the people here," Bertie admonished. "Many, young and old alike, have come under the spell of the trite pap that their Chris Cadia and others serve up on a regular basis. They all want to profess to be lovey-dovey, green and sustainable, and the world will right itself. But these people simply don't understand human nature. They don't really realize who we are or what we are: we're greedy, combative, competitive apes. And by being what we are, that's how our civilization worked itself to this advanced state. That's also why our country has the rule of law and a strong Constitution that we mutually agree to live by."

"But are you certain these old folks are aligned in revolt with the terrorists, and against the status quo?" McClelland inquired, attempting to get his friend back on track.

"So it appears," Stanton sighed, calming. "Like I said, it's very possible they are lending material support to the younger revolutionists actively promoting revolt. I tell you, I think this whole region has caught a fever and is in the process of going collectively insane against their own country."

Or, Stone thought, maybe they've seen the insanity of those in power that control, manipulate, and subjugate their own people. Keeping such thoughts mute as much as the collateral realization that one of the geezer networks might well be providing Chris Soles material support in the form of a safe house, Stone took another tack.

"In accepting the possibility that a 'geezer network' is out there," McClelland posed, "what's the likely reaction and operational thrust against these 'graying' insurrectionists?"

"We're monitoring them now even as we speak," Bertie assured him. "We will go after any and all we find in cahoots with the revolutionists. This is a war against our government that will not be tolerated on any level – be they young or old. We're afraid they're all uniting behind this Chris Cadia of Future Generations. And that's why it's absolutely vital that you help us get to him, and stop all this madness in its tracks."

"You mean Chris Soles, don't you?" Stone suggested, correcting his friend.

"Chris Cadia, Chris Soles – what difference does it make?" Stanton shrugged his shoulders. "At this point it's all the same thing."

Before McClelland could comment, the Pirate's Palace waitress arrived with their meals. Bertie eagerly launched himself into his cheeseburger as soon as the waitress departed. Before beginning with his salmon, however, Stone returned to a previous observation that didn't quite fit the circumstances.

"So Bertie," Stone queried, "if Chris Soles and his rep are parties to the Future Generations terrorist movement, why would he be supplying information about a shift of tactics to active assassinations?"

Speaking with his mouth full of cheeseburger, Bertie shot back, "It's simply disinformation, or he's using it to undertake something bigger."

Stone acknowledged the possibility, then with his fork took a bite of his salmon.

And yet his gut feeling was less mixed. Mostly it told him that Chris Soles was telling the truth.

***

"You fart in here," Kiri whispered in warning into their confined chamber, "and I'll kill you."

Tightly spooned together in darkness, Chris laughed and replied, "If I fart in here, it'll kill you – before you can get to me."

With her elbow, Kiri jabbed back at him and he hugged her tighter, as they listened to the motor home roar over the final miles toward Port Townsend.

After Sapphire had departed back to Bainbridge Island nearly a week ago, Kiri and Chris had visited with Bob and Donna Carlson. At the time, Donna was cleaning up after baking and Bob was down in his woodworking shop, a short distance from their house.

Chris and Kiri explained to Donna what they needed while she set a pot to boil on the stove for tea. While the water heated, the septuagenarian great-grandmother loaded a cookie tin with goodies still warm from the oven, as Kiri and Chris continued to speak. When the tea was finally ready, all three carried something down towards Bob's shop, be it teapot, cookie tin, or cups.

As they approached, Bob was already lounging at the picnic table outside his shop.

"No wonder you never get anything done around here," his wife playfully chided. "You're always just sitting around."

Bob's glasses had slid to the tip of his nose and he looked over them with arched eyebrows.

"I saw Chris and Kiri coming over here from the shop window," he reproached her in the sternest voice he could fabricate. "I also knew you were baking and it would only be a matter of time before you all came down here. So I took an early break."

"Oh, Lordy, how did I ever end up with such a sly old devil?" Donna moaned in feigned exasperation.

Amidst mutual laughter, they all joined Bob at the picnic table. Then, over cookies and tea, Kiri and Chris shared with Bob what they had spoken to Donna about in the kitchen. They told him because of the desperate straits in Cascadia, at a time when the people were being severely oppressed by their own government, they needed new ideas from those that had learned the wisdom of many years. They told Bob, as they'd told Donna, about desires to convene a meeting of whatever Elders were available, in Port Townsend once again, and as soon as possible.

"Consider it done," Bob stated succinctly. "I think that's a splendid idea and I'll start making phone calls this afternoon."

"That's exactly what I told them in the kitchen," Donna beamed, taking a sip of tea.

"That's great," Kiri smiled, yet then followed it with a frown. "But Chris and I have another problem and that's how to get there. We'd never get through all the roadblocks."

Bob and Donna looked quizzically at one another. Seconds thereafter, Donna's face lit up.

"It's no problem at all," she exclaimed. "We'll just take the motor home."

Chris and Kiri had no clue how that was a solution to their problems, but Bob explained.

"You see," he said with a smile directed to his wife, "Donna likes to take too much stuff on motor home trips, so I built in an extra luggage compartment under the bed frame."

"And you wouldn't even know it's there," Donna affirmed. "I think you two can fit in there just fine."

"Yeah," Bob agreed, "it'll be tight, but it'll probably work."

The hidden compartment under the bed turned out to be quite tight, and very dark.

They'd already stopped at two roadblock checkpoints and the third and final one awaited them just outside Port Townsend.

The first checkpoint had been on the outskirts of Poulsbo and the second one was set up at the Hood Canal Bridge. Military personnel at both sites asked for formal ID so as to enter it into their computers; they requested the destination and purpose for travel; they also insisted on coming inside the RV for a physical inspection.

At the Poulsbo stop, Chris and Kiri could barely hear the conversation Bob and Donna carried on with the soldiers, though they did catch Bob's explanation for the journey, as practice with friends in Port Townsend for an upcoming shuffleboard tournament.

At the checkpoint before crossing the Hood Canal Bridge, Bob actually showed the military people inspecting the interior his rack of custom made shuffleboard cues and the box of discs resting on the bed above them. It was all a little unnerving for Kiri and Chris, but at both roadblocks they were waved through without incident. Now, they were somewhere on Highway 19 rolling on toward Port Townsend.

"One good thing about this hidden compartment – or trap as they call it in the smuggling biz," Chris whispered into Kiri's ear, "is that out of all the insects in the whole wide world, there're absolutely none in here."

"Except for you," Kiri shot back. "A big cockroach in the darkness."

She playfully jabbed him once more with her elbow. "But for sure, there's no water."

"What do you mean?" Chris protested. "I've been needing to pee for the last half hour."

"Urine doesn't count," she assured him. "It's processed."

"Well then," he suggested, "why don't you roll over and I'll give you a great big wet and watery kiss."

"Doesn't count again," Kiri informed him. "I couldn't possibly roll over in here and saliva is processed too. Sorry, bub, there's no water in here."

Chris was ready to reply, but suddenly they were both aware the motor home was slowing down. Seconds later, Donna was knocking on the exterior wood frame of the bed that hid them.

"Okay, kids," she announced, "sit tight and be quiet. We're almost at the last checkpoint before we enter Port Townsend."

Whispering in Kiri's ear, Chris wondered, "What else can we do but sit tight?"

Kiri playfully reached back and playfully pinched his thigh.

"You can be quiet."

***

After all had arrived and enjoyed a casual meal prepared by Mister Q's B&B staff, they convened much as before in the great room of the Port Townsend Victorian mansion. Because of travel restrictions, however, attendance was much smaller than the July Fourth meeting that had filled the place to near capacity.

Sapphire MacKenzie had requested and received special documents to visit her parents home in Port Townsend. She had walked the twenty minutes from there to Quimper Jones's Victorian home with an overnight bag and disguised as an elderly woman with a cane.

Sitting next to Chris and Kiri, they faced the eighteen or nineteen Elders of whom they had requested their presence. Chris opened his remarks by thanking all for attending at short notice and under such difficult travel conditions.

"You all know basically why we are gathered here," he continued. "It's necessary to discuss the repercussions of the current State of

Emergency, tell you about some things you may not know, and mostly to solicit suggestions regarding the best course we should take forward into the future under the present circumstances."

Chris turned to Sapphire. "Maybe you could review for everyone what the current State of Emergency means to the Free Cascadia movement and activism in general," he requested.

With a nod of her head, Sapphire addressed those in the great room, saying, "To be blunt, it means we're between quite the rock and a hard place. When Section 1021 of the National Defense Authorization Act and other similar rules were invoked, we lost our constitutional right of dissent. Our activists and protestors have been arrested and jailed, and the military patrols our streets.

"All in Cascadia have been subjugated and hogtied – but at the same time, we're not dead yet," she stated defiantly. "And then there are abhorrent injustices and dire grievances that have occurred on an individual basis, and that still haven't been rectified. Chris, can you tell them about Tomas Hernandez?"

"Yes," he replied gravely. Then, slowly and solemnly, he reiterated the story of the abduction of Tomas Hernandez for those that may not have heard it through the grapevine. He also spoke of the horror and terror Linda Hernandez and their kids had endured the night of the abduction, and how Tomas was still missing.

"And the cause of all this appears to be an overreach reaction to the destruction and violence initiated by Future Generations," interjected Kiri matter-of-factly.

"Indeed," Mister Q concurred from his seat among the Elders. "But what has happened to them?"

Sapphire and Chris let Kiri respond.

"Future Generations has virtually disappeared, for the time being,"

Kiri acknowledged. "But I can tell you all now that we have a source within that organization, and as soon as credible information is known it will be passed on to us."

"Tell them what else you've learned, Kiri," urged Sapphire.

"From what we've been told by our source, their tactics are changing," Kiri revealed. "Instead of concentrating their efforts on the destruction of infrastructure, Future Generations will soon be focusing on assassinations."

An Elder behind Mister Q voiced, "Assassinations? Who is going to be assassinated?"

"At this point we can only guess," replied Kiri. "But it's likely to be one of the Kingpins of Carbon, or a lieutenant down the line."

"Or anyone dealing in fossil fuels," said someone else.

"Or anyone dealing in fossil fuels," Kiri agreed.

A quiet moment of shock was shared among those in the room.

"So that's where we are," announced Chris. "At this point, we're more or less at a standstill, or in the best case scenario, drifting without a rudder."

"And we're in this pickle because of the violence and destruction," declared a female voice in the back.

Looking closer, Chris could see it was Sasha Tharp who had spoken. She was sitting next to her husband Todd; they were the Elders he and Kiri had stayed with in Maple Valley after their last trip to Oregon.

"I don't know if you all remember my friend Molly Boxwell from Bend, Oregon, and what she talked about in this room on the Fourth of July," Sasha carried on.

"Remind them," pressed her husband, Todd.

"Molly said eco-terrorism would get us nowhere," stated Sasha Tharp. "It would only create a backlash against us and the repression of our causes. And events have proven that Molly was right!"

There was a general murmuring of agreement throughout the room, before Chris Soles took another turn to speak.

"Future Generations has caused great strife and misery in Cascadia," he acknowledged. "But precisely because of that, we should also realize what they've done without intending to, in galvanizing and promoting our true quest toward Cascadia. The people must fully begin to understand that violence is the wrong path to get to the right future."

"So how do we get to that right future?" asked Quimper Jones.

"What?" asked Chris, somewhat taken aback by the question. Before he could say anything further, however, an Elder sitting next to the Carlsons began to talk. His name was Dan Wilson and he was from Port Angeles on the Olympic Peninsula; Sapphire knew him well, but Kiri and Chris did not.

Wilson spoke of rumors he'd heard about the State of Emergency being lifted soon. Business leaders throughout the region complained of a slowdown of commerce and many feared if restrictions were in place too long, a genuine revolt might be triggered among a resentful populace.

"Well, it's got to end at some point," declared Bob Carlson, "and when it does we'll all be better off for it."

"So Chris," Mister Q was again addressing Soles, "if things do slowly get back to normal, or even if they don't, what are *you* going to do?"

"What am I going to do?" Chris was once again baffled by the question from Quimper Jones. "I came here with Sapphire and Kiri seeking suggestions from all of you, not to propose solutions."

348

"We've got your back, Chris," Cascadia Elder Todd Tharp spoke up. "But the solution is up to you. We respect you as being the one to carry us all forward.

"But I'm only one person," Chris protested.

"So what are you going to do?" repeated Mister Q.

Helplessly, Chris shrugged his shoulders while he stewed in thought.

"Well, for starters, I truly believe there's nothing more important than trying to do the right thing – no matter the circumstances," he eventually surmised. "So I guess all we can do going forward is to work as hard as possible to forestall any more violence."

Quimper Jones nodded his head then gazed among his fellow Elders. There didn't seem to be any objections, so he announced it was time to play shuffleboard while there was still enough light outside.

"Shuffleboard?" Chris countered.

"Sure, we've got everything here settled," Mister Q stated confidently. "And all of us old folks can use a little exercise before we retire. Plus, it's something for Empire's satellites above to enjoy in case they're watching."

After the Elders had departed the great room for the shuffleboard deck outside, Chris, Kiri, and Sapphire talked and laughed for some time together. They had all been given separate guest rooms on the third floor, but as the mansion grew quiet later in the evening, Sapphire and Kiri stole into Chris' room.

The bed here was noticeably smaller than in the Poulsbo cabin, yet they all cuddled and snuggled close together making it delightfully comfortable.

Full in the throes of all that cuddling and snuggling, Sapphire whispered to the other two, "I can't wait until we can really consummate this threesome!"

Chris laughed. "Well, it won't likely occur tonight; we can't be waking the Elders with a lot of moaning and screams of pleasure."

"Especially if it's coming from you!" Kiri whispered in his ear loud enough for Sapphire to hear. "Don't worry though, it will occur: it's been foreseen. But it will occur in ways unexpected, and bring about – as yet – unfathomable consequences."

"Oh Kiri, I love you so much," said Sapphire as she rose above Chris in the middle to kiss her full on the lips.

"I love you too, Sapphire, and we both love you so much, Chris," Kiri exclaimed after the kiss from Sapphire. She then took her turn smooching with him, as did Sapphire thereafter.

Snuggling in tight together much as they did a week ago, the three of them relished a sweet yet temporary happiness – even in the midst of knowledge of storms on the horizon, which might possibly overwhelm them all.

CHAPTER TWENTY-EIGHT

"Tomas is alive!" they heard Linda blurt over their speakerphone, "but he's not doing well."

Almost simultaneously, Kiri said, "Thank goodness!" as Chris replied, "That's the best news we've heard in a long time!"

Kiri asked, "So what's going on?"

"A hiker found him unconscious near here – at Meadowdale Beach Park – early yesterday morning in the parking lot," Linda explained. "They think he was dumped there during the night."

"By whom?" asked Chris.

"That's anybody's guess at this point," stated Linda. "Anyway, the first responders took him to Swedish Medical Center in Edmonds and discovered he was severely malnourished, dehydrated, and apparently in some kind of drug induced state of quasi-consciousness."

"Who the hell would do something like that?" Kiri exclaimed.

Linda carried on without answering Kiri's question.

"Of course, Tomas had no ID on him because of the abduction," Linda noted, "so the hospital staff had no clue who he was for the longest time. It actually took a day and a half before he could come around enough to be able to tell them his name."

"How's he doing now?" wondered Chris.

"Better for sure," Linda responded, "but his mind is still pretty foggy. Apparently the police attempted to interview him, but he doesn't seem to recall – at least not yet – what happened during the time following his abduction. Right now he's just trying to get his head straight and his strength back."

"I bet Cassie and Kyle are overjoyed to know their father's back," said Kiri.

"Yeah," Linda replied tentatively. "I've visited Tomas, but I don't want to take the kids in to see him until he's more lucid. I told them Daddy's okay, but he's in the hospital for a while."

"Well, at least he's alive," Chris declared, his tone colored in relief.

"And with the hospital's help, I'm sure Tomas will be back to being himself in no time," Kiri tossed in.

"I surely hope so," Linda said with a sigh. "But how are you two doing? I didn't even ask."

"Still on lockdown, just like the rest of Cascadia," replied Chris.

"But don't even worry about us," Kiri insisted. "Just take care of Tomas; give him our best and get him healthy."

"And thanks so much for calling, Linda," Chris added. "We're so happy for you, Tomas, and the kids."

***

Not fifteen minutes after hanging up with Linda, one of Kiri's secure phones began ringing in the bedroom. Snatching it up from the top of the dresser, she realized this was the only phone she used anymore to communicate with Carolyn Maxwell. With equal amounts of hope and apprehension, Kiri answered it.

"Hi, Carolyn,"

"Hi, Kiri, how are you?"

Kiri's chuckle was sardonic. "As a friend says, still on lockdown, just like the rest of Cascadia."

"I know what you mean," Carolyn concurred. "It's getting to be very repressive, isn't it?"

"It's ridiculous."

Changing the subject, Carolyn simply said, "I may have something for you – or I may not. I don't really know."

"What is it?" asked Kiri.

"Well, I told you about the encrypted email program they put on my computer that keeps spitting out garble about meetings and 'beheadings' in language that makes no sense, right?" Carolyn began. "And I'm still getting a lot of the same stuff; here, let me read you an example that I printed out with the other message."

Kiri could hear the shuffling of paper in the background and then Carolyn's voice once more.

"Yeah, some of them are longer than this, but they're all gobbledegook nonsense," stated Carolyn. "Here we go: 'Convene in the onion milk table around earwax-thirty to conjure beheading of big dog baker and porcupine whelp.'"

Kiri laughed. "It must mean something to someone."

"Or intentionally nothing to me," Carolyn countered, "especially in light of what came in overnight."

"What did it say?"

"It almost, more or less, made sense," admitted Carolyn. "And that's what scares me – because I don't know why it almost makes sense."

"So what did it say?" Kiri asked once more.

"I printed it up on this paper too in order to make sure I got it right," Carolyn replied. "It said, 'The car is loaded and ready for planting on the route the D.I. rep takes to meet the N. in B. on T.'"

"Yeah," Kiri agreed, "that almost makes sense, but not quite."

"And that's what bothers me," conceded Carolyn. "It makes me wonder if I'm being set up – I don't trust Garf Taylor at all – or if the message is a slip up and there's a legitimate threat out there to someone or something."

Kiri took a moment to deliberate before responding and as she did, Carolyn shuddered. Every time she thought about Garf Taylor, she could feel his fingers inside of her as lifted her up against her apartment wall.

"It could go either way, I agree," Kiri was back speaking in Carolyn's ear. "I don't want to put you in harm's way, but at the same time I don't want someone else hurt and see this madness continue – especially if it's preventable."

"Kiri, I'm already in harm's way," Carolyn jumped in, "and there's nothing I can do about it. I just realized right now that I called you for a lot more than to just share something with you. I called because I don't want to see anyone else get hurt or killed – and that includes my brothers. So see if you and your friends can make sense of that message, or if it even makes sense."

"I'll do whatever I can," she promised. Suddenly, however, Kiri was struck by a prescient escapist fantasy. "I'll tell you what Carolyn: when all this is over, let's make plans to visit my cousin Ingri in Norway."

"Do you mean it, Kiri?" Carolyn said excitedly. "I'd love to go see my most favorite ex-roommate in the whole wide world!"

"Count on it, Carolyn," Kiri declared assuredly. "Keep it in the back of your mind at all times that when all this is over, one way or another, you are going to Norway."

"Oh, Kiri, I love you," gushed Carolyn, quite happily. "I'll keep it in the back of my mind and totally look forward to it!"

***

"Yes, I read the entire interrogation report," Theodore Dellenbach replied to his son's question over the phone, "but most of the subject's statements were rambling and incoherent. Others made me worry."

"Part of the incoherence was surely from the constant flow of drugs administered to him," Whitley Dellenbach explained. "And part of it might have been from the editing process that attempted to compile and organize babblings ejected over several weeks."

"One thing that surprises and frightens me though, is how well these commons people are organized by their respective interests," stated the elder Dellenbach. "This movement is more advanced and a bigger threat than I anticipated.

"And after this interrogation, it's clear they have no connection with the Future Generations terrorists," the old man observed, "yet I believe it still serves our interests to use our media people to portray them in league with the terrorists."

"I completely agree, Father," said Whitley, "and I'll have our surrogates working on that directly."

"From the report, it also appears that the Commons movement was itself disrupted by the terrorism, became somewhat emasculated, and refused to respond with the people in protest against the government," noted the father. "Do you believe there is any way we can strike them while they're down – and eliminate them much quicker than the decades it took with the labor unions?"

"I'd be very cautious there, Sir," the son responded. "I think the current state of things within the commons people may only be temporary. Once these Future Generations terrorists are caught and put away, I sense the resilience amongst the commoners is deep and they may well come back much stronger than before."

"That can't be allowed to happen," the elder Dellenbach snapped. He then slightly altered the subject matter. "During the interrogation, I see in the report that many names were spilled by the subject. What do you intend to do with those?"

"We've already started background checks and investigations on many of those names," Whitley informed his father. "Eventually we'll have them all under the microscope."

"But what do you intend to do with the lot of them after they're investigated?"

"We watch and wait for now," replied the son. "If things become problematic with the Commons movement or individual commoners, we take action against them."

"What kind of action?"

"You remember how our ex-DEA man was told assassinations were coming?"

"I damn well do!" Theodore Dellenbach thundered over the phone. "And that's a personal and deliberate threat against us and our business partners."

"Well, we can easily create a back-up plan based on a similar strategy," surmised Whitley. "For the most troublesome we create a fear factor that prevents action."

"How do you accomplish that?" the old man wanted to know.

"As serenely as possible," the younger Dellenbach explained to his father. He added that such a fear factor might include "accidental" deaths, rumors and innuendo, or strong-arm tactics by "vigilante" gangs.

"Hmm, interesting," murmured the father. "And what are your intentions regarding the name that the subject was most queried about – that being Chris Soles?"

"As I'm certain you read in the report," began Whitley, "the subject knows him well. But under repetitive questioning regarding the whereabouts of Soles, the interrogators believe the subject doesn't know the actual location. He merely rambled on about 'the Peninsula.' Which of course could be the Olympic Peninsula, the Kitsap Peninsula, the Quimper Peninsula – or whatever other peninsulas they may have out there. It's all such a huge area that none of that helps."

On a positive note, Theodore Dellenbach declared, "But we do definitely know that Chris Soles has the stolen list of subversives and revolutionaries originally compiled by the crackpot former Gaia/Universe leader. We need to get hold of that in order to eliminate enemies in deep cover that seek to overthrow our very way of life."

"Yes," agreed the son, "the subject admitted he himself was on the list and that's how Soles connected with him. And yes, we understand the vital importance of seizing Soles and taking back that list he stole from cousin Alice as well."

"But even if this business with the ex-DEA agent is making incremental progress, it's frightfully slow," the elder Dellenbach declared. "We must move more forcefully if we intend to stop the Future Generations terrorists and capture Chris Soles, and get the list back, so we can put them all away."

"I intend to do just that," Whitley replied with supreme confidence.

"May I ask how?" his father replied.

"Certainly," assured the son. "I've planned all along to exploit whatever connection my unwitting dupe of an informant Sapphire MacKenzie has with Chris Soles. Very soon, when the time is right, I will meet her in Seattle and pry precisely what I need out of her head."

"So she's just going to tell you what you need to know, eh?" Disbelief was in the old man's voice.

"I have my ways," Whitley lobbed back, slyly. "And I promise it won't take weeks of drugs, sleep deprivation, and incoherent ramblings to get a report like our last interrogation subject."

"That's what I like to hear!" Theodore Dellenbach roared. "This has all gone on too long and we need to refocus entirely on our business matters. Get it taken care of, Son!"

"I fully intend to, Father," the younger Dellenbach responded, once again superbly confidant.

***

"What kind of gibberish is that?" Stone McClelland asked angrily.

"It's the best gibberish you're going to get all day," the voice in his ear assured him. "And now I'm going to repeat it; make sure you write it down and get it right. Ready?"

"I'm ready," McClelland replied dourly.

"That's better," commended the voice. "Okay, here we go: 'The car is loaded and ready for planting on the route the D.I. rep takes to meet the N. in B. on T.'"

After a short delay, Stone stated, "I've got it. Now what do I do with it?"

"I'm sure some of your friends have supercomputers," the voice said rather snidely. "Let them play around with it and run all the possibilities. And in return for that little gem, I need some information from you."

"That's not how the rules in the game of trust work," McClelland protested. "You give me something that proves true, *then* you ask me to reciprocate."

"If you still want to play the game with me, the rules are changing."

"What do you want?"

"I want to know who abducted Tomas Hernandez and why," the voice simply requested.

"What is this Tomas Hernandez to you?"

Dodging the direct question, the voice explained Hernandez was abducted from his home by thugs in front of his family. McClelland also learned that Hernandez recently turned up in a park near his Edmonds home in a drugged and debilitated state, and that the police and all authorities his family had spoken to hadn't any idea as to his abductors.

After learning of Hernandez's story, Stone compromised. "I'll make inquiries about Hernandez, while checking out if your gibberish is of any value. Along with that, and since the rules in the game of trust are changing, I want to know precisely when I can meet Chris Soles and get past his rep."

"That's very simple," the voice said pleasantly. "You can meet him when he deems you trustworthy and understands why you set him free in Arizona."

"What if I'm not sure why I set him free in Arizona?"

"Make sure you're trustworthy," was the last thing McClelland heard before the connection clicked silent.

CHAPTER TWENTY-NINE

"Linda's on the line," Kiri told Chris, entering the kitchen, "and Tomas is home."

"How is he doing?"

"You can find that out for yourself," she said handing him the phone. "Linda said he's still pretty weak, but wants to talk with you."

"I'll put it on speaker," said Chris as he laid the phone on the kitchen table.

Kiri sat down beside him.

"Hello, Tomas," Chris spoke first, "how are you doing?"

After a delay, the words that came out on the speakerphone were hoarse and hesitant. "Not good, but getting better. I think. But that's not why I'm calling."

"Well, we're just glad to hear you're alive and back with you're family," consoled Chris.

"That's not why I called," Tomas repeated. "For your own safety, you don't want to deal with me anymore. I'm damaged goods."

"No!" Chris strongly objected. "You're a good friend; you'll never be 'damaged goods.'"

"Look Chris, it's time to be realistic," stated Tomas, his speech wan and pallid. "I was captive in a drug-induced state for weeks. At this point, it's sheer luck I don't know where you live or surely you'd now be rotting in one of their jails. Or dead. Anything else I told them gives you diminishing hope with each passing day."

"I don't need hope," Chris asserted. "I have a true friend; that's what Empire doesn't understand."

"You got to be kidding me," Tomas replied haltingly. "You have to assume that I gave everything I know about you away."

"It doesn't matter," Chris avowed. "Unwavering friendships are the most valuable and powerful thing one can possess in this life. We all take care of each other and move forward together, even in the face of insurmountable adversity. Instead of Empire's competitive lust for greed and dominance of others, our friends work cooperatively towards the goal of mutual benefit for all. And that's what gives us our courage to stand up to them in the end."

Lightening up, Tomas moved in a more positive direction. "You're correct of course, Chris; we stand together against all odds. That's what our friendship, our quest toward Cascadia is all about."

"You got it," agreed Chris. "I have no worries going forward. You are not damaged goods: you are my friend."

Before the silence on the line could become awkward, Kiri spoke up.

"And when you're well enough, Tomas," she said encouragingly, "Sapphire wants to send a small video production crew to visit you."

"What for?"

"A reenactment of the abduction and its aftermath," stated Kiri.

"I couldn't put my family through that," Tomas responded without hesitation.

"Don't worry," she assured him, "that's not what we're talking about. Sapphire can get fill-in actors for everyone else, but she wants you depicting your story."

"And then what?"

"Sapphire will post the video on the Free Cascadia Internet movie site with followers numbering in the hundreds of thousands," said Kiri.

"I'll talk it over with Linda," Tomas replied, after deliberating for some time. "I think I need to go now though; I need to rest."

"You get plenty of rest and get better, Tomas," Chris stated positively. "Cascadia needs you back at full strength."

"Much remains before us all in the upcoming weeks," added Kiri, sensing portents of things others couldn't quite see.

* * *

"Well, I suppose you've heard what happened up here today," said Stone McClelland, after his wife answered the phone for their nightly conversation.

"I don't think I've heard anything else since I finished with my last acupuncture patient," replied Lorien. "I must say though, it all adds up to a pretty big news day from the Northwest. Does it also add up to me getting my husband back home in Arizona soon? And did you have anything to do with all that?"

Stone chose to answer the latter question first.

"Certainly there was nothing I did to provoke The Seven on the Supreme Court to schedule a major 'assemblage' in Idaho on the last weekend in September, a little more than a week before their next session begins on October 7th — the first Monday in October," McClelland stated. "But I might have had a hand in foiling the car bomb plot in Bremerton."

"How so?"

"Oh, a so far reliable informant passed along some gibberish," Stone told his wife, "then I passed it along to people that might be able to figure it out – and figure it out they apparently did. I'll probably learn more about it all tomorrow when I meet my FBI friend for lunch."

"On the news I watched after getting home," Lorien injected, "it was reported there were enough explosives loaded into the car to do some serious damage."

"All I've got to say is that it's a good thing the bomb squad people got to it before anybody was hurt," declared Stone.

"Do you think foiling the bombing plot had anything to do with the announcement later on in the day that the State of Emergency was being lifted?" wondered Lorien.

Stone acknowledged that it was possible the two events were connected.

"But I think lifting the State of Emergency and easing the restrictions was bound to happen sooner than later," he surmised. "The business leaders around here were getting louder and louder with their complaints about lost revenue, and the people in general were getting pretty upset. My guess too is that whoever is in charge began to realize that they'd driven the Future Generations terrorists so far underground that they'd never find them with such stringent restrictions in place. And now I'm wondering how long it'll be until they're implemented again."

"What do you mean by that?"

"I'm afraid it's going to be a security nightmare for the authorities over in Coeur d'Alene and Hayden Lake, Idaho," noted Stone. "Every protestor, demonstrator, and advanced nut case in the Northwest is going to show up."

"You'd think they'd realize that," exclaimed Lorien. "Why didn't they schedule their assemblage in some conservative bastion like Texas, or Kansas? They're just asking for trouble in the Northwest."

"To my mind, I believe it's a very calculated move," Stone projected. "I imagine the powers that be want to demonstrate they are fully in control after all the unrest, and the assemblage is a blatant and commanding response to stamp out any further murmurings about a free and sovereign Cascadia."

"Well, I still think they're just asking for trouble," Lorien repeated. "And that's especially true since it was also announced that free speech rights will be observed and demonstrations allowed."

"Yeah," replied Stone, "but only in the streets of Coeur d'Alene, and not up by the town of Hayden Lake which is four or five miles to the north. You can be quite certain the compound by Lake Hayden, where The Seven gather, will be on a tight lockdown."

"You know, I almost feel sorry for the two liberal, female Justices on the Court," remarked Lorien. "The press is treating it almost derisively and laughable how The Two subsequently scheduled an 'assemblage' – also in the Northwest, and at the same time as The Seven."

"Well, I suppose they've got to do whatever they can to get attention when they're such a weak minority," said Stone.

"I heard The Two were meeting at some family waterfront house near Seattle owned by one of the Justice's husband," Lorien added.

"And that's probably the last you'll ever hear about it too," Stone could nearly guarantee. "All the focus will turn on northern Idaho, especially if the President and prominent supporters in control show up as I've heard in various news reports today."

"Do me a favor, Stone."

"What's that?"

"Try to stay away from all that, okay?"

"I will if I can," he promised.

"So when are you coming home?" she asked again. "For good?"

"I'm working on it."

"What do you mean by that?"

"I've got a credible source," Stone patiently explained, "with a line to Chris Soles – the man everyone is hunting for – and who I released in Arizona. It's all moving in the right direction. With a little luck, I'll soon meet up with him, get my own questions answered, and maybe even help straighten out this mess here in what they call Cascadia."

"I hope you can do all that and soon," Lorien spoke tenderly. "I want you back here for good."

"I'm working on it," he assured her.

***

"The key to solving your gibberish turned out to be pretty simple," Bertie told Stone, as he sipped his water. "It was apparent from the get-go that 'the D.I. rep' most likely spoke to being a representative of Dellenbach Industries as the victim of a car bombing on the way to keep an appointment with someone."

"Okay," acknowledged McClelland, tasting the local microbrew the waitress had delivered after taking their orders, "so the first part of the gibberish being, 'The car is loaded and ready for planting on the route the D.I. rep takes,' was easy enough. But what about the rest of it concerning where the rep would 'meet the N. in B. on T?' It seems like that could contain endless possibilities."

"It probably could," Stanton agreed, "but our people received a good deal of help from the security people of Dellenbach Industries, who had uncovered similar threats."

Stone nodded, but said nothing. Of course Dellenbach Industries were aware of an impending plot because he had also passed the same gibberish onto his handler, Roger, and ultimately Whitley Dellenbach.

"Going over the schedules of the Dellenbach people here in the Northwest, it didn't take long to realize a car bomb was planted along the route their employee would take to meet with the Navy in Bremerton," Bertie informed Stone. "The only uncertainty then was if it was to occur on Tuesday or Thursday. Working with the D.I. security people, it was narrowed down to Tuesday, the car was found, and the plot was foiled."

Stone took another sip of his beer, looked about at others dining in peace, and was relieved by the outcome of events. They were in the same outdoor restaurant they met in weeks ago below the Pike Place Market and with a stunning view of Elliott Bay. The clear Plexiglas barrier surrounding the dining space was as useless today as it had been then, yet with the approach of colder weather in coming weeks its value in repelling the wind would once again become apparent.

"So after the bomb squad people disarmed what was in the car," Stanton continued, "the explosives were traced back to the excavation company where the younger Maxwell brother worked and where he stole the same."

"Where do you go from there?" asked McClelland.

"Some of our FBI agents interviewed the younger sister of Billy and Timmy Maxwell up in Everett," replied Bertie.

"Did you learn anything new?"

"Not much," said Stanton. "She said she hasn't heard from them in weeks. Apparently, the girl is worried about her older brothers but doesn't want to be involved, preferring simply to tend to her job and her life."

"Do your people buy into it?"

"Pretty much," Bertie grunted. "We've had a tail on her for weeks and there's no real reason to doubt her. Overall, however, this whole car bomb plot smells bad to me."

"Why do you say that?" McClelland wondered.

"It was too easy," Stanton stated nebulously. "The whole shebang should have been more difficult to solve. My guess is that Soles, Garf Taylor, the Maxwell brothers, and their suicide squads are setting us all up for something else down the road."

"Like what?"

"My gut tells me the Future Generations terrorists are setting us up for something bigger, more deadly, and dangerous," Stanton declared.

"You mean something like an attack on The Seven when they convene in Idaho in a few weeks?" asked McClelland.

"Precisely," Bertie replied. "Now, this is speculation on my part – and way above my pay grade – but what if the all-knowing in control back in D.C. wanted The Seven to meet in Cascadia, not only to publically display their power and grip over the revolutionists here, but also to lure the Future Generations out of hiding with a bait they couldn't resist so as to be captured or killed?"

"I'd say that's pretty high risk bait," observed Stone.

"Not really," objected Bertie, "not once you become familiar with the venue."

"I heard it was on a large piece of property on the north side of Lake Hayden," said Stone.

"It's on an absolutely defensible piece of lakefront property," Stanton took pains to point out. He went on to paint a picture of a sprawling forty to fifty-acre parcel, dotted with magnificent homes built with massive timber beams and high-pitched roofs. Several tennis courts could be found within the compound, as well as swimming pools. High fencing surrounded the curving three-sided perimeter on land, and the open area facing Lake Hayden to the south featured steep cliffs with only a private gondola down to the beach and boathouse.

"There's enough outbuildings and servant housing to easily camp a small army of security people, which is precisely what will happen," stated Bertie. "And it's all owned by one of Idaho's most prominent citizens."

"Who might that be?" asked Stone.

"None other than the Northwest lumber tycoon, former conservative Idaho senator, and current Supreme Court Justice, Dudley

Gassack," Stanton informed his friend. "And no one will even get close to The Seven at that place."

"But the gathering of The Seven will surely bring the grumbling masses in the Northwest out of the woodwork in droves," McClelland easily assessed.

"And that would most likely include Chris Soles and his Future Generations terrorists, I suppose," Bertie stated with a smug smile.

Stone didn't immediately reply. Instead, he returned to his crab salad and allowed Stanton to inhale the other half of his sandwich. When McClelland had enough to eat, he washed it all down with healthy swig from his microbrew. He then asked Bertie for some reciprocal knowledge he needed to keep the game of trust in play.

"So what did you find out about what my informant wanted to know?" inquired Stone.

Bertie looked up from picking at his French fries. "You mean something about who abducted that Hernandez fellow?"

"That's what I need to know."

"I haven't a clue," Stanton stated, his black face lighting up with a wry grin.

"What do you mean by that?"

"The FBI has no knowledge of who abducted Tomas Hernandez, nor of any motive to do the same," Bertie declared forthrightly. "Was it vigilantes, somebody fighting the Commons movement? You might as well make up your own motive, because I wasn't able to uncover any trace of who abducted him, or why."

McClelland took another sip of his beer, while retreating into thought. That directly contradicted what Roger had told him. Roger informed him that his sources were able to verify that FBI counterterrorism teams took Hernandez in for intensive interrogation.

"But I think the bottom line at this point," Bertie was saying, interrupting Stone's reveries, "is that we need to bring your informant in as soon as possible. To put it quite simply: he knows too much. Once he's in custody, we'll break him down to get everything he knows, snare Chris Soles, and end this thing without the probable loss of many lives when The Seven come to Idaho."

With a straight face, Stone assured his old friend that he would do his best to carry through with that request.

But that's exactly the same thing he told Whitley Dellenbach through Roger, when they also demanded that he deliver his informant with all haste to them.

The bottom line here, as Stone McClelland saw it, was that there was no contradiction whatsoever when it came to the FBI or Dellenbach Industries wanting the head of Chris Soles' rep – and surely Chris Soles' head as well – on a platter. And that made Stone uneasy, especially in light of the relationship he was building with his informant. Contrarily, and without rational justification, McClelland wondered if Soles shouldn't be set free – again.

But that was enough to chew on for a while.

Stone smiled at Bertie then enjoyed another taste of his Seattle microbrew, as the two old friends discussed lighter and less consequential matters during the remainder of their lunch together.

***

That evening, just before Stone's nightly call to Lorien, his phone rang. The caller ID listed a number he'd never before seen, and would likely be as untraceable as all the rest.

Nevertheless, he believed he knew who it might be so he answered. And once again, the voice was in his ear.

"It seems my intelligence proved useful," was said without preface.

"So far, I guess," replied McClelland.

"What do you mean – so far?"

"I don't know your motives."

"Building trust is primary and comes first," the voice responded. "At least that's what I presumed."

"Your presumption is correct," Stone fired back. "But I don't know where you're going."

"That doesn't matter now," snapped the voice, cutting to the quick. "What about Hernandez? Who abducted him and why?"

"It's hard to say," McClelland stated ambiguously.

"What do you mean by that?"

Stone McClelland sighed. "My trusted source inside law enforcement says they don't know who abducted Hernandez, nor why. Other sources tell me it was FBI counterterrorism forces behind the abduction."

"So who do you believe?"

"Both and neither, I guess," muttered McClelland. "But what I believe, or don't know, doesn't matter. In this instance, it's up to you to make the right assessment based on limited knowledge, and go from there."

"That's not very good intelligence from your sources," observed the voice. "Wouldn't you agree?"

"Without question, but that's where we're at," Stone admitted. He then added, "Good luck."

"Good luck!" exclaimed the voice into McClelland's ear. "Is that all?"

"It's the best I've got right now," he admitted.

"You've got to do better than that if we're going to move forward in the right direction," the voice admonished. "You're in a very pivotal position in the greater scheme of things."

"I realize that more with each passing day."

"I'm glad you do," the voice lauded, "so I'd urge you to get as busy as the proverbial beaver."

"I'm working on it," replied McClelland, and the phone line went dead.

CHAPTER THIRTY

When he opened the hotel room door, he couldn't believe how drop-dead beautiful she was. And the short, tight red dress only made her brilliant blue eyes radiate all the more.

"I'm sorry I'm late, Whitey," Sapphire said with a smile, "but our meetings about the upcoming Idaho protests lasted longer than expected."

"I said whenever you got here, it would be fine," he replied, drawing her inward and closing the door behind her.

They exchanged hugs as Whitey asked Sapphire if she found her room okay.

"Of course I did," she giggled, "it's just down the hall from you. I also took a little extra time to shower and freshen up, so that I'd be ready for wherever we go to eat."

A momentary shadow crossed Whitey's Aryan features. "I've already ordered dinner from room service; I think it's best we aren't seen together in public for reasons that will soon become apparent."

Obviously puzzled, Sapphire merely shrugged her shoulders and uttered, "Okay."

"And while we're waiting for room service to deliver," Whitey remarked as he led her further into the commodious hotel suite, "why don't we share some champagne and toast to finally getting together in Seattle?"

"That sounds good to me," Sapphire replied with a smile.

From the ice bucket stand near the dining table, Whitey extracted the champagne bottle that room service already opened upon delivery. He had placed two glasses on the dining table that he now filled.

Handing Sapphire one of the glasses, and raising the other, Whitey declared, "To finally being able to spend some time together after all these years!"

Sapphire clinked her glass with his, saying, "I couldn't be happier," and they both took a sip.

"This champagne is wonderful," she exclaimed.

"It's frightfully good, isn't it?" he agreed. "Why don't we enjoy it on the couch in front of the entertainment center?"

"Sure, why not?" Sapphire said, as they began walking across the suite, past the bedroom door, and finally to the couch.

The lights were lower here than back by the dining area, and soft symphony music was coming from the entertainment center stereo. The plush sofa could easily have held five or six people, but Whitey and Sapphire found it more than comfortable to be seated quite close together.

Conversationally, Whitey asked her how the planning for the Idaho demonstrations was coming along, and that launched Sapphire into a lengthy digression that also included a refill of their champagne glasses.

She spoke first of the convoluted permitting process they faced to demonstrate on the streets of Coeur d'Alene. Sapphire then went on at length concerning the sheer logistical challenge of organizing the tens of thousands that would be participating to protest The Seven, and their ill begotten decisions that so adversely affected the common people of the country. She also had her people looking into options for housing, food, sanitation, and safety for so many.

It was time to fill the champagne glasses a third time when they heard a knock on the hotel room door. Whitey rose and answered it; he then allowed three room service wait staff to set up the dining table with fancy cloth napkins, sparkling silverware, covered dishes, glasses of water, and more wine glasses. One of the room service waiters also brought in another ice bucket stand with a champagne bottle that he opened before departing.

Whitey tipped the waiters generously before they closed the door behind them. He then turned to Sapphire who was still sitting on the couch before the entertainment center.

"I hope you enjoy lobster thermidor, for that's what's on the menu," he announced. "I know it's usually only for very special occasions, but I think this qualifies."

"It sounds wonderful," Sapphire smiled, as she rose from the sofa and approached the dining table. "And what accompanies the lobster?"

"You will also be treated to roasted asparagus spears with a particularly tasty Hollandaise sauce, and a side of rice pilaf," he informed her, as he pulled back Sapphire's chair.

She seated herself as Whitey filled their glasses with fresh champagne, then joined Sapphire at the table. He removed the covers from their plates and steam was jettisoned aloft by the warm food before them.

Their previously voluble flow of conversation on the couch now slowed as they tested and savored the creamy mixture of cooked lobster, egg yokes, and cognac stuffed into a lobster shell. Sapphire told Whitey she had never tasted anything so wonderful and he was visibly pleased that she was enjoying it so.

The asparagus and rice were delightful as well, and the bubbly continued to flow throughout the meal. As both Sapphire and Whitey were finishing up their meals, and enjoying another refill of the champagne glasses, Whitey's mood abruptly became more somber and serious.

Sapphire was instantly aware of it from the look on his face.

"Is there something wrong?" she asked.

"Uh, no," he muttered, then began shaking his head. Whitey was unable to speak for several seconds, until speech found him. "But yes, there is something wrong, very wrong."

"Were there problems with the lawyers you had to meet with here in Seattle?"

Whitey sighed. "No, nothing like that; the problems run much deeper," he admitted.

"Tell me about them," she requested.

Once more, Whitey shook his head. "I don't want to burden you with any of it."

Tenderly, Sapphire reached across the dining table and placed her hand upon his.

"I'm here to listen," she assured him.

Exhaling heavily through his mouth, Whitey initially said he didn't know where to start then blurted, "I think I'm at a crossroads in my life."

"What do you mean by that?"

"It's my wife, it's my family, and it's about who I am," he said. "I'm at a crossroads in my life."

"Tell me what's happening," Sapphire spoke kindly. "I'm here to listen."

Whitey took a sip of champagne, and continued to stare into the glass as he began to speak.

"I recently had to institutionalize my wife in an assisted living center," he revealed. "It's the hardest thing I've ever had to do in my life."

"I'm so sorry," Sapphire replied with great honesty.

"It's all hush-hush of course, but doing that made me rethink so many things in my own life that I had previously taken for granted," Whitey continued. "I put everything under the microscope: my extended family, my work, the future of our planet for coming generations – even you."

"Even me?" she wondered. "What is that supposed to mean?"

Whitey looked deep into her brilliant blue eyes. "You don't even know who I am, do you?"

The question was mildly humorous to Sapphire and she chuckled. "You're a real nice guy I had to teach how to float down a river in Idaho. Then you kept in contact and were interested in supporting causes I believed in. You helped me out financially for years to support those causes, and I'm very grateful for your generosity and friendship."

"No, you don't know me at all," he shot back. "You don't know my family."

"I never needed to know your family," she stated. "I knew my friend Whitey from a distance and that's all that was important."

Point blank he asked her, "Have you ever heard the name, Dellenbach?"

She pondered for a moment, then queried, "You mean like, 'Dellenbach Brothers – the arch enemies, the destroyers of the planet, and the evil oligarchs?'"

"Of course you've heard of them," he noted. "The Dellenbach Brothers are my father and uncles. My real name is Whitley Dellenbach. Our family might as well represent everything you are against."

"Then why have you been helping me out for so many years?" Sapphire wanted to know.

"You're not the only one I've been aiding unbeknownst to my family," Whitey admitted. "In my position, with our supposedly iron strong family ties, it was all I could do to assuage my conscience. But now I don't think it's enough. I'm at a crossroads."

Sapphire said nothing, for it seemed Whitey still had more on his mind. And indeed he did.

"I've come to the conclusion that I must do all I can to put the future of this planet and the common people on a sustainable course," he earnestly declared. "I intend to do all I can to work with you and those fighting with you. I will fund the rebels and the rebellion, even if it means going against my own family. With my wife as good as gone, and with no children, I have little choice but to try to change the world. But I have to do it from within – I must still pretend to be a full-on member of the Dellenbach family – and no one but you can know."

Sapphire was visibly shocked. She stood as if jolted from her seat.

"What is it?" he asked, standing as well.

"I've got to go to my room down the hall," was all she said.

"Why?"

"I'm going to get my luggage," Sapphire informed him. "Because I'm going to stay here tonight with you. Pour some more champagne and I'll be right back."

After she departed his room for hers, Whitey collected the dinner dishes from the table, placed them on the tray room service had left, and deposited everything on the hallway floor outside the room.

When she returned, Sapphire put her small overnight suitcase on an available luggage stand in the bedroom. She then retrieved what she wanted, while informing Whitey that she would be in the bathroom changing into something more comfortable. Sapphire suggested he might do the same thing, and then they could enjoy champagne on the couch.

"And don't laugh about what I'm wearing when I come out, because it's what I wear at home when I want to be comfy," she warned, as she closed the bathroom door behind her.

As instructed, Whitey removed the dress slacks and button down shirt and tie he'd been wearing, along with shoes and socks. He then slipped into a tee shirt and shorts he extracted from the bottom of his suitcase. By the entertainment center, he topped off their champagne glasses once more, and reclined on the sofa to wait for Sapphire.

A few minutes later she approached with a smile on her face.

"Now why would I laugh about what you're wearing?" he wanted to know. "There's nothing wrong about a nightgown on top and sweat pants underneath. It looks comfy indeed."

"It is," she said, snuggling in next to him on the couch.

Whitey handed Sapphire her champagne glass from the small table before them. They toasted to nothing in particular, and he put his arm around her after the glasses were returned to the table.

"So how are we going to work as a team going forward?" Sapphire wanted to know.

For the following five or ten minutes, they talked over logistical scenarios concerning how they could strive for the greater good when coordinating their efforts together. Whitey promised he'd get her whatever information he could regarding all the fossil fuel kingpins including the Dellenbachs, as long as it didn't ostracize him from his own family. Among other items, Sapphire promised to consult with him on all major decisions the Free Cascadia movement planned regarding the upcoming Idaho demonstrations, and he promised he'd help grease the wheels for her people in Coeur d'Alene.

Somewhere during the course of their discussions, Whitey's arm around her shoulder had transformed from dangling placidly, to a hand emphasizing its clasp of one of Sapphire's breasts — and she had willingly allowed it.

Now, as their discussion was coming to a close, Sapphire excitedly said, "I'm so excited we'll be working as a team. We'll both be so proud of what we accomplish together."

Whitey responded with nothing verbal in reply; instead he leaned over and kissed her softly on the lips. Sapphire came back with much more physicality, fully engaging him in a vigorous kiss and wrapping herself around him.

For several minutes they enjoyed themselves as such, until Sapphire slipped a hand up into his shorts to find him already fully erect.

"C'mon," she announced, untangling herself from him and standing, "we're going to the bedroom."

Holding her hand and without protest, Whitey followed her with relish. When they reached the bed, Sapphire dropped his hand and yanked back the covers. Effortlessly, her sweat pants fell to the floor, her nightgown came off over her head, and suddenly Sapphire was fully naked.

She turned to see Whitey had just removed his shirt, but nothing else as yet. Helping out, Sapphire pulled down his shorts and then his underwear. Whitey's erect member stood up proudly, as she grabbed and stroked it.

"Now, do you have a condom with you?" she wanted to know.

Whitey admitted he didn't. "I didn't exactly plan on all this occurring."

"Well, I've got one in my purse," Sapphire informed him. "I don't have sex without a condom."

She instructed Whitey to lie on his back in bed while she reached for her purse. After Sapphire retrieved the prophylactic, she unwrapped it then went down to her knees at the side of the bed. Up and down she sucked him for a minute or two, then applied the condom over his very stiff unit. Sapphire rose to turn down the lights, and then joined Whitey in bed.

For a minute, maybe two, they kissed and passionately squirmed together with joy. She was already quite wet when he entered her and, for what seemed an eternity, they shared and enjoyed one another immensely.

***

Afterwards, and following individual trips to the bathroom, Whitey and Sapphire snuggled spoon-like, naked and satiated. Neither was quite ready for sleep yet, so they found opportunity to talk.

Speaking softly into her ear, Whitey asked Sapphire how best he could help her friends.

"Could I, for instance, offer financial support to Chris Soles?" he wondered.

"He doesn't need it," Sapphire replied dreamily.

"What do you mean by that?" Whitey asked. "Everybody can use money to advance their causes."

"Chris doesn't need it," she repeated. "The people of Cascadia, the Elders, they all stand behind him. He'd never take your assistance."

"Everybody needs money," Whitey insisted. "The world revolves around money and money is for helping friends."

"Not Chris," she objected. "Money doesn't matter in the least to him; besides, he's a minimalist. On top of that, he cares more about his principles, about his quest for Cascadia. He's on a different plane; he plays by rules the rest of us haven't yet learned."

"What do you mean by that?"

She laughed at him. "Suffice it to say he treads on sacred footpaths; he's not like the rest of us."

Yeah, yeah, yeah, thought Whitey. He then asked, "How do you know so much about him?"

Sapphire giggled and backed her body in even closer to him. "We're in a threesome."

Whitey was immediately disgusted. The picture that came to mind was Sapphire getting plugged by two dicks in both her lower holes. "It's a threesome – with whom? Some queer?"

Sapphire reached behind her and grabbed his limp member. "Don't even say such things. Our other partner is my missing sister that I never knew. The three of us are very much in love."

"So why are you in bed with me then?" Whitey demanded to know.

Still snagging his penis, with a laugh she gave it a shake and let go. Totally in control, Sapphire said, "I've always wanted you since your first fumbled attempt at getting onto a raft on the Salmon River."

"I wasn't that bad," he protested, "otherwise you wouldn't want me now."

"Not that bad," she allowed, "but I hope you learned a few things tonight."

"Learned and loved it," he said magnanimously. "But really, what can I do to help Chris Soles and your young female friend?"

"Nothing at all," Sapphire said once more, trying to emphasize her previous point. "Chris has it all — or most of it, anyway — figured out. Since Arizona, he has had the most excellent and comprehensive plastic surgery. If you were to put one of the old wanted posters next to the way he looks now, you'd see two different people. He's even been in contact with some ex-DEA agent he knew in Arizona and the guy doesn't have a clue that it's the same person. That's how good the plastic surgery is."

"But maybe I can still help," Whitey pressed. "You must have other friends that could use my assistance."

Stifling a chuckle, Sapphire said, "Sure, why don't you just ring up Garf Taylor and see what he needs done. Oh, wait, you can't do that after all: he's so far underground that nobody can find him."

"Who is Garf Taylor?"

"He's the one running the Future Generations group," she informed him.

"How does one get a hold of him?"

"Like I said, I don't think anybody can get in touch with him anymore," replied Sapphire, "especially after all the havoc they've created. I used to be able to contact him, but certainly no more."

Sapphire realized she was stretching the truth a little, but it didn't really matter. She still had a number that might work, but had promised never to use it except in a dire, life or death emergency.

"Well, how does Chris Soles coordinate with Garf Taylor?" Whitey wondered.

"He doesn't," Sapphire said simply. "Chris has a totally different philosophy; he tries to deter Garf and his people."

Saying nothing, Whitey couldn't accept that. Obviously, her devotion to the threesome had clouded her discernment and judgment.

"Don't worry," Sapphire spoke sleepily, "it'll all shake out in northern Idaho. Dissent is allowed and our Free Cascadia movement will be there."

She rolled over and kissed him on the lips, then snuggled back into her previous position.

"That reminds me," she said with a yawn, "I have to be in my Bainbridge office early for meetings about demonstrations in Idaho, so it's time for sleep now."

With an arm wrapped around her, Whitey promised, "I'll be there to support you from behind the scenes no matter how it shakes out in Idaho."

Sapphire felt safe in his presence. "I can always count on you Whitey, can't I? To do the right thing?"

"Always," he assured her, before they both drifted off to sleep.

***

The following morning, after Sapphire had departed to catch a ferry to Bainbridge Island, Whitley cleansed himself thoroughly as a result of performing his duties the previous evening. He dressed, then

383

summoned room service for breakfast.

Fifteen minutes after he finished eating, he called his father at the prearranged time.

"So did you meet with her as scheduled?" asked the old man.

"I did indeed," replied the son.

"And what did you learn?"

"I learned a lot, Father."

"Such as?"

"First of all," Whitley began, "Soles has had extensive plastic surgery since Arizona. Most likely it was Soles himself meeting our ex-DEA agent and not a representative."

"We've got to move on that," the elder Dellenbach urged.

"I'm fully prepared to do so," the son assured the father.

"What else did you discover?"

"I was given the name of the individual running the day-to-day of the Future Generations terrorist group," Whitley revealed. "It's someone called Garf Taylor. The name means nothing to me right now, but I'll have my people run it to ground."

"You do that," said the old man. "And how does Soles control this Garf Taylor and Future Generations?"

"My unwitting informant says they are not in cahoots," replied the son, "but I don't believe her. Instead, I think she and Soles may have a romantic entanglement, and she may be attempting to cover for him."

Whitley didn't mention third party involvement in the triangle because he was still working on how he could use that knowledge if needed.

"So is your unwitting informant at the end of her usefulness?" wondered the elder Dellenbach.

"No, not at all, Father," the son stated definitively. "She's going to Idaho to lead protest demonstrations against The Seven. I'll feed her disinformation and thereby keep tabs on her, and maybe even snag Soles through her. It'll all work out okay, I assure you."

Theodore Dellenbach enjoyed a hearty chuckle. "Just like your Uncle Walter was, you've become quite the puppeteer."

"I have a lot to learn from you and Uncle Paul about being a truly successful puppeteer," Whitley admitted, while accepting the compliment. "I'm still in awe at the mountains you moved to get The Seven out to Idaho to bring all this unrest to a head, and finally resolve it."

"Those mountains weren't that hard to move," the old man noted. "The politicians and law enforcement people receiving our donations simply convinced a reluctant number of Justices to convene at Justice Gassack's compound. We'll force the terrorists and revolutionaries into the open, and in the process destroy them."

"That's fine, as long as The Seven will be safe," Whitley agreed.

"Don't worry, Son, a virtual army will be there with them," the elder Dellenbach assured. "They'll be safe and our great country will subsequently be rid of the revolutionists."

CHAPTER THIRTY-ONE

Stone McClelland was purposely early for his appointment at the downtown Seattle hotel with his handler, Roger. Rush hour traffic being what it was, he much preferred to avoid the normally snarled mess on Interstate 5 and find a parking space without any hassle.

Entering the lobby of the swanky hotel, Stone checked in with the clerk at the front desk. He informed the young lady of his name, and whom he had an appointment with.

"Yes," she said, scanning a computer monitor before her, "you are expected in Mr. Roger's room number 2402 at 8:30 A.M."

The young lady then checked the current time on the same computer screen.

"Oh, but you're quite early," she observed. "Why don't you enjoy our complimentary continental breakfast, a selection of some of Seattle's favorite coffees, and today's newspaper here in our lobby?"

McClelland looked about the spacious lobby, spotted the breakfast station, and replied, "Thank you very much; I'll do just that."

Stone meandered toward the food, while picking up a morning paper on the way. He poured himself a cup of coffee from one of several pots available, and secured a couple Danish pastries on a small plate. Of the several open chairs and tables at this hour, McClelland chose one toward the back wall of the lobby. It was a space where he'd have his privacy and at the same time where he could leisurely observe the comings and goings of an early morning.

It was a little before 7 A.M. when he sat down, and foot traffic through the stately hotel lobby ramped up appreciably during the following half hour. Occasionally, Stone would glance up to see who might be passing through, but for the most part he focused on the latest news while absently sipping on his coffee and finishing off his pastries.

Somewhere right around 7:20, however, from the corner of his eye McClelland caught sight of a tall, pretty woman exiting the elevators, and striding across the lobby toward the exit doors. When she was halfway across the room, Stone realized who she was.

Without a doubt, it was Sapphire MacKenzie. And she appeared much more buoyant and bouncier than when he last saw her, back when she was angrily throwing him out of her offices on Bainbridge Island. Now, with a merry smile, she wore a very satisfied, just-fucked look, if he'd ever seen one.

MacKenzie didn't turn her head as she made her way to the revolving exit doors and then she was gone.

At precisely 8:30 A.M., Stone McClelland was knocking on the door to room number 2402. It took a moment for the door to open; yet when it did, McClelland was flabbergasted.

"Please come in," invited Whitley Dellenbach.

Stone McClelland did so and Dellenbach closed the door behind him.

"I was expecting Roger," stated McClelland, adding, "I thought you said I'd never see you again."

"I sent Roger on an errand," Dellenbach snapped. "There are matters of import we must discuss. Please take a seat at the table."

Stone followed Dellenbach to the fancy suite's dining table. Dellenbach was sharply dressed in suit and tie, and looked ready for business.

When both were seated, Dellenbach announced, "I've going to make this short and sweet. I have attorneys on the agenda and two other meetings this morning before I fly back East at noon."

Stone said nothing. He was repulsed, however, by the same condescending preppy vibe he'd first picked up on when they met at the Scottsdale restaurant. Of course there were more important people than Stone McClelland to meet with, but the way he put it on display made him a bona fide jerk.

"Our people have gathered important tidbits of information that can probably assist you in capturing Chris Soles," declared Dellenbach. "And we must apprehend him soon – before he has a chance of attacking The Seven in Idaho."

"That would be a good thing," Stone patiently agreed.

"First of all, and very important in your dealings with your contact," Dellenbach went on, "is that it's very likely the 'rep' of Chris Soles you've been interacting with, is actually Chris Soles himself."

"How could that be?" countered Stone.

"A good plastic surgeon can work wonders," Dellenbach replied.

"I don't think so," Stone begged to differ. "A lot of criminals we took in when I was with the DEA tried to alter their looks, and none of them was anywhere close to what you're suggesting."

"Get used to the idea," insisted Dellenbach, "and keep in mind that's precisely why you have to schedule another meeting with his 'rep'

— so as to take the real Chris Soles down."

"What else have you got?" McClelland asked dourly.

"There's someone named Garf Taylor that's supposedly running the day-to-day of the Future Generations terrorist group," Dellenbach stated. "Obviously, we want to take him down too when we snag Soles, so do what you can to find out how they coordinate."

"That won't be easy."

"Work on it," prodded Dellenbach. He added, "And there's one more thing you might use as a bargaining chip. I don't know how exactly to utilize it, but make it something that works to your advantage."

"And that one thing is?"

"Soles appears to be involved in a romantic threesome relationship with two women," revealed Dellenbach. "Like I stated, I don't know how best to use that, but maybe it can be part of how you get him out in the open again, so he can be captured. Try to remember, as I do daily, that among his many other crimes, he killed my cousin and he must be brought to justice."

After Stone left Dellenbach's luxury suite, he rode the elevator down and began crossing the lobby to exit the hotel. Casually and without intent, he glanced to where he'd been sitting earlier this morning. Suddenly, he was struck by the realization he'd seen Sapphire MacKenzie exactly where he was now.

Stone McClelland froze in place. All at once, his feet refused to move any further.

She was exactly where he was now. And she was coming from...Whitley Dellenbach's room?

What the hell was going on here, wondered McClelland.

In his very first meeting with Whitley Dellenbach, Stone was told to contact her, but also to never mention Dellenbach to her.

What the hell was going on here?

And where did Dellenbach get the information he just told Stone about? Was Sapphire MacKenzie working for him? Was she a spy, a mole undermining her own movement?

"Impossible!" McClelland stated aloud. Sapphire MacKenzie was too idealistic and headstrong; she was wholly dedicated to a free and sovereign Cascadia.

So what the hell was going on here?

***

The two telephone calls came in almost simultaneously.

First, it was from a phone near Chris on the kitchen table. The caller ID told him Tomas was on the line, so he moved to answer. Before Chris could put the call on speakerphone, however, another phone began ringing from the bedroom.

Kiri immediately rose from her seat at the kitchen table and disappeared into the bedroom.

About ten or twelve minutes later, Chris and Tomas ended their conversation. He could hear Kiri still talking to someone in the bedroom, but it sounded like they were finishing up. And sure enough, a few seconds later she was walking into the kitchen.

Without saying a word, Kiri had Chris turn his chair and himself away from the table enough so she could be comfortably seated upon his lap. Kiri then wrapped her arms about him to deliver a soft kiss. Without warning, her tongue bypassed his lips and began passionately exploring his mouth.

At the same time, Chris discovered he couldn't resist and suddenly they captivated by the most ardent embrace they'd ever experienced. They were breathing heavily and both sensed they wanted more but suddenly, Kiri backed off. She disengaged from the kiss, removed her arms from him, and slipped off his lap. Kiri returned to the chair she'd been in before the phones began to ring, and smiled.

"That kiss was from Sapphire, who made the other call," Kiri explained. "She said to give you a kiss from her that you'd remember. Are you going to remember it?"

"Am I going to remember it?" Chris gawked at her in disbelief. "Every time I look at you I'll never forget it."

"Well, don't get any ideas," she warned. "That kiss was from Sapphire and I'm surely not going to do anything to encourage you to break your vow to my parents."

Staring at such a close companion – and pretty woman – Chris knew he was in a tough spot. Without much alternative, he changed the subject.

"So what did Sapphire have to say?" wondered Chris.

"She wanted to send that kiss to you because we probably won't see her for a while," replied Kiri. She then added, "Unless of course we go out to Idaho."

Chris shrugged his shoulders noncommittally.

"When is she leaving?"

"This afternoon," Kiri stated. "She said that even though the big weekend for The Seven to meet and all the demonstrations is still over a week and a half away, there was too much work to do on the ground before them."

"So where is she staying?"

"With a friend's family in Coeur d'Alene," explained Kiri, "a friend that is in the Idaho chapter of the Free Cascadia movement."

"I wonder if she'll be close to Tomas," Chris remarked.

"What do you mean by that?"

Chris replied that one part of his conversation with Tomas concerned his decision to join the protests and demonstrations in Idaho as a representative of the commons. And yet, Chris explained to Kiri, it was only a small part of what they discussed at the end of their talk.

Mostly, Tomas had called to say he was doing much better. He also talked about completing the video reenactment of his abduction with the production team Sapphire had sent over. Further, he remarked that he was much improved mentally as well, because the reenactment process had been remarkably purgative and regenerative. The whole family had taken part in it and being successfully together again sparked a collective sense of overcoming adversity, and seemed to make everyone stronger when the filming was done.

So stirring had the experience been, Tomas and Linda talked it over and decided the best thing for Tomas to do would be to represent the Commons movement and Commons Rising in Idaho, even if he couldn't get the rest of the commons to join. Linda and the kids would stay at her mom's house, and when Tomas returned from Idaho, they would look for a new house a few miles north in the Meadowdale area. Even though the filming of the abduction reenactment had helped, the family agreed they would never sleep another night in the old Edmonds house.

"Where is Tomas going to stay in Idaho?" asked Kiri.

"He's got a dependable friend in Coeur d'Alene from Commons Rising that helped him out when some thugs roughed him up after a meeting," replied Chris.

"When did that happen?" wondered Kiri. "I never heard about it."

"I hadn't either until just now," said Chris. "I guess it was after a Commons Rising meeting in west Seattle. It appears that someone's been after Tomas for a while and it's all made him even more determined to pursue what he believes in."

Staring directly into his eyes, Kiri asked Chris, "So when are we going to Idaho, Chris?"

"As soon as Tomas can locate a safe house for us," he assured her, adding, "at least that's what he said he was going to do."

Kiri sighed heavily.

"I'm very leery of it, Chris," she admitted. "I sense great danger approaching from multiple directions over there."

"There will be great danger," Chris agreed. "And even though I'm still learning how to use it after many years, I've consulted the I Ching of late and there appears to be great opportunity wrapped with danger out there. I think we should go."

With mischief in her smile, Kiri, "I don't know, Chris, it could be an unmitigated disaster."

"Why do you say that?"

"I fear we might be overwhelmed by the world's billions of insects," she plainly stated. "A plague of locusts will likely descend upon us, cockroaches will finally be able to conquer the world, and bedbugs will disrupt the sex lives of all lovers in Cascadia."

"Oh no," Chris disagreed. "It'll get much worse than that before it gets better. No doubt the waters of Lake Hayden will rise, sweep away The Seven, and naturally the little folk will be blamed for it. Retribution will be swift and, of course, unjust."

"And we'll go anyway," Kiri added, as she laughed at their nonsense, before recalling something else. "Oh, and I almost forgot."

From a pocket of her shorts, Kiri withdrew a piece of paper.

"This has a telephone number Sapphire wanted me to write down and give to you," she said, handing it to him.

"Whose number is it?"

"Sapphire didn't know or wasn't saying," explained Kiri. "She said it was a dead letter account number."

"What the heck is that?"

"As I understand it," Kiri began, "Sapphire said it was something like a dead letter at the post office that can neither be sent on, nor sent back. In this case though, it's a phone number belonging to a fictional entity most likely; no one ever calls it and it never calls out. It was probably paid for long ago, and paid for as well far into the future."

None of this made sense to Chris.

"So if nobody ever calls the number, and no one ever calls out, what good is it?" asked Chris. "And what am I supposed to do with it?'

"Sapphire said it's a phone number of last resort," replied Kiri. "She wants you to give it to your ex-DEA contact and have his friends track it if it surfaces. If the number's being used, she just wants it followed and then for us to get back to her with the locations."

"That could have all kinds of implications and complications," Chris observed. "It could be used to identify the numbers it makes contact with and an entire network could be identified. It could be something deadly for many."

"I'm certain Sapphire understands the risk," Kiri stated assuredly. "I trust her, and you should too."

"Oh, I most certainly trust Sapphire," Chris declared, staring at the ten digit phone number on the paper, "and because I do, I'll pass it on as she requested."

***

"I think I have something that eventually might prove mutually beneficial for the both of us," the voice cooed into the phone.

"That's good," Stone McClelland averred. "Why don't we get together again and discuss it?"

The delay in response time made Stone worry that he'd fumbled the ball. The suspicious tone he next heard in his ear confirmed his fears.

"What – aren't our phone conversations enough?"

"There are things that I think we best go over in person, that's all," said McClelland. "You've got to trust me; I need to pass along some documents that Chris Soles will find interesting and I can't do it over the phone."

"Documents can wait," declared the voice. "In the meantime, if I can't trust you over the phone, I can't trust you in person. And likewise the other way around."

McClelland realized he'd blundered, pushed where he shouldn't have because everybody wanted Soles brought in, and made a misstep in the game of trust. He sought to go on the offensive so as to cover his bases.

"That brings up a major problem," McClelland asserted. "I need some way to contact you."

"Don't worry about it; I'll be in touch with you."

"That's not good enough anymore; it's too one-sided and doesn't advance the game of trust," stated McClelland.

Pausing to ruminate on the matter, the voice eventually replied

"Fair enough. Are you on social media?"

"Don't know much about it."

"Well, it's time to familiarize yourself with it," commanded the voice, giving him three social media services to try. "I have an app on my phone that will pick up handles or hashtags when they're used, and when that alert goes off, I'll get back to you."

McClelland didn't have a clue what was being spoken about, so the voice explained the handle was like a user name on the social media site, and along with the identification of subject matter, the two were often denoted by "@ and #," respectively.

"For example," explained the voice, "you might be '@deahulk,' for a name identity, and we could use the subject matter of '#trustand/ordeception' for a hashtag, whenever you want to communicate."

"That might work," McClelland replied skeptically, "except, I'd prefer '@exdeahulk.'"

"Fine by me," acknowledged the voice.

"Okay, I'll check into it," Stone grudgingly agreed. "So explain to me, how well do you know Chris Soles?"

"Fairly well, as you might guess," the voice replied. "But sometimes I don't know where his motivations come from."

McClelland laughed.

"Sounds familiar," he stated, reflecting honestly. "Sometimes I don't know where my motivations come from either."

"Like when you released Chris Soles in Arizona?"

Somewhat stunned by the question, Stone answered honestly, "I guess that fits in a box that could be checked affirmative."

"So really, why did you let him go?"

"So why did he kill his girlfriend, Alice," McClelland countered, "and their unborn child?"

"He didn't," blurted the voice, without any forethought. "Snipers did it."

Goading him, the ex-DEA agent stated, "That's not what the news reports, media, and wanted posters said."

"It's all rigged," the voice snarled. "Empire is scamming him for their own nefarious ends. His girlfriend, Ali, with her very pregnant belly, was reclining on a rock in the sun. Soles was sitting next to her in a chair. The snipers could have easily taken him out, but they went after her first."

"How do you know so much?"

"He's a good friend," offered the voice, "someone who has the best interests of Cascadia and a grand awakening of the planet close to his heart."

"Can you prove that Soles didn't kill Alice Cope and the unborn child?" demanded McClelland.

"Can anyone prove he did?" the voice tossed back. "It's all rigged."

Stone McClelland realized they weren't getting anywhere, but didn't want to lose the connection. Very amicably, he asked when Chris Soles would be going to Idaho.

"Who says he's going to Idaho?"

"Everyone's going to Idaho," McClelland pronounced grandly. "The Seven will be there along with so many government forces you can't begin to imagine. Sapphire MacKenzie and the entire Free Cascadia movement will be there. And if The Seven are there, you can be certain the Future Generations terrorists will be there too, attempting to upset the entire apple cart, by attacking to assassinate The Seven."

"Don't forget commoners and the Commons movement in general," suggested the voice. "They'll be there too."

"Okay," Stone agreed, "toss in the commoners as well. But if what you've told me is true, if Future Generations will be in northern Idaho, Chris Soles will be there as well to deter them."

"That's a pretty big burden to put on the shoulders of Chris Soles."

"It's a big burden that he's assumed, if I'm reading him right," McClelland admitted. "And it still remains to be seen if he can truly match wits with Future Generations and Garf Taylor."

Completely shocked, the voice asked, "How do you know that name?"

"There are people getting too close to Soles, that perhaps shouldn't be," was what Stone offered. "Possibly he should be more wary and cautious with the people around him, and less trusting."

"What's that supposed to mean?"

"Let me ask you a question," proposed McClelland. "Do you think Chris Soles might imagine he's being compromised if his adversaries are close enough to perceive he's in a threesome relationship with two women? If that's the case, I'd think he might surely want to be a little more cautious."

The voice went quiet for an extended time.

At the same time, McClelland realized that particular bargaining chip of information probably wasn't played precisely as Whitley Dellenbach may have wished, yet nevertheless it could likely work to Stone's advantage.

"All that's the business of Chris Soles," the voice finally spoke. "I'll pass along your information, but I'm not involved."

"You better tell him that," McClelland affirmed. "There are people on the outside getting very close. And that's my tidbit of intelligence for today; what have you got for me?"

"Some of it depends on your motives," declared the voice. "Do you intend to trap Chris Soles, or go with what's honest in your heart?"

"Sorry, that's no good," the ex-DEA man fired back. "It's a trick question and that isn't how the game of trust works. I give you something of value and you give me something of value in return. So what have you got for me?"

"What I called you about to begin with."

"And what might that be?"

"Have you ever heard of dead letter phone accounts?" asked the voice.

"They don't exist anymore," McClelland snapped, "if they ever existed in the first place. With today's technology they'd be routinely eliminated."

"Well, let's give a number that's supposed to be one a try and see what happens," suggested the voice. "I suppose you have friends that can pinpoint the location of phone calls."

"I have friends," Stone replied curtly.

"That's wonderful," the voice was congratulatory. "I have friends too. Here's the number."

As the voice read the ten-digit number, McClelland wrote it down.

"Now, I might suggest that your more aggressive friends don't run out and clog things up by making raids and arrests right away when tracking this number," requested the voice. "But if it gets used, you might simply follow the location, or locations it turns up at. If and when your friends have some results, maybe then they can get them to you. And maybe then, you can pass them along to me when I call, and I'll pass them to my friends that gave me this number. Does that make sense?"

"I suppose so," Stone said without much enthusiasm.

"Then we have a deal?"

"For now."

"For now works – for now," concluded the voice, before hanging up and ending the conversation.

***

The hike up to the bluff overlooking the Bangor submarine base had been invigorating and salubrious.

Upon returning to their safe house cabin in the woods, Chris volunteered to pour a cool drink for the both of them, while Kiri opted to check their extra phones on the dresser in the bedroom.

The only phone showing any activity was the one she used exclusively for keeping in touch with Carolyn Maxwell. The icon on the phone indicated a text message had come in. Tapping the display, Kiri opened and began reading the panicked message with shock and dismay.

"Kiri – you've got to help me! My brother Timmy and three thugs I don't know are in the process of kidnapping me and taking me to someplace they're calling Asshole, Idaho – wherever that is. I'm in the bathroom right now and they don't know I have this phone, which I'll drop in the reservoir for the toilet water after this text message is sent. Please Kiri, find me in Idaho and save me. You're the only one I can count on!"

In the kitchen, Chris had already poured iced tea into two glasses and was on his way to return the pitcher to the refrigerator. Before he could, however, Kiri gently place her hand on his forearm, delaying him.

"Stop what you're doing," she pleaded, "and listen to this text message I just received from Carolyn Maxwell.

Slowly, deliberately, Kiri read the message to Chris. When she was finished, Kiri gazed intently up at him.

"So, Chris, when are we going to Idaho?"

He looked deep into her eyes.

"As soon as we safely can," he assured her.

CHAPTER THIRTY-TWO

"Billy, this is the last time I'm going over it," Garf stated as patiently as he could, while seething inside. "They are both over there – in Asshole, Idaho – for the cause. You got it?"

"But it's still my brother and sister, my only family," Billy Maxwell weakly protested.

"They both betrayed and disobeyed us," Taylor shot back. "They are in Asshole, Idaho, as bait and distraction; they merely run interference for our ultimate plan to finally ignite full-on revolution in Cascadia."

"But Garf, you don't have a clue how hard it is to sacrifice your only family," replied Billy.

Taylor sought to reassure his friend, for he needed his help. "It's probably not going to happen anyway. Most likely they'll merely be arrested. And maybe if they're clever enough, they might escape. But whatever they get, it's what they deserve for their transgressions against Future Generations."

Billy said nothing, so Garf took it as a sign to carry on.

"You're fucking brother Timmy killed a cop on an evening he wasn't even supposed to go out. It wasn't someone in the goddam fossil fuel Weapons of Planetary Destruction employ; that would have been all right. But no, your fucking brother Timmy kills a cop. And that jumpstarted a State of Emergency that set us back weeks in initiating the revolution."

Billy didn't reply for perhaps he already knew what was coming next.

"And then your traitorous sister has been feeding info to who the hell knows," Garf nearly shouted. "That's precisely what I always suspected and why I brought you in on the con to test her loyalty with the car loaded with explosives in Bremerton. And you know what Empire did with that!"

Billy Maxwell's head bobbed in acknowledgement.

"That's why they're in Asshole, Idaho, with others of their kind that don't truly respect the revolution," Taylor declared unequivocally. "And also why they've been given prominence in our decoy ploy – while we're getting on with the real thing."

Recognizing the reality of the situation, Billy nevertheless murmured, "But they're still my only family."

"Look," Garf began, a little exasperated, "my former lover Sapphire MacKenzie always said, 'Revolutionists have no family, except for the revolution.' Simply put, are you with it, or are you against it?"

Billy was quick to answer. "I spent all those years in Monroe because I believed in the future of this planet and Future Generations. They are my only family – but let the chips fall where they will."

"Okay," declared Taylor with some finality, "so that's that."

Maxwell wasn't done, however. "I still think you should let me go out there with you; it'll help make them believe in the plan. Besides, I'm about sick to death of this Birch Bay safe house."

Although Garf didn't say anything initially, he didn't want Billy anywhere close to his brother and sister: it might weaken his resolve.

"No," Taylor objected, "you stay on this side of the Cascades taking care of our little fishing expedition. That's more important."

"And what the hell are you going to do out there?" Billy queried. Even though he knew the answer, he required the reassurance.

"I'm going to make certain they can pass through the perimeter the authorities established allowing only residents living near the fenced compound where The Seven are meeting," said Garf. "Like I told you long ago, we have a homeowner we've paid off and is loyal to the cause to make certain it works."

"And you expect my brother and sister and the others to cause a distraction with explosives at various points next Saturday on the final day The Seven are at the compound?" asked Billy.

"They'll be told it's a distraction for the drone strikes that will come in from above shortly thereafter to take out The Seven, many of their supporters from the oligarchy, and maybe even the President and some of his billionaire/millionaire cabinet," Taylor stated grandly.

"But it's all a fake." Billy's voice was leaden. "None of that will ever happen."

Garf nodded in acknowledgement. "It will all be over Friday night and the fires of revolution will have been ignited from sparks no one could ever have anticipated."

Billy Maxwell sighed. "Man, that's a high price to pay."

"Desperate circumstances require desperate measures," stated Taylor, without emotion. "Now, the time has come for me to be off to Asshole, Idaho."

***

"Sorry if I'm catching you too early," McClelland apologized over the phone to Bertie, "but I'm off soon and wanted to make contact before I go."

"It doesn't matter when you call on Monday," Stanton replied sourly, "because it's Monday and anytime stinks. And that's especially so when you have to go to Vespers on Sunday evening."

"Vespers?"

"Yeah, Vespers," Bertie confirmed. "I don't know if all of us Baptists condone the practice, but our church seems to view it favorably, as does my family at times. So after attending morning services, my family determined it was my fate to join them by spending last evening singing hymns and worshiping as well."

"And now it's Monday," cracked Stone, with good heartedness in his tone.

"Yes, it is," agreed Stanton, "and thanks loads for being my first caller of the day. So where are you going – any chance it's northern Idaho?"

"How did you guess?"

"Well, let's see," Bertie began, "this is Monday, the demonstrations begin Wednesday when The Seven and all their friends start to arrive, the gala dinner for all the anointed is to be held Friday night, and it's rumored even the President will be in attendance on Saturday, the final day of meetings and speeches at the compound on Lake Hayden. So why wouldn't you want to go there for all the fun and games as well?"

"I'm not so certain it'll be as much fun as pin-the-tail-on-the-donkey," Stone allowed, "because I'm hoping to run into reprobates like the terrorists of Future Generations if I'm fortunate enough."

"And Chris Soles?"

"And maybe Chris Soles," McClelland acknowledged, "though I haven't been called by his rep now for a while now."

"Where are you staying?" asked Bertie. "I've heard there're no accommodations remaining over there whatsoever."

"I got a room at some place on Lake Coeur d'Alene," said Stone, reaching for the name he'd scribbled down on a piece of paper. He read Bertie the name.

"Wow, fancy place," Stanton exclaimed. "That must have cost a pretty penny."

"It was one of the only places available," McClelland replied, even as he had no clue of room's cost since his handler Roger had made the arrangements. "Are you heading over there too?"

"Nah, as of now, I don't think so," Bertie said with some disappointment in his voice. "I reckon they'll station me here to keep my nose to the grindstone."

"Are you making any progress?"

"Maybe," mustered Stanton, "and maybe not. Those that aren't focused on the events in northern Idaho are still looking into the possibility of an old geezer network lending material support to Chris Soles and Future Generations. And there might be some promising leads with that improbable stuff. Seems a lot of them traveled to Port Townsend a few weeks ago to practice for a – believe it or not – shuffleboard tournament, which might well have been cover for a secret meeting."

"What makes you think that?"

"Well, according to other reports our analysts have compiled," Bertie explained, "another similar meeting might have occurred at the same old Victorian mansion in Port Townsend on July Fourth – that initiated this reign of terror by Future Generations. In any case, we're seriously starting to monitor any and all of these old geezers that might be involved."

"Anything else?" wondered McClelland.

"Not much," Stanton responded. "Our people are watching that 'dead letter' phone number you gave us, but nothing yet. In fact, we can't determine that it's ever been used, although it is active. Like speculated, the number was signed up for a long time ago by a fictional business entity, and paid for far into the future – but never used. So we'll just keep watching it, as if we've got nothing else to do."

"Well, let me know if it suddenly lights up," Stone requested. "It's very important to somebody, and that might make it important to us."

"And what have you got for me?" Bertie wanted to know.

"Currently, not a heck of a lot," McClelland admitted. "Like I said, the rep for Soles hasn't called since he gave me the 'dead letter' phone number. I was actually going to ask if you could obtain something for me."

"What might that be?"

"How about a dossier?" suggested Stone.

"What kind, and about whom?" Bertie shot back.

"How about a dossier on everyone who is on the guest list for the circus provided by The Seven this week in Idaho?" Stone requested.

"What do you want that for?"

"Bait," McClelland simply explained. "You told me the compound The Seven and all the others are staying at was impregnable, right?"

"Yep," Bertie responded. "Plus, there will be so many armed forces stationed there that a successful attack is totally implausible."

"Then we needn't worry if a tempting dossier is tossed out as bait to trip up Chris Soles, and maybe even Future Generations," proposed McClelland. "It might be a way to bring him out in the open; it might make the plots of Future Generations more transparent."

"I'll do what I can," Stanton promised. "Anything else?"

"I don't think so."

"Okay, then," replied Bertie. "Enjoy your vacation by the lake; I'll be here hard at work – or attending Vespers."

***

"Do you think this is public enough?" asked Tomas uneasily.

"I have my reasons," Sapphire smiled smugly, "but I'll get to that."

They were seated at the outdoor restaurant of the five star hotel sipping coffee drinks. The hotel was on the edge of Lake Coeur d'Alene with an excellent view of the rows of boat docks below them. Even if rain was forecast intermittently later in the week during the demonstrations, they both relished the fine, sunny weather today.

"Thanks for taking time to meet me here for a break," Sapphire stated kindly.

"I probably have a lot more free time than you," noted Tomas. "How are your preparations going for the rest of the week?"

Sapphire smiled and sighed at the same time. "Oh, it's madness, of course. I've got meetings all afternoon and tomorrow's preparations are basically the same. Then on Wednesday, when The Seven begin flying into Fairchild Air Force Base southwest of Spokane, and get shuttled via helicopter to the Lake Hayden compound, we'll already have people marching through the streets of Coeur d'Alene. The marching demonstrations will culminate with an hour or two of speeches in McEuen Park – which is just over there," she said, pointing to the east.

"And then on Thursday?" inquired Tomas.

"Thursday is about the same as Wednesday," replied Sapphire, "but Friday and Saturday will be when it gets more interesting."

"Why, what happens then?"

"First, on both days," she began, "we have thousands of kayakactivists launching for a southern approach from the lake. While that is happening, the central body of protesters will see how far we can get on the main road toward the north entry of the compound. Some want to attempt to breach the main gate, but I'm persistent in my opposition to that approach. We don't need to be slaughtered by all the military forces that have been mobilized; we just want to bring greater awareness to the plight of Cascadia and the world with The Seven and their enablers in control and destroying the future of the planet."

"Does that mean you're bracing for violence regardless?" wondered Tomas.

"It's generally assumed something unnecessary will transpire," Sapphire admitted. "There are always infiltrators attempting to give Empire an excuse to crack skulls; it goes with the territory."

Tomas sipped his latte. "So why was it so pressing to meet me here today? I can imagine you have more important things to do than sitting around drinking coffee."

Removing her sunglasses, Sapphire stared deep into Tomas's eyes.

"Are you aware of what's happening regarding the abduction reenactment video you made with your family?" she asked.

Visibly uncomfortable, Tomas recalled that his wife had told him last night during a phone call that a lot of people had watched it.

"It's gone viral on the Internet," Sapphire affirmed. "Since it was posted on the Free Cascadia video channel, it's had over three million views. And counting."

"So Linda told me," Tomas admitted.

"And because of that, it's prime time to capitalize on such momentum," exclaimed Sapphire.

"What are you proposing?"

"Another video. A short one."

"What kind of video?"

"Tomas, you have the power right now to fuse the Free Cascadia movement and the Commons movement together," Sapphire asserted. "It's much bigger than simply bringing more bodies into the streets; it's all about the merging of ideologies for a brighter future in the long run. All I'm asking you to do is record a call for all commoners and commons to join in solidarity with Free Cascadia for this week — and let the future take care of the future."

Tomas chuckled. "And that's why you're not afraid of meeting in such a public place?"

Sapphire smiled back at him. "It's not everyday you get to have coffee with a viral Internet star."

Growing more serious, Tomas asked Sapphire what she wanted him to do.

"The same video crew that filmed the reenactment is here in Idaho," she informed him. "If you're willing, they could produce a clip this afternoon and then we'd append it to the reenactment video, so all viewers going forward will hear a call to joint action. I think you might just have another hit on your hands."

Laughing, Tomas agreed to meet the video people, then changed the subject.

"You know, I still haven't been able to find a safe place for Chris and Kiri to stay," he noted.

"I talked to Kiri this morning," mentioned Sapphire. "She's worried to death about her friend that was kidnapped by Future Generations and taken to some place they're calling – Asshole, Idaho."

"Yes, Chris told me about that yesterday when I talked with him about a lack of places to stay," said Tomas. "He was waiting to hear back through the Elder network, but if something didn't develop they were going to leave Tuesday regardless."

"And tomorrow surely isn't soon enough for Kiri," Sapphire stated ominously.

* * *

On Monday evening, Kiri was watching the nightly news on TV while Chris was in the bedroom on the phone. The stories were all about the massing swell of humanity in northern Idaho, as well as the abundant military troops to defend The Seven and other dignitaries.

With all the protesters and soldiers gathered in one region, Kiri knew it would eventually be a mess one way or the other. It was a situation anyone in their right mind would avoid, but she knew they had to get out there. And the sooner, the better.

They had to get moving.

Even now, Kiri could see the cabin wall behind the television in flames. The fire was coming and they had to get moving. There would be nothing left of this place; she could foresee it as clearly as anything she'd ever foreseen.

The effects on Kiri were claustrophobic and panic provoking. They had to get moving – and Carolyn's life might depend on it.

What was taking Chris so long on the phone?

She glanced back at the TV to see a video about The Seven soon to be landing at an air force base near Spokane, and some of the massive helicopters that would shuttle them to the sanctity of their Lake Hayden compound. Then the reporter with the background story cut to the demonstrators already at the entry to the air force base.

It all made Kiri ever more nervous and antsy. Of course, she realized they needed a safe place to stay. They couldn't just go out there and get arrested, or worse, put other good people at risk. But they had to get moving.

Kiri wondered whom Chris was talking to now. He said he was going to speak to more Elders and the ex-DEA agent as well. She had great misgivings about the former drug cop, even though Chris said the I Ching and his own gut told him it was okay. "Ambiguous," is the word he used, which Kiri took to mean it could work out well – or not at all. And if something was ambiguous, at least in her experience, it was better to avoid if possible. But Chris was the Teacher, and sometimes she had to let things play out as they would – and hopefully for the best.

It was only a few minutes later when Chris finished his phone calls and joined Kiri on the couch in front of the television. She asked him how it went.

"I just got off the phone with Stone McClelland," he explained. "He says he's already in Coeur d'Alene and wants to pass some documents along to Chris. But I fear a trap."

"And well you should," Kiri stated definitively. "Any luck finding a place to stay?"

"Unfortunately, no," replied Chris. "Tomas said it was probably better to not even come under the circumstances."

"Are you kidding me?" Kiri was outraged. "Doesn't he know about Carolyn?"

"He knows," Chris said patiently, attempting to calm her. "He was just stating the reality of the situation out there right now. And according to the Elders I spoke with in the area, many of them believe something foul is afoot."

"What do you mean by that?"

"Many are under the impression that people are watching them," he told her. "And that might well be the case if Empire thinks they can get to us through them."

"It sounds like it could just as easily be paranoia on the part of the elderly," Kiri observed.

"It could be," Chris allowed, "but most of the Elders are incredibly attentive. After all, what else do they have to do besides a few games of shuffleboard, puttering in the garden, and going to bed early?"

Kiri came directly to the point that had been bothering her for days.

"So, Chris," she asked, "what are we going to do?"

"We're going to leave in the morning for northern Idaho and wing it," he simply stated. "My gut and my reading of the I Ching say it'll all work out."

"As in work out – okay?" she demanded to know.

"Hopefully," said Chris. "The I Ching is just a partially open window on the future as my old mentor Wimp would often say."

Shaking her head dubiously, Kiri blurted, "Well, at least we're getting out of here; we've got to find Carolyn."

"Oh yeah," Chris began, recalling details of his recent phone conversation, "McClelland told me something else."

"About what?"

"You remember that 'dead letter' phone number Sapphire gave us to watch?" Chris asked.

"Yeah, and?"

"He told me the phone was used once this afternoon," he explained.

"Were they able to track it?" wondered Kiri. "What was its location?"

Chris nodded his head. "It was calling from – where else – but northern Idaho."

CHAPTER THIRTY-THREE

"I just wanted to make certain you were comfortable with it, Father," spoke Whitley Dellenbach over the phone.

"I think it's a splendid idea your ex-DEA man has," lauded the older man. "If he wants to chum the waters, so to speak, with us and our friends as bait, I say let him do it – especially if it proves a temptation to bring Chris Soles out into the open."

"As long as you're not worried about our safety in doing so," cautioned the son.

"Why should I even be concerned?" Theodore Dellenbach laughed robustly. "We'll have a sizeable chunk of the U.S. military defending us in Idaho. How is this dossier of all attending The Seven's little party being compiled?"

"It's coming from a friend of his involved with Federal law enforcement."

"That's grand!" the old man recognized. "We're all working in harmony."

Whitley was still hesitant, however. "And our friends that will be in attendance; will they be of the same mind as you in these matters?"

"If they aren't initially – if they even find out – I will make sure they will congeal and are wholly united on the matter," the elder Dellenbach assured his son. The troops are already there and their presence is overwhelming. All will be well on the inside of the compound."

"But not on the outside, I fear," Whitley countered.

Theodore Dellenbach agreed. "It's not likely at all on the outside. But on the inside it will be a grand celebration – silently, of course – of our effective control on all facets of government. We are in cahoots with and thus control the Administration, we own the Congress, and this gathering of The Seven will celebrate our ownership of the Judicial System.

"Our corporations and those of our friends," continued the old man, "control those in government, and our unwitting working class goons control the populace when the police can't or have to look the other way.

"So when the great unwashed and unnumbered choose to come after us in desperation in northern Idaho or elsewhere," the elder Dellenbach thundered on, "they will only reduce their numbers by the guns of our troops, or by getting skewered on our bayonets. We are in control; the masses must understand their subjugation and accept it. Otherwise, inevitably, they die!"

Letting his father have his say, Whitley eventually asked if he was still planning his arrival in northern Idaho for Friday morning.

"Yes," he acknowledged. "I still have much on my schedule for the rest of today, as well as Wednesday and Thursday, but will fly to Spokane on Friday. And you, Son, is your arrival still set for Thursday afternoon?"

"Indeed it is," replied the younger man, "and the transit to the military helicopter waiting at Fairchild that you arranged will be escorted and seamless. But there is one thing more I must mention before seeing you there."

"And that is?"

"I'm sure you recall our commons 'informant' Tomas Hernandez?" inquired Whitley.

"I do," the father answered, "and I also recall the superb job your people did in compiling that report under difficult circumstances."

"That's kind of you, Father, but there is something new you're probably not aware of concerning Hernandez," Whitley stated. "Not long ago, Tomas Hernandez released a short abduction reenactment video clip on the Internet and it's gone viral. He's in Idaho now and is becoming a strong force that we might have to deal with."

"Do you see him as a manageable threat?"

"I have people watching him," Whitley assured his father. "If he's not manageable, in the chaos of the next several days it's likely he can be easily neutralized."

"Take care of it however you must, Son," the old man ordered.

"I will, Father; you need not worry about that."

***

Kiri was up earlier than Chris; it was the fire that woke her.

The walls of their beautiful little cabin hideaway were burning – everything was in flames – but not yet.

She couldn't let the place go. They'd shared too many good hours here. And it was where Sapphire stayed when they became a threesome. It was where she'd learned so much from him and learned to love him like no other. It was a place like no other...

But it was all going up in flames. Or would be, soon enough. They had to get out, get away.

In the silent, peaceful dawn, Kiri let him sleep as long as he might. The day, the trip would be trying enough. There was no reason not to let him have his rest now. This evening in northern Idaho would inevitably beset them with its chaos, with its darkness closing in. Yes, she would let him sleep for now. In spite of the coming flames.

It wasn't until ten-thirty, or nearly eleven that they finally got away. Purposely, they delayed to miss the Tuesday morning rush hour traffic in Seattle, and then one thing led to another and suddenly it was approaching eleven AM.

The trip east across Washington State would probably last somewhere around six or more hours, and Kiri was in a sullen mood from the start. She didn't want to see their cabin burn; she spoke nary a word until they crossed over the Cascades on Interstate 90 and were passing through Ellensberg.

Another thirty miles or so to the east, they dropped into the gorge and crossed the mighty Columbia River, which flowed more or less north/south through central Washington. Close to George – yes – George, Washington, Chris took I-90 almost due east for what seemed to Kiri miles and miles of interminable boredom.

They stopped for gas in Moses Lake and used the facilities as well. Another forty or so miles later they passed through Ritzville, on the "hypotenuse' of Future Generations' prior sabotage earlier in the summer. With memories of the first suicide sacrifices in the Ritzville post office on both their minds, neither Chris nor Kiri made mention of it. Looking at each other, shaking their heads, seemed to say all that was necessary.

Now heading northeast towards Spokane, it only took Kiri five or ten miles for her mood to alter dramatically. She opened the four or five different maps she'd brought along of eastern Washington and northern Idaho. Feverishly, she began combing through them.

Kiri's sudden burst of activity didn't escape Chris's attention.

"What are you doing?" he wanted to know.

Looking up from her maps, Kiri explained, "Carolyn has been kidnapped and is being held against her will somewhere in northern Idaho. I'm going to find out where we go to rescue her."

"I thought we already knew she was in Asshole, Idaho," noted Chris.

Turning back to the maps, Kiri blew him off. "You just keep driving; I'm going to figure out where Carolyn is."

It was shortly after Chris first started seeing signs for the Spokane airport on the west side of town that Kiri lit up with excitement.

"I get it!" she proclaimed exuberantly. "I get it, I get it – I got it!"

"What have you got?" asked Chris.

"I know where Carolyn is!" Kiri exclaimed jubilantly. "She's being held in Athol, Idaho."

"I thought we already knew that," Chris tossed back.

"No, Chris. It's not Asshole, Idaho; it's Athol, Idaho," she strongly objected. "It's spelled A-t-h-o-l: Athol, Idaho."

Chris chuckled mischievously. "And I suppose it's just down the road from its sister city, Anath?"

Kiri playfully thumped him on the leg.

"I'm serious, Chris," she declared. Kiri pointed to her map. "Athol is right here; it's a small town north of Coeur d'Alene, and north of Hayden, on Highway 95. That's where Carolyn is being held prisoner, and that's where we're going to go."

"You are serious, aren't you?" Chris said with a smile.

"I'm certain Athol, Idaho, is where she's at," Kiri stated triumphantly, "and we're not stopping until we get there!"

***

The dockhands in Poulsbo that rented him the eighteen-foot inflatable boat for the beautiful week of weather that was forecasted didn't hold back their opinions. They flat out told Billy Maxwell that he was wasting both his time and money.

"There ain't no fish left in Puget Sound," barked a swarthy bearded guy with chewing tobacco remnants smeared amongst his teeth.

His buddy in a greasy work shirt embroidered with the name "Carl" chimed in, "And anything you do catch is probably closed to recreational harvest by the state."

"Absolutely for fucking certain, though," continued the bearded dockhand, "you won't be catching any salmon because there ain't any no more. And that's just the way it is."

Billy told them it didn't really matter. "Because I've got a cooler full of beer."

"Well, at least you'll catch a buzz," stated Carl, before Billy shoved off.

The boat was just what he needed. It had a one hundred horse outboard mounted on the back, next to a smaller 9.8 horsepower, four-stroke outboard for trolling. Billy would be able to get where he wanted quickly enough and − best of all − he could easily land on any beach, especially when the tide was out.

Maxwell charted a southwest course from Poulsbo down Liberty Bay using the full power of the big outboard motor. In spite of the roar of the engine, it was otherwise a sunny, peaceful day on the water. It wasn't long before he passed the small town of Keyport to the west, yet he hardly gave it a second glance. Hugging the shore to his port side, Billy eventually motored around the southerly protruding landmass of Point Bolin.

With the waters opening up more around the Point, Maxwell changed course, heading now north northeast into the Agate Passage. In the distance he could make out the Agate Pass Bridge that connected Bainbridge Island to the Kitsap Peninsula.

Upon drawing close to the bridge, Billy crossed the Passage so that he floated near the Bainbridge shore side. Here he let the big outboard motor idle while he fired up the outboard for trolling. When certain the smaller engine was firing well, Billy shut down the big outboard.

He baited up his fishing gear and opened a beer from the cooler. Then, for the next four and a half hours, Billy trolled up and down the northwest Bainbridge shore from the Agate Pass Bridge to Manzanita Bay, a distance he guessed to be about four or five miles.

While leisurely floating along, Billy wished he could have traveled with Garf to Idaho to help solidify the planning. Garf had called him the previous evening from his special phone to tell him everything was going okay; nevertheless, Billy had mixed emotions about the whole thing.

He was naturally worried about his brother, but more particularly about his sis.

Whatever Timmy got later this week, Billy had to admit, would be whatever he unfortunately deserved. His drinking routinely put him in the way of trouble and he never should have killed that cop up by Marysville.

His sis was another matter entirely though. She hadn't willingly joined Future Generations, so Billy still thought Garf should cut her some slack. Nevertheless, she had apparently been the one giving them away. Regretfully, Billy wished he could be in Idaho to keep an eye on Carolyn and set things straight.

As he slowly turned the boat about in Manzanita Bay once more to head north toward the bridge, Billy cracked another beer. He would have preferred to go to Idaho, but this floating around on the water wasn't bad duty either.

The dockhands were right though: the fishing sucked. He'd only caught three dogfish in over four hours, and he hated those little bastard sharks. Fortunately, with a steel leader they weren't biting through his line, yet those little bastards really sucked.

But like he told the dockhands in Poulsbo, it didn't really matter. He was out here to drink beer. And scrutinize the docks and houses on the northwest shore of Bainbridge Island.

***

Chris and Kiri arrived in Athol, Idaho, a little after 5:30 PM.

If they had taken some alternative, more diagonal route after crossing the Washington-Idaho border it most likely would have been faster, because the traffic around Coeur d'Alene was horrendous.

Turning off Interstate 90 and heading north on Highway 95 in Coeur d'Alene, they were almost immediately confronted with near gridlock. To drive the mere five miles to Hayden took thirty-five minutes – a span of time that began to edge Kiri ever closer to absolute frustration. It seemed the closer they got to Athol, the more antsy and anticipatory she grew. And the snail's pace traffic was clearly taking its toll.

Chris recalled earlier travels through the same area being slow, but nothing like this. Kiri said it had to be because of all the demonstrators that had flooded the area. Agreeing, Chris noted that many of the more aware in Cascadia had surely found their way to northern Idaho.

When finally they reached Hayden the congestion on the road began loosening, and with fewer cross streets meeting the highway it became more freeway-like. At the turnoff for Hayden Avenue, there were scores of protesters with signs. Kiri and Chris glanced at each other, acknowledging without words that soon The Seven would be gathered at the compound only a few miles to the east, and all hell would likely break loose outside the gates.

Arriving in Athol about fifteen minutes later, they turned off the freeway and headed west on Highway 54, which seemed to be the main route through town. There were a couple eateries where they first turned off, and then further on was the post office. Nearby was, at first glance, a small motel called the Traveler's Inn that only appeared to have five or six rooms in front, yet wrapped around in the back to contain three stories and several more rooms.

They came upon a couple churches, an auto repair shop and a steak house restaurant as well. It was necessary to wait before the double set of railroad tracks while a BNSF two-engine train hauling mostly empty flatbed cars passed before them. Graffiti cluttered whatever space was available on most cars, while to their left and down the tracks was what looked like a big lumber milling operation.

When the train was finally past and the gates lifted, they drove by an ancient and solitary structure called the "Good Times Tavern." From the outside the tavern appeared to be an assemblage of add-on structures and the old metal roof had as much rust as it did paint. Even though there were bars on the windows, a welcoming neon, "OPEN" sign bid passersby inward. Parked in the dirt lot outside were a couple motorcycles, several cars, and a solitary work truck with side panels for tools. Beyond the tavern, Highway 54 proceeded directly west uphill and out of town.

There had been hardly any traffic on the main road through the small town, so Chris was able to execute a u-turn without any complications. They motored back past the Good Times Tavern, across the railroad tracks once more, and on impulse Chris took the first right he came to, heading south down 1st Street. Here they could plainly see to their right the large lumber yard with stacks and stacks of milled dimensional wood.

Wandering about, they turned onto a street named Menser and slowly followed it east. There were children out riding bikes and kicking balls, and a lady walking her dog gave Kiri and Chris a friendly wave as they passed. They slowed by a water tower that proudly and prominently displayed "ATHOL" on the tank, and then were quickly abreast of the Athol Elementary School.

For the next fifteen minutes they drove down nearly every street in the small, modest town, before Chris finally pulled over.

Turning to Kiri, he said, "I don't know where we're going to find Carolyn."

"I don't either," she grudgingly admitted, "but I know she's here."

"Well, I know I'm getting hungry," Chris replied. "Do you want to get something to eat?"

"Yeah, sure," Kiri said, with some disappointment in her voice.

"Where would you like to go?"

"I don't know," she said wistfully. "We passed a pizza joint, a couple of cafes, a steakhouse, and an old tavern. You make the choice."

"Okay," agreed Chris, "how about the old tavern? That place looked like it had some character."

"Fine by me," was all Kiri could say.

It only took them a minute or so to get back on Highway 54, and then a few minutes more to drive back across the railroad tracks to the west end of town and the Good Times Tavern.

The parking lot had a few more cars and pickup trucks than when they'd last passed by. Finding a place to park their van was relatively easy regardless, yet as they entered the restaurant/bar it proved to be moderately busy for a Tuesday evening.

The pool table toward the back looked popular with more men than women around it; still, the eight or nine people there seemed to be having a good time. A baseball game was playing on the TV in the corner of the room, while next to it an electronic dartboard console sat unused.

Several patrons were seated at the bar, laughing and joking like regular customers. The bartender was busy mixing drinks as he plucked various bottles stacked on four ascending levels in front of a long mirror. Another television hanging from the ceiling on the far right end of the bar was playing the same baseball game as the one at the back of the tavern.

A waitress had noted their entry and asked if they intended to eat dinner. Kiri replied affirmatively; they were informally told to take any open table. Seating themselves, Kiri took a place facing the entry door whereas Chris, across from her, could keep an eye on the pool table towards the back. The menu, with its limited fare, was in a plastic holder at the center of their table.

When the waitress returned with water and to take their orders, Kiri selected the house salad. Chris requested fish and chips along with a draft beer. The waitress asked Kiri if she wanted anything to drink, but she said she was satisfied to stick with water.

Chris could tell Kiri was disappointed and somewhat despondent. Because Carolyn's whereabouts were irresolvable – at least for the time being – neither mentioned her, although she was on both their minds.

Even though it was fairly loud in the tavern, especially back by the pool table, when their meals came Chris and Kiri began speaking about where they should spend the night. Chris mentioned he had seen a sign for a campground a few miles before turning off the highway for Athol, but Kiri didn't think that was the best idea. She suggested it might be better to slip off onto some side road in the woods and sleep in the van, because Empire would likely be monitoring most campgrounds.

They talked about how they both wanted to see Sapphire, yet were afraid that would be too dangerous as she would surely be in the public spotlight for the entire week. Chris mentioned he had to get in touch with the ex-DEA agent to see if he had any new information for him, and how they needed to contact Tomas Hernandez if possible.

Later, after the waitress had taken their plates and they waited for the bill, Kiri suddenly sat bolt upright in her chair as first a man, and then a woman, and others entered the door to Good Times Tavern. The woman and Kiri locked eyes. The woman was Carolyn Maxwell.

Even as Carolyn recognized Kiri, she spun and fled back through the entry door. The others with her quickly followed suit.

"You stay here, Chris!" ordered Kiri. "I'm going to catch up with Carolyn!"

Before Chris could protest, Kiri had snatched up her purse and was gone.

A few minutes later Chris paid their bill and was ready to follow Kiri. But just as he began to rise from the table, Kiri was walking back in the door. She marched over to their table, yet didn't sit down.

"Chris, you've got to stay here and don't say anything," she pleaded. "Carolyn didn't want me to get involved and that's why she ran out of the tavern when she saw me. But I caught up with her and now I'm involved. Carolyn's been made so the Future Generations are taking me so I don't report them. They've already taken my purse and phone; Carolyn needs me and I'm going with her."

"What about me?" wondered Chris.

"I told them I got your name off a ride board at the university, and barely knew you," Kiri replied hurriedly. "They're waiting and I've got to go or I lose Carolyn. Give me the keys to the van so I can get my backpack and stuff, and I'll leave them on the driver's seat."

Stunned, he handed her keys. Chris made the point, "These people are dangerous, Kiri. Are you going to be okay?"

"Probably not," she stated with conviction. "Just make sure you come back here every evening for a few hours, because if we can get away we'll come here and meet you. Okay?"

"Of course I'll be here – if you're sure about this," he assured her.

"Good; I've got to go," Kiri said desperately. "Give my love to Sapphire – and give me several minutes to get away before you come outside!"

CHAPTER THIRTY-FOUR

"I'm sorry if I'm calling too early," apologized Chris.

Sapphire laughed robustly. "You can call me anytime you want – you know that. And don't worry; I've been up for an hour and a half already. As a matter of fact, I was on another call and told them I'd call back when I realized it was you. I suppose you two are in north Idaho by now?"

"Yes, Kiri and I arrived yesterday, but we're not together now," he replied.

"What do you mean by that?"

"Kiri was abducted," Chris blurted, then added some fine tuning, "or willingly abducted."

"What are you talking about?" Sapphire demanded to know.

Briefly, Chris recalled the events of the previous evening.

"Oh my god!" Sapphire nearly shouted into the phone. "This can't be happening!"

"Unfortunately, it is," Chris noted dejectedly. "But Kiri's strong; she can handle it."

"Chris, we've got to do something for her," Sapphire said helplessly.

"I'm going back to the same tavern every night," he told her. "That's where she said we'd meet if she and her friend could escape."

"There must be something else we can do," she pleaded.

"I've been picking my brain all night about it and as a result didn't get much sleep," Chris admitted. "Something will work out, but there is another thing I have to tell you about as well."

"What's that?"

"I got an alert from the app on my phone that I told McClelland to use if he had to contact me," stated Chris. "So I called him back."

"What did he have to say?" Sapphire wondered warily.

"He told me the dead letter phone number that you gave us went operational once on Monday, and three times yesterday," Chris replied. "And each time the phone was tracked to the Coeur d'Alene and Hayden, Idaho, areas."

"So he's using the phone of last resort, eh?" posed Sapphire.

"Who?"

"Don't worry about it for now," she requested. "Just keep me informed when and where it's used again. Did he say anything about where the calls were being received?"

"No, he didn't mention it," said Chris. "But I have to put a call into him later today and I'll ask."

"That might be helpful to know," she mused. "And in the meantime, find Kiri. I want the three of us together again – and soon."

Chris smiled into the phone. "I'll do what I can. You know that."

"Stay in touch, Chris," Sapphire spoke softly. "And find Kiri for both our sakes."

∗∗∗

"Sorry about that Whitey," said Sapphire, when he came back on the line, "but I had to take that call."

"That's not a problem," he kindly replied. "Is everything okay?"

"To tell the truth – no," she sadly declared. "A close friend of mine was abducted last evening by the Future Generations people, and I'm terribly worried about her."

Dellenbach was suddenly very interested. "Where did all this happen?"

"At some tavern in northern Idaho; that's all I know," sighed Sapphire.

"It could be very important to know," Whitey pressed.

"Friends are already working on it," she assured him, cutting short any further discussion on the matter. "Besides, there's nothing I can do about it and I've got four full days ahead of me filled with protests and demonstrations."

"Yes," Dellenbach said, restraining himself about what he really wanted to know, "and before your other call came in you were telling me about today and tomorrow which are basically street marches in Coeur d'Alene, and speeches in a park. What about Friday and Saturday?"

"Those are the big days because all of The Seven will surely be in attendance and tens of thousands of protestors will have gathered," she explained. "Some are exceedingly important strategic allies that we never imagined would be joining forces with us in the protest."

"What allies?"

"The Commons movement, of course," Sapphire responded.

"I think I heard something about that," Whitey stated warily. "But can you trust them?"

"Absolutely," she fired back without hesitation. "They are being led by the husband of a close friend I used to raft guide with in Idaho years ago."

"Is that the guy named Tomas Hernandez?" Dellenbach inquired, though he already knew the answer to his question. "I think I heard something about him before."

"It sure is," Sapphire replied, "and he's brought thousands and thousands in the Commons movement throughout Cascadia to north Idaho."

"Well, I hope they can successfully further your efforts," Dellenbach mouthed politely, while silently cursing Hernandez and vowing to himself to have some people keep tabs on the activist and provide some bumps in his road.

"But anyway," Whitey continued, "you were telling me about what would happen later in the week with the protests."

"Yes," she agreed. "Friday will be very important since the march shifts north to Hayden and Hayden Lake, and we test the security perimeter about the compound. There will also be hundreds and hundreds of kayakactivists on the water below the compound and that's colorful because it always draws a lot of media attention."

"It sounds like testing of the security perimeter could cause clashes though" he observed.

"I hope not, but it's always a possibility," she honestly responded. "If anything like that were to happen, my guess is that it would transpire on Saturday instead."

"Why do you say that?"

"Because on Saturday, the national press will be allowed in for a live speech by the President inside the compound when he arrives for a few hours," Sapphire explained. "That also means maximum press coverage for the demonstrations on the outside. And I wouldn't be surprised if there will be infiltrators or rogue elements that want to cause a ruckus."

"No one needs that," Dellenbach assured her. "Where will you be?"

Sapphire shrugged her shoulders before she spoke. "As we stage a mass confrontation from all sides of the perimeter and from the water, I'll be somewhere in the midst of it all – of that I'm certain. I figure if The Seven, the President, select members of Congress, and supposedly many of the oligarchs that pull the strings behind the scenes will be there, why shouldn't I be there as well?"

Whitey laughed. "Just be careful, okay?"

Sapphire was still caught up by her previous thoughts, however. She asked him if any of his family would be attending the gathering of The Seven.

Sighing in frustration, Dellenbach admitted that he didn't know.

"They don't include me in their plans," he told her, feigning a heavy heart, "and that's another reason I'm siding with you and your friends. All I've heard from my father is that the names of the attendees – aside from The Seven, the President, and select members of Congress, of course – is a closely guarded secret so as to protect their security."

"More likely it's to forestall additional criticism of collusion in controlling the country," Sapphire snorted.

"Be that as it may," he replied in a measured and tender tone, "if I knew, I'd surely tell you."

"Responding to his kind words, Sapphire spoke sincerely. "You know, Whitey, I really like you.""

"And I really like you as well," Dellenbach said mirthfully. "I can't wait to share another night like Seattle — when it works with my schedule, and if I can somehow be absent from my sick wife during this terrible time."

"Oh, Whitey," Sapphire exclaimed with a warm glow, "you are such a special soul."

"As are you, my dear," he declared. "Let's talk again when you get a chance."

***

"I'll inquire, but I doubt if he wants it," the voice assured him. "It smells like a document your so-called friends are using to bring Chris Soles out in the open."

"It's nothing like that at all," Stone McClelland objected. "It's good solid information on everyone attending The Seven's little party. It's stuff that nobody else has access to."

"Chris doesn't need it," the voice shot back. "Empire and The Seven are despicable, but he doesn't care in the least who is at their little party. His interest is in stopping Future Generations from further violence that will only endanger the greater awakening, the more transformational revolution, that he is seeking in Cascadia.

"Besides," the voice continued, "it's my understanding that the VIP's and any bootlickers they bring with them are totally protected by an overwhelming contingent of military and police. Isn't that correct?"

"It's absolutely correct," McClelland affirmed. "With the collective force gathered in north Idaho right now, there is no way any of the dignitaries attending are at risk."

"Then all of Empire is in greater danger than they can possibly realize," the voice flatly stated. "Perhaps it's time to give you some advice you could put your trust into – in our little game."

"What do you mean by that?"

"Have you not read the writings of Lao Tzu, Confucius, or Sun Tzu?" asked the voice. "Particularly topical is Lao Tzu who once said, 'Fill your bowl to the brim and it will spill. Keep sharpening your knife and it will blunt.'"

McClelland blew him off. "Sorry, never had time for it. I was busy catching criminals during the War on Drugs."

Laughing, the voice merely asked, "And how well did that work out?"

Stone was stymied, not comfortable with any reply he might muster. Eventually he simply mouthed, "Let's just say I'm no longer pursuing that profession."

"And let's also say Empire is creating a most dangerous opening unto themselves by such a display of power and force in north Idaho," asserted the voice. "They've unwittingly allowed the possibility of a great danger of which they're not aware to stealthily sneak up on them."

"How do you know that?" McClelland demanded. "And what specifically is the danger?"

"I don't know what it is," answered the voice, quite honestly. "But I have read Lao Tzu and the others."

Stone McClelland was frustrated; he wasn't getting anywhere so he changed the subject. "Where are you now?"

"I'm in northern Idaho," the voice replied, "just like you. And not doing all that well at the moment, I might add."

"Why is that?"

"A companion of mine was abducted by the Future Generations people last evening," admitted the voice. "Do your contacts have any current intelligence about Future Generations in north Idaho?"

Stone didn't know if he was getting the truth or bullshit about an abduction. He simply replied, "You probably know a lot more about them than me. Did you pass along my information about the dead letter phone becoming active again?"

"I did, and thank you very much," the voice responded. "Do you have any idea who is being called?"

McClelland snorted. "We have somewhat of an idea. One call yesterday and the call the day before were made to the Seattle area to what apparently is another dead letter phone. The other two calls yesterday were picked up by probable burner phones in this area."

"Well, it makes no sense whatsoever to me," stated the voice, quite genuinely. "Nevertheless, I'll pass it on to my friend that gave me the number."

"After that," McClelland urged, "pass along any information back to me when that number does make sense to you."

"I'll keep it in mind," the voice promised.

***

After making his phone calls Wednesday morning to Sapphire and McClelland, Chris attempted to call Tomas Hernandez. Unfortunately, Tomas wasn't available, so he left a short message to call back when he could. Chris didn't leave his name – Tomas would recognize his voice – and he didn't mention anything about Kiri or anything else in case the phone fell into the wrong hands.

Like Kiri had suggested before being abducted, he parked the van on a little used forest road near Athol and slept in it there. Now, after the calls, Chris spent some time pouring over Kiri's maps of the region wondering where the Future Generations people could have taken her.

Looking at it realistically, he had to admit there were many relatively close places they could have taken her to hide out. To the west there were a couple lakes called Spirit Lake and Twin Lakes. They each had several named beaches on their shores, plenty of access roads and, Chris imagined, probably several lakeside cabins, some of which could likely be rented this time of year.

To the north, probably about thirty minutes away, was Sandpoint, Idaho. When traveling through there previously, he recalled beautiful and large Lake Pend Oreille and a farmer's market he had happened upon and the tasty blueberries he'd purchased. It was the largest town in that area and would likely have many potential hideaways the saboteurs could disappear in.

Pretty much directly east of Athol was the southern tip of Lake Pend Oreille and then acres and acres of Coeur d'Alene National Forest. They might be holed up on some lonely forest road out there, but his gut told him no.

To the south were of course Hayden, Hayden Lake, and the nearby compound where the honored henchmen of Empire were convening. Another five miles or so south was Coeur d'Alene where Sapphire and the tens of thousands would be marching and listening to speeches throughout the day. Future Generations might have dragged Carolyn and Kiri down there, though Chris doubted it. Marches and demonstrations were not their thing; Future Generations was hellbent on destruction.

Thus, Chris reasoned, they were likely hiding out somewhere relatively close to the Lake Hayden compound where The Seven and other accessories of Empire were to gather, and most probably plotting something over the top for maximum effect on Saturday – when the brash and impetuous President was supposedly arriving.

There was a chance they'd been scared off of Athol after abducting Kiri, yet odds seemed low in that regard. That would mean finding another safe place to hide out while simultaneously getting plans in order for their spectacle of upcoming violence. No, his gut told him as well, they had said they were going to "Asshole, Idaho," via Carolyn's message to Kiri, and then they showed up in the Athol tavern. It was most probable that they were currently holed up somewhere nearby – and he just had to find them.

So it was that in the early afternoon Chris parked the van on a dead end side road on the outskirts of town, after deciding to take an extensive walkabout through Athol. Donning a wide brimmed hiking hat so he was less recognizable, Chris slowly and purposefully stalked his way throughout the small town for hours.

It was probably around five-thirty when Tomas called him back. A half hour before that Chris had returned to the van feeling footsore and flustered regarding his search for Kiri. He had driven into the forest a few miles west of Athol and was having a beer from the cooler when Tomas rang.

"I'm sorry I couldn't get back to you any sooner," Tomas apologized. "It's been a very busy day."

"Just glad to hear your voice," responded Chris, "but I have some unfortunate news to tell you."

"If it's about Kiri, I'm terribly concerned as well," sympathized Tomas. "I was with Sapphire on and off throughout the day. She told me about it, but it wasn't possible to get back to you until now."

"It's okay; Kiri's strong," Chris stated, attempting to reassure Tomas and himself. "She can handle whatever comes along."

"Where are you staying?"

"In the van, in the forest," replied Chris. "Mostly out of sight. Tell me what happened today in Coeur d'Alene."

Briefly, Tomas spoke first of the march that began around mid-morning. After the thousands gathered in the city beach park on Lake Coeur d'Alene, the permitted route led east to normally busy 4th Street and then north for about a mile and a half. The throngs then turned left, headed to 3rd Street, and turned south to return to the park where they had started.

Explaining the walk in each direction would normally take around a half hour each way, Tomas said that because of the sheer number of marchers it took several hours to complete and reassemble the masses back in the park.

Further, he mentioned that it was all conducted under the watchful eyes of hundreds and hundreds of military and police in riot gear along the way. It was quite peaceful, Tomas noted, as were the hours of speeches in the park that followed the march.

"It seems like you're playing a bigger role than you expected," noted Chris.

"That's because of the reenactment video that was made about my abduction," Tomas remarked. "It became a big hit on the Internet and as a result thousands of commoners have joined us here in Idaho. We all had a very successful day, but I fear there's trouble to come."

"I know there's trouble to come," Chris shot back.

"What are you going to do about Kiri?"

"There's not a lot I can do at the moment," complained Chris. "Right now, I'm near a small town called Athol, which is north of Coeur d'Alene and north of Hayden. Athol is what Future Generations were calling 'Asshole, Idaho,' and Kiri figured it out. I'm supposed to wait at a place called the Good Times Tavern every evening in case she shows up – and that's how you can help me out if need be."

"Whatever you need, name it and I'm there," Tomas assured his friend.

"That's great," said Chris. "Listen, if anything happens to me, you need to be there for Kiri."

"Not a problem whatsoever," confirmed Tomas. "Just let me know and I'll be waiting for her. Is there anything else I can do?"

"Nothing now," Chris replied. "Thanks though, and I'll be in contact."

After hanging up with Tomas, Chris readied himself to spend the evening in the Good Times Tavern – waiting for Kiri, and hopefully Carolyn, to escape and show up.

CHAPTER THIRTY-FIVE

Matt Mason, from the renowned alternative energy think tank, was Thursday morning's last speaker before the day's marches through Coeur d'Alene. He was already well into his lively delivery when Sapphire MacKenzie attempted to tune back in.

She had of course been ecstatic when Mason accepted the invitation to attend the protests in northern Idaho, but at this point there was so much on her mind she barely heard snippets of what was sending the vast crowd into nearly delirious cheers.

"Only a free Cascadia," Mason was now telling the receptive masses, "can deter a world globalized and enslaved by the oligarchs from sleepwalking over the greatest cliff humanity has ever faced! Only a free Cascadia is poised to address the challenges of climate change, of species eradication, resource exhaustion, and the hypnosis of consumerism!

"And how will a free Cascadia become the impetus that pulls us all back from the brink?" Matt Mason continued, only to answer his own question. "A free Cascadia will turn corporations into cooperatives, a free Cascadia will turn its back on The Seven, on the bought-and-paid-for Congress and the bait-and-switch President, and make economic localization the solution to a global problem. And that is just the beginning! We are The Thin Green Line! And I say: Free Cascadia!"

As if exploding from a volcano, cheers erupted from the masses on Coeur d'Alene's beautiful waterfront park with Cascadia Doug flags pumping vigorously up and down.

From the stage and behind the podium where the speaker was delivering his booming proclamations, Sapphire gazed upon the sea of demonstrators occupying every square foot of grass available in the park and spilling over onto the waterfront walkways, as well as in boats on sparkling Lake Coeur d'Alene. And, for as far as Sapphire could see, Cascadia Doug flags filled the air.

She was well aware that live TV feeds were beaming their protests to satellites and around the planet, and again her mind drifted to what she must yet do to make Day Two of Four a success. In a matter of minutes, Sapphire and Tomas Hernandez would descend from the stage and prepare to symbolically lead together the Free Cascadia and Commons movements and everyone else through the designated route of Coeur d'Alene streets that would eventually lead them back to this park.

The stage had been erected on a mound at the north end of the park; to the south was the lake and to the west the lakefront luxury hotel and additional boat docks. To the east were the library and various public buildings, but it was by passing the stage – and going up 4th Street – was where the march would commence.

Normally, 3rd and 4th streets were the dedicated multiple-lane, one-way roads, and the two busiest routes servicing the entry and egress for downtown Coeur d'Alene. That was why many local residents and businesses had vigorously protested the route during the permitting process, fearing possible violence and property damage during the demonstrations. City leaders nevertheless approved the necessary permits and thankfully, thought Sapphire, only a boon in business had been a result, without any collateral violence. And hopefully it would remain that way on Day Two.

Matt Mason was ending on a triumphant note, telling all that a free Cascadia was well prepared to courageously tackle the oncoming shitstorm future years would bring and this set the crowds into a frenzy of elation.

Sapphire's Free Cascadia colleague, Polly Hawser from British Columbia, was scheduled next to pump up the crowds a little more for the march, remind them of the insistence upon non-violence, and of the sharing of food upon their return to the park – compliments of the local farmer's commons and food co-ops.

As Polly rose to take the podium, Sapphire smiled at Tomas Hernandez seated nearby, and both rose to depart the stage. Together they descended the rear stage stairs and walked to their predesignated stations on the 4th Street promenade, from which they would lead the march.

Once more, they were ready to conduct the tens of thousands through the streets of Coeur d'Alene and Sapphire prayed everything would be peaceful. Indeed, she thought, peace had to prevail today because it was very likely it wouldn't during the following two days when things were planned to be more confrontational. When the demonstrators and marchers moved up to Hayden and Hayden Lake to test Empire's defense perimeter about The Seven's compound the shit was very likely to hit the fan.

***

At a greasy spoon breakfast joint in Sandpoint, Timmy Maxwell and two of his buddies were drinking coffee and waiting for Garf Taylor to show.

His cohorts, Tom Wilcox and Buzz Razmussen, were two members of the triad Timmy had joined up with several weeks ago when they captured a cop that had followed them into an electrical substation –

442

and Timmy had later put a bullet into the back of his brain. The third member of the original triad, Kyle Anderson, had been left at the motel in Asshole to keep tabs on the women along with the other triad Taylor had put in charge of this mission.

Wilcox and Razmussen were grumbling about Garf being late, and what the day had in store for them. Razmussen's complaints centered around the possibility of another tedious day of training for their roles on Saturday, while Tom Wilcox stated with certainty they would only have to put up with Taylor for a short meeting this morning, as he would be spending the rest of today and all day Friday with the drone drivers near the airport.

Maxwell listened to their grousing without entering the conversation, mostly because he wasn't all there. He wasn't hung over from the previous evening's partying, as much as he was still intoxicated and musing about his sister's friend they'd taken into "protective custody." A nice piece of snatch she was, Timmy had to admit, if ever he'd seen one. The problem was that he had to work around his sister to get to her, but he'd have her friend if not tonight, tomorrow night for certain.

"So why did you let Kyle stay with the other triad to watch the women this morning?" Buzz asked again since Timmy had missed the question the first time around.

Maxwell's reply was surly. "Because I was afraid you'd be in the sack with Mindy or Hope again, and not paying attention to guarding the rest of them. Simple as that."

"Mindy or Hope? You gotta be fucking kidding me!" Razmussen fired back. "I'd take Lucy any night instead of those other two pigs, but she just wants to screw that tall guy Derrick of the other triad. So I'm kind of focusing on that friend of your sister that we 'sheltered' the other night. I'd go after your sister, but Tom here has got his eye on Carolyn; her friend, on the other hand, looks at me like she knows I got a big dick."

"You keep your paws off my sister's friend," warned Timmy. "She's not for you. And as far as Tom and Carolyn go, Tom has nothing but respect for my sister."

Buzz Razmussen laughed in his face. "You're just saying that because she's your sis. Wilcox is no different from you, me, or the rest of us when trying to score some ass."

Timmy Maxwell's notorious temper was beginning to surface, but was prematurely snuffed out when he spotted Garf Taylor. The leader of Future Generations was entering the restaurant with a smartly dressed, suburban looking fellow, with wavy hair and a pudgy face, and wearing brown loafers, slacks, and a preppy green golf shirt.

In total command as he approached, Garf and his guest comfortably took two of the open three chairs at the table. He then introduced his companion.

"This is Mister Delaney," Taylor told everyone, quite business-like. "He will take three of you through the outer security perimeter to his home, so you can be in position for the assault on the inner security ring at the compound early the following morning. Is that understood?"

Timmy, Tom, and Buzz nodded their heads but said nothing.

"Okay then," Garf continued, "to get through the outer perimeter checkpoints, you'll each need official passes and here they are."

From a manila envelope he'd brought along, Taylor spilled the contents on the table. Extracting particular I.D.'s from the pile, Garf handed Tom and Buzz their passes with phony names and pictures from the photos taken earlier in the week. To Timmy, however, Garf granted two passes, both with his picture and fake name upon them.

"As you can see," Garf spoke to Tom and Buzz, "Timmy has been given two passes. That can be easily explained." He turned to his suburban companion. "Mister Delaney, can you please show the others your pass."

"Certainly," he responded. From his wallet, Mister Delaney removed his pass and put it on the table before everyone.

"The passes are exactly the same," explained Taylor, "except below his name Mister Delaney has the word, 'Homeowner,' whereas the rest of you have printed instead, "Certified Visitor.' And below that, all passes have Mister Delaney's home address."

"All of them except for my second pass, which has a different address," Timmy Maxwell interrupted.

"Quite correct," Garf declared. "That is because you are going on the mission regardless, because you are leading. Mister Delaney's brother-in-law, Mister McGrath, will pick up three others of your task force fifteen minutes after Mister Delaney picks up the first three."

"That goes back to our prior discussions, doesn't it?" interjected Tom Wilcox.

"Indeed it does," replied Taylor. "As we spoke earlier, the task force is made up of two triads and one leader, that being Timmy Maxwell. The six members of the two triads will draw straws, so that one person – other than Timmy Maxwell – will remain at your base to protect Carolyn Maxwell, and so that Carolyn and whoever stays can insure your safe exit if you are lucky enough to make it back to the base without incident. Understood?"

While heads nodded about the table, Timmy was relieved Garf apparently didn't know anything about the other women at the Asshole Motel. Taylor replaced the passes of the others not currently in attendance back into the manila envelope. He then handed the manila envelope to Maxwell.

"So Timmy has two valid passes, each with a different address,"

Taylor continued. "From whichever triad the short straw is drawn, Timmy goes with them in that vehicle and to the respective house within the exterior security perimeter."

Interrupting himself, Garf Taylor examined his watch. "I have to depart very soon towards the airport to meet with the drone drivers for the rest of today and tomorrow, before the actual assault on Saturday during the President's speech. But before I go, let's review the basic plan once more, okay?"

Again, heads were nodding.

"Great, here we go," said Garf. "The first group of three will meet Mister Delaney at 11 PM in the parking lot of the supermarket at the corner of Highway 95 and Hayden Avenue. In the northeast corner of that lot, there is a container with stairs climbing up to its rear entry doors. Park somewhere close, and when you see Mister Delaney's brown Lincoln town car, meet up with him and get in. The same thing goes fifteen minutes later for the next three with Mister McGrath. He will be driving a black, Chevy Suburban.

"From there," Taylor continued, "get some rest at your drivers' respective houses, because as you well know, at 3:30 AM you are on your way. Both triads will meet up where we discussed close to the inner security perimeter, then in groups of two, you plant your remotely controlled, diversionary explosive packages at our prearranged points just outside the compound fencing itself. Plant your explosives and don't worry about them after that; one of the initial drones will have the controls to set them off before the remainder of the drone fleet arrive, and launch their missiles of death and destruction. Just plant your explosives and get the hell back to either Mister Delaney's or Mister McGrath's house.

"They will get you past the outer security perimeter by 7:30 AM," Garf went on, "under the pretext of having breakfast before things really get busy regarding the protests and demonstrations. Then, with all haste, get into your vehicles and return to your base. Collect Carolyn Maxwell and whoever was left with her — and get the hell out of the whole region as soon as possible."

Garf scrutinized Timmy, Tom, and Buzz. "Are you ready to take on this mission?"

"Damn straight we are!" Buzz shot back, falsely enthusiastic.

"Then I wish you the best of luck," Garfield Taylor replied quite seriously to all.

***

It was another night in Athol, Idaho, for Chris Soles, and another frustrating evening waiting for Kiri to show up at the Good Times Tavern.

He had passed the time tonight much as he had the previous evening, taking a seat at an open table early, facing the door, and scrutinizing all that entered. To be certain, Chris had met his share of characters, especially as the tavern grew crowded toward the dinner hour and seats at tables became scarcer.

Last night, a young couple in their early twenties, fresh from the day's marches and speeches down in Coeur d'Alene, had asked if they could share his table. They intended to have a quick meal, as they were on their way further north to Sandpoint for the evening. Glad to oblige, Chris introduced himself and they said they were Doug and Shelly.

After his table companions reviewed the limited menu items, they caught a passing waitress and ordered. While waiting for their meals to come, Doug launched himself into a review of the events in Coeur d'Alene, as they were still fresh in his mind.

By the time their food arrived, Shelly more or less took over the conversation from her boyfriend while he began tearing into a burger and she picked at a salad.

"We're totally behind the protest against The Seven and the corporate governance," she told Chris, "but what we mainly drove all the way here from northern California for was the parties."

"The parties?" mused Chris.

"You bet," Shelly beamed, while stabbing a tomato with her fork. "We knew the parties around this event would be great and if the wild one we attended last night on the Spokane River was any indication, we are in for some awesome times."

Doug took a breather from his burger momentarily to inform him they were headed to Sandpoint tonight for what was supposed to be another outrageous evening. He also invited Chris to accompany them if he so desired.

"Thanks, but no," Chris replied. "I'm waiting for a friend to show up, but I'm not sure when she'll arrive."

The young couple passed the remainder of their mealtime in small talk with Chris, and then departed toward party land after finishing and paying their bill.

For the rest of the evening, and always with an eye on the entry door, Chris mingled with several other patrons of the Good Times Tavern. Most notable was Athol resident Grant Gilbert, who wore a "Free Cascadia" ball cap, and worked for the local lumber milling operation a short distance away.

Chris met others yesterday as well, but in the end there was no Kiri to be seen.

And unfortunately, Thursday evening was beginning to hint at similar results as the hours wore on. It was beginning to get late when Grant Gilbert once more joined Chris at his table. He had his "Free Cascadia" ball cap on, and told Chris he was surprised to see him again in the Good Times Tavern.

"Oh, I'm just waiting for a friend," he explained, "and I don't know if or when she'll arrive."

Grant let it go at that, leaving Chris to his own business.

"How was it at the protests today?" inquired Chris.

"It was about like what I told you yesterday," Grant replied. "Everything was peaceful and respectful, with several astute speeches and good food. I'm almost glad I can't take off tomorrow though, because it might turn violent."

"Let's hope not," replied Chris. He was ready to say something else when suddenly a beeping from the phone in his pocket erupted.

Chris asked Grant to excuse him momentarily while he examined the phone. It was an alert from the app that told him when a certain handle or hashtag was used on select social media sites. Rapidly, he tapped the alert that instantly redirected him to the social media website. It was a post from Stone McClelland.

After Chris read what the ex-DEA agent had left for him, he looked about the tavern. The crowds were thinning because the hour was late. Once again, he judged Kiri wasn't going to make it.

Hastily, but politely, Chris bid Grant Gilbert farewell. As he made his way to the door, all he could think of was McClelland's message: *"Call me ASAP. Have info that may – or may not be – pivotal in the game of trust."*

***

"So, I just got a call back from the rep for Chris Soles, or Chris Soles, or whoever it is I'm talking to," McClelland stated as soon as his old friend picked up the phone.

"What did he say about what I passed on to you?" Bertie wanted to know.

"He was absolutely non-committal; he was playing dumb, or was just plain dumb," stated Stone. "Once again, he said he'd pass it along, so that was it."

"That was it?" Stanton gasped. "Does that mean we're still stuck in the same old waiting game?"

"No, that means it's time for us to get to work; there's too much action shaking out in Seattle according to what you told me and what I passed along. Everything should be happening here in Idaho," McClelland countered. "Bertie, you've got to fly to Spokane tonight; we have to lay a trap. The time has come; I need you."

Incredulous, Stanton fired back, "What are you fucking talking about? Why would I want to come to Spokane tonight?"

"You just gotta trust me: it's my intuition, my gut," Stone assured his old pal. "I think all this will draw Chris Soles out into the open. Things are happening in Seattle and I might need your help."

Bertie couldn't believe what he was hearing.

"Oh, man!" he asserted. "Do you know what that means? Well, I'll tell you. First, since I'm supposed to be in the office tomorrow, I'd have to clear the trip with my superiors. And that would likely mean coming up with some lie that would eventually find its way into my personnel file and possibly culminate in disciplinary action.

"Next, I might well miss the special Friday evening Vespers service at our church," Bertie warned warily, "and that might result in a very important personal relationship being compromised and my falling out of favor as a consequence. So I ask you, do you have anything better than instinct or gut feelings to go on?"

Stone McClelland grinned into the phone. "Just get your shiny black ass on a plane to Spokane tonight and I'll pick you up!"

"No doubt in your white luxury limo, eh?" Bertie laughed. "I'm on my way as soon as I hang up and make a plane reservation, old buddy. Just get a decent place for me to get a few hours of decent shut-eye before tomorrow's excitement. And make sure it's not as uppity as that hotel-on-the-lake joint you been hanging out in."

"Don't worry," McClelland chuckled. "There comes a time in everyone's life when it's apropos to downsize. I'll get a hotel room close to Spokane International with two queen beds as soon as I hang up."

"That works," Bertie assured him. "Just answer one question for me though."

"Okay."

"What made you think I'd agree to your 'gut' feelings anyway?"

"Maybe because of a – gut feeling?" offered Stone. "Call me back when you get your flight scheduled and I'll pick you up."

"Your gut feelings really suck," Stanton declared. "Do you know that? And what else do they portend?"

"Nothing but trouble, simple as that."

"Then, for sure, count me in," Bertie exclaimed jubilantly. "Mine say the same thing; it'll be just like the old days working together in the Southwest."

***

Even as Chris was readying to call Sapphire, she was already ringing him.

"I was just about to call you," he said, surprised.

"I had to call you first before anyone else," Sapphire nearly wailed into the phone, "because it's just terrible."

451

"What's terrible?"

"It's my parents," she blurted. "They've been in a horrible car accident on the Olympic Peninsula, but both are still alive – so far!"

"I'm so sorry," Chris expressed with sadness. "What happened?"

"All I know is that they were on the way back to Port Townsend and not far out of Port Angeles – where they were visiting old friends and hiking with them in Olympic National Park," she burst out somewhat hysterically, "when a driver going the opposite direction on Highway 101 crossed into their lane and it resulted in a head-on crash."

"Do you know how they're doing?"

Sapphire sighed heavily. "Only vaguely. I was told my mom is in better condition than my dad. They took her by ambulance to Olympic Medical Center in Port Angeles. But dad had to be airlifted by helicopter to Harborview Medical Center in Seattle where they have a Level 1 trauma center."

"So are you flying over to Seattle tonight?" asked Chris.

"At this point it's too late," Sapphire replied. "I've already checked and the last flight from Spokane to Seattle tonight is leaving before I could get to the airport. There's nothing I can really do there tonight anyway, so I booked an early flight for tomorrow morning. My car is in a parking lot near SeaTac, so I'll pick it up first thing and go to Harborview to check on my father."

"Is there anything I can do?" Chris inquired.

Without a second thought, Sapphire shot back, "Did you find Kiri yet?"

"No."

"I guess that's all you can do then: find Kiri," she replied.

"I'm real sorry to hear about your parents," consoled Chris. "Before you rang me though I was ready to call you, but the little I've got pales in comparison to what you're dealing with."

"Tell me anyway," Sapphire said warily.

"I just got off the phone a while ago with McClelland," he explained.

"What did he have to say?"

"Stone McClelland told me his sources said the dead letter phone number we gave him became very active this afternoon," remarked Chris. "It made nine calls out."

"Yeah, so?"

"Sapphire," Chris began emphatically, "the calls were all from the Seattle area and made to other phones in the greater Seattle area. Does that mean anything to you?"

A gasp was all Chris heard in response.

"Give me a minute to think," she requested.

Silence reigned for easily thirty to forty seconds. When Sapphire came back on the line, she asked Chris if he had something to write with.

"Sure, I've got pen and paper right here," he told her. "Go ahead."

Sapphire gave Chris her flight information for her morning flight to Seattle and he dutifully wrote it down.

"Okay, now that you've got that," she carried on, "when we get off the phone you need to book a flight on the same plane."

"What? Why?"

"Can't you see?" Sapphire countered. "He's going to kill them!"

"Who is killing whom?" Chris wanted to know in exasperation. "And whose dead letter phone number is that anyway?"

"It's Garf Taylor's number, of course," Sapphire stated, as if she'd already mentioned it. "And he's going to kill The Two to jumpstart the Revolution."

"That's insane," Chris snarled.

"That's revolutionary," Sapphire shot back. "It's perfectly in line with the way Garf thinks. The Two are the last bastion of hope for the people and Cascadia. Albeit of miniscule promise, if that last bastion of hope is gone the people will have no choice but to take to the streets. If The Two are gone, Garf likely foresees a general uprising because there's nothing else left that the people can do."

"But that's crazy," Chris protested, "totally wacko."

"When you're crazy, only crazy makes sense," countered Sapphire. "That's Garf's plan – and you've got to stop him because he's going to do it tomorrow night."

"How do you know that?"

"Same thing," she stated, "it's his style. He'll have a chaos of diversions going then."

"How so?"

"Look, everybody thinks Saturday is the big day in Idaho," she stressed herself to patiently explain. "That's perfect for Garf. He lets everybody believe it's all happening then, so he'll likely create a diversion Friday night in Idaho – which will merely be a diversion for the main thrust of his attack on The Two on Friday night in western Washington."

"Are you sure?" Chris asked dubiously.

"I tell you, Chris, I know him," Sapphire avowed with certainty. "He'll probably also have a whole series of diversions on the west side of the Cascades that will further distract from his real target – The Two. Trust me; that's how it'll all come down. You've got to stop him from his ultimate target on Friday night – killing The Two!"

Chris was flabbergasted. "So how do I do that?"

"You'll figure a way," she assured him. "Just make sure you're on that plane to Seattle tomorrow morning."

"What about Kiri?" he demanded to know.

"You said she's strong and I agree," Sapphire declared with confidence. "She'll survive. Just have Tomas wait for her at the tavern. He'll do that, won't he?"

"Of course he will," Chris avowed, "and gladly."

"Good," she affirmed, "because it's totally up to you to stop Garf Taylor and Future Generations!"

CHAPTER THIRTY-SIX

At the appointed hour early Friday morning, Theodore Dellenbach and his son met downstairs in the great room of the massive timber hewn mansion designated for their party on the compound. The help had laid out a full breakfast buffet for them all, even though the others wouldn't likely be down for some time.

"How was your flight, Father?" inquired Whitley. "Sorry the hour is early and that I didn't wait up for your arrival last evening."

The elder Dellenbach smiled broadly as he puffed on his first cigar of the day.

"The flights were quite commendable," he remarked, "both via our jet and on the military helicopter shuttle here. And the early hour? Oh, pshaw; don't you remember what I always taught you?"

Whitley chuckled. "Certainly I do:

Early to bed, early to rise,

Makes a man healthy, wealthy – and easy to despise."

Both father and son laughed at the recollection.

"That's my boy," lauded the old man. "And how was your dinner last evening with Justice Gassack and some of his closest friends on the Court?"

"It was everything I imagined it would be," Whitley declared with satisfaction. "The money expended on Sir Dudley joining the Court was a shrewd investment."

"Well, of course you realize," Theodore Dellenbach tossed in, "that he was a great friend of your Uncle Walter."

"Indeed, Father," concurred the younger man, "and that's how I met him as a novitiate at my uncle's side when Justice Gassack was the junior Senator from Idaho."

Altering the subject, the elder Dellenbach asked his son if he had scrutinized the agenda of events for the next few days here at the compound.

"Does everything meet your approval?"

"Things seem to be in quite the proper order," Whitley assured his father. "I know Mother will especially love the ballroom dancing scheduled for this evening after the dinner feast and speeches. It will be perfect."

"And as far as security goes for our friends?"

"Impeccable," the junior Dellenbach honestly declared. "The barbarians may well be at the gates rattling their tin cups, shouting sophomoric slogans, and shooting their cap guns into the air. But Mother and the others will never know as we dance the night away. And when our billionaire President that joined forces with us arrives tomorrow, and tells us how great we all are – it will be a weekend to treasure forever!"

"And revel in it we will!" the old man exclaimed triumphantly, his famous and fabulous hanging jowls quivering excitedly. "Things are as they have always been."

Conspiratorially, Theodore Dellenbach drew close to Whitley with a whisper.

"Come, Son," he spoke slyly, "before the others are awake, let's steal some sweets from the buffet line!"

"Indeed," the younger Dellenbach laughed, "to us the spoils!"

***

Tomas Hernandez awoke in the same spare bedroom of his commoner friend Wade Nash's house, as he had for the last several mornings. And as had been the case for several days, he was uncertain at first where he was.

Hernandez was groggy to be certain, though it wasn't from drink. The last few days had been inordinately busy with too much stimulus, creating a resultant surfeit that was necessary to work through the following mornings for a while.

The last thing he recalled the previous evening was speaking to Linda, and the kids, who were up past their bedtimes to speak with dad. The conversations had been joyous and laden with homesickness, but after his wife put the children to bed, Linda had called him back.

Tomas mostly remembered telling her about the marches so far, and how much he was worried about likely violence on Friday and Saturday. He didn't tell Linda, however, about the hombres that had been verbally and personally calling him out from the sidewalks during the marches. Nor did he reveal anything about the cars that had been following Wade and himself whenever they drove somewhere.

Thinking about the calls from home last evening led him to check his phone for messages. The indicator icon on the phone for voice mails told Tomas two messages were waiting that must have come in after he fell asleep.

The first one was from Sapphire and it was a shocker. She said her parents had been in a car accident and she was flying to Seattle in the morning. She also asked Tomas to coordinate with Polly Hawser in her absence, while hoping she might return Saturday for the climax of protests against The Seven.

Immediately, Tomas called Sapphire back but all he got was her voice mail. Somewhat at a loss for words, he expressed sincere condolences for her parents' accident, and wished them both a speedy recovery.

The next voice mail message was from Chris. It was curt and troubled, saying he had pressing business and he must depart to Seattle for it the morning. Almost plaintively, he seemed to plead that Tomas wait nightly for Kiri in the tavern, as he could not. He also mentioned a "friendly" in a Free Cascadia ball cap might be there.

Tomas shook his head and sighed. Whatever was drawing Chris to Seattle must be extremely important for him to ask Tomas to wait in his stead, especially considering how close Chris and Kiri were.

Without hesitation, Tomas sent Chris a text message saying he would be there for Kiri if by chance she showed up – and that he need not worry.

Tomas then pulled himself out of bed – preparing to face the day of demonstrations without Sapphire, but with the hombres shadowing him again, and with the real possibility of violence during the march – and a thousand other worries.

***

Because of construction delays just past Rathdrum on his route to Spokane International, Chris consequently arrived just as his plane was beginning the boarding process.

Hurriedly, he parked and scrambled to the terminal building. At a kiosk Chris printed up his boarding pass and made it through security with no questions about his phony Canadian passport supplied by the Elders in Victoria.

The airline ground crew was calling out the final rows for boarding as he slipped in line with the others at the end. Slowly the trail of passengers worked its way onto the plane. By the time Chris finally entered the cabin, he immediately spotted Sapphire sitting in the third row aisle seat on the starboard side of the jet. She had apparently been looking for his arrival; she smiled broadly when their eyes met.

As the line of passengers plodded forth and those before him haltingly disgorged their carry-on baggage into overhead bins and found their seats, Chris passed by Sapphire quite languidly as well. When he was finally standing beside her, Sapphire reached up to clasp his forearm and he hers. Again, they smiled pleasantly at one another until it was time for Chris to move on as the ribbon of passengers found their seats.

One of the last to be seated, Chris took his assigned spot in number 25D, an aisle seat on the same side as Sapphire, but twenty-two rows behind her.

All seemed quite normal and unremarkable as the crew prepared those aboard for the flight, even if both Sapphire and Chris paid no mind to the black man sitting in seat 1C, the aisle seat on the port side of the craft in the first row. And certainly, neither Chris nor Sapphire could have known about the big man posing as a pilot in proper uniform back aft in the flight attendants' station, that had observed all arrivals through a peephole in one of the doors.

For the most part, the one-hour flight from Spokane to Seattle was uneventful. That is, it was uneventful until the announcement came onto the plane's public address system that the jet was on final approach, passengers must return to their seats, tray tables had to be locked away, and seats returned to their upright position.

As all aboard secured themselves for landing, and flight attendants made their last trash collection of the flight while simultaneously checking for fastened seat belts, the big man posing in pilot's uniform left the flight attendants' station and marched the few rows forward to seat 25D.

When the man dressed as a pilot towered above him, Chris did a double take. He was stunned. The face shouldn't have been in this situation and those clothes.

"Don't say anything," warned Stone McClelland. He handed Chris a small notebook that was bound. "This is the dossier I promised you. Skim it quickly and then give it to your girlfriend in 3D."

"Girlfriend?" Chris queried evasively.

"Don't fuck with me," McClelland snarled in a low voice. "You likely won't see her the rest of the day, and you haven't much time on this flight. Tell her to look specifically at the bios on pages 18, 19, and 20."

With that, the ex-DEA agent in pilot's uniform turned and walked briskly toward the cockpit. Chris watched him depart, then saw McClelland knock on the cockpit door. A few seconds later he was admitted and the door closed behind him.

Without delay, Chris opened the booklet. The first page had an official FBI seal and was marked classified. Briskly, he turned to the pages McClelland had spoke of. The content of these two and a half pages had to do with members of the Dellenbach family who would be in attendance at the meeting of The Seven.

It all meant honestly nothing to Chris, so he unbuckled his seatbelt and scurried up the now empty main aisle of the cabin to seat 3D. He barely had time to place the booklet in Sapphire's hand – and tell her that Stone McClelland had suggested she read pages 18-20 – before an aging flight attendant was fast upon him and administering a scolding for leaving his seat. Chris was unceremoniously herded back to his place twenty-two rows aft.

In the meantime, Stone McClelland was staring through the peephole in the cockpit door until it was time to take his jump seat. He had observed Soles delivering the dossier pertaining to all those invited to attend the meeting of The Seven, and now it finally got to where he always wanted it to go.

Ever since the day he had seen Sapphire MacKenzie in the downtown Seattle hotel lobby, and then met later with Whitley Dellenbach, the delivery system had been the problem. And now MacKenzie was presumably scrutinizing the suggested pages. Was the dossier booklet an adequate catalyst to promote a reaction? Stone McClelland could only watch and wait.

At the same time, Sapphire had already flipped through the pages with the photos and biographic sketches of the elder Dellenbach Brothers and their wives, when she came upon a picture and bio of Whitley Dellenbach – who had told her he would not be attending the gathering. It pissed her off, but the photo and bio below Whitley made her livid.

It was a picture of a beautiful woman named Darlene (Smythren) Dellenbach, who was said to be the wife of Whitley Dellenbach. The bio mentioned the Dellenbach family's penchant for privacy regarding family members down the generational line, yet it had been doubled down upon in the case of Darlene Smythren, the former budding professional tennis star who still competed in celebrity pro-am competitions under her maiden name.

The dossier further stated that Darlene (Smythren) Dellenbach would be departing the gathering of The Seven early Saturday morning as she was scheduled to participate in a tennis competition over the weekend in Southern California.

After Sapphire slammed the booklet closed, both fists began to clench. How could Whitey do this to her? There was no way she could begin to gauge the depths of his treachery and betrayal. So he had a sick and dying wife? Not quite, it seemed.

A red sheet of bitter anger swept over Sapphire. Even though the plane's nose was decidedly down and the tail was up, she was unaware as she released her seatbelt and stormed back toward the rear of the cabin to find Chris.

When she discovered him in his aisle seat, Sapphire emphatically heaved the classified dossier at him.

"What the hell did you give me this for?" she yelled in outrage. "I didn't need that!"

"It was Stone McClelland," Chris tried to feebly explain.

By then, two flight attendants had arrived from the rear and were sternly forcing Sapphire to her seat. To the utter surprise of nearby passengers, she began vocally calling Chris out in a blind rage.

"I'll tell you what," she shouted as she was urged away," I never want to see you again! Don't call me, don't stop by, and forget that you were ever a part of my life! And I can't believe you had the gall to do this on the day I have to see my parents in the hospital after a tragic car accident!"

The two flight attendants had Sapphire back in her seat shortly before the jet touched down for landing. They themselves had scurried to the closest open seats on the not completely full flight and rapidly strapped into seatbelts.

Landing and taxiing to the terminal was without further incident. Chris worried that Sapphire might face legal issues regarding interference with a flight crew, and hoped that wouldn't come to pass. He had no idea what in the dossier had set her off like that, yet felt bad that she was so upset.

The passengers in any proximity to Chris treated him like a leper by giving him plenty of room as they slowly off-loaded the jet. He could feel many pairs of eyeballs picking him over as they made their way forward, but was too worried about what was going on with Sapphire to care.

Sapphire was long gone when Chris was finally ready to turn out of the main aisle and up the jet way to the terminal. For some reason though, a black man with salt and pepper hair still sat in the first row in seat 1C. As Chris turned to the jet way, the black man stood up behind him, facing the rest of the oncoming passengers. He flashed a badge and asked everyone to please wait.

Thinking this was curious indeed, microseconds later a massive force in the form of Stone McClelland exploded from the jet way, slamming Chris into the rest room on the starboard side of the plane. McClelland smothered him into the fuselage interior wall above the toilet, even as Bertie Stanton followed them both in and locked the lavatory door behind him.

"We've got you now, Chris Cadia!" Stanton exulted jubilantly. "And we're going to lock you away, until the death penalty is fulfilled."

"Help me turn him around so we can zip tie his hands," Stone snapped at Bertie.

"Before we do, let me take a quick photo."

Bertie already had his phone out. He took several shots of Chris's face, then immediately forwarded them - with "Chris Soles" appended – to his FBI office here in Seattle.

"Now," Stanton took pleasure in announcing again, "we're going to lock you away forever!"

***

Both Kiri and Carolyn were fully awake at this point, but lost in their own thoughts and saying nothing at all.

Sharing the king size bed again in the third story motel room, they were fully clothed. After being locked in for the night following a major donnybrook in one of the rooms below, they wordlessly knew the clothing they wore was their last defense against nighttime intruders – just in case – besides kicking, scratching, and fighting back for their lives.

Eventually, it was Kiri who spoke first.

"We're getting out of here today," she said.

"How?" Carolyn wondered.

"One way or another."

"Well, we can't hardly walk out the front door since they turned the deadbolt around and locked us in here for as long as they choose," Carolyn objected. "And with plywood nailed over the windows from the inside, we're prisoners at their mercy."

"One way or another, we're getting out of here today," Kiri stated with resolve. "My friends are out there waiting, and they'd be here now if they knew where we were."

"We've got no hope left." Carolyn's voice was filled with dejection and desperation. "I believe Garf Taylor has purposely doomed us all. My brother Timmy's friends and those other goons certainly aren't of the suicide mindset that Garf expects of his minions. Something tells me he assigned all those guys here as a sacrifice to serve some bigger scheme he's concocted."

Kiri sighed in agreement. "Yeah, your brother and the others here would rather party than blow things up or kill people. And I think, even if they don't admit it to themselves, it's why they don't give a fuck about anything at this point – especially us."

"What do you mean?"

"As far as your brother and the others go, I think they're sucked into a last ditch, gloom mentality thing," Kiri explained. "They sense whatever mission they're assigned to carry out late tonight and early Saturday morning could be their end. So they're going to have us before they go down – and have us tonight."

"Shit," Carolyn exclaimed, "it's only because Buzz Razmussen and my brother got in a knock-down, drag-out fight over you that we didn't get raped by somebody last night."

"Yeah, we got lucky – last night," Kiri concurred. "But I fear much worse tonight, especially if they start drinking early again this afternoon."

"So what are we going to do?" Carolyn replied fearfully.

"We're getting out of here today," Kiri declared with resolve.

"How?"

"I don't know," Kiri dithered. "Maybe jump out of the window in the bathroom. They didn't nail plywood over that."

Carolyn was dubious. "That's a pretty small opening. Can we even fit through it?"

"We're getting out of here one way or another," Kiri assured her friend. "Even if it's through the bathroom window."

"And then what?" Carolyn objected. "We fall three stories to the concrete patio below which adjoins the room where that Derrick guy and his girlfriend are always going at it?"

"Listen, Carolyn," Kiri stated almost harshly, "we're getting out of here one way or another – before we get raped, and likely killed along with the rest of them!"

***

With the threats of being locked away forever from McClelland's black friend ringing in his ears, Chris shifted his focus to the ex-DEA agent that had once released him and who had just shed the pilot uniform jacket.

"Is this how the game of trust is now being played?" he demanded pointedly.

"It depends on what you have to offer," the big man fired back.

To Stone McClelland's mild surprise, both Bertie and Chris Soles seemingly accepted his reply.

"Let's get him out of here," Stanton interjected. "We've got TSA waiting in the terminal."

Immediately thereafter, with McClelland and the FBI agent each iron-gripping his biceps, Chris was manhandled up the jet way. Flanked by six well-armed TSA security men, they broke onto the concourse leaving passengers gawking in their wake. Chris was hustled into a small interrogation room behind a TSA station and firmly slammed into a seat at a table with his hands still zip tied behind him.

Without delay or mincing words, Bertie Stanton demanded to know where Chris and his terrorist comrades of Future Generations intended to launch their attacks.

Soles purposely looked at Stone McClelland when he spoke. "I am here to thwart the attacks, not at all join in them."

"So where's it all going down?" Stanton shot back, ignoring the substance of the reply.

Chris calmly transferred his gaze from McClelland to his pugnacious black friend.

"Well, I reckon it could be just about anywhere," he remarked rather snidely. "For starters, the target might be the massive oil storage tanks on the Columbia River north of Clatskanie, Oregon, in order to halt the transshipment of oil to ship. Or maybe the focus might be out at the series of new terminals at Grays Harbor, with the well-documented reports of poor security. Then again, the massive fossil fuel export terminal at Cherry Point north of Bellingham will always be a tempting target. And that's just a start. I can guarantee you there's plenty of inadequately protected objectives when everybody is looking the other way toward Idaho."

"Look, asshole," Stanton snarled, deciding to play hardball, "we can just take you in and get everything we need out of you."

"Probably so," Chris agreed, "but most likely not in time. Especially so, since it's all going down tonight."

At once, Stanton turned himself away from the prisoner to confer in low tones with McClelland. While they spoke, Chris mentally mused on the actual target's whereabouts he had researched on the Internet after concluding his conversation with Sapphire last night.

Though virtually no one cared, it was easy enough to pinpoint the specific location since all eyes were instead on The Seven and their gathering in northern Idaho. All he needed to know had been readily online, but now this detention by McClelland and his partner complicated how he would get there to thwart the assault. ...Or maybe it didn't.

Turning back to Chris after their conversation, McClelland again allowed his partner to take the lead.

"You know, pal, if you really wanted to stop this attack that you say is coming," Stanton bargained, "all you have to do is tell us where it is and we could have a small army there waiting."

Chris shook his head. "That's precisely what you cannot do. They'd sniff it out from miles away and your best opportunity will be gone forever. In fact, there's only one way it'll work."

"And that is?"

"You take me with you."

"Why in the fuck would we need you?" Bertie grumbled.

"You have no other source," Chris simply replied.

"And since I'm your only resource," Chris continued to inform them, "I'll dictate the terms of my assistance." He looked directly at Stone McClelland. "It's merely a continuation of the game of trust."

Stanton and McClelland contemplated one another knowing, whether they liked it or not, they were hogtied.

"But there's one more stipulation if we're to play this game of trust," Chris added. "You both may keep your guns, but I confiscate your phones and discard them on the way out of here."

Stanton's reply was instantaneous. "Not a fucking chance in hell, partner. We'd be walking into a trap with no back-up."

Chris directed his focus back on McClelland. "You better help your friend get the gist of what's happening here. Either we play the game of trust, or we don't play at all. And if we don't play at all, Future Generations wins by default."

Stanton and McClelland exchanged glances, then both returned their gaze back on Chris. From his pocket, Stone extracted his phone and placed it on the table in front of Chris.

Turning to his partner, McClelland said, "Give him your phone, Bertie."

"Are you out of your goddam mind?" the FBI agent raged. "It's a trap."

"Listen, we both still have our guns," Stone stated patiently. "If it's a trap, you shoot him first and I'll make sure he's dead. Give him your phone, Bertie; it's the best choice we have."

Very reluctantly, Stanton was shaking his head as he passed Chris his phone.

"Now, if you'll cut my hands free," Chris said cheerily, "we'll get going."

"Where to?" McClelland wanted to know.

"It doesn't go down until tonight," he reminded them, "so what do you say if we spend the afternoon fishing?"

Turning on his partner, Bertie Stanton exploded. "You gotta be fuckin kidding me, McClelland! You still want to let this guy lead us into a trap with the rest of his terrorists?"

Stone sighed and weighed his friend's words.

"This is the best option we got, Bertie." McClelland looked at his friend, and then at Chris, shaking his head.

"Let's go fishing," was all he could muster.

CHAPTER THIRTY-SEVEN

The wisecracking dockhands in Poulsbo that rented them their inflatable boat told Bertie Stanton that Puget Sound was fished out, and he likely wouldn't catch a thing. Fortunately for Chris, Bertie took their comments as a personal affront.

After all, throughout his youth Stanton had fished the Sound and still fancied himself quite the angler. And after he powered the rental boat toward the waters off the northwest shores of Bainbridge Island at Chris's request, McClelland's partner found himself quite content to be absorbed in his various attempts at trolling or jigging as the afternoon hours slid by.

The fishing fortunately subdued Stanton's growing ire regarding Chris's many requests – the FBI agent called them "demands" – that he had made since they departed the interrogation room at the airport. First was the clean rental car that wouldn't have hidden phones or guns that one of their personal vehicles might. Chris requested his captors to acquire the same and McClelland paid for it, then there was the rental boat in Poulsbo that Stanton had to put on his personal credit card, as well as the fishing gear and bait, extra clothing, and food, water, and sodas. Stanton had also been especially upset when Chris stipulated that he be allowed to keep his own phone – the singular phone between the three of them – only to make a show of throwing it overboard on the ferry from Seattle to Bainbridge Island.

Stanton's fuse had been growing shorter by the minute until the monofilament hit the water; thereafter he was mentally transported into a far better realm for a time. Stone McClelland, on the other hand, felt himself as uncomfortable as Chris Soles looked. Both of them said little, but kept their eyes on each other as they alternately drifted and motored up and down the Bainbridge Island shore.

Soles had yet to reveal Future Generations nighttime target, yet McClelland took note of Chris's avid interest in a pier that jutted out from shore whenever they passed it by. The tide had been going out through the afternoon and at this point there was less and less water below the pier every time Chris scrutinized it.

About a hundred yards north of the pier looked to be a beach park where the public could secure access to the water. A couple of families with kids had been there earlier, but at last pass the beach access park was deserted.

Most of this Stanton didn't pay much attention to, for his focus was seemingly upon his fishing. He was successful too, bringing to the surface several small shark fish that he immediately threw back, as well two undersized salmon that he returned to the Sound as well. While jigging, he also caught a spiny fish with big eyes that McClelland declared was "the ugliest fish on the planet." Bertie thought it was some kind of cod. He was also very cautious regarding the creature's spines as he removed the hook and returned the animal to the water.

At this point in the early evening, however, with the sun going down and setting as the air turned decidedly cooler, Bertie Stanton's pole and line were out of the water as his thoughts returned to their prisoner that held them hostage.

Tearing into one of the submarine sandwiches that were to serve as dinner, Bertie couldn't take it much longer. In measured and snarling tones, he threatened Chris Soles. He promised in no uncertain terms to pitch Chris overboard – and soon – if he didn't reveal what was going down regarding his terrorist comrades.

Heading in a northerly direction and at the wheel, Chris requested, "Give me about five minutes."

"What are you talking about?" barked Stanton.

"It's up there," Chris explained, "about five minutes away."

Stone McClelland gazed through the dimming light toward the pier Chris had studiously considered each time they passed off shore. He could tell low tide was either fully upon them or just passed as the fifteen to twenty foot barnacle encrusted support posts at the end of the pier were now almost totally out of the water.

Soles pointed to the pier. "That's where we're going."

"And why the fuck are we going there?" the FBI agent demanded to know.

"That's where the attack will be," Chris remarked factually.

"Attack on whom?" Stanton shot back.

"On The Two."

"On The Two? You mean like The Seven?" Bertie queried incredulously. "Who cares about The Two? They're irrelevant."

"Unless you believe that by killing them," Chris countered, "the last psychological hope for the masses is eliminated, and the only option remaining for the people is a general uprising in the streets."

"That's insane," Stanton muttered.

"Not just insane," Soles agreed, "but as someone once told me, it's revolutionary."

"So," Stone McClelland interjected, "what do you propose to do?"

"The estate, of which that pier up there is part of, is where The Two elderly female Supreme Court justices are cloistered away this weekend with their husbands and probably others. It's been in the family of Justice Sislak's husband for decades. They are certain to have some kind of security personnel around them, so we'll just be extras to deter and/or capture the leaders of those from Future Generations that attack the estate this evening."

"That's your plan?" Stanton bullied back, in disbelief.

"Pretty much," admitted Chris.

"Is there anything else?" McClelland prodded.

Chris nodded in the growing darkness. "A little ways up from the pier is one of Bainbridge Island's road-end beach access parks. I say we tie the boat up there, then climb the steps in order to sneak across the neighboring property to that of The Two, and then wait for the leaders of Future Generations to show up."

"And if they don't show?" Stanton asked skeptically.

"I guess you can take me in," Chris replied, shrugging his shoulders.

"We should have done that in the beginning," grumbled Stanton. He then asked, "What do you think, McClelland?"

Stone took his turn at shrugging shoulders. "At this point, what have we got to lose? Besides, I'm ready to get out of this boat and take a piss."

With great doubt, the FBI agent said, "Okay, we'll go along with it. But remember one thing, Chris Cadia."

"Sure. What?"

"No matter what happens up there," Stanton began, "if you betray us even the slightest amount to your terrorist friends, I promise I'll have a bullet saved especially for you."

***

Hustling in through the door of the Good Times Tavern, Wade Nash noted, "They're still behind us."

"And probably coming in here as well," remarked Tomas Hernandez. "How many you think?"

"It's getting dark so I can't be certain," Nash replied. "But I'm pretty sure there were four carloads; maybe ten or twelve guys."

"Hmm," murmured Tomas, "it might be a rough evening of waiting around here tonight."

"So did you say we were supposed to meet someone here tonight?" asked Wade.

"Maybe," said Hernandez. "I was told a guy wearing a 'Free Cascadia' ball cap was friendly."

Wade Nash was already smiling at a fellow engaged in conversation sitting not far from the pool table. He wore a Free Cascadia ball cap and was oblivious to their arrival.

"You mean like that guy over there?" Wade asked Tomas, pointing.

"I guess so," Tomas mustered.

Without hesitation, Nash marched over to fellow in the ball cap and demanded, "What are you doing in this bar?"

Stunned equally by surprise and excitement, Grant Gilbert leaped to his feet as the two engaged in a vigorous bear hug.

"I haven't seen you in so long," Wade exclaimed.

"How the hell you been doing?" Grant shot back.

When Hernandez joined the two apparently old friends, Nash introduced Gilbert.

"We go back a long ways," Wade explained.

"Yeah," Grant joined in, "we were in grade school together and then all the way through high school in Coeur d'Alene."

Grant asked Wade and Tomas to join him at his table.

"It's good that you could run into each other again," Tomas congratulated them as he sat down. Abruptly, however, he changed the subject; Tomas wanted to know if Gilbert was the same person that had spoken with his friend the last couple nights.

"You mean that guy that was waiting for a gal to show up?" wondered Gilbert.

"Yeah," Tomas acknowledged. "She's a friend of mine too and we're waiting to see if she makes it here tonight."

"But unfortunately," Wade Nash interjected, "we're being trailed by some scavenger feeder sharks." He nodded toward the tavern's entry door. "I count nine of them so far."

Grant and Tomas glanced warily at the thugs.

"Don't worry," Gilbert assured them. "I know the bartender and he can have the cops here in minutes if there's trouble."

Tomas shook his head. "We'd like to avoid involving the authorities at all costs – especially if the lady we're waiting for shows up with her friend."

Both Nash and Gilbert found Hernandez's statement peculiar.

Shifting the focus, Grant Gilbert mentioned, "I couldn't get off work today to attend the protests, but was it as bad as the news I heard this afternoon?"

"Probably," Wade replied, while Tomas kept a wary eye on the hombres that had meandered over to the bar. He then went on to explain how the thousands had marched east up Hayden Avenue to the outer security perimeter only to be ultimately repulsed by force.

"It began with hecklers and instigators throwing rocks and bottles at the military and police riot squads," recounted Wade. "Then nightsticks came out and eventually the tear gas. Tomas and Polly from the Free Cascadia movement did all they could to pull their people back, but there were still a lot of arrests. And tomorrow with the arrival of the President it will likely be much worse."

"That sucks," was all Gilbert could say for a moment. He then stood and announced he was going to the bar to buy his friends a beer.

Entirely forgetting the thugs that had followed Hernandez and Nash into the tavern, Grant Gilbert waded into the crowd surrounding the bar. At the same time, five of the hombres sauntered away from the mob barking orders at the bartender and approached the table where Tomas and Wade were sitting.

Surrounding them, the hombres said nothing at first in a show of bullying intimidation. But Hernandez would have none of it.

"What do you dickwads want?" he demanded.

For a moment, none of them replied. Then the apparent leader spoke.

"You commoners shouldn't start thinking you're too safe in here," he snarled. "Because if you don't go outside after you finish whatever drinks your friend at the bar is ordering, we'll take you down in here."

"Get lost," Hernandez fired back defiantly.

The hombres towered above them for a few more long seconds, then slowly dispersed back toward the bar as Grant was returning with three bottles of beer.

Sitting down and passing the others their bottles, Gilbert remarked, "Those are some nice friends you let tag along."

"What happened to you?" asked Wade.

"A couple of them up there warned me that I should move along," he said, "if I didn't want the trouble you were going to get. Rather sinister they are, I must admit."

"They told us we have one beer's time," Wade tossed in.

"What do you intend to do after that?" Grant wanted to know.

"I'm going to wait right here to see if our friends show up," Tomas declared. "It's that simple."

***

Once on the property of refuge for The Two, McClelland and Stanton quickly agreed on their station of ambush and defense.

Crouching behind two massive driftwood logs that must have been wrangled from the Sound at high tide, they positioned Chris between them for safekeeping. The logs were arranged at right angles to each other with seats carved and rounded in them for a bit more comfort to enjoy the fire pit behind. Being at the Puget Sound end of the property, Bertie and Stone would be assured of observing any intruders that might storm the grounds from the waterside.

This was doubly true, for bright spotlights from atop the residence fully illuminated the spacious backyard. They could clearly see the lit swimming pool perhaps forty yards away from them, and a solid brick structure closer to the main house that was likely used for barbecuing and smoking of meats and fish. A semi-meandering walkway of pavers led from pier to house.

For some time, the three of them hid silently behind their defenses. Occasionally Stanton or McClelland would peer over the rounded out seats in the log, but all was still and quiet otherwise. Chris began wondering if the focus of Garf Taylor and Future Generation's attack had been an erroneous assumption on Sapphire's part.

Before twenty minutes had passed since they'd taken up their hiding place, they began to hear multiple explosions far away – likely in Seattle – and they went on for an extended time. As if in answer to the distant noise, two or three bombs suddenly exploded much closer to them. Chris guessed those explosions were perhaps in the town of Winslow, maybe close to where the ferry came into Bainbridge Island from Seattle.

And suddenly, several detonations erupted from the front of the house that was the refuge for The Two. Immediately following those blasts, multiple gunshots rang out to signify a battle had ensued from the front.

Then, from the direction of the pier, came the sound of running feet. Coming into view and running past them was a triad of heavily armed attackers. With an easy angle and short distance, Bertie Stanton lifted his gun to take them down – when Chris Soles suddenly put his hand on Stanton's forearm lowering the gun.

Urging him to stop, Chris said, "That's not who we're waiting for."

In a rage that he'd missed his opportunity, Bertie backhanded Chris in the chops, sending him to the ground next to the fire pit.

"You do that again," Stanton snarled in warning, "and you're dead."

Stone McClelland kept an eye on the interaction of his companions, but he also followed the approach of the terrorists as they dashed up the paver walkway to the residence. And even though the battle in front of the house was still pitched, someone was watching the back and shots began ringing out from inside as the attackers advanced on the rear of the residence.

McClelland observed one of the assailants dive into bushes across from the entry while the other two took temporary sanctuary behind the brick barbeque. Then, after what appeared to be a quick conversation, one of the raiders using the barbeque as a shield dodged around its side and out of sight.

It was then Bertie Stanton drew a bead on the only attacker he could see. Rising above the driftwood log to get a clean shot, Stanton fired and the terrorist by the brick barbeque structure fell in a heap.

Only a second after the attacker dropped, however, shots from an automatic weapon in the bushes by the house took Bertie down. Falling backwards atop Chris Soles, he then rolled into the fire pit.

A hail of gunfire from the house was aimed into the bushes without any shots being returned. All became silent and no movement whatsoever transpired for several minutes.

Stone checked on Bertie to discover his old friend fading fast. He had taken two bullets to the head and likely more to the chest. Unfortunately, McClelland didn't have time to dwell on his buddy because suddenly the lights were going out.

In rapid succession, three of the four massive spotlights on the roof were shot out – apparently by the attacker that slipped around the other side of the brick barbeque. A salvo from inside was launched in the direction of something McClelland couldn't see behind the barbeque; consequently, it appeared the remaining light had been salvaged.

Immediately thereafter, the terrorist reappeared back behind the brick structure and Stone readied to take a shot. He didn't get a chance as the madman unhesitatingly rushed the residence on the path of pavers. Gunshots were fired from the house but it didn't seem to matter, for when he was close enough to the deck and doors at the back, the attacker detonated the suicide jacket he wore.

A tremendous explosion of glass and building materials was lifted upward and outward; it rained down upon the grounds all the way out to the swimming pool.

Then all was silent once again. Even the gunfire in front of the house had ceased.

Alarmingly, in the stillness McClelland and Soles could now hear the padding of more feet coming from the pier. It was counterintuitive that again people could come from the pier, thought Chris, when it was low tide and the boat landing stuck out of the water high and dry.

McClelland wasted no time on such considerations though; he was prepared to take out whoever was coming at them without a second thought.

***

Dusk was imminent as the door slammed behind them and the deadbolt was driven home.

Once locked inside, Carolyn gasped at Kiri.

"I can't believe you said that to my brother!"

"What else could I do?" she fired back. "He was already putting his hands down my pants and his friend Tom was all over your boobs!"

"But you just encouraged them!" Carolyn nearly shrieked in protest.

Kiri begged to differ. "I bought us time."

"And what's that good for?" Carolyn demanded to know. "Just to shave our pussies like you offered so they could lick us and we'd all 'share a most memorable night?'"

"I had to do – I had to say something," Kiri snapped back. "I bought us a little time and we're getting out of here."

"So how do you propose to do that?"

"The only way possible," stated Kiri. "We're going through the bathroom window. It's the way out; it's the only window they didn't plywood over."

Carolyn marched over to the motel unit's bathroom and fully opened the door.

Quite dubiously, she objected, "I'll never get my big butt through that. Your skinny ass might make it through – but then what? We drop three stories to the concrete deck below? I don't suppose the motel supplied any rope to climb down."

"No, we don't have any rope," Kiri acknowledged as patiently as possible. "But the bed has sheets and a blanket, so we're going to knot them all together and climb down out of the window."

"It'll never work," balked Carolyn. "There are not enough sheets to get us all the way down."

"Dammit, Carolyn," Kiri countered angrily, "we're getting out of here and we're not getting raped. Now, help me get these sheets off the bed so we can get going."

The growing rage in Kiri's voice prodded Carolyn to action. She aided Kiri in removing sheets and blanket from the bed, and then assisted in tying them all together. They then tested each knot by forcefully pulling from opposite ends.

The knots held, but Kiri worried that perhaps Carolyn was correct in presuming the joined sheets and blanket were not nearly long enough to reach the ground. The problem was compounded by the fact they somehow needed to anchor their escape linens before shimmying down.

Kiri eliminated that issue by sliding one end of their sheet/rope between the bathroom's door and its jamb and tying an anchoring knot on the other side. She tested it by tugging upon sheets once more and was convinced that the hinges for the door were secure. The only drawback was the distance to the ground would be further increased because of the need for the anchor knot to connect in the doorjamb.

But that couldn't be helped, Kiri thought to herself. She was ready to toss their escape sheet/blanket rope out the bathroom window when sustained pounding began on the motel unit's entry door.

"You ready in there?" hollered out a clearly intoxicated male voice.

Carolyn glanced at Kiri wide-eyed with fear. Kiri shook her head and sauntered toward the entry door.

"We need a few more minutes," she begged through the door. "I'm done, but Carolyn is still shaving in the bathroom."

"Well, hurry up," the drunken sot slurred. "Timmy wants to get it on so we can leave for the mission on time. If you're not ready when I come back, I'm taking you down as you are."

"I'll tell her to hurry," Kiri responded.

As whoever it was departed, Kiri bolted back to the bathroom, slid the window fully open, and cast their sheet rope out the small window. Sticking her head out the window, she observed that it terminated after only a story and a half. They'd have to drop from there to the concrete deck below.

Without hesitating, Kiri darted out of the bathroom and returned with the chair that had been at the small desk in the main room. She started to step up on it, then glanced at the window while having second thoughts. They were going to need all the space available to squeeze out the opening, so she lifted the sliding portion of the window out of the frame and set it down by the bathtub.

Kiri climbed atop the chair below the window and turned to Carolyn.

"Listen, Carolyn," Kiri demanded, putting it all on the line, "the sheets don't reach all the way to the ground. You've got to go as far as you can, then drop the rest of the way."

"I don't know if I can do that," Carolyn replied dubiously.

"It's either that," Kiri warned, "or you stay here, get raped, and possibly killed when Empire catches up with Future Generations. Now, watch what I do and follow me down."

On top of the chair facing the window, Kiri first positioned one leg out the window and then the other. Moving fully forward as far as possible, she turned onto her stomach while securely gripping the sheets she'd been sitting upon. Wrapping her legs tightly around the sheet/blanket rope, Kiri little by little lowered herself down toward the second floor.

The bathroom below them had the light on, but as Kiri passed by she looked in to see that, fortunately, it was empty. When her legs and feet ran out of any blanket or sheet to clasp, using only her arms she cautiously lowered herself as far as possible. Dangling in the dark, Kiri could nonetheless see that the distance from her feet to the concrete deck was only about a story, not a story and a half.

Small consolation, she thought, as she let herself go.

The concrete deck came up quickly. Kiri landed on her feet only to fall on her butt, which proved to be a sufficiently good cushion.

Carolyn had been watching everything from above and suddenly she was certain she wasn't going to be left behind. Hurriedly yet very guardedly, she mimicked Kiri's descent almost exactly. The only variation was that Carolyn tweaked her ankle upon landing.

"Are you okay to run?" Kiri whispered.

"I'll make it wherever I got to go."

"Okay, my friends should be waiting; let's get moving."

In the small town of Athol many of the yards were unfenced. This was the case near the motel so Kiri figured they would likely be able to avoid most of the main road to the Good Times Tavern – especially if Timmy and his friends came after them.

They had only started into one overgrown backyard of a darkened house nearby, when suddenly two soldiers with rifles and night vision goggles popped up off the ground before them.

With both rifles trained on the women, one soldier asked, "Just where do you think you're going?"

CHAPTER THIRTY-EIGHT

Four attackers were coming from the pier and into Stone McClelland's crosshairs. His plan was to eliminate them from behind just as the last one passed them by, so as to assume the advantage he had in surprise but lacked in numbers.

With only one spotlight now atop the roof, it was difficult to ascertain who was charging at them. Nevertheless, judging by sheer mass and girth, it had to be Billy Maxwell leading the assault with someone close at his heels that Chris didn't recognize.

Watching them pass and waiting for the others that were coming, McClelland turned enough to draw a bead on one of them, knowing he couldn't miss a shot.

Immediately behind the first two, Chris spotted Garf Taylor in spite of the paltry amount of light, and then – *Sapphire!*

No – it couldn't be her, he panicked, but it was!

Much as he had with Bertie Stanton and the first round of attackers, Chris interrupted Stone before he could get a shot off.

"Don't fire!" he hissed at McClelland. "That's Sapphire MacKenzie who is with them!"

Shaking Chris off, all Stone replied was, "Then she's with the wrong people."

By now, the four had reached the shield of the brick barbeque. Without delaying any longer, McClelland rose and assumed a shooting stance.

His first bullet struck the assailant that Chris couldn't identify. The man fell without a struggle.

Before Stone could get off another shot, automatic weapon fire resounded from the same bushes that had felled Bertie. McClelland took a couple slugs, but somehow managed to pinpoint precisely where the gunfire was coming from. Three times his gun barked toward the bushes and there was no return fire whatsoever.

And then Stone McClelland collapsed behind the driftwood logs.

Chris's attention was fully focused on the ex-DEA agent that had long ago set him free. It was obvious McClelland was in great pain, yet he was still fairly lucid. And he was handing him his gun.

Chris Soles was dumfounded.

"Take the gun," Stone demanded, as he wheezed and strained, "take the gun and do what you must to finish it...if you can."

Shaking his head, Chris rejected the notion in its entirety.

"Take the gun," McClelland insisted. "It's how the game of trust continues."

"But I don't even know how to handle a gun," protested Chris.

"It ain't rocket science," Stone declared, his breathing becoming more labored. "You just point and shoot. Now, take it!"

Gingerly, Chris plucked the proffered weapon from the big man's hand.

"One more thing," McClelland mustered, "if you make it back here alive, put the gun back in my hand before you go."

"What?"

"Just do what I say," Stone ordered, beginning to drift away. *"I trust you."*

***

Initially quite stunned, neither Kiri nor Carolyn could find their voices to respond.

Again the soldier queried brusquely, "Just where do you think you're going?"

"Anywhere!" Kiri blurted. "We're trying to get away from those monsters in the motel room that were going to rape us."

"We had to climb down sheets out of the third story bathroom to escape," added Carolyn.

With rifles still trained on the women, the second soldier said, "We know, we watched you. How long have you been there?"

Kiri lied outright. "We met them in the tavern a while ago. They seemed nice so we went to party with them."

"Obviously, our mistake," Carolyn tossed in.

The first soldier asked, "How many of them are there and how many rooms do they occupy?"

Kiri shrugged her shoulders. "I think there's six or seven guys and some of their girlfriends as well."

"And rooms?"

"Maybe five or six rooms," estimated Kiri, "and I think they're all on this side of the motel."

"Who is in the other rooms?" demanded the soldier.

Again Kiri shrugged her shoulders. "I have no idea for sure, but probably demonstrators protesting The Seven."

The first soldier glanced at his companion who merely remarked, "Collateral damage."

"Call in the intelligence, will you?" requested the soldier that had first confronted them. While his fellow trooper quickly went onto the radio he carried to pass along the information about those in the motel, the other soldier spoke threateningly.

"Let me ask again," he said, his tone chilly, "where do you think you're going?"

Carolyn started to say something but Kiri overrode her. "We're going back to the tavern a few blocks away. Some friends are supposed to show up later."

The second soldier, coming off the radio, said, "Let them go; we've got more pressing matters. Besides, this whole town will be on lockdown within fifteen minutes anyway."

"Okay," he agreed, "now scoot!"

Carolyn and Kiri needed no further prodding. As rapidly as possible with Carolyn's twisted ankle, they headed straight to the main road running through Athol, confident that the military would intercept Timmy and friends if they chose to pursue them. Upon reaching Highway 54, looking to the west they could clearly see the Good Times Tavern on the other side of the railroad tracks.

By the time they made it to the entry door of the bar, multiple police cars with lights flashing were swarming toward them. Kiri and Carolyn rapidly ducked into the tavern.

489

Inside, Kiri quickly understood the reason for the police activity. A fight was underway, or rather – a beating. With the victim's back to the entry door, two men were restraining his arms on either side, while a third person was pummeling his gut. Five feet away, two other young men struggled against those preventing them from coming to their friend's rescue.

With Carolyn trailing, Kiri moved through the surrounding crowd to see that the person being beaten was – *Tomas Hernandez!*

Without thinking her actions through whatsoever, Kiri approach the man punching Tomas and began shrieking, "The cops are here, the cops are here!"

Nonplussed, the suddenly interrupted assailant gawked at her.

"Can't you see the freaking lights through the windows?" Kiri screamed. "The cops are here!"

Becoming aware of the situation as red lights from squad cars ricocheted from wall to wall inside the tavern, the thugs holding Tomas allowed him to drop to the floor. Immediately, Kiri and Carolyn were under both his arms and helping him to his feet.

"We're getting out of here!" Kiri announced.

Although groggy, Tomas noted the flashing red lights and objected, "We shouldn't deal with the police. What about your friend here?"

Tomas was worried about Carolyn, but Kiri was insistent. "We can't stay here; we're going. The whole town is going to be on lockdown soon."

"If it isn't already," Carolyn added dourly.

By now, Tomas's two friends had been released as well and they helped the women get him to the door. They were ready to follow outside, but Tomas asked them to stay.

"Wade, Grant, sorry to drag you into this," Tomas apologized. "I can face the police alone, if that's what I have to do, but can you stay here to make sure none of the hombres slip out before they can be identified?"

Both Wade Nash and Grant Gilbert were pleased to do their friend's bidding.

Stepping outside the door, they confronted a semi-circle of cops in riot gear. Just beyond was an officer who was apparently in charge busy giving orders to others.

Still being supported by Kiri and Carolyn, Tomas shuffled laboriously toward the officer in charge. Apparently sensing no harm, the surrounding cops parted enough to let them through.

Without hesitation, Kiri announced, "This is the guy that was getting beaten up in the brawl."

"What brawl?" the lead officer asked incredulously.

"The fight in there," Kiri stated, pointing back to the tavern. "Isn't that why you're here?"

"Nobody called us," replied the cop. "We're here for other reasons."

Kiri studied the officer. He looked to be about the same age as Tomas, yet appeared rather stern and forbidding.

"You got some ID, buddy?" he asked Tomas.

Hernandez reached for his wallet then handed over his driver's license. Stepping away for a moment or two, the lead officer called in to someone using the microphone on his shoulder hook. When he returned, the officer conspicuously turned off his communications equipment.

The cop scrutinized Tomas, then his ID, and then Tomas once again.

He then inquired, "Who are these women?"

"My interns," Hernandez replied without batting an eye.

The trooper then asked, "Are you Tomas Hernandez – of Commons Rising?"

"Yes."

"Were you and your family in a reenactment video of your abduction?"

"Yes," Tomas assured him.

The nod of the cop's head was consolatory. "Then you, my friend, are free to go with your two interns. I have children about the same age as yours, and I hope your kids weren't irreparably damaged after what they went through."

"Your kindness is exemplary," Tomas stated with graciousness. "My best wishes to your family."

"I thank you," replied the officer. "Now, get into whatever vehicle you've got and go straight west on this road before everything is totally shut down."

***

By the time Chris worked his way past the brick barbeque through the explosion rubble of glass, wood, and other debris, he discovered he'd walked out of the light from the sole spotlight on the roof. Everything would have been shrouded in darkness if not for a fluorescent light still shining from inside the severely damaged house.

With the aid of that singular backlight, Chris could discern three figures on what remained of the back deck, although they could not easily see him in his darkness. And what he saw was shocking.

Billy Maxwell had apparently gotten the drop on Garf Taylor, for his automatic weapon was trained directly on Taylor, whose weapon was at his side and pointing downward. A short distance away from both men stood Sapphire MacKenzie, stunned and inert.

"You leaked their whereabouts to Empire; you ordered my brother and sister killed!" Maxwell berated Taylor. "They were my only family!"

Speaking as calmly as possible, Garf stated, "They were incompetent and traitorous. The diversion in Asshole Idaho was necessary if we were to succeed in killing The Two and sparking a true Revolution of the people."

Hardly listening, Billy irately shot back, "You ordered my family killed — for what?"

"We've been over it a hundred times," Taylor patiently sighed. "To jumpstart a revolution in the streets of Cascadia and eventually the rest of the world, we needed a small diversion. Now let's do our part and finish the job by eliminating The Two."

Interrupting from the darkness, Chris Soles boomed, "No one will be killing The Two tonight. Now, drop your weapons!"

Billy Maxwell's attention was diverted in the direction of Chris's voice, while Garf Taylor's focus was never distracted. Raising his weapon without a sideways glance, Garf dropped his former comrade-in-arms with three quick shots.

Before Chris could respond — if Chris could respond — Garf Taylor wrapped an arm around Sapphire's neck, pulling her in tight and using her as a human shield.

Squinting out into the darkness, Taylor marginally recognized who had entered upon the scene.

"Oh, it's only you," Garf laughed derisively. "It's Chris Cadia, the legend — the *myth*. Now, isn't this rich! Mister non-violence crashes a gun party."

"Put your weapon down, Garf," Chris replied.

Scornfully, Taylor laughed once more. "Put my weapon down? Never. Not while successful Revolution in the streets is within our grasp!"

"You're deluded," Chris replied flatly. "Killing The Two will only lead to a continuation of the same male dominance mistakes we've encountered for thousands of years."

"You're so weak and pitiful," chided Taylor. Abruptly he pushed Sapphire away. "Here you go Mister *Myth*, Chris Cadia; take a free shot at me."

Chris had a perfect target, but he couldn't pull the trigger.

"I knew you didn't have the balls to do it," Garf belittled Chris.

Immediately, Taylor turned to grab Sapphire's wrist and exclaimed, "Now let's go kill The Two and declare a Revolution."

Just as Garf turned to drag Sapphire inside, a bullet exploded from the gun Chris held in the direction of both. Chris didn't have a clue how to fire a pistol and had no idea what the outcome might be.

As Garf Taylor began to fatally fall, Chris hustled to Sapphire. She was seemingly still in shock, while Chris was beginning to hear multiple sirens approaching in the distance. Gently, he took hold of her gloved hand.

"C'mon Sapphire, we've got to go," urged Chris.

Silently she joined him, and as they ran into the light past the brick barbeque she broke into tears.

"Chris, I'm so sorry," she wailed as they dashed toward the Sound. "I was pissed at my own stupidity with Whitey Dellenbach and blamed it on you giving me that dossier. I was so pissed that after I saw my father unconscious in the hospital in Seattle, I contacted Garf and said I'd join him."

Chris didn't fully understand what she was saying, yet he tried to console her. "Don't worry about it; we've just got to get out of here now."

As they came upon the driftwood logs, Chris delayed to replace Stone McClelland's gun back in his hand as instructed. Placing a finger up close to Stone's nostrils, he could still feel breathing going on.

Hopping back over the log, Chris told Sapphire they needed to cross the property next door so they could get the inflatable boat that McClelland's friend had rented.

"That won't do us any good," objected Sapphire.

"Why not?"

"Garf thought it looked out of place, so he had Billy slash it," she explained. "We'll just go down the rope ladder and take the one I came in."

"You came up on a rope ladder?" mused Chris.

"Yeah, Garf knew it would be low tide when we arrived," Sapphire replied, "so he had the first triad affix it before they attacked so it would be easy-in and easy-out."

"Well, we best give it a try then," Chris suggested.

Quickly, they dashed out upon the pier to where Sapphire pointed at the rope ladder. Without hesitation, they scrambled down to the beach and untied Garf's inflatable rental boat from a barnacled post supporting the pier. Chris asked Sapphire to get in first; he then pushed off and jumped in at the same time.

"I'm going to take the wheel," commanded Sapphire. "I grew up on the waters off Port Townsend and can probably handle this boat better than you."

"Fine by me," Chris responded.

The motor fired on first try, Sapphire pulled back on the throttle, and they launched themselves toward Liberty Bay.

They were maybe half a mile out when Chris caught sight of spotlights from two helicopters that were sweeping the grounds of the residence of The Two. A few seconds later, one helicopter remained focused on the property, while the other was scanning surrounding properties and the beach.

Slowly, the spotlight from that second helicopter advanced further and further from shore, and drew ominously closer to them. Glancing back at one point, Sapphire feared the helicopter would catch sight of their wake and it would all be over.

They had no choice but to keep going on.

***

Spotting his father finishing a conversation near the punchbowl and open bar, Whitley approached the old man. Theodore Dellenbach was beaming as his son drew near.

"Well, are you having an enjoyable evening?" the elder Dellenbach inquired.

"As my wife said earlier, it is a 'magical gathering of special people,'" Whitley replied with a broad smile upon his face. "Who could complain about such a wonderful dinner, all the dancing, and the surprise early arrival of the President?"

"And the speeches," interjected the father, "did you enjoy the speeches after the meal?"

"Why, certainly," the son laughed. "They were all self-laudatory, pointedly preaching to the choir, but that's precisely what we all wanted."

The old man couldn't help but chuckle. "And you and Darlene met with the President and First Lady. I saw Justice Gassack introducing you; how did it go?"

"Splendidly, Father," Whitley exclaimed. "Darlene and the First Lady got along famously. My sweet little tennis star wife was even invited to visit the White House next month."

"That's wonderful," Theodore Dellenbach emphatically declared. "It is always wise business to personally cultivate those we've chosen to work for us."

Nodding his head in agreement, Whitley Dellenbach's demeanor grew darker.

"I do have another piece of news, however, that I should share with you," he stated.

"Alas, it's from the outside, I fear," the old man sighed, "and no doubt bleak after the violence that erupted today."

"I wouldn't exactly call it bleak at all," the son countered. "After an anonymous tip, our forces surrounded a motel about an hour ago in Athol, a small town about fifteen miles north of here."

"What did you call that town?" interrupted the father.

"Athol."

"That's a curious name, don't you think?"

"Probably," Whitley shrugged. "But anyway, the troops discovered where the Future Generations terrorists were hiding, assumedly in preparation for a strike tomorrow. The hundreds of military and police officials on the scene demanded the terrorists surrender – but instead they started shooting from inside the motel."

"I can already guess the outcome," the elder Dellenbach said ominously.

"Our forces had no option but to obliterate them," Whitley gravely replied. "The troops used heavy armaments and incendiary devices, yet Future Generations fought back to the bitter end. Eventually, all the terrorists perished as the motel was burned to the ground."

"And what of Chris Soles," the father interjected, "can we assume he perished as well?"

"It's too early to know," Whitley responded hesitantly. "Some of my other people back in D.C. did pass along some additional information though. Late tonight, Section 1021 of the National Defense Authorization Act will be enacted for this entire region. That means by tomorrow morning everything in this area will be on lockdown and there will be no further demonstrations. Soldiers will be on every street corner and no one will be allowed to go anywhere at least until Monday."

"And by then, we'll all be gone and any protests will fizzle," observed the father.

"We'll be long gone," agreed the son.

"Whitley, do you know what this means?" the old man inquired. "Do you know what we now must do?"

"No, Father, what?"

"Dance the night away, of course," he winked. "I'm going to go find your mother."

Whitley smiled back. "Yes indeed, let's dance the night away!"

***

Motoring slowly and quietly up Liberty Bay's west shoreline, Sapphire searched for an unobtrusive site to put in. The tide was still out and she debated as her eyes searched the shore whether to set the inflated loose after they found a landing point, sink it, or simply tie up somewhere.

Eventually, she spotted a small public launch area about the size of a driveway with four or five small boats scattered about it. All were beached because of the low tide with anchors extended before them towards land.

In a similar manner, Sapphire piloted their boat on to the beach and then both she and Chris scrambled out and dragged their boat relatively close to the others. Discovering a folding grapnel anchor and line in an equipment box back by the outboard, she hustled toward shore and dug two of the anchor flukes into the rocky soil that would soon be covered again by the tide. After securing the other end of the line to a bow ring, Chris urged Sapphire to make haste with him up the boat launch and towards the cabin he and Kiri had shared.

They had been lucky so far, but honestly, Chris didn't know how long their luck would hold. The helicopter that had been sweeping the waters behind them hadn't gone out far enough from Bainbridge Island to spot them, and fortunately turned back. Multiple obstacles would no doubt block whatever pathways they chose in the coming hours and days, yet their choices were made simpler for the time being by following the singular objective of making it to the safety of the cabin.

Once Chris figured out where they were on Viking Avenue NW, the main road running down the west side of Liberty Bay, it only took them another fifteen minutes to reach the cabin. Whenever headlights approached, they leaped off the road to let the vehicle pass. Chris had some difficulty figuring out a few connecting back roads in the dark, but they eventually made it safe and sound.

In spite of the vigorous hike from where they'd parked the boat, both Sapphire and Chris were still wet, cold, and clammy after their escape from Bainbridge Island. Exhausted and overstressed, they made a direct line to the shower without any verbal discussion on the matter.

Shedding their clothes and preparing to step into the small shower tub, Sapphire realized she still had her gloves on.

Chris smiled at her. "Are you going to wear those in the shower?"

Sapphire laughed back as she removed the gloves. "I almost forgot I was wearing them. Ever since I was a little girl my hands get especially cold when I'm out on the water and I made Garf stop at the marine store before we got into the boat so I could buy them."

Once inside the shower with the curtain pulled tight behind them, Chris and Sapphire relished long minutes under the hot water by holding tight onto one another. Occasionally, one might kiss the other's cheek, or nibble on an ear as the water cascaded down, but mostly they just embraced each other tight.

Drying off afterwards, Sapphire stated quite definitively, "I worry about Kiri."

"I do too – all the time," replied Chris. "I hope with all the hope I've got left that she isn't dead."

"Kiri is alive," Sapphire quickly fired back, "and I'm certain she'll be joining us soon."

After Sapphire had blown her hair dry as much as necessary and they'd hung up their towels, they didn't pause an instant to break for food or clothes. Without a second thought, Chris and Sapphire headed straight to the bed.

They relished each other under the covers. Passionately kissing, exploring one another's mouth, hugging and squirming, they celebrated finding themselves together after a long and turbulent day.

Easily, she soon had him as hard as a rock.

Into Chris's ear, Sapphire whispered seductively, "I want you entirely and fully: I love you."

Chris was more than willing to comply but suddenly he hesitated.

"Sapphire," he balked, "I don't have any protection."

"You don't need to worry," she cooed. "Everything is taken care of – now love me!"

Unencumbered, Chris couldn't resist. Slowly he entered her and everything became better and better for both of them. When he was in as far as possible, very gradually once again he began to pull out. When the terminus was nearly reached, he plunged unhesitatingly back in and she responded exuberantly. As the joy in one another became all the more vigorous and heartfelt, the more they pursued it.

After the moment came, he resided fully within her for many blissful minutes.

And following a long, stressful day, that was precisely how they both fell asleep.

CHAPTER THIRTY-NINE

In the dark, early morning hours, the pounding on the cabin door brought them to their senses.

"Chris, Kiri – wake up! Empire is coming and you've got to run!"

"Who is that?" Sapphire gasped, quite startled.

"You know him," replied Chris, "it's Bob Carlson, the owner of this cabin."

Slipping on some shorts then dashing to the front door and swinging it open, Chris greeted his benefactor while noticing how his old work pickup was backed up to the deck with it's motor running.

"What's going on, Bob?" he asked.

"Chris, you and Kiri have to get out of here immediately," the older man warned in a rush. "Take my truck and go!"

"Why, what's happening?"

"In the last half hour we've been getting word from others on our shuffleboard team," he explained rapidly. "They say Empire is making a sweep on everyone of us looking for you. Grab only what you absolutely need and go, because this cabin and everything in it will be demolished and all traces of you eliminated."

"How are you going to do that?"

Although in a hurry, Carlson tried his utmost to be patient.

"Chris, earlier in my life – for over two decades – I was a fire investigator," he stated. "Believe me, I can make this cabin go up in total flames within minutes."

"That's a shame," sighed Chris. "It's such a cozy refuge."

"Don't worry: it's insured," Bob replied, "but you're not. So, get going!"

Carlson turned to go, but suddenly remembered something else. "Also, check your phone. There's supposed to be a vitally important message on it for you. And when you get to where you're going, send me a message about where you leave my truck; Donna and I will pick it up. *Now go!*"

Sapphire was almost fully dressed when Chris reentered the bedroom.

"That was Bob and he said – "

"I heard everything," she snapped. "Let's get out of here!"

Chris dressed quickly and was about to follow Sapphire out to the idling truck when he recalled Bob mentioning a phone message. The next second, he was stunned, recalling how he'd tossed his phone overboard into Puget Sound yesterday when crossing from Seattle to Bainbridge Island.

But that was okay – he had a spare in the top dresser drawer. Snagging it and the charger, Chris rushed out the front door to join Sapphire in the truck – hoping the phone still retained enough power to get the message.

***

Behind the Fish House restaurant in Poulsbo where Sapphire had left her car yesterday, Chris couldn't believe what he was hearing.

"You're going to do what?" he exclaimed incredulously.

"I'm going straight to the Poulsbo police," she said again.

"That's crazy!"

"No, it's the smartest thing I can think to do," Sapphire objected. "Somehow I have to account for the time since I left my father at Harborview Medical in Seattle until right now. I've got to have a credible explanation of why I haven't yet made it to my mother's hospital room in Port Angeles."

Chris was astonished. "So what are you going to tell the cops?"

"First, I tell them that after I picked my car up at the airport, then visited my father in the hospital in Seattle on the way to visit my mother in the Port Angeles hospital, I stopped here to tell my old Port Townsend classmate, Beth — who owns this restaurant with her husband — about my parents," she said. "We've always been close and it would seem like a perfectly acceptable thing to do."

"And then?"

"Then I tell them as I got out of my car here in the restaurant parking lot," Sapphire continued, "a van suddenly pulled up and I was abducted by several men wearing ski masks. They covered my head as well and drove me to some room — maybe in a motel nearby — where they removed my mask and interrogated me all night."

Dubious, Chris asked, "Now why would the cops believe that?"

"Because I'll tell the police how they continually drilled me about my involvement with Commons Rising and the de-privatization movement," she began. "Because I'll remind them about the same kind of people that abducted Tomas and the reenactment video that's been viewed literally millions of times. And because I'll make a plain and simple case that after leaving my father in intensive care in Seattle, I'm now just trying to get to my mom in the Port Angeles hospital after their car accident – where lives might well be in the balance."

So forceful was the presentation of Sapphire's words that Chris believed she might well be successful with the police. He nodded in accession to her strategy and wished her luck.

"Okay, I've got to go," she stated firmly, "but before I do, let's hear whatever message is supposed to be on your phone."

Chris had nearly forgotten about the message. Removing the phone from his pocket, he turned it on and was encouraged that it still held a charge. This phone had been synced with the one he had thrown overboard yesterday, so in theory he figured he should be able to get whatever was supposedly waiting for him.

It turned out there was indeed one message that came in very early this morning and it was from Tomas Hernandez. Chris turned on the speakerphone and tapped the "play" icon.

"Chris, this is Tomas. I have Kiri and her friend Carolyn with me and we're on our way to Seattle. We are okay, but you are in grave danger.

"We're still on the east side of the Cascades and just stopped at an all-night diner in Ellensberg. They had a 24-hour cable news station running in the restaurant and your picture was all over it. Mind you, it's not a shot from those old wanted posters, but a current photo instead. An all points bulletin has been issued; you are currently the most hunted man in all Cascadia.

"You must keep out of sight at all costs! Call me as soon as you get this and we'll try to have something planned for you."

"Shit," Chris muttered as the voice message from Tomas ended. "I should have figured that was going to happen."

"How did they get your photo?" asked Sapphire.

Chris sighed. "McClelland's FBI friend snapped it on the plane when they were taking me captive."

Sapphire shook her head and leaned over to solidly kiss him.

"I've got to go," she said tenderly. "You call Tomas and do what he suggests. Be safe; I love you."

He kissed her back. "I love you too."

Chris watched as she slid out of the old work pickup and determinedly marched to her car. She backed out of her parking spot, and gradually accelerated to the streets of Poulsbo.

He then called Tomas who picked up after the first ring.

"Chris, I've been waiting to hear your voice," Tomas exclaimed excitedly. "Are you okay?"

"For the time being," Chris mustered.

"Where are you?"

"Poulsbo."

"I thought you might be somewhere over on that side of the Sound," stated Tomas. "We've been waking lots of people out of bed early this morning and making all kinds of contingency plans. So let me explain what you're going to do next..."

* * *

Everything had gone well so far, but then he'd followed the instructions Tomas had given him to the letter.

506

From Poulsbo, Chris had made the twenty-minute drive to Kingston where the ferry came in from Edmonds. He was specifically advised neither to approach the ferry nor to park in the public lots nearby. Instead, Tomas told him to park on a side street and walk briskly to the Kingston marina adjacent to the ferry landing.

Dawn was beginning to break after he parked Bob Carlson's old pickup and Chris began to grow concerned about surveillance cameras. Searching behind the seat of the truck, he found a ratty and aging cowboy hat so he put it on. It wasn't much of a disguise, but it was the best he could muster.

No one was in sight as he crossed the mostly empty parking lots that served both ferry and marina. He had been instructed to proceed directly to Dock D. The entry gate to the dock was normally self-locking and a pass card was necessary to enter, but Tomas told him he would nevertheless be able to access the dock. And, sure enough, he was able to get in because the entire locking assembly had been wrapped with duct tape, rendering the latch incapable of engaging.

About halfway down Dock D Tomas said he should find a thirty-six foot powerboat with the name of "Seeker." He was to give three quick knocks on the hull, delay two or three seconds, and then deliver two more knocks. Chris did precisely that and from somewhere inside the boat and forward, a deep male voice resounded saying, "Permission granted to come aboard."

Without engaging anyone on board, Chris was then supposed to go below deck and as far aft as possible where he'd find a small engine room. Once inside the engine room, he closed the cabin door behind him.

Five minutes later, the motor he was sitting next to came to life. It startled him and was loud, but not unbearable while it idled. After ten to fifteen minutes more passed, Chris sensed the boat was beginning to move. Tomas had guessed the journey across Puget Sound to Edmonds would take thirty to forty-five minutes. Although it seemed longer to Chris, it was perhaps because the noise from the engine was less tolerable at higher speeds and wore on him more the further they went.

Finally, when the motor began revving down Chris guessed they must be entering the Edmonds marina. Another five or ten minutes at a slower speed brought the powerboat to what Tomas had said would be a covered slip. After the boat had tied up and the engine turned off, Chris was to wait ten minutes and then exit as he had entered, without encountering anyone.

He'd watched his cell phone battery draining away for what seemed an endless ten-minute countdown, and then exited the boat without incident. Walking up the dock and out the gate, in the parking lot beyond he easily found the silver four-door hatchback whose last three digits on the license plate were "422." As Tomas had promised, the driver's side door was unlocked and the car keys were under the front seat.

Also under the front seat were back-up directions to his destination, though he didn't really need them since the pre-programmed guidelines from the vehicle's GPS worked just fine.

Tomas had warned him to be on the lookout for roadblocks on his route, although he also guessed they probably wouldn't be fully established until later in the day. As it turned out, Chris didn't come across any checkpoints during his half hour journey.

On a meandering course that took him north and east of Edmonds proper, he eventually found his way back down to the Sound again in the direction of Picnic Point Park, a popular beach accessible location on the other side of the rail tracks that ran north-south on this side of Puget Sound.

Just prior to the Park, however, the GPS instructed him to turn south. Going uphill there were several large, expensive residences, yet he was directed to park in a double driveway of a small, dark green, one-bedroom cabin without a garage. Tomas had mentioned the cabin was built in the 1930's or 40's and had a million dollar view of Puget Sound. He was not to enjoy the view from the outside deck in back. Instead, Chris was advised lock himself inside the cabin and look out the window if he wished.

Well, Chris thought to himself as he surveyed the inside of the little cabin, so far so good. All he had to do now was wait until the evening hours when Kiri would be arriving with a meal – and whatever plans The Elders were concocting during the day.

***

Following a nap that lasted long into the afternoon, Chris took an invigorating shower to fully wake up. At a table beside the picture window that truly did have a million dollar view of Puget Sound, he snatched up his phone.

It had been on the charger since he decided to rest and now was fully prepared for whatever might be needed. Without a second thought, Chris sent Bob Carlson a text message telling him where his old pickup was parked in Kingston, and thanking him for everything.

Half an hour later, in a series of text messages, Bob noted that things had finally calmed down on his property. He said the cabin was fully engulfed in flames within fifteen minutes after Chris departed, and five minutes later fire trucks arrived – along with a swarm of Feds – just like others on their shuffleboard team experienced. And yet, Bob continued, there was little for authorities to do but ask a few questions and watch the fire. His final text message again noted all was now calm, though it ended in warning, "Be extraordinarily careful: your photo is everywhere!"

For better or worse, there was no television in the cabin so he couldn't watch lurid stories about himself; instead, for several hours Chris stared out the window at Puget Sound.

When Kiri finally arrived, he didn't hear her car pull up outside. It was the knocking on the door that retrieved his thoughts from wherever they had been while gazing out the window. Through the peephole in the front door, Chris saw it was indeed Kiri and he flung the door open wide. She leaped into his arms as they joyously entwined, kissing and hugging.

When they eventually disengaged, Kiri said she had carryout dinner in her auntie's car that she had to bring inside. Following, Chris offered to help but she quickly turned on him.

"No, I'll get it," Kiri stated sharply. "You should not be seen anywhere if possible. The authorities and in turn the media have everyone in a panic. As a result, the public is repeatedly being pressed to call in anything at all they see that might be even remotely suspicious. And in their manufactured fear, people are responding."

Returning with two bags and a six-pack of beer, Kiri did allow him to disperse the food on the table by the window. Opening two beers, they launched themselves into a Mexican meal, with tacos, burritos, and enchiladas filling their plates. And as they ate, they spoke of events that had transpired since they'd last seen one another.

Initially, it was mostly Kiri that explained what had been happening in the larger scheme of things for she had been able to witness them all day where Chris had not. She told him first of events in Idaho where everything had been on lockdown with military troops in strict command.

That led her to an explanation of how she and Carolyn had escaped from their Future Generations captors at the motel, how they found Tomas and were allowed to depart, and how – as they drove west out of Athol – they had seen a fireball erupt behind them into the night sky that emanated from the motel.

Kiri also related how the attack on The Two on Bainbridge Island had put military and police forces on full alert throughout western

Washington. Further, she recalled how news reports stated The Two and family members with them had holed up in an armored safe room during the attack. It was speculated by experts that the plastic explosive the dead attackers had carried would have been sufficient to destroy any supposedly "safe" room – if they had not been killed first.

"I also spoke to Sapphire for a few minutes this afternoon," Kiri noted.

"Is she okay?" Chris interrupted.

"She is doing as good as possible, given the circumstances," replied Kiri. "When I caught up with her she was in the hospital in Port Angeles with her mum and preparing to drive back to Harborview Medical in Seattle because her father's condition was growing more dire with each passing hour."

Chris shook his head. "That's a tough situation."

"Sapphire also told me," Kiri continued, "that you saved her life."

"We were both lucky to get out alive," he shrugged, attempting to mitigate and discard any notion of saving someone's life.

"Well, all I can say is: thank you very much" Kiri stated sincerely and with a smile. "Now it's your turn; tell me what happened to you since we parted."

Without lingering too much on details, Chris recalled how Sapphire had surmised Garf Taylor's real plot, how he had traveled on the same plane to Seattle with her, and how Stone McClelland and his FBI friend had subsequently taken him into custody. He then told Kiri how he'd convinced his captors to disrupt the assassination attempt on Bainbridge Island, and was ultimately able to escape with Sapphire across to Liberty Bay and eventually to their cabin on Bob and Donna Carlson's property.

"Then this morning Bob woke us up while it was still dark and said we had to leave because Empire was coming," said Chris. "And to destroy any evidence of us, he set fire to the cabin."

Kiri said nothing, yet Chris could see tears forming in her eyes. "What?"

"I foresaw that coming," she replied softly. "I'm sorry, I truly loved living there with you."

After they finished eating, they cleaned up and Chris opened another beer before they returned to the table. It was growing dark outside so Kiri closed the blinds and began telling him about future plans.

"Many people have been very busy on our account," she mentioned, "and not only on our account.

"Carolyn, for example, is leaving on a redeye flight with forged papers to Norway tonight where she'll be living with my cousin Ingri," stated Kiri. "I don't know how they did it all so quickly, but maybe with so many of Norwegian descent living in this area they were somehow able to produce the necessary paperwork this afternoon to get her on her way."

Chris was encouraged. "Good for her," he smiled. "And maybe by completely disappearing the authorities will believe she perished in the Athol Traveler's Inn motel inferno – if they could even be certain she was there."

"That's certainly one hope everyone held today," nodded Kiri.

The Elders of Cascadia had also been very busy on her own account, Kiri told Chris. Someone had visited her parent's house in Cumberland on Vancouver Island, retrieved her original Canadian passport and B.C. driver license from her top dresser drawer, flew it down to Seattle, and eventually to her uncle's house in Mukilteo – where Tomas, Carolyn, and Kiri had driven to after escaping Idaho.

Others, Kiri had been told, had hacked into bus line and Customs records to establish she'd crossed the U.S.-Canadian border through the Peace Arch last Thursday to visit her aunt and uncle.

"I'm going back tomorrow," she further informed him. "I'll be taking the ferry from Port Angeles across to Victoria on Vancouver Island. Since my sister goes to UVic, the University of Victoria, she's going to pick me up and give me a ride up to Ladysmith, where our parents will meet us, and drive me home to Cumberland."

Smiling, Chris was fascinated by the aura Kiri had assumed since last they were together. Something had transformed, transmuted, as a result of her experiences in northern Idaho. It was almost as if she'd successfully passed through trials to become quite self-assured, capable, even confident like a commander in the midst of chaos. And he very much liked what he saw.

"And what's in store for me?" he wondered aloud.

"Oh, there was some talk about you too," she laughed. "Are you still comfortable in the backcountry?"

"I believe so."

"Well, the plans are for you to disappear in the Olympics for a while for your own good," she explained. "When we get to Port Angeles, and specifically at Laurel Street, we go in opposite directions. I'll go towards the water and the ferry, and you'll go the opposite way — more or less south — down Laurel Street. There is a hill with cliff sides that parallels most of the waterfront in Port Angeles. But on those cliff sides is a ravine, at Laurel Street, where a set of stairs was constructed that you can ascend on. There's also a beautiful mural at the bottom of those stairs, so you can't miss it.

"At the top of the stairway are some condos, motels, and apartments. There's also a parking lot that you walk directly into at the top of the stairs. In that lot will be a Toyota pickup with a backpack and all the gear you need to sustain yourself for some time in the backcountry.

"From there you drive west on Highway 101 for not too many miles until you see a sign for the Elwha River and dam. If you don't see it, don't worry. You'll also have a pre-programmed GPS that will take you directly up the river to the old dam – the old dam that was destroyed several years ago and now the salmon can swim back up the river again. You leave the truck in the small parking lot and that's where you head into the backcountry and disappear. And don't worry about the truck; someone will retrieve it."

Chris had been listening patiently to every detail, but now he said, "I have one question."

"Yes?"

"I'm guessing it's about a two hour trip or more via ferry and road from Edmonds to Port Angeles," he noted. "And if they're looking for me like I've been led to assume, there will be roadblocks and checkpoints from the ferry to random stations along the road. So just how do we get safely from Edmonds to Port Angeles?"

Kiri smiled. "Simple. We fly over it all."

"How do we do that?"

Briefly, Kiri explained that an Elder who years ago started one the region's float plane services volunteered to fly them over to Port Angeles. She told him that there would also be two French tourists flying with them that were going over for the crab festival and staying for several days.

"The crab festival?"

"Yes, the Dungeness Crab and Seafood Festival," replied Kiri. "It's become quite a big deal over the last several years."

"That's all well and good," Chris declared evenly, "but by doing that for me, the pilot is putting his life at great risk."

"His life is already at great risk," Kiri shot back curtly.

"What do you mean?"

"Don't worry about it," she said sternly, ending the discussion.

Kiri looked into his eyes to see he'd let it pass.

"Okay, so that's most of what we're doing tomorrow; I'll explain the rest of the details about Port Angeles in the morning," she stated. "What we're doing tonight – is going to bed."

"Huh?" Chris muttered, not prepared for the abruptness.

"I took a shower this afternoon," she told him. "Do you need to take a shower first?"

"No, I took one this afternoon following a nap."

"Oh, you took a nap, eh?" Kiri exclaimed slyly. "Then you better be ready to go all night."

"What?" Chris was perplexed, at a loss. This was not where she was normally coming from.

Kiri took his hand and he followed her into the cabin's small bedroom. She pulled back the covers on the bed and then untied his shoes. She had him kick those off; she then removed his socks. Standing, Kiri had him help her remove his shirt. Next, she loosened his belt and dropped his trousers. His underwear followed the pants to the floor.

In like manner, Kiri briskly disrobed and both were suddenly naked, staring at one another.

Rather formally, she declared, "You are released from your vow to my parents."

"What do you mean?" Chris asked incredulously.

"You are no longer my Teacher, and I am no longer your Student," she stated.

Taken aback and speechless momentarily, Chris soon began to smile.

"Well, you know what they say:" he offered, "When the student is ready the Teacher will appear. When the student is truly ready, the Teacher will disappear."

"Is that from one of your old Chinese guys?"

"Yes," Chris nodded, "Lao Tzu."

"I guess he might have known a thing or two," she allowed.

Kiri turned out the lights and then playfully grabbed his wiener, leading him to bed. She pulled the covers back atop them, then snuggled in close to Chris.

Whispering into his ear as she wrapped her arms around him, she said, "I want it slow, steady, and delicious. You lick me until I gush, and I'll suck you until you throb. And then I want to love you like I've never loved you before, and you love me like you've never loved me before."

Hours later, in the dark of the middle of the night, Kiri was suddenly awake and lucid. In fact, never before had everything – simply everything – become so incredibly lucid. Never, ever, before had she perceived things like *this*.

And then she began to laugh. Outrageously.

In the midst of her chortles, she jabbed Chris in the ribs.

"You, dickhead," she chuckled, "wake up!"

As Chris fought toward consciousness, Kiri smiled, saying, "It was all a koan; I should have known! It was all a koan, wasn't it?"

"What?" he finally mustered, waking enough to converse.

"The quantity of insects versus the quantity of water on the planet," she laughed. "It's exactly the same thing, isn't it? Everything suddenly comes together; it's the same thing – just like you and me."

"You seem to have hit upon something," he lauded her with a dry attempt at humor.

"Everything comes together; it is one," Kiri repeated once more, amidst her giggles. "Can you handle it, Chris? We're going to lust the night away!"

He felt her gripping him, as she began stroking once more.

Smiling into the darkness between them, Chris replied, "So be it: let's lust the night away!"

CHAPTER FORTY

Relatively early the next morning, Kiri was motoring her auntie's car toward Perrinville Corner, a location a little more than half way from the Picnic Point cabin to the Edmonds marina where the float plane would hopefully be waiting.

Located at an intersection of two of the more prominent roadways in a largely residential area, the small burg of Perrinville was originally established in the late 1930's. Toward the end of the 1970's, a shopping center was designed and built to mimic a historical town. Today it was a "town" of quaint buildings, antique dealers, a deli, and even a post office. Over the years, Perrinville Corner had also become known for attractive young women in skimpy bikinis making money washing cars in the summer, with male drivers backed up sometimes for miles waiting for their turn at a clean car.

This morning, however, the delay had nothing to do with scantily clad young ladies washing cars, but everything to do with local police staffing a manhunt checkpoint. Because it was still early on a Sunday morning, the light traffic moved through the roadblock at a fair pace and it didn't take long for Kiri to be directed toward one of the two officers inspecting cars as they drove through Perrinville Corner.

The cop that Kiri rolled her window down for was a young guy, maybe a few years older than she. Kiri smiled as he asked her for identification and the car registration. Willingly, she handed him both her Canadian passport and British Columbia driver license, and from the glove compartment, the registration for the car.

With some kind of hand-held device, the officer scanned first her passport, and then her license. He then scrutinized the car registration for several minutes.

Seriously, he queried, "Who is the owner of this car?"

"It belongs to my auntie in Mukilteo," she replied glibly. "I've been visiting the last several days and she let me use the car this morning."

The electronic device in the policeman's hand beeped and he began concentrating on some kind of readout.

"This says you traveled over the border last Thursday," he noted. "Is that correct?"

"Yes, to visit my uncle and auntie," Kiri reiterated.

"And how long do you intend to be here?"

"I'm going back to B.C. today," she informed him. "After I meet a girlfriend at the Crab Catcher restaurant in Edmonds, my uncle and auntie gave me an early birthday present of a scenic float plane trip from Edmonds to Port Angeles. From there I catch the ferry to Victoria, and back home."

"What about this car?"

"My uncle and auntie will pick it up this afternoon after my uncle gets off work," Kiri explained.

The officer seemed satisfied with her replies. "Okay, but I have to search your vehicle."

Glancing behind her toward the back seat, the cop asked, "What's all that?"

Kiri sighed, then smiled. "To say the very least, my auntie's an avid gardener. We were shopping in Everett yesterday and she found a late summer/early autumn deal on potting soil, peat moss, and dried manure. That's what all those big bags are and there's more in the trunk – along with all kinds of pots that she bought as well."

"Can you pull the trunk release to open it, please?" he requested.

"Sure, no problem."

The police officer poked around in the rear of the vehicle for only a few seconds, before closing the trunk and returning to the driver's side window.

"Okay, you're free to go," he stated, before kindly yet formally saying, "Enjoy your travels," even as he began flagging the next vehicle in line forward.

The remainder of the drive to the Edmonds marina was uneventful. The coalition of Elders that had aided in plotting the escape for Chris were truly detail oriented, even to the point of where she should park at the marina. They said there were four parking spaces together that were blocked from the surveillance cameras by a light post and part of the Crab Catcher restaurant sign, and it was in any one of those she was instructed to park.

Fortunately, at this hour on Sunday morning, three of the four spots were open so Kiri pulled in and parked the vehicle.

After turning the motor off, she turned to the rear and asked, "Are you okay back there?"

From underneath the bags of potting soil, peat moss, and dried manure in front of the seat came a muffled, "I think so."

Kiri told Chris that she could see the float plane waiting at the fuel dock with two passengers outside.

"Give me a minute or two, then come out from under those bags and meet me at the plane," she instructed. "Oh, and don't forget the mask. Okay?"

"Okay," came the reluctant and muffled response.

After Kiri departed it took Chris several minutes to heave the heavy bags off of him and onto others atop the back seat. When he was finally free, he grabbed the mask he had chosen – although in his mind it was not much of a choice.

At such short notice as the Elders had to finalize plans for his escape, the only masks they were able to scour up were an old Richard Nixon mask and a Guy Fawkes/Anonymous mask. Chris didn't really want to wear either, but in the end chose the Guy Fawkes/Anonymous mask. He couldn't really stomach being Richard Nixon; if anything, he preferred to be anonymous – if that was indeed at all possible at this point. The mask and the Seattle Seahawks ball cap that Kiri suggested he wear was his entire disguise.

Without hesitating any longer, Chris got out of the car and began walking toward the marina and boats. Before he was ready to turn down the ramp to the fuel dock and waiting float plane, a passerby coming in the opposite direction started staring at him, which immediately transformed into suspicious gawking. A few seconds later, he jerked his cell phone out of a pocket and began dialing.

While the guy concentrated on his phone, Chris briskly turned down the ramp to the fuel dock and float plane at the end. All other passengers had loaded into the plane and the pilot waiting outside hustled Chris on as well, even as he was removing his mask. Casting off lines that secured the plane to the dock, the pilot followed Chris on board. He locked the door and seated himself in the cockpit, while requesting everyone to make certain seat belts were buckled.

The plane had been idling and now the pilot slowly taxied to the marina entrance. As they gradually gained speed and eventually took off, from up in the air Chris could see multiple police cars with lights flashing and coming from various locations – and all converging on the Edmonds marina.

***

Although Kiri told the officer at the Perrinville Corner checkpoint that she was going on a "scenic" plane ride from Edmonds to Port Angeles on the Olympic Peninsula, she hardly took the time to look out the window.

She was seated on the port side of the aircraft behind the French tourists who were busy talking with the old pilot whenever he had the opportunity. Chris was seated across the float plane's small aisle on the starboard side near the cabin entry/exit door. For the duration of the hour or so flight, they said next to nothing. Instead, they held one another's hand across the aisle, while sharing both squeezes and smiles.

After landing near the entrance to the Port Angeles marina and taxiing around inside the marina a bit, the pilot got out and tied the aircraft to the dock below the small U.S. Customs building. The French couple was kind enough to invite Kiri to share their pre-arranged and waiting cab if she wished. Overhearing the offer, the old pilot noted that it would be a good idea, because the ferry was on the way to the Crab Festival and it would save her the walk of about a mile.

Watching his passengers load into the taxi and depart, the pilot shrugged then ambled up the ramp from the dock to the Customs office to turn in his paperwork.

Entering, he immediately caught sight of the administrative assistant he'd known for years, and greeted her cheerfully, chiming, "Well hello, Margie, you're looking as young and stunning as ever!"

"And you're as full of bullshit as you've always been, Gregory," she tossed back, laughing.

The old pilot handed her his passenger manifest with a few other pieces of paperwork. He acted as if he was ready to depart but his friend was shaking her head.

"Don't be in too big a rush, Gregory," she said, "Howard wants to talk with you in his office. You can go right in; he's waiting for you."

The pilot once more shrugged his shoulders as he opened the adjoining door to enter. The Custom agent's office had a sweeping view of the marina, enabling one to easily observe the comings and goings on the water. Now, however, his attentions were focused upon some papers on his desk.

"What's up, Howard?" the old pilot asked without sitting down.

"Barely glancing up from his desk, the Customs officer said matter-of-factly, "I saw you taxi down through the docks before you tied up."

"Yeah, so what?" the pilot replied defensively. "I often give my passengers an extra thrill by touring the marinas a bit after we land. You know that."

"Yeah," the Customs man said looking up, "but you don't often drop a passenger halfway down a dock so he can bolt toward the ramp at the end and disappear."

"Who says I did that?"

"I watched it all through binoculars, Greg."

In full denial, the old pilot said, "I'd never do a thing like that."

"Don't worry about it," the Customs agent spoke calmly. "I already called in an alert."

The old pilot was offended.

"Why, you officious little prick," he shouted in denunciation. "You're still the same slimy weasel you were when we were classmates back at the old Shoreline High School. You haven't changed a bit; you've always been destined to be one of Empire's lackeys."

"And you're still the same swaggering jerk you always were," the Custom's man countered, "full of bluster and hot air. You dropped off Chris Soles, didn't you?"

"I'm not certain who I dropped off," stated the old pilot. "But in Cascadia we take care of people valuable to us and the future."

"What are you talking about, Greg?" wondered the government man. "Chris Soles is the most wanted fugitive in the entire Northwest right now."

The pilot shook his head. "Whomever it was that I dropped off is favored by the Elders of Cascadia, an inspiration for those coming of age, and everyone else in between."

"He's a criminal," the Customs officer flatly replied. "He will be captured or killed."

"And if you do that, you only hasten Empire's inevitable demise by making him a martyr," the pilot fired back. "The Revolution is at your doorstep; Cascadia will emerge victorious."

"Greg, slow down and get a grip on your senses," the Customs man urged. "You are presently in the city of Port Angeles, in the state of Washington, in the United States of America. North, across the Strait of Juan de Fuca, is the city of Victoria, in the province of British Columbia, in the sovereign nation of Canada. There is no such thing as Cascadia. It's a delusion, a figment of the imagination."

"Are you fucking kidding?" the pilot exclaimed hotly and incredulously. "Is it even possible that you're completely unaware of the Quest for Cascadia?"

Contemptuously, the Custom's agent blew him off with a wave of the hand. "You might best just take a seat and wait. More of 'Empire's lackeys' will be here soon enough to interview you."

"I'm not hanging around to wait for some trumped up interview," the old pilot announced defiantly. "I've got an appointment."

"You might as well wait here," the government man suggested, "because they'll come after you back in Seattle just the same."

"Nope," the pilot firmly fired back, "I've got an appointment with Mount Olympus."

A moan emerged from the man behind the desk. "You're not dredging up that tired tale again, are you?"

"Howard, I've told you many a time that's what I intend to do," declared the pilot. "Today is the day. I fly south from here into Olympic National Park and formally meet up with Mount Olympus."

"Why today?" queried Howard. "Just to avoid an interview with government agents?"

The old pilot shook his head. "The cancer's inoperable and the pain grows worse with every passing week. Today I meet Mount Olympus head on and go out with a bang."

"Out with a bang?"

"Out with a big bang," the pilot affirmed, "which is diametrically opposed to the whimper you'll likely depart with after months of morphine and suffering when it's your time to go. I'm out with a bang!"

"You're making a big mistake," the Customs man cautioned. "Crashing your plane into a mountain isn't the right solution."

The pilot shrugged his shoulders. Turning toward the door to exit, he merrily replied, "See ya, Howard. I gotta go."

***

Before departing the Picnic Point cabin, Kiri had explained the details of what would transpire in Port Angeles after their arrival by float plane. She told Chris how the pilot would drop him off in the marina half way down a dock, and how he could easily exit through a ramp at the end.

Kiri further revealed how an unlocked bicycle would be leaning on the side of a restaurant that served the boat basin patrons and surrounding marine related businesses. She then guided his attentions to the map app on her phone as she pointed out the simple directions he must follow to get to Laurel Street, and the staircase to the escape pickup truck.

All that was necessary for him to do was ride the bike out of the harbor area by means of the short Boathaven Drive, to where it met the busier thoroughfare of Marine Drive. He would then follow that road mostly east until it met West 1st Street. From there, Laurel Street was less than half a mile and he could leave the bike in a rack near the bottom of the staircase. All told, the total distance from the harbor to the Laurel Street stairs was around a mile and by bike should only take five to seven minutes, or so said the Elders planning his escape.

The Elders had also cautioned that Chris should not be carrying any of his forged identity documents, nor his phone – both of which might endanger others in an investigation if he was taken into custody. The ID warning was in effect already complete; he'd dashed out of the cabin in Poulsbo yesterday morning without wallet or paperwork. And the phone was taken care of easily enough: Chris drowned it in the toilet reservoir at the Picnic Point cabin and left it there in the water for dead.

After landing in Port Angeles, the plan Kiri had laid out for his escape worked perfectly at first. He left the Guy Fawkes/Anonymous mask on the plane – it had already garnered undue attention – but he did wear the Seattle Seahawks ball cap if only to engender some kind of solidarity with those he might meet on the street. Chris was dropped off down the dock, exited the plane, and scooted up the ramp and away without any issue he could detect.

He found the bicycle easily enough and was on Marine Drive closing in on West 1st Street when things began to go south. Chris thought it might have been a nail or a tack, but when he stopped to investigate the suddenly flattening rear tire, he found it to be a large treble fishhook that had punctured the tire.

There wasn't much he could do to fix the bicycle tire at this point; regardless, as there was a gas station ahead and just before the turn onto West 1st Street, he wheeled the bike around the back of the station and propped it up against the wall.

It was at that moment that he heard what was to be the first of many sirens in the distance.

Trying not to appear suspicious, at a brisk pace he departed from the rear of the gas station. Chris made it off Marine Drive and onto West 1st Street just as two military humvees with lights flashing went screaming past in the opposite direction toward the marina. He knew he had less than half a mile to go to get to the Laurel Street ravine and stairway so he quickened his pace.

More and more sirens began piercing the air of downtown Port Angeles, and suddenly there was one coming up from behind on the one-way West 1st Street. At that moment Chris was passing a mini shopping mall so, as inconspicuously as possible, he dodged to the right and in through the open mall doors.

When the state trooper's patrol car sped by, Chris had no other alternative but to follow it in the same direction if he was going to make it to Laurel Street. The trooper turned left on some street in the distance and Chris carried on.

Soon enough he came to the Oak Street intersection and crossed it, with the U.S. Federal Building now to his right. From what Kiri had shown him from the map on her phone this morning, he recalled that Oak Street was last street before Laurel so he was almost there.

He heard a car turning left from Oak onto West 1st Street behind him, but hearing no sirens didn't give it a second thought. Unfortunately, the vehicle was a local Port Angeles police cruiser with neither siren nor lights activated. Chris believed he was fortunate nevertheless and breathed a sigh of relief when the vehicle passed by him without incident, and then turned left at the next intersection that was Laurel Street.

As the mural at the base of the staircase came into view on his right, so also did he spot to his left the police cruiser that had just passed him. The cop was turned around, waiting, and apparently on his radio. Within seconds, the sound of multiple sirens filled the air and they all seemed to be converging upon him.

All along it had been his intent to ascend the staircase in the ravine to where his escape vehicle was waiting; now there was no other alternative. In passing, Chris glanced towards the fifteen or twenty foot high mural to see a pastoral scene with the snowy Olympic Mountains in the background, a blue lake in the foreground, and some deer as well. But that was absolutely all he had time to take in.

On the left side of the mural, the first set of stairs — maybe ten to twelve of them — led to the first of what later proved to be several landings. From there Chris turned right and scrambled up another fifteen or twenty stairway treads to a larger observation platform above the top of the mural.

From here, he could look four or five blocks north to the ferry terminal where Kiri would soon be departing from; yet more pertinent to his present situation was the sheer show of armed force that was gathering before the mural in the intersection of Laurel Street and West 1st Street.

Quickly turning in an uphill direction, Chris hustled up to the next landing by taking the thirty-five or forty steps two at a time. This platform jutted out on both sides to accommodate small benches where weary stair climbers could rest if they wished.

Dashing on past this landing to get to the escape truck that waited only thirty or forty more stairway steps above, Chris suddenly came to an abrupt halt.

Above, at the very top of the staircase, a solid line of troopers in riot gear and with weapons pointed at him began to form not only at the top of the stairs, but also across the entire width of the ravine as well.

Shocked but not stunned, Chris automatically turned about and nearly leaped to the landing below with the benches on either side.

Looking down upon the intersection of West 1st Street and Laurel though, he was now stunned to inaction by the sheer mass of troops that had swarmed streets — with all their weapons trained upon him as well.

There was no going up and no going down. Realizing the hopelessness of the situation, Chris concluded there was nothing he could do but peacefully surrender.

Setting the Seattle Seahawks ball cap down, he slowly raised both hands above his head. In that pose, Chris then stepped up passively onto one of the benches, offering no resistance whatsoever.

Nothing at all happened for a moment. Then a single round was fired at him – only to be followed by hundreds and hundreds more. Caught in the middle of a crossfire from above and below, there wasn't a thing he could do.

In seeming disbelief, Chris Soles stood there defenseless, with hands high above his head, for several seconds into the brutal fusillade. Then, tilting forward and definitely off kilter, the ultimate human bullet sponge plummeted headlong over the side of the stairway railing and into the ravine below.

***

Thanking the French couple for the ride as they dropped her off, Kiri walked the short distance to the terminal for the ferry to Victoria.

Inside, at the ticket booth, she presented the documentation that was requested and paid her toll for the trip. In the holding area for foot passengers within the terminal, Kiri had barely found a seat to wait for the ferry departure when she heard the first sirens out on the Port Angeles streets.

She was alarmed and became more so as the quantity of the sirens rapidly escalated by dozens. Kiri knew it could only mean one thing. She attempted to console herself though, rationalizing that as long as they were screaming helter-skelter about town, he was still on the run and still had a chance.

Unnervingly, the piercing noise continued for several additional minutes until they began to convene in her general area – no doubt now – surely on Laurel Street, only four or five blocks south of her.

And then, hardly a minute or two later most of the sirens were muted. An eerie quiet and calm held sway for a couple minutes more.

When the scores and scores of guns exploded almost simultaneously, tears began to form in Kiri's eyes.

She knew precisely what had happened because she had foreseen it months ago. At the time she hadn't known when or where, only that it would transpire.

Kiri hadn't cried then; accepting the coming reality was all she could do. But now that the reality had set in, there was nothing else she could do.

And so the tears flowed relentlessly, on and on.

CHAPTER FORTY-ONE

Savoring a mood of utmost contentment, Whitley Dellenbach sunk graciously into his plush home office chair. A bottle of his late Uncle Walter's premium forty year old Scotch was on the desk before him, along with a glass that was begging to be refilled.

Glancing about his late uncle's private study, Whitley acknowledged to himself how he had always coveted this special room with its stately raised wood panels, the wall of books on one end, and even the lingering scent of his uncle's favorite cigars.

He had always assumed the multi-acre walled and gated estate in one of Boston's oldest and most respectable neighborhoods would someday be his, and indeed it was, albeit after the delay he should never have suffered. Following his death and without any surviving immediate family members, it was discovered Uncle Walter had willed the estate to his cousin, Alice Cope. If she was unable to assume possession, it was only then alternatively willed to Whitley.

As things turned out of course, Alice was eventually to be found hiding out at a remote cave in southern Utah with Chris Soles. In a gun battle, she was killed and Chris Soles somehow escaped. And with her death, Whitley was awarded possession of the Boston estate he had yearned for since his youth.

Yes, Whitley thought to himself, he was truly happy here — especially in light of the events that had transpired in the last several days. First, there had been the wholesale elimination of any threats posed by the Future Generations terrorist group last Friday night both in Idaho and Washington. Then on Saturday, with everything in northern Idaho on lockdown, there were no demonstrations or disturbances, and all went off without a hitch; the gathering of The Seven had been judged an unqualified success.

To top it off, when his private jet arrived back in Boston late Sunday afternoon, Whitley learned that Chris Soles had been killed on the Olympic Peninsula in Washington State. For the next several days the Internet, newspapers, and the video media had been filled to the brim with stories and commentary he couldn't get enough of. Articles with titles such as, "Future Generations — Destroyed!" and, "The End of Future Generations!" were a natural draw; some Whitley had even printed up and were still scattered about the desk before him.

Today, Thursday, a special private courier delivered a full and confidential summary of evidence regarding the events of the last several days in the Northwest. The information for the most part would likely be released in the upcoming days and some of it was incredibly damning. Nothing more so, however, than conclusive proof that Chris Soles had been the leader of the terrorists, as his prints were discovered all over the escape boat found across the bay along with those of his accomplices that died in the Bainbridge Island shootout.

Still unknown though, was how Soles lured Stone McClelland and his FBI agent partner into the trap at the Bainbridge Island refuge of The Two. For that reason alone, Whitley hoped McClelland might live; yet that was still in doubt even today. In grave condition, he had teetered on the brink of death for days with little change. Still, if he lived or died, McClelland would surely be recognized as a hero, since ballistics in today's report had identified the bullet that killed Chris Soles' second-in-command, Garfield Taylor, had come from McClelland's gun. He then somehow made it back to his fallen comrade from the FBI before he fully collapsed.

Another puzzle remaining was how the slippery Chris Soles evaded capture or death once again on Bainbridge Island as he had at the Utah cave and many times in between. Perhaps McClelland would have some answers about that as well – if he lived.

Equally strange was Sapphire MacKenzie's tale of being abducted on Friday evening. She told local police Saturday morning that after visiting her father in the Seattle hospital following a car accident, she stopped by a close friend's restaurant on the way to see her mother in another hospital. There she was purportedly taken away by masked men who queried her most of the night about her connections with the Commons movement, before releasing her unharmed in the morning.

Curious indeed, yet there was nothing whatsoever tying her into the events of the night before only a short distance away, so she was allowed to depart for her mother's hospital on the Olympic Peninsula.

When Whitley attempted to call Sapphire following her father's death a couple days ago, he discovered she had blocked his number. He reasoned that she was understandably upset and grieving over her loss but, given time, he knew he would retain her good graces and confidence for many years.

Dellenbach finally yielded to the summons of the impatiently waiting glass on the desk by pouring two fingers of the precious liquor into it. He sipped it down and allowed himself time to contemplate upon consequences.

Finally, with Chris Soles dead – killed, it was reported, attempting to escape into a ravine when his flight from justice was blocked from above and below – events had satisfyingly turned full circle in Whitley's favor, in the oligarchy's favor, as it must inevitably be.

Soles, a most vile member of the rabble had seduced and turned his cousin Alice against the family, against the hegemony of the elite through the generations, and he blamed her for hastening their Uncle Walter's death as well.

At the hospital that day, Alice had arrived late but had been requested to visit the old man on his deathbed before most others. Whitley had missed the majority of what transpired between them, but upon slightly opening the door to Uncle Walter's hospital room, he clearly heard and couldn't forget what his cousin Alice said.

"I hope you suffer a miserable death after what you've helped do to all the fine people I knew at Gaia/Universe." Her voiced had hissed with acerbity and the medical monitors began sounding their alarms.

Alice had bolted from Uncle Walter's hospital room so consumed by her passions that she didn't even register Whitley standing by the door. Now, and ever since that day, Whitley fully believed what she said had pushed the venerable old man over the edge and to his death.

And so, when his contacts learned of the hiding place in Utah for Alice and Chris Soles, Whitley had given instruction to kill the future. Or, more specifically, that the baby to be spawned as the fruit of Alice and Chris Soles would be killed first and foremost. If everything else failed, at least it would kill off the conjoined future of Alice and Soles. Alice was to be eliminated next, for there was no room for traitors within an oligarchic family.

Orders were given for Chris Soles to be captured, or killed. If captured he would have been made an example of before his ultimate trial and execution. If killed, that was a satisfactory resolution as well.

But, most unfortunately, Chris Soles had escaped to cause infinite troubles. Yet finally, that had all ended last Sunday, and ended satisfactorily.

From the President, to the Supreme Court and the full Congress as well, even unto the people themselves – all were under the ultimate sway of the oligarchs, especially the fossil fuel oligarchs of the most successful corporations in the history of the planet – which controlled and ruled from the shadows.

Whitley realized that insurrections would always be out there waiting to rise, yet those were petty threats to the world the oligarchs were forging. There would always be some grit in the grease that oiled the wheels of future progress and control, but in the long run that was merely a minimal disruption and distraction. For people like he would always be on guard.

Smiling with an inherited and rightful pride, Whitley Dellenbach poured himself more premium Scotch.

CHAPTER FORTY-TWO

Partially because of the unusually beautiful weather for early November, Kiri Thorson had chosen to walk to Comox Lake rather than take her mother up on the offer to borrow the car and drive. With no rain for two days in the Comox Valley and much of Vancouver Island, it felt more like late summer than full-on fall.

Kiri was in a merry mood. She knew it would be a special day because of a special call she would receive. And no matter that the cell reception was often spotty at the lake, today it would be reliable.

Departing her parent's house on Dunsmuir Avenue in Cumberland, Kiri traveled in a westerly direction until Dunsmuir met Comox Lake Road, which would take her to the lake. When they were kids, Kiri and her sister, and half the neighborhood, would easily trek the three and half kilometers to enjoy hours of summer fun on the lake's shores. It usually took only about thirty-five or forty minutes, and today Kiri was gazing at Comox Lake before she knew it.

Her destination was actually a little further on, past the boat docks and the campground at the end of the road, to what she'd always called her "Thinking Rock." As a teen and needing to get away from it all, Kiri would take the path through the woods past the campground where eventually there was a waist high boulder with a splendid view of the lake and the mountains on the other side. Then, as now, she climbed atop her "Thinking Rock" and relished the view on this spectacular morning.

The rock was the perfect place for today and there was much to think about.

Since the Picnic Point cabin when she'd been Awakened to the solution of a koan, her inner awareness had accelerated into almost another dimension altogether. Simply put, she had been transformed in ways that words could not capture nor describe. Everything was separate, yet interpenetrating to be tied together at the same time; all coalesced into a singularity while retaining individual uniqueness. And all, inherently ineffable.

For Kiri, the lucidity, the clarity of mind, she had experienced when stirred from sleep by the koan that night had remained and intensified for several weeks. Outwardly, all her senses were overcharged and over stimulated as well. The colors in flowers were intense, mind-blowing, dew on the leaves sparkled electric, and the clouds throbbed with life as they passed overhead. And she found she could sit still for hours, merely meditating upon what was going through her mind.

With ear buds in and connected to her phone for later, it so happened that deep reflection was precisely what she engaged in until the call finally came.

Kiri smiled as she answered the phone. "I've been waiting for your call."

Sapphire was puzzled. "We just talked a couple days ago."

"No, I've been waiting for this call."

"Why?"

"Prescience, I guess," Kiri stated with a shrug. "That's all."

"What do you mean?"

"I'm fully prepared," declared Kiri. "It's time to fully bind for the sake of Cascadia."

"What?" replied Sapphire. "What are you talking about?"

Kiri laughed. "First, tell me what you're calling about."

"Okay," Sapphire began, "but some of it's good and some of it's bad."

"I hope the bad is not about your mother," Kiri said warily.

"No, thankfully she's doing much better and now full recovery is eventually expected," Sapphire spoke happily. "She's staying with her younger sister, and she's doting on mom."

"Okay then, tell me the bad first and let's be done with it."

"Good idea," Sapphire remarked. "Do you remember Mister Q – the librarian in Port Townsend?"

"Of course I do," said Kiri. "He was such a charming little man."

"He was indeed," agreed Sapphire. "But Mister Q died; he had a stroke and passed away about a week after my father's death. I don't think I ever mentioned it to you in our calls; it was such a hectic time for me."

"That's a shame," Kiri commiserated. "I'm so sorry."

"Yes, me too," said Sapphire. "So that's the bad part. Ready for the good part?"

"Sure, why not?"

"Well, it goes like this." Sapphire paused. "A lawyer working on the will of Mister Q called me out of the blue. She said Mister Q had left me his property on Marrowstone Island across from Port Townsend, as well as a generous monthly stipend."

"That's fantastic for you, Sapphire!" Kiri exclaimed.

"It's fantastic for both of us," Sapphire fired back. "I want you to come live with me on Marrowstone Island."

"Of course I'd love to do that," Kiri replied excitedly. "That way we can raise *his* children together."

"What do you mean?"

"You missed your period too, didn't you?"

"How do you know that?"

"It's that prescience thing again," smiled Kiri, "that's all."

Sapphire was incredulous. "Then we're both having *his* children?"

"That is how events have come to pass," Kiri replied with a hint of mystery.

"I can't wait to live with you on Marrowstone Island," Sapphire declared exuberantly. "We will raise *his* children together and simultaneously foster a true revolution in Cascadia. The revolution is not over in the least. The momentary setback that we've suffered will only make us stronger. Cascadia will unite more than ever after the murder and martyrdom of Chris Soles – *Chris Cadia*."

"And I have all his lists from the Gaia/Universe days on a thumb drive, as well as what was compiled during his years in Cascadia," Kiri tossed in.

"On top of that, the Free Cascadia organization has been energized by the recent events – and the Elders pledge to have our back more that ever," vowed Sapphire.

"Even more," Kiri added, "Tomas Hernandez is now a recognized leader of the Commons movement and the common people in rejecting the rule by the elites and oligarchs."

"What Empire is blind to," noted Sapphire, "is that in Cascadia the sands of power and control that they rely upon are eroding underneath their feet unbeknownst to them. As the people walk away in Cascadia, Empire will lose all power and control."

"We cannot and will not lose in our Quest for Cascadia," Kiri affirmed.

"I agree," Sapphire stated. "Only in the darkest of nights do the grandest of opportunities unfailingly arise. We are The Thin Green Line. This is our time; our time has come."

"I'm so excited, I'm going to start packing for Marrowstone Island today," exclaimed Kiri. "Listen, you and Tomas have touched the hearts of the people and I'm conversant with the ethereal realm. And *he* has given all of us the template with which to work. I say, let *our* Revolution begin!"

Sapphire was compelled to vigorously agree. "Yes, indeed: Let the Revolution begin!

###

Connect with Mike Penney Online:

Twitter: http://twitter.com/mfpenney

Website: http://www.mikepenney.com

Other Titles:

WALKING AWAY FROM THE KING

THE COMING TSUNAMI

BEHIND THE GATES WITH THE 1%

MIKE PENNEY

ABOUT THE AUTHOR

Mike Penney was born in Colorado and attended the University of Colorado in Boulder, where he studied Philosophy and Literature. Following college, he lived in various locales throughout the West, including California and Washington State. After sailing his boat from Ventura, California to Honolulu, Hawaii, he was fortunate enough to reside on the Big Island for over a decade and a half. Presently, Mike once again calls the Colorado Rockies his home.

Made in the USA
Columbia, SC
07 August 2017